THE
GAMMA
RECUITS

JAMES PELKMANS

GammaPubs.com
Copyright © 2022 James Pelkmans

ISBN Paperback: 979-8-9858144-1-5
ISBN eBook: 979-8-9858144-0-8

ACKNOWLEDGMENTS

I would like to thank my beautiful wife, Fleur, for her encouragement and patience during the long process of writing my first book, and my sister, Carol, for providing feedback on a half-dozen iterations of my manuscript without a hint of diminishing enthusiasm. I would also like to thank fellow Stratford, Ontario native, and High School friend Tyson Erb for providing enormously valuable editorial advice on character development, pacing, and perspective that helped make my storytelling more compelling.

This book is dedicated to my boys, Connor and Owen, and the diverse new generation of scientists and engineers like the ones I have the pleasure of working with every day.

Chapter One

THE CANOES APPEARED AS a pair of dots below the horizon off the distant southwest tip of Moloka'i a little after sunrise. Ruan Van Zijl raised his binoculars to get a better look. They were still too far away to be recognizable, but he knew it was the same fishermen he'd been tracking every few days for the last two months. Each time they appeared, they chose a different spot off the south side of his island to set up for a few hours of fishing, working their way gradually eastward toward his vantage point with each visit.

Aside from the considerable distance they traveled, there was nothing remarkable about the unwelcome visitors. Their small, two-man outriggers, clothing, and gear were typical of what he'd observed among the locals when he first arrived. It was possible they were just trying to find the most bountiful place to cast their nets, but the hairs pricking up on the back of his neck told Ruan otherwise. It felt like a recon operation.

Having served four years in the South African National Defense Force Reconnaissance Commando, specializing in long-range, overland infiltration, Ruan understood recon. The disappointing culmination of a childhood dream, by the time he'd made it through the brutal selection process there was little action left for a Recce.

The youngest of his mother's siblings and a family outcast, his uncle had regaled him with stories of clandestine missions behind enemy lines during the Angolan Bush War. The stories, far too graphic to be appropriate for a ten-year-old, had convinced Ruan to one day follow in his uncle's footsteps. He enlisted in the defense forces on his eighteenth birthday and applied for Recce selection at the first opportunity.

The calculated cruelty of the selection process for earning the laurel dagger of the Recces had tested his physical and mental endurance far more than he'd anticipated. The penultimate challenge of the four weeks of hell was a one-hundred kilometer, thirty-six hour, non-stop simulated recon mission through bush country—with a full ruck. When it was over, he'd collapsed into a deep sleep without the strength to tend his bleeding feet.

A few hours later, woken by gunfire, he and the others were ordered to strip naked and swim across a crocodile-infested pond. Most of the exhausted men had refused to risk their lives, preferring to save that for actual combat. They were dismissed on the spot without a chance to reconsider, leaving only Ruan and two others from his cohort to join the elite ranks of the Recces. It turned out to be a hollow victory. Prime Minister De Klerk had already handed South Africa over to mob rule, and Ruan was left serving a country he no longer recognized.

When his service ended, he joined his uncle and dozens of other SANDF Special Forces veterans as a private security contractor in Afghanistan and, later, Iraq. It was there he finally got the action he was looking for, and an opportunity to put his deadly skills to use. Although technically sanctioned and legal, there was little oversight and even less accountability for the activities of private contractors. He and his brothers-in-arms took full advantage, often favoring force over diplomacy.

There were few similarities between the bleak landscapes of the Middle East or the unforgiving extremes of Afghanistan and his lush island paradise. Even so, his work as a contractor had been the ideal preparation for his current and final mission a world-and-a-half from home. Unconstrained by oversight or rules of engagement, he was free to deal with the persistent fishermen approaching his rocky perch from the southeast however he saw fit.

Based on his current elevation and their relative position below the horizon, Ruan estimated the small, two-man outriggers were no more than ten kilometers from shore. Moloka'i was forty kilometers away, and even on this relatively calm day, that was seven or eight hours of hard, nonstop paddling.

They would have had to start their journey around midnight to be so close this early in the day, and it was hard to imagine that a few hours of fishing was enough to justify the level of effort. More likely, he thought, his instincts were right, and they were trying to provoke some kind of reaction. He maintained watch for another thirty minutes as they drew slowly closer against a backdrop of inky-black water and scattered whitecaps.

Early start or not, it would still be more than an hour before they arrived. There was plenty of time for breakfast and a tactical nap to keep his senses sharp. He rolled onto his back and eased himself safely out of sight below the ridgeline before sitting up to reach for his rucksack. Though unnecessary under the circumstances, it was a programmed precaution exercised without thought. Rooting through the dirty, faded pack, he retrieved a beat-up thermos and one of about a half-dozen neatly wrapped banana leaf packets.

Ruan took a sip of lukewarm water, imagining it was steaming hot, black coffee. There wasn't much he couldn't survive, but he'd be surviving it a lot better if he had some coffee. The mixture of poi and dried fish was equally uninspiring. He picked it absent-mindedly from the leafy pouch with his fingers until it was nearly gone, and then dumped the remaining morsels into his mouth. Laying back against the incline of the ridge, he shifted his weight around until he felt relatively comfortable and closed his eyes, allowing his thoughts to wander.

Following his work in Iraq, a seemingly inconsequential job in the summer of 2011 had set his life on an unlikely course to minor celebrity status, and the moderate wealth that had come with it. Being familiar with the region, he had been recommended to work security on an American reality show set in the Okavango Delta region of Botswana. After two weeks on the job, the producer had confronted him with the intent to send him packing.

"Nobody's seen you for days," he'd complained. "You're supposed to be making sure the contestants and crew are safe, not fucking off and disappearing."

Ruan calmly explained that he preferred to deal with threats before they came close enough to cause harm. He pulled out a map to show the angry producer the perimeter he had established, and the places where he'd encountered a couple of hunting parties, politely advising them to avoid the set. More alarmingly, he'd documented the movements of a group of poachers to the northwest, and identified the chokepoint where he intended to dispatch them if they got too close.

The producer was horrified. Not out of concern for the poachers, but by the implications of a murder investigation and the associated trouble with the local authorities. Ruan assured him the park wardens would not ask questions about a few dead poachers, but ultimately agreed to a less extreme deterrent to any threat they might pose. The producer, satisfied Ruan should keep his job, listened with rapt interest for hours while he described his experiences as a soldier and security contractor.

A few months after production wrapped, the producer reached out to pitch an idea, and '*Survival Stories with Ron Van Zeal*' was born. The premise was straightforward. Each episode would feature him re-enacting real-life survival situations, historical and contemporary, and documenting the actions leading to the protagonists' success or failure. It had proved popular enough with a niche cable audience to keep him on the air for five seasons and fifty total episodes. By the end, they were struggling to find good stories, and his personal life was in crisis.

Ruan woke suddenly, sensing he had slept longer than intended. Lifting his head slowly, he looked around to get his bearings before deciding it was safe to sit up. To his relief, the sun was still low in the sky, and he estimated he'd only been asleep for about ninety minutes. He took a sip from his thermos and hastily tucked it away in his pack, eager to see what progress the paddlers had made.

Although not the highest peak on the island, the location of the ridge on the south-facing promontory made it the ideal place to keep watch. Any approach was likely to be visible from there, and he had a clear view of several places where visitors might choose to come ashore. He eased his way forward as he approached the top, not wanting to draw attention from anyone below who happened to be looking in his direction.

The fishermen had arrived offshore and positioned their outriggers about a hundred meters apart on the far side of the reef, just west of his vantage point, where the ocean floor dropped off steeply, and the fishing was especially good. Ruan raised his binoculars, looking for any hint in their gear or comportment to indicate they might not be what they seemed—anything to explain their repeated and unwelcome visits.

On the nearest boat, one man swung a weighted net effortlessly over his head and released it at just the right moment, allowing the angular momentum to open it into a near-perfect circle by the time it splashed down on the surface of the water. A couple of minutes later, both men worked in unison to haul it back in, dumping its writhing contents into their canoe. They squatted down to examine the catch, throwing back whatever they deemed unworthy of keeping. If they were acting a part, they were undoubtedly convincing.

Occasionally, the men yelled back and forth between the two boats and shared a laugh. He imagined they were making fun of each other's fishing prowess, or perhaps commenting about who may have seduced whose sister the evening before they had set out. Of course, even if he could hear them from such a distance over the sound of the surf, there'd be no way for him to know what they were saying.

Ruan kept watch from his hidden perch as the sun climbed steadily to its midday apex, and the men continued the skillful display. It was about the time of day when they'd have to haul in their nets one last time and start the long journey home to make it back before dark. He could see it had been a good day. They'd filled both canoes with glistening fish of all colors and shapes, warranting a triumphant return to the families waiting for them on the other side of Moloka'i.

The two boats moved alongside each other, and the men chatted as they passed around food and gourds of fresh water to ready themselves, he imagined, for the demanding trip home. When they finished their meal, they carefully stowed the remaining loose gear and retrieved their paddles.

Instead of heading back the way they had come, as on previous occasions, they turned westward and began paddling along the shore. He edged along carefully behind the ridgeline to keep them in sight, hoping they would eventually turn back to the southeast. However, they continued steadily westward for two hours before finally disappearing into the mouth of a sizeable lagoon. There was only one explanation for why they would go there with such a large catch. They were coming ashore and planning to stay awhile.

The elevation difference wasn't that much—a bit more than two hundred meters from the top of the ridge down to the flat, grassy patch where Ruan had built a small hut. He'd made the steep decline of tight switchbacks and near-vertical faces passable using makeshift bamboo ladders bound with coconut fiber. Navigating it quickly and efficiently, but without undue haste, he made a disciplined descent to the isolated plateau that had been his home for the last ten years.

Though his heart was pounding by the time he reached the bottom, it was more from the excitement of imminent contact than the exertion of the descent. A plan was taking shape before he reached the entrance of his hut.

Chapter Two

THE ISLAND OF MOLOKA'I grew steadily larger, drifting past the left-side windows as the plane passed through ten-thousand feet on the descent into O'ahu. Jayson held up his phone and snapped a picture. After examining it for a moment, he loosened his seatbelt and slid down to take a few selfies with the island in the background. Scrolling through them, he chose one that would make a good post and did a few adjustments to the contrast before disguising the puffy bags under his eyes.

"We're in our final approach, Mr. Reilly," the attendant informed him as she took his half-full glass of Coke and stowed his tray for him.

Startled, Jayson glanced up from his phone.

"Yeah, cool. Thanks."

Cool was an understatement, he realized as he lowered his footrest and eased the expansive leather seat into the upright position. After passing through U.S. customs at Vancouver International Airport, he'd gone directly to a private lounge where he was met by a chauffeur and driven out to a waiting Dassault Falcon 6X. The comparative luxury made his first-class flight from Toronto seem ordinary. Onboard were just himself, the pilots, and an attendant dedicated to his every need. It was a recruiting experience worthy of the next LeBron James or Connor McDavid.

But Jayson Reilly was not a star athlete. He was a graduate student in Sustainable Agriculture at the University of Guelph in Southwestern Ontario. 'Moo U,' it was colloquially called for its prominence in livestock research and location in the heart of Canada's dairy country—not exactly a prime target for high-tech billionaires to recruit talent. Nonetheless, here he was escaping a soul-crushing late spring snowstorm back home and descending into paradise on a private jet.

The trip, his recruiter had explained, was an opportunity to tour the campus of a new venture funded by billionaire Anton Kamaras, the richest man on the planet, and to interview with the managing director. Kamaras wanted to do 'something real' to make the world a better, more livable place, and was prepared to spend billions of his own money. If the fit was right, perhaps Jayson would be part of it.

The plane touched down at Wheeler Army Airfield, northwest of Honolulu, near the center of the island of O'ahu. He disabled airplane mode on his phone and waited impatiently for a connection so he could check up on his hitz. Notifications began popping up.

> Mom has hit you!
> Paul Beekman has hit you!
> Two stories you're following have new hitz!
> Sheryl Decker added you to her hitzlist!

The notifications kept coming. Jayson opened the Hitz-It app and skimmed through his messages. Then, he created a new hit with the selfie he'd taken during the descent and added a caption: *'Just landed in Hawaii on Anton Kamaras's private jet!'* It was nice to be the one bragging about doing something exciting for a change, he thought to himself as a flurry of immediate reactions from friends and family filled his screen.

Focused on his phone, Jayson didn't notice the plane had rolled to a stop outside an unmarked hangar at the west end of the runway, and the crew was preparing to disembark.

"Mr. Reilly?" prompted the pilot, trying to get his attention. "Welcome to O'ahu."

He was standing by the open door, gesturing for his passenger to exit the plane. Jayson grabbed his carry-on from under the seat next to him and started for the stairway.

"Thanks," he replied, extending his hand awkwardly.

The pilot smiled and offered him a firm handshake. "Enjoy your stay."

He stepped out into the dazzling sunshine and took in the surroundings. The immediate area was flat, drab, and uninspiring, but the emerald peaks rising to the east and west hinted at the beauty of the place. A familiar voice caught his attention.

"Jayson! Welcome to O'ahu. Aloha."

The recruiter he'd met just a few weeks earlier at a coffee shop on the University campus was almost unrecognizable, wearing cargo shorts and a gray t-shirt in place of the expensive suit and tie he'd sported at their first meeting. He already had Jayson's suitcase in tow behind him.

"Hey Mr. Young, good to see you," he replied. "I didn't expect you to meet me personally."

"No way I'd invite you to my home and not offer a proper greeting. That's not the Hawaiian way. And please, call me Cal."

Descending the last step, Jayson offered his hand, and Cal took it enthusiastically, pulling him in for an unexpected embrace.

"Aloha. That's hello, right?"

"Aloha is everything here, Jayson," smiled Cal, as he clapped him on the back.

He was more casual than when they'd met on the University Campus in Guelph, and Jayson was sure he was 'Calvin' and not 'Cal' during the first interview. His host rolled the bag towards the back of a black Mustang convertible and tossed it into the trunk.

"Get in, Jayson. Let's roll."

Jayson set his carry-on on the back seat and got into the car. It smelled brand new. He noticed as they drove that the other planes and helicopters on the tarmac were all military aircraft.

"This isn't the main airport?" he asked.

"No. This is Wheeler Army Airfield. It's easier to get to our facility from here. Less traffic. Mr. Kamaras has an agreement to use it when he needs to."

Leaving the base, they turned right and headed south.

"We'll be down to Waipi'O in thirty minutes, or so."

"Waipi'O?"

"Pearl Harbor," explained Cal. "Mr. Kamaras leased the vacant land on Waipi'O Peninsula at Pearl Harbor from the government for the next hundred years. It's where he's headquartered his Center for Sustainability Research."

"Hundred years, huh? I like his optimism."

Jayson doubted there was anything that could be done in a thousand years, let alone a hundred, to fix what humanity had done to the planet and keep it livable. He doubted Anton Kamaras believed anything could be done, either. A billion-dollar publicity stunt to pay lip service to sustainability was nothing for a man like him. He made that in a week while continuing to profit from the status quo.

Maybe that was harsh, considering Jayson's own hypocrisy. After all, he'd jumped at the chance to take a private jet halfway around the world to interview for a job that was probably just bullshit. How could he justify the environmental impact of his little joyride? *'Screw it,'* he'd rationalized to himself, *'why be the only one making sacrifices if we're all fucked anyway?'*

The highway crossed over a ravine and swept to the right, revealing a large swath of agricultural land to the west.

"I didn't expect it to be so rural here."

"Yeah. There's a lot of land like this on O'ahu. I mean, for its size," explained Cal. "Most of the population is packed pretty tight in Honolulu."

"It's nice. Not too different from back home in the summer."

"Sure," laughed Cal, "and how many days of the year is that?"

"Not nearly enough," conceded Jayson with a smile.

Soon, the fields gave way to light industrial buildings as traffic got a bit heavier. They crested a gentle rise, and the Pacific Ocean appeared in the distance below them.

"Still look like home?"

"No," replied Jayson, shaking his head. "No, it does not."

The ocean disappeared on the horizon as they headed down the other side of the rise into increasingly urban surroundings.

They exited the highway a few minutes later, passing a high school and traversing a small bridge before the water reappeared on the east side of Waipi'O Point Access Road. On the right, a beautifully manicured golf course stretched into the distance. They continued down the road to where it swept around towards a public soccer complex. At the midpoint of the curve, Cal turned left onto a narrow road obstructed with a lift gate, and came to a stop at an unmarked guardhouse.

An enormous guard lumbered out of the building and approached the convertible. Jayson imagined he must be a native Hawaiian, not that he knew much about the demographics of the islands.

"Good afternoon, Mr. Young," he greeted. "Who you got with you today?"

"Hello Makani," responded Cal. "This is Jayson Reilly. He's on the list."

"Hello, Mr. Reilly. Can I see some ID?"

Jayson pulled the crisp new passport from his right front pocket and handed it over.

The guard smiled and gave it a cursory look before handing it back.

"All good. Have a nice day."

He returned to the guardhouse and raised the gate, allowing them to continue down the road.

"Doesn't exactly look like a multi-billion dollar operation," said Jayson.

"We prefer to keep this place low profile. This gate is just for local travel. The big stuff comes into the port by container ship."

"Why low profile? Don't you want to show the world all the good you're doing here?"

"Did you do a search on the Center for Sustainability Research before coming?" asked Cal.

"Yeah," admitted Jayson.

"And what did you find?"

"To be honest, not much. Some governmental filings, registration information, and a vague, single-page website with no contact options."

"Exactly. This place is about results, not public relations."

Jayson noticed an enormous array of solar panels between the road and the harbor on the left. It continued around the corner as far as he could see.

"That looks promising for a sustainability research center."

"We can't take credit for that. It belongs to the U.S. Navy," explained Cal. "We're doing a bit of solar, but working on other stuff, too."

They encountered a second gate beyond the solar array, much more serious-looking than the first. Solid steel and twelve feet high, it obstructed the only means through an imposing concrete wall topped with a ribbon of fierce-looking razor wire. No guard was there to greet them, but arrays of mounted cameras and other electronic equipment meant somebody knew they were there. The gate began opening even before the Mustang could come to a complete stop.

They passed through the gate into the Center for Sustainability Research compound. On either side of the gravel road were dozens of small, neatly divided plots of land. A few tractors, trucks, and other miscellaneous agricultural equipment sat idly here-and-there in the fields and at the side of the road.

"Sunday," explained Cal. "Not much happening today, but tomorrow it'll be buzzing."

"What's going on with this stuff?" asked Jayson.

"This is why you're here," he replied with a smile. "Right now, we've got people prepping all this land back to the soil conditions that were native to the area before we showed up. Lots happened here with the military before and during World War Two, and we want to make sure it doesn't mess with your research."

"My research?"

"Yours—or whoever we end up bringing in to run the agricultural stuff. We want to make sure we start with the right control conditions."

"And then what?"

"And then we look for ways we can augment the soil," continued Cal, "with only native, natural materials from the island to make it best suited for various test crops."

"No fertilizers or pesticides?"

"Nothing chemical. Just whatever you can make or find naturally. Like guano, or whatever."

"So I'm here to haul bird shit?"

"Of course not. We've got people for that—and they didn't fly in on a private jet," assured Cal, "You just tell 'em what to haul and where to haul it."

"To what end?" asked Jayson. "What are you trying to do here?"

"Well," he paused. "I'd summarize it as maximizing production while minimizing impact."

"That's a nice little garden project, I suppose, but I don't see how that saves the world."

"By itself, it doesn't," conceded Cal. "It's just one piece of a very large and complex puzzle. But it's an important piece. Critical, even."

The road continued past the fields, toward Pearl Harbor. Some large, two-and-three-story buildings appeared ahead, but their presence was overshadowed by the massive spectacle anchored offshore just beyond them.

"Holy shit," remarked Jayson.

"Yeah. That's the USS Ronald Reagan," explained Cal with pride. "It's usually stationed at Yokosuka Naval Base in Japan, but we're borrowing it for a few days."

"You can borrow an aircraft carrier?"

"You and I can't," he laughed, "but Mr. Kamaras can."

"Should I ask why he would need to do that?"

"We're experimenting with fusion as a source of sustainable energy. Do you follow fusion research at all?"

"Just enough to know it's always ten years away," smiled Jayson.

"We've cut that in half, and now it's always five years away," quipped Cal.

Jayson laughed to be polite.

"Anyway," he continued, "it takes a huge amount of power to do fusion research, and the Hawaiian government wasn't thrilled with the idea of letting us build our own fission reactor here on-site to support it. We borrow power from the ones on Navy ships like the Reagan when we need to run big tests."

"What does the Navy get out of it?" asked Jayson.

"Fusion reactors, if we're successful. So a pretty good deal both ways."

Massive cables ran out of an opening on the carrier's side and down to the water below. Jayson traced the shoreline and saw where they resurfaced to come ashore near one of the buildings. Impressive as it was, the thought of collaborating with the military made him uneasy. Still, if it meant less radioactive waste from nuclear carriers and subs, he supposed that was probably a good thing.

"Be good to the earth while going to bomb the shit out of some poor, brown villagers on the other side of the planet," he remarked. "A kinder, greener brutality."

"I get that this isn't exactly the kind of image that goes well with making the world a better place," conceded Cal. "Mr. Kamaras approaches his goals like he approaches a chess match. Sometimes he makes calculated sacrifices, but the end goal is still to win."

"It's hard to argue with his track record," admitted Jayson.

"We'll start with a facility tour tomorrow," explained Cal as they drove past the first set of buildings and headed southeast towards the water. "It's past 9:00 eastern now, so you're probably getting pretty tired."

"Yeah. A bit."

But he wasn't tired. His mind was still processing everything he'd seen in the last few minutes. Maybe it wasn't all bullshit. It was hard to imagine the United States Navy would commit the resources of an aircraft carrier—a carrier group, even—to a billionaire's vanity project. Thousands of personnel? Tens of thousands? He had no idea what kind of manpower and money it took to support a carrier group, just that it was probably a lot.

They pulled into the circular drive at the main entrance of a long, modern-looking, boomerang-shaped building with a sweeping curved roof and a raised, circular central hub with windows all around. Feeling like a posh hotel minus the glitz, everything about the place was clean and functional.

"This is the main residence for all of our researchers and support staff," explained Cal as he led Jayson through the automatic sliding glass doors into the large open foyer. "Up the main stairs here, you'll find the cafeteria and common areas."

It was bright and airy. On the mezzanine above, Jayson could see a few people milling around and talking. They were back lit by sunlight streaming in from the towering windows of the building's central hub.

"Nice," he nodded in genuine awe.

"Down here on the main floor, through those doors, you'll find the gym, swimming pool, and laundry facilities. Use any of it while you're here."

They continued down the northern arm of the building until Cal stopped at a door. He fished around in his pocket and produced a badge with Jayson's name and picture on it. It was marked with 'visitor' in bold, red letters.

"Here we are. This will get you into your room."

Jayson took the card and examined it for a moment.

"Thanks."

"Oh, and that'll get you access to everything else in here, too. Pool, laundry, whatever," he added, pointing at the badge. "Don't go anywhere without it."

"Got it."

"I'll meet you in the lobby at eight. Get some rest."

Cal passed Jayson his suitcase and clapped him on the shoulder.

"See you tomorrow."

"Thanks, Cal. See you tomorrow."

Jayson passed the badge over the door sensor. It buzzed agreeably and flashed green. He walked in, trailing his suitcase, and looked around. It was a little larger than a standard hotel room with a small kitchenette and some living space with a couch and TV. A large closet and the bathroom were adjacent to the entrance.

He left the suitcase by the closet, tossing his carry-on onto the bed on his way to the eastward-facing floor-to-ceiling window at the far side of the room. The view was spectacular. Ford Island and the aviation museum, along with Joint Base Pearl Harbor-Hickam, were directly across the water from his window. Beyond that, he saw the gleaming city of Honolulu against a backdrop of soaring emerald mountains, and began to understand why the place was called paradise. Jayson took a smiling selfie with the view in the background to post in another hit, unaware that Kamaras's fusion team was making history only a few hundred meters away.

Chapter Three

THE CENTER FOR SUSTAINABILITY Research Fusion B building comprised several modular units. They could be disassembled for easy transport and reassembled in less than seventy-two hours, thanks to clever couplings that linked the structural, electrical, plumbing, and networking components. Presently, it was fully assembled and drawing a tremendous amount of power from the twin reactors aboard the USS Ronald Reagan.

That it was a Sunday afternoon did not matter. The critical Alpha test intended to prove Dr. Olujimi Akindele's theoretical work could only be performed during brief windows of convergence that arrived without consideration for what anyone thought might be reasonable working hours. Besides, Dr. Akindele's team had invested too much in the project to let frivolities like a Sunday afternoon with family interfere with its success.

High-level representatives from Hitz-It.com and the Navy were in attendance to witness the outcome firsthand. Pacific Fleet Commander, Admiral Spencer Daniels, who had invested enormous political capital getting the Navy to support the project, had come to see if that investment was paying off. Rebecca Steinman, the right hand of Anton Kamaras, was in the control room with him.

From their vantage point, they could see the activity in the test chamber below through panes of thick plexiglass. It was an expansive, rectangular room approximately thirty-five meters long and ten meters wide, dominated by a pair of axially aligned ring assemblies three-and-a-half meters in diameter. One of the assemblies was fixed to the chamber wall with heavy steel brackets. The other, only inches away from the first, was mounted on a dual rail system that allowed it to slide back and forth to fine-tune the gap between them.

Other than their mounts, the two assemblies appeared identical. Each consisted of a freely rotating inner ring adorned with copper coils housed in a stationary outer ring wreathed in thick bundles of multi-colored wires that ran up to connection points in the ceiling.

"Time to window?" called out a tech in the control room.

"Eight minutes," came the measured reply.

"Okay. Let's verify the sample and clear the chamber."

A few techs in radiation suits gathered equipment and placed it on a cart. In front of the rings, two more techs focused on the sample—a small cube of silvery-gold metal, one cubic centimeter in size, resting atop a waist-high pedestal.

"Dr. Akindele?" asked Admiral Daniels, leaning uncomfortably close to the physicist.

"Yes, Admiral," he replied without taking his eyes from the array of monitors in front of him.

"How long is the Alpha window?"

"Thirty-seven milliseconds."

"And what's the sample?"

"Two milligrams of cesium-136."

"That's all?" he asked, wrinkling his brow.

The physicist looked away from his screen with a scowl.

"Admiral, we only need measurements today. The sample size is irrelevant. Please do not speak to me again until after the test concludes."

Admiral Daniels blinked in surprise as his face flushed with anger. He raised a finger and started to speak, but was restrained by a gentle touch on the shoulder.

"Spencer, why don't we let Dr. Akindele focus on his work for a moment?"

It was Rebecca Steinman.

"There's a bank of monitors set up for us over here," she added, gesturing to the back of the room.

Admiral Daniels changed the subject to distract from the embarrassing rebuke he'd just received from the arrogant physicist.

"I'm surprised Anton isn't here for such an important test."

"He won't be onsite personally until Epsilon."

"I see," he replied, wrinkling his brow.

"There are a lot of things that need to come together, and he applies the appropriate focus to each of them. He has a strong team here, and Richard has everything under control."

"Where is Richard? I haven't seen him yet today."

"Just taking care of a few details. He won't miss the test."

A tone sounded on the speaker overhead, followed by an announcement.

"Three minutes to window. Initiating power sequence."

A hum filled the room, and the floor vibrated. In the upper left corner of a screen in front of them, a timer was ticking down. The rest of the screen displayed a close-up of the test specimen in the chamber, while a second monitor showed a wider angle where the inner rings of the apparatus began to rotate in opposite directions.

A side door opened, and a tall, thin man with short, salt-and-pepper hair rushed into the room.

"Richard," greeted the Admiral. "Glad you didn't miss the excitement."

"I wouldn't dream of it, sir," he responded with a smart salute.

"Rebecca," he added as he shook her hand and offered a deferential nod.

"Good to see you, Richard," she replied. "Everything taken care of?"

"Absolutely," he assured her. "Ready for the show."

The room grew quiet with anticipation. A few technicians speaking in hushed tones and the clicking of keyboards were the only sounds apart from the low, throbbing hum. Whether directly through the observation window or via monitors around the room, all eyes were fixed on the accelerating rings. Ghostly patterns of concentric waves, like ripples in a pond, emanated from them.

"We're locked on to the target waveform," announced one of the scientists, staring at his monitor. "Initiating synchronization with source."

The rail-mounted ring and pedestal supporting the sample moved slowly closer to the fixed ring, and the waves began interfering, creating an intricate pattern of dancing, iridescent light. The gap between the rings continued to close until, finally, the interferences merged into a perfect standing wave, the form of each successive one identical to the last, creating the illusion they were frozen in midair.

19

With ten seconds left, there was no dramatic audio countdown—just the numbers ticking down in unison on all of the monitors in the room. The precision required meant the computers now controlled everything, relegating the scientists and technicians to mere observers.

Milliseconds before the timer reached zero, a pneumatic actuator drove into the side of the small cube of radioactive cesium, launching it through the center of the rings, and there was a momentary flash. The standing wave pattern collapsed, and the hum slowly faded as the room fell silent. On the monitors, the sample appeared to be gone, but everyone turned their attention to Dr. Akindele for confirmation. He stared at the data feed in front of him.

"Superposition achieved," he started. "Tracking resultant waveform."

There were a few nods around the room, but tension was still high.

"Sample entanglement—," he continued slowly, "confirmed. No losses detected, and no inconsistencies in decay."

The room erupted in cheers. There were high-fives, a few hugs, and even some tears as the enormity of their accomplishment sank in. Admiral Daniels clapped Richard on the shoulder and embraced Rebecca.

"This is incredible." he said with wide eyes. "I can't believe it."

"We never had any doubts, sir," assured Richard.

Rebecca was beaming. The cheering subsided, replaced by excited chatter as team members gathered in small groups to review test data. Richard made his way to the middle of the control room, shaking a few hands along the way.

"Everyone," he called, "can I have your attention for a moment?"

The chatter faded while everyone turned their focus to Center for Sustainability Research Managing Director, Dr. Richard Vandergroot.

"This incredible success today is not an end to our work. It is just the beginning. Even so, we must take some time to recognize the significance of what we have achieved here. This is the single greatest scientific breakthrough in the history of humanity," he paused for dramatic effect, "so far!"

More cheering and clapping erupted from the assembled team. Richard looked around and smiled, trying to make momentary eye contact with each person in the room as he waited to continue.

"Now, I would like to invite the COO of Hitz-It-dot-com, Rebecca Steinman, to say a few words on behalf of Mr. Kamaras."

Polite applause greeted her as she raised a hand to the room.

"Good afternoon, everyone. First, let me say congratulations to the team, and a special thank you to Dr. Olujimi Akindele, without whose leadership and vision we would not be here today."

Another round of applause. Dr. Akindele glanced around appreciatively but uncomfortably. His hands balled into tight fists; he was pushing nervously against the cuticles of his fingers with his thumbs.

"Second," she continued, "I want to express how important your work is to Mr. Kamaras, and convey his deepest gratitude. He's looking forward to meeting each of you one day soon to express his appreciation personally."

More applause from the excited team.

"Richard? Back to you."

"As you all know, there is a lot still to do, and time is precious. Tomorrow morning, we will begin disassembling Fusion B for transport to the Beta site. But first," he said, "I would like you to join me this evening in celebration so we can properly memorialize today's events."

The applause started again, but Dr. Akindele silenced it with a wave of his hand.

"Okay, enough of these distractions. There will be no celebration tonight if we do not secure the chamber and complete the diagnostics first. Back to work."

As the scientists and lab technicians dispersed at the doctor's suggestion, returning to their post-test checklists, Admiral Daniels approached Richard and Rebecca.

"Listen," he started, "I was hoping to discuss invitations for Epsilon."

"Don't worry, Admiral," assured Richard, "your list is confirmed."

"Yes. It's just that—"

Dr. Akindele interrupted him mid-sentence.

"Richard, we still don't have adequate capacitance for Beta, and we are running out of time."

"Relax, doctor. The two largest capacitor networks on the planet are on a cargo ship from Taiwan," he assured. "They'll be here in plenty of time."

"Two?"

"Listen," he explained, "the specifications were very challenging."

"The specifications are critical," insisted Dr. Akindele. "I don't need two capacitors that don't work. I need one that does."

"They work. Guaranteed to discharge within spec, but—" Richard paused.

"But what? What is the problem?"

Richard hesitated, not wanting to elaborate, but now the Admiral and Rebecca were clearly interested in the conversation and waiting for him to answer.

"They can't guarantee more than one good discharge. In fact," he continued, "there's a pretty good chance the networks won't physically survive."

"What? Are you serious?"

The others, too, were showing looks of concern.

"Listen. The specs are unheard of. We're lucky to have any solution at all."

"What are the risks?" asked Rebecca, displaying her usual pragmatism.

"Minimal," insisted Richard. "We've enclosed each network in a reinforced container with built-in fire suppression."

Anticipating the next question, he added, "and we've calibrated the control system to compensate for the additional cable needed to keep it a safe distance from the rest of the equipment. The two on the way now cover us through Gamma, and there's two more in production for Delta and Epsilon."

"Why am I just learning this now?" asked Dr. Akindele.

"Because it's not your job to know, Jimi," he shot back. "Equipment and logistics are my responsibility. You can stick to the physics."

"I told you never to call me that. Only my mother calls me Jimi," huffed Dr. Akindele before turning on his heel to walk away.

"Fucking guy," snorted Richard.

"He has a point, though, Richard," said Rebecca. "Why are we just learning this?"

"Because it's under control," he replied. "The only time I'll bother you with details is when things are not under control."

"Look," interrupted Admiral Daniels, "so far, you've been on top of everything, Richard, and you have my complete trust."

"Yes," conceded Rebecca. "Today has been a good day, Richard. You've done well."

"Now, about the Epsilon invitations," continued the Admiral, "I could really use a couple more."

"No problem. Just take Jimi's," offered Richard. "And his mother's."

"Don't even joke about that," whispered Rebecca. "I don't want to deal with the shit show that would cause."

Chapter Four

THE SOCIAL MEDIA FEEDBACK from the East Coast slowed to a trickle and finally stopped as friends and family turned in for the night. Jayson found himself unable to stay still. Wandering his room, he compulsively checked the empty drawers and cabinets, and tested the faucets. Just as well, he thought, his best bet to avoid jetlag and stay functional would be to hold off on sleep until the appropriate local time, anyway. He decided to expend some nervous energy passing the few hours before dinner exploring the Center grounds.

The boomerang shape of the residence building, he discovered, matched the curve of the shoreline on the point where it stood. Between the building and the beach was a neatly maintained trail that was not overly manicured. The adjacent gardens were planted with some species that he recognized as indigenous and others he could not immediately identify. He took a mental note to look them up later.

He walked south, away from the cluster of buildings he'd passed on the way in, towards more natural-looking surroundings. The path took him along the length of the residence, and he counted the windows as he went. Some rough calculations led him to estimate it could house as many as four hundred people. He wondered how many of the rooms were still vacant, waiting for people like him to arrive.

His phone vibrated in his pocket. He pulled it out without adjusting pace to see a news alert from Hitz-It on one of his tracked topics. '*Atlantic Meridional Overturning Circulation Collapse Accelerating.*' The critical processes of the world were shutting down or changing irreversibly everywhere he looked, and the grim, daily news alerts only served to increase his anxiety. He shook his head and wondered why he continued to read them with such morbid eagerness.

Well past the residence, the trail disappeared into a wooded area and diverged. On the left, some scattered benches sat facing the harbor, and it seemed like a good place to sit for a while to read the article. He headed for the nearest one and noticed a young woman sitting alone on a bench a little further down the path. He decided he was in the mood for real company instead of the impersonal companionship of his social media apps. Besides, he figured, it was an opportunity to get a different perspective on the Center instead of relying exclusively on the one offered by Cal.

Despite the view, the young woman was staring at her phone. As Jayson approached, she looked up and smiled.

"Hello," she greeted.

"Hi," he replied. "I'm Jayson."

She offered a hand and said, "Samaira."

"Nice to meet you, Samaira. Do you work here?"

"No," she replied. "Just interviewing. Same as you."

Jayson cocked his head and raised an eyebrow at her.

"Your badge," she explained, pointing at her own. "The big red 'visitor' gave you away."

"Oh, yeah."

"So, what's your field of expertise, Jayson?" she asked.

"Sustainable agriculture. You?"

"Organizational psychology."

Jayson didn't want to admit he had no idea what that was.

"Interesting," he replied. "How does that fit into the whole sustainability thing?"

"You can't change the world if you don't change human behavior," she explained simply.

"Of course," he nodded. "That makes sense, but sounds—daunting."

"That's an understatement," she admitted.

"Hey, you mind if I hit you?" he asked suddenly, reaching for his phone.

"Why not? We might end up being colleagues, after all."

They tapped their phones together gently to make a connection on Hitz-It, sharing their profile and contact information.

"Oh, wow," commented Jayson as he scanned her profile. "So it's not just Samaira. It's *Dr.* Samaira."

"Yeah, but I don't let it go to my head," she said with a laugh.

"I'm still a grad student myself," he admitted. "Not really sure what I'm doing here, to be honest. It seems like I might be punching a little above my weight."

"Oh, I doubt that. I'm sure there's a good reason you're here."

"I guess. I just keep thinking maybe it was a mistake, and they're going to be pissed off when they find out they wasted a private jet on me."

"Private jet?"

Jayson suddenly felt he might have put his foot in his mouth.

"Uh, yeah. They flew me from Vancouver on a private jet," he said. "How'd you get here?"

"I flew commercial from Atlanta."

"Probably I just got lucky. Like the jet was already there, or something."

"Maybe," she said with a smile. "Or maybe you're just a little more special than you think."

If she was upset or jealous, Samaira didn't convey it.

"Someone back at the residence told me this path goes all the way around the point," she continued, changing the subject. "They said it's about a two-and-a-half-mile loop with some okay views. If you'd like to join me for a walk, I think we'd be back right around the start of dinner at the cafeteria."

"I've been dreading the idea of eating dinner alone," he admitted. "So, yeah. Count me in."

The trail took them through a flat landscape of sparse forest with intermittent, open grassy areas. Throughout the walk, Jayson pointed out various flora that he recognized and talked about some of their more interesting characteristics—how their seeds spread, what kind of soil they preferred—anything notable that came to mind. Samaira was mainly quiet, but showed interest and politely acknowledged his observations. The silences in between made him uncomfortable, but she didn't seem to mind.

Towards the end of the peninsula, there were places where the land was still scarred from whatever abuses the Navy had subjected it to before the Center took it over. Derelict buildings and the scattered, decaying carcasses of abandoned military equipment offered more clues to the peninsula's past.

"It's such a shame," he said, gesturing at a ratty old tent and a pair of abandoned jeeps. "This is such a beautiful place, and they just left all this crap here."

"It is a shame," she agreed.

"I wonder how many places like this there are in the world," he continued. "Places where we've come in, taken what we wanted—done what we wanted—and just left behind a pile of garbage. How is that fair to the ones left to deal with it all?"

"Sometimes the things we can't change overwhelm us, and we forget about the things we *can* change."

He considered that for a moment. '*Suck it up, buttercup. There's work to be done.*' Is that what she was trying to say? If so, she'd done it subtly.

The conversation for the rest of the walk was superficial, but comfortable. They engaged in the perfunctory small talk of strangers, and Jayson started feeling more at ease with the intervening periods of silence. His compulsion to break in with random observations abated as he enjoyed the quiet companionship of their afternoon stroll around the point. Samaira was easy company.

The sun was beginning to set as they arrived back at the residence lobby. Passing through the sliding front door, they noticed a group of people gathered on the mezzanine above, looking out of the west-facing windows.

"There's still time to catch the sunset if you hurry," a young woman called down to them.

Jayson looked at Samaira, who replied with a casual shrug. They took the wide, spiral staircase two steps at a time and arrived at the top just in time to view the spectacle. A couple of people stepped aside to ensure the newcomers had an unobstructed view of their first island sunset, and they found themselves standing next to the woman who had called down to them.

"It's not the best place on the island for sunsets," she explained, "but there's no such thing as a *bad* sunset on a day like this."

Her accent was slight, but familiar. Growing up near the melting pot of the Greater Toronto Area had exposed Jayson to a variety of ethnicities and their various accents. He considered himself something of an expert on the subject. Still, he couldn't place where she might be from. He glanced around to acknowledge those standing behind him, and was struck by the youth and diversity of the group. It looked like they were gathered for a stock photoshoot for some impossibly progressive college brochure.

They stood in silence until the last glimmering sunlight disappeared on the horizon, and the buildings' lights came on gradually to compensate for the waning daylight. Quiet conversations rose behind them as people started gravitating towards the cafeteria.

"My name is Hitarthi," offered the woman.

"Samaira. Nice to meet you."

"Jayson," he added.

"We're just about to have dinner," she said. "Will you join us?"

"Of course. Thank you," answered Samaira for both of them.

They made their way through a set of automatic sliding glass doors where a sign posted at the entrance read, '*The cafeteria lanai is closed this evening for a special event. We apologize for the inconvenience.*'

"Is it closed?" asked Jayson with a frown.

"No, not closed," explained Hitarthi. "We just have to eat inside tonight."

The cafeteria was spacious and bright. They found a relatively empty area to one side and pulled together a few tables to accommodate everyone, leaving a few pairs of sunglasses to claim the space while they went to the service area to select their meals.

An abundance of choice greeted them. Vegan, kosher, and halal options were available, and all items listed the sustainability considerations such as place of origin, water sources, fertilizers, and cultivation techniques. Jayson imagined his own contributions could soon be represented in the cafeteria selection if he got an offer to join. It struck him how quickly he'd gone from dismissing the opportunity as frivolous to already visualizing himself as part of the team at the Center.

Returning to the table, Jayson was careful to take a seat at the end near Samaira and Hitarthi. He felt more comfortable if he didn't have to sit in the middle of too many new people all at once.

"Red badges, I see," observed Hitarthi as he sat down next to her.

"Yep. Interviewing tomorrow," he replied.

"A word of advice? Don't let Dr. Vandergroot intimidate you. He's quite nice once you get to know him."

"Thanks. I'll keep that in mind."

Samaira acknowledged with a nod as she chewed a bite of food.

"What do you do here?" asked Jayson.

"Materials science," she explained. "The Center is funding my research at Rice University on durable biodegradables. We're trying to create a broader range of material properties to replace plastics in short and medium lifespan products."

"Impressive."

"My dream," continued Hitarthi, "is that someday you'll be able to throw your old cellphone or laptop into the compost, and it will break down into harmless organic compounds and fertilizer."

"Is that even possible?"

She laughed.

"Not even remotely. At least not with the technology we have now. That's what makes it a dream. Touch screens, circuit boards, processors—there's so much to consider. For now, I'm hoping we can introduce compostable outer shells for electronic gadgets we throw away every few years."

"That's a fantastic start," replied Samaira.

"We shouldn't be manufacturing things that survive hundreds or thousands of years past their useful life," continued Hitarthi. "That's not even engineering. It's just lazy."

"The Wonderful One Hoss Shay," said Samaira with a smile.

"Huh?" asked Jayson, furrowing his brow.

"It's a poem written by Oliver Wendell Holmes in the mid-nineteenth century," she explained. "It's about a deacon who builds a one-horse shay—a two-wheeled, horse-drawn carriage—designed to last exactly one hundred years.

On the one-hundredth anniversary of its construction, it crumbles to dust all at once."

"*That* is what I call perfect engineering," smiled Hitarthi.

Two more from the group returned from the service area with full trays. The first sat down next to Hitarthi, and the other sat opposite him, next to Samaira.

"Hey," the man greeted casually, "I'm Parth."

"Luping," added the woman. "Nice to meet you."

Samaira and Jayson introduced themselves to the new arrivals.

"Luping works with construction materials for buildings and roads," explained Hitarthi. "And Parth is a civil engineer. They work together a lot."

A loud pop and an eruption of cheers and laughter from the large group gathered in the outdoor dining area cut the introductions short. Through the windows, they saw a tall man with salt-and-pepper hair holding a newly opened bottle of champagne; the foaming contents overflowing onto the floor. Despite the growing mess at his feet, he was grinning widely.

"What's going on over there?" asked Jayson.

"Not sure," replied Parth. "That's the fusion team. Must have had a breakthrough."

"This kind of thing happen a lot?"

"First time I've seen it, but I've only been here a couple of months."

Hitarthi shrugged in agreement.

"What's the matter, Richard?" one of the celebrants yelled. "You never open a bottle of champagne before?"

There was more laughter from everyone in response to the good-natured ribbing.

The tall man, still smiling, replied, "You mean I'm not supposed to do this?"

He shook the bottle vigorously and used his thumb to create a nozzle effect, spraying the pressurized contents at the assembled team. He then dumped the remaining champagne on his head, evoking more applause and laughter. One man, however, was not laughing. He rose from the end of the table opposite his champagne-drenched host and walked inside—towards the cafeteria exit.

"Oh, he's pissed," observed Jayson.

"That's Dr. Akindele," said Parth. "He's always pissed."

"He is not very friendly either," added Luping. "I tried to talk to him about his work once. He told me he'd rather explain it to a monkey because the monkey wouldn't ask stupid questions."

"Ouch," remarked Jayson.

"I wouldn't judge him too harshly," said Parth. "Dude is definitely on the spectrum."

"You have a background in psychology," Jayson prompted Samaira, "what do you think?"

"I'm more geared towards organizational psychology, not individual," she deflected.

"But you studied it, right?" he urged.

"Yes. But I'm really not comfortable diagnosing someone I've never met before based on anecdotes."

"He doesn't even live here at the residence," continued Parth. "He stays over in West Lock Estates with his mother."

"And she drives him to work and picks him up every day," added Luping.

"Still not comfortable making a diagnosis?" asked Jayson with a laugh.

Samaira just smiled and shook her head.

The boisterous laughter in the lanai subsided, and the young researchers in the cafeteria continued chatting over their meals. Their new colleagues introduced Jayson and Samaira to a few more people within earshot of their end of the table. By the time dinner was over, they'd connected with all of them on Hitz-It. The jetlag was catching up with Jayson, so he was relieved when people began picking up their trays and excusing themselves for the evening. He thanked Hitarthi for her hospitality and said goodnight to Samaira before returning to his room.

Once inside, he gave his messages a last look for the day, and responded to a few he had missed. Everyone he knew was on Eastern Time, and he wouldn't likely be getting any more hitz before morning. A recommendation for an article popped up on his screen: *Top ten places to see before they become unlivable.* He settled in to read it before going to bed.

Chapter Five

JAYSON WOKE EARLY BECAUSE of the time difference and caught the sunrise alone on the cafeteria lanai with a cup of coffee. Though from a machine, it was still superb. After the kitchen staff arrived and others began filling their trays, he enjoyed a leisurely breakfast while catching up on his hitz. By 8:00, when Cal walked in, he was waiting on a lobby couch with his head buried in his phone.

"Good morning Jayson. I trust you had a pleasant evening?"

"Hey. 'Morning, Cal. Yeah, it was great."

"You do much after you got settled in?"

"Not too much," he replied. "Went for a walk, met some of the other researchers watching the sunset, and joined them for dinner in the cafeteria."

"Great! Glad to see you're getting comfortable. Now, let's go for a tour and meet the man in charge."

They took the path Jayson had followed around the point with Samaira the evening before, this time heading north towards the cluster of buildings and the massive aircraft carrier still moored offshore.

"It's not that far, and I figured it would be nice to go for a walk," said Cal.

"Yeah," agreed Jayson. "Great day for it, but I do like your car."

"I have to admit that was a bit of a flex," he laughed. "I just rented that to pick you up yesterday. It doesn't really go well with the whole green image."

"I didn't even make the connection," admitted Jayson.

"We have a small fleet of electric cars you can borrow if you need to leave the facility," explained Cal. "And there're golf carts on-site in case it's raining, or you have to haul some gear around the fields."

Jayson nodded his approval of the arrangement as though it would be a consideration for his acceptance of any forthcoming offer.

"The power cables from the carrier are gone," observed Jayson as they passed a large, windowless warehouse next to the docks.

"Yeah. They concluded the test yesterday, and the Reagan is getting ready to head back to Yokosuka."

"I saw the party last night in the cafeteria with the fusion team. Do you know what happened?"

Cal stopped, looked around, and leaned in close, as if about to reveal some forbidden secret.

"I can't say too much about it," he said in a hushed tone, "but I can tell you a viable fusion reactor is now always two years away."

"Very funny," replied Jayson. "I had a feeling my joke was going to age poorly."

They resumed their walk, and Cal started the tour in earnest.

"The largest building is home to the Center's administrative offices, and where most of the sustainability researchers are working. Next to that is for research that is not directly related to the center, but Mr. Kamaras still wants to support."

"What kind of stuff?"

"Medicine, cultural studies, linguistics—all sorts of things."

"So he gives out grants and provides facilities?"

"He has something much more valuable than that," explained Cal. "I know you're not naïve, Jayson, and you know what makes Hitz-It unique are the algorithms that analyze and commercialize user data."

"Yes," acknowledged Jayson. "I get the concept that I'm the product for sale when I'm using a *free* app."

"Well," he continued, "we can use those algorithms for more altruistic purposes. When combined with our quantum computing capability, we can help make better antibiotics, better cancer treatments, better language translators to increase understanding among cultures, and so on."

"Giving back," summarized Jayson. "I like it."

"Exactly," agreed Cal.

"And those smaller buildings?"

"The one closest to the path is Fusion A. That's where the fusion team has their offices and meeting rooms. Closest to the water is Fusion B, where we house the test chamber and control room."

A team of workers in orange vests and hard hats were milling about Fusion B. One of them was guiding a crane hook into position with a series of hand signals.

"What are they doing?"

"They're disassembling it. The building is modular so we can take it apart and move it when necessary."

"Wow. That's pretty cool."

"The next test is going to be quite a bit bigger," explained Cal, "and the Navy is a little touchy about the whole 'blowing up Pearl Harbor' thing ever since the second world war."

"Is that really a risk?" asked Jayson.

"We don't think so, but we're relocating to a more isolated secondary location on the southeast corner of the island just to make the neighbors feel more at ease."

Like those at the residence, the grounds immediately surrounding the research facilities were neat but not heavily manicured. A central plaza provided seating in the shade of a few acacia trees and wooden pergolas covered in vines and flowers. They entered the most prominent building via automatic sliding doors adjacent to the plaza, and Cal offered the receptionist a smile.

"Monica, you are radiant this morning."

"Good morning, Cal," she replied with mock embarrassment.

"This is Jayson Reilly. He's here to meet Richard."

"Dr. Vandergroot is running a little late this morning," she explained. "Perhaps you could start Mr. Reilly on a tour in the meantime?"

"No problem," assured Cal. "We'll start with the main floor labs."

Jayson gave the receptionist a polite nod and followed Cal through another set of sliding doors into a wide, brightly lit corridor. It was lined with windows into the laboratories on either side.

"This side of the main floor is dedicated to materials and fabrication techniques," said Cal. "Everything from eco-friendly plastics to new materials for roads and skyscrapers."

Jayson recognized Luping wearing a lab coat and safety glasses as she peered into a test cell. Cal described what she was doing.

"That's Dr. Zhang. Right now, she's conducting a compression test on a new type of concrete. It's embedded with metal-coated carbon fiber for strength and energy storage."

"Like a battery?"

"Exactly. She's expanding on some work done at Chalmers University of Technology in Sweden to increase the energy density of the fibers. One day, buildings like the one we're in right now will serve as giant batteries, storing up energy from power-generating windows for use when it's dark."

"Or storing power from the grid overnight when peak demand is lower and using it during the day," suggested Jayson.

"Yes, exactly. Leveling out energy production requirements from conventional sources," agreed Cal.

They continued walking leisurely down the hall as Cal described the equipment and activities they saw behind the glass, and Jayson tried to ask relevant questions. When they rounded a corner and passed through another set of doors into a new section, Jayson could feel the increased humidity and greedily inhaled the sweet, musty scent of compost and soil.

"Here's where you'd be contributing your expertise. We've been experimenting with yields and nutritional content on various types of grains, vegetables, fruits, and so on. So far, it's all been in ideal, controlled conditions, and now we need to understand how to best translate those results out into the real world."

"Some aspects of sustainable agriculture involve the use of controlled, indoor environments," said Jayson. "It's not realistic to get the best out of every crop outdoors, nor is it necessary."

"Sure," conceded Cal, "but we want to spread the benefit as far as possible—not just to the industrialized world where that sort of thing is possible."

"Can we go in and take a closer look?"

Cal checked his phone and shook his head.

"No. It looks like Dr. Vandergroot is ready."

They took the elevator up to the third floor, where the administrative offices were located. Dr. Richard Vandergroot occupied a corner suite on the southeast side of the building with sweeping views of Pearl Harbor and Honolulu. When they arrived, his inner office door was closed, and they could see through the windows he was on the phone.

"I've got to go," said Cal, tapping his left wrist where a watch would be if he wore one.

"No issues," assured Jayson. "I've got this."

Cal left Jayson alone in the outer office to wait for Dr. Vandergroot to finish his call. As he sat waiting, he took out his phone and hit Samaira.

Going into interview
When is yours?

1hr
Breakfast now
Break a leg

He was reviewing the list of new articles recommended to him by Hitz-It when Dr. Vandergroot emerged from his office.

"Mr. Reilly?"

"Yes. Jayson. Nice to meet you, Dr. Vandergroot."

He rose for the requisite handshake and was surprised by his interviewer's height. Jayson was over six feet tall but felt short standing next to the lanky managing director.

"Come in and have a seat," he invited, motioning towards a pair of chairs at his desk. "And, please, call me Richard."

Both men sat down, and Richard picked up a handful of papers, briefly studying them before speaking.

"Canadian, I see."

"Yes, sir," confirmed Jayson, although it wasn't really a question.

"From Brantford, Ontario. The home of Wayne Gretzky," observed Richard with a smile."

"That's right," laughed Jayson. "Our most famous export, I guess."

"Not a huge place, but still pretty urban, right?"

"About a hundred thousand people. And pretty close to Toronto."

"How does a city kid end up interested in sustainable agriculture?"

"My father is a schoolteacher in a nearby rural elementary school—kindergarten through grade eight, actually. That's where I went to school and met most of my friends. During summer breaks, I used to earn a few extra bucks helping out on their farms."

"And you got seduced by the simple life?"

"I wouldn't exactly call it simple. There's more tech packed into a tractor these days than in any car I've ever seen. You need to be part computer geek to be a farmer anymore. I once helped a guy side-load a modified operating system into a half-million-dollar combine harvester so he could bypass the subscription services."

"That's an amusing visual," replied Richard with a laugh. "A manure-covered hick with coke-bottle glasses pecking away at a keyboard like some kind of hacker."

"I guess," allowed Jayson with an involuntary frown.

Richard flipped through a few more pages, pausing to read some handwritten notes in the margins before moving on with the interview.

"Jayson Reilly."

He let the name hang in the air as he studied Jayson intently.

"That's an Irish name, but you don't look Irish," he continued.

Still unbalanced from the comment about the 'manure-covered hick,' Jayson was stunned by the statement, and didn't know how to respond. Of course, he had heard things like that before, but never in a professional setting.

"Uh, yeah. That's me."

"But you weren't born a Reilly," insisted Richard.

"No," admitted Jayson. "I was adopted as a baby."

"I thought so. Native, right?"

"Yes. That's right."

"What tribe?"

"My father was Cree, I think."

"And your mother?"

"Not sure," he admitted. "I've never been told much about her."

"Do you know anything about her at all?"

"Sorry," deflected Jayson, "but I kind of expected this to be about my work."

"Your work speaks for itself," assured Richard. "I'm just trying to get to know more about you as a person."

"I don't remember anything before my adoption. Everything about me starts with my family—the Reilly family."

"I don't believe that, Jayson. We're the sum of our experiences *and* everyone that came before us."

He decided it wasn't a question and waited for Richard to continue.

"My parents moved to the United States from the Netherlands in nineteen sixty-two, and I've been back there with my family a few times. I feel a connection to my history there, and want my kids to feel the same thing."

Jayson swallowed hard.

"Sounds nice," he offered.

"What about you, Jayson? Do you feel a connection to your history?"

"Not really," he admitted. "I mean, I think about it *sometimes*. About who my ancestors might have been and how they might have lived."

"But no connection?"

"No. Not really."

"So," continued Richard, "Cree. What makes you think that?"

Jayson squirmed uncomfortably in his chair, wishing that Richard would just let it go.

"It's what my parents, the Reillys, told me," he replied. "Based on where I was born, it seemed most likely."

"And where was that?"

"Fort Albany, Ontario. Way up north on James Bay."

"Wow. I bet you'd be having quite a different life if you'd stayed up there."

"You've got that right," he agreed with a nod.

"How did you end up getting rescued by the Reillys?"

"My mother just kind of disappeared, and my father," he hesitated, "he died when I was a baby."

"That's terrible. How did he die?"

"I'm not really sure," he lied.

"Your mother disappeared, you said?"

"That's what they tell me."

"And she was native as well? Cree?"

"I have no way of knowing. Her name isn't even listed on my birth certificate."

"So there's a significant piece of your history that's just missing? Doesn't that bother you?"

"I don't spend a lot of time dwelling on it, I guess."

"Do you ever feel guilty about not seeking to connect with your culture?"

"No," replied Jayson with growing annoyance.

"I can't imagine not having that grounding," prodded Richard. "I think I'd be lost without it."

"It's great you have that luxury," shot Jayson.

"Really? How are we that different? What luxury do I have that you don't?"

Jayson took a deep breath and closed his eyes for a few seconds to calm down.

"Let me explain some history to you, Dr. Vandergroot," he started. "For generations, my ancestors had their culture physically and psychologically tortured out of them by the Catholic Church with the full knowledge of the Canadian government."

Richard leaned in.

"They claimed it was to help integrate natives into Canadian society," continued Jayson, "but they never let us in. They left us stuck between cultures, without an identity, to rot on isolated, poverty-stricken reservations. I'm not connected to the culture of my ancestors because it's been wiped away like it never existed."

Richard nodded solemnly as Jayson leaned back in his chair and crossed his arms to show the subject was closed.

"Did your father have any substance abuse problems that you know of?"

Jayson's eyes widened in disbelief as he struggled to maintain control.

"I have no way of knowing the answer to that."

"What about you? Do you have any substance abuse problems? It's not uncommon with your people."

"You know what?" he blurted. "Go fuck yourself. I don't need this bullshit."

Jayson shot to his feet and stormed out of the office. In the hallway, he briefly forgot what direction to turn for the elevator. His head was spinning with rage and confusion, and he wanted nothing more than to get out of the building as quickly as possible. He slammed the elevator call button with the side of his fist repeatedly until it arrived. Though it was only a few floors down, the ride seemed interminable. He paced back and forth like a caged animal, swearing under his breath. On the ground floor, he burst from the elevator, sidestepping a pair of startled Center employees waiting for its arrival. As he fumed his way back to the residence, Jayson tried to comprehend the bizarre interview with Dr. Vandergroot.

It wasn't the first time he'd heard the tired substance abuse trope. At fourteen, he left the isolated safety of his small school for high school in the city, where he and his friends found themselves among throngs of unfamiliar students. As though the surroundings weren't intimidating enough on their own, they faced the predictable taunts of privileged city kids calling them hicks and making animal sounds at them in the halls. Bafflingly to Jayson, their new tormentors had singled him out with his own unique nickname.

"Hey, Chug!" they'd call out with self-congratulatory amusement while tapping their hands to their lips in a mock war cry.

He endured their taunts stoically for weeks, assuming the bullies would eventually get bored. Instead, it became an ingrained, reflexive behavior that spread out slowly among a growing number of students, and more people knew him by his derogatory nickname than by his real name.

One of the few people outside of his close friends who *did* know his name was a pretty brunette named Harper Wentz, who sat next to him in math. She was effortlessly popular and always friendly. Jayson was even considering asking her out, if he ever got up the nerve. One afternoon, after class, she caught up with him in the hall.

"Hey, Jayson. I need some help."

"What's up?" he asked, his heart skipping a beat.

"Polar coordinates," she confessed. "I don't get it at all."

Instead of using the opportunity to see if she was trying to get some time alone with him, he began excitedly explaining the concept as they walked to their next class.

Focused on Harper, he accidentally collided with another student exiting the boys' washroom.

"Watch it, Chug," he snarled.

Jayson turned beet red, first with embarrassment, and then with anger.

"What the fuck does that even mean?" he demanded, clenching his fists.

The boy raised an invisible bottle to his mouth and replied, "Chug, chug, chug."

Despite his anger, Jayson stood there frozen as the asshole laughed at his own cleverness, and others looked on with varying degrees of shock or amusement. Harper slinked off unnoticed during the short confrontation, and they never had another exchange that lasted beyond a few brief pleasantries. He still thought about the incident occasionally, imagining different outcomes if he'd just had the courage to do something.

Before that eye-opening encounter in the hallway, Jayson had never really felt any different from those around him. He'd been living under the naïve assumption that superficial differences, irrelevant to this point in his life, would always be so. Like a soldier with PTSD, he became hypervigilant, examining every interaction for a potential slight, and even found himself resentful of his parents for ignoring his race and failing to prepare him for reality.

Still, Jayson managed to find some comfort in the hopeful belief that people like his old high school bullies ended up pumping gas or working the late shift at McDonald's, where their ignorance would have limited impact. It was disheartening to realize that some of them, like the managing director of the Center for Sustainability Research, had done well for themselves. He took out his phone to say goodbye to Samaira.

> This place isn't for me
> Nice meeting you

He waited a few seconds for a response, but there was nothing immediate. To avoid the embarrassment of having to explain what happened to her, Cal, or any of the others he'd already met, he pulled out his phone to see if he could find a cheap flight home as soon as possible and get away from the Center unnoticed.

***

Samaira wasn't responding because her recruiter was already touring her through the facility. Although Samaira's work was directly related to the sustainability project, her tour had started in the guest researcher facility. There, her recruiter explained, she would have access to the Hitz-It algorithms and the enormous computing power needed to develop a means of fostering environmentally friendly behaviors on a global scale.

By the time Richard was ready to see her, there was no time to go through any of the labs in the main building. She was whisked straight past the reception desk and up the elevator to his suite, where her recruiter excused herself and left Samaira to wait for him to finish a phone call. She sat patiently, studying the artwork and photographs on the wall.

"Miss Adams," he called as he opened the door to his inner office, "please come in."

"It's Dr. Adams, sir," she corrected with a polite smile.

"Of course, yes. Forgive me, Dr. Adams. I hope you didn't take any offense."

"Not at all, Dr. Vandergroot."

"Please, call me Richard."

"Samaira," she replied, as she shook his hand.

"Please have a seat, and we'll get started."

She sat down across the desk from him and looked out the window.

"You have a lovely view from here."

"Thanks," he replied. "It's a nice perk of the job."

"I imagine you must enjoy having this view, considering your background."

"How's that?"

"The photographs in your outer office," she explained. "You're a Navy man."

"Yes," he smiled. "I worked for the Office of Naval Research many years ago."

"That makes sense to me now. I noticed your doctoral certificate from MIT, and wondered why a physicist would join the Navy."

"There's an impressive group of scientists and engineers of all imaginable backgrounds supporting naval research."

43

"Weapons research?"

"Some, yes. But not me. I was doing early theoretical work related to quantum computing. It was up to others to figure out the practical defense applications."

"And I saw that you've met Mr. Kamaras as well," she redirected. "I hear he's quite reclusive."

"I started working for him right after I left service, when Hitz-It.com was just a startup," he replied. "I posed for that photo with him the day I signed my first contract."

"It's a nice photo. It must be very special to you."

"It is," he agreed with a smile. "But we're here to talk about you today, not me."

"Of course," she apologized. "I didn't mean to derail your agenda."

"Not at all."

Richard sorted through a few loose papers on his desk, ostensibly referring to some notes about her background and qualifications.

"You showed your promise quite early," he started. "Graduated high school at sixteen with a perfect GPA *and* voted class valedictorian."

"Yes. That's correct."

"And we're not talking about some dump in the ghetto of Lakewood Heights," he continued, "Atlanta Girls' School is a top-notch private high school."

"It is an excellent school," she agreed. "I enjoyed my time there very much."

"Were there a lot of girls like you there?"

"It's a very diverse school," she assured him.

"Undergrad degree in psychology at Spelman. I'm curious about that."

"Yes?"

"A perfect GPA at an expensive private school, and then Spelman?" he said, wrinkling his brow. "You could have gotten a full ride at a good Ivy League college, especially as a black woman."

"Spelman was a perfect fit, and it just felt like the right choice for me," she replied. "I really can't imagine my undergrad experience being anywhere else."

Richard studied her for a moment.

"Then it was graduate studies and doctorate at the University of Georgia in Athens," he continued.

"Yes. I loved it there, and I loved the city. It had a great, positive vibe."

"I'm curious about your choice for postgrad. Why organizational psychology?"

"Corporations have a great deal of influence. I realized I could impact many lives if I could impact the culture and values of corporations."

"If it's about helping people, then why not be a *real* doctor?"

"For me, it's a matter of scale and persistence. When you change culture, you have a greater reach—and continue to change behaviors even after you're gone."

Richard frowned doubtfully.

"You say it like it's so simple, but is it really possible to establish a culture?"

"Sure," she replied, "Let me give you an example. This country was founded primarily by immigrants from England, yet our culture is distinct from what you find there."

"I concede that," he nodded, "but how did it happen?"

"It's not a simple answer, but it started with a vision."

"A vision?"

"Yes. A clear and compelling picture of a preferable alternative to the status quo, stated in powerful terms."

"And what was that vision?"

"We hold these truths to be self-evident," she quoted, "that all men are created equal, that they are endowed by their creator with certain unalienable rights, that among these are life, liberty, and the pursuit of happiness."

Richard nodded again.

"Did you feel that?" she asked.

"Feel what?"

"When I said that," she continued, placing her fist at the base of her sternum, "you felt something right here."

"I did," he admitted.

"That's it. That's your culture speaking to you."

"You said it *starts* with a vision. What else?"

"Well," she continued, "You need norms and values to act as guardrails to behavior, and you need a way to guide the everyday work of getting where you're going."

"Apply that to your analogy for me," he urged.

"The constitution would be the guardrails. Laws, policy, etcetera, give the daily guidance."

"So that's it? A bunch of words?"

"Of course not," she smiled. "We have our shared mythology of heroes like Abraham Lincoln, Neil Armstrong, and Rosa Parks. We have symbols like the flag and the American eagle. We have rituals like the pledge of allegiance, and we sing the national anthem before football games. We celebrate the fourth of July, and watch our athletes win gold at the Olympics. All of these are aspects of a culture we've sustained generation after generation."

Richard nodded as he listened to her explanation.

"But now that we've achieved our vision, what keeps us going?" he asked after a momentary pause of consideration.

Samaira's measured façade cracked for the first time during the interview. She sighed and smiled at him with a slight shake of her head.

"That they are endowed by their creator with certain unalienable rights, that among these are life, liberty, and the pursuit of happiness," she repeated. "The men who signed that document bought and sold other men as property."

"That was a long time ago," protested Richard.

"I'm not saying that as an indictment of the country," she explained. "Just an example that an enduring vision evolves to mean more over time. It's always just out of reach. Even today, many people would argue the pursuit of happiness isn't possible for them."

"So, no matter what, there's always more work to be done?"

"Yes," she asserted. "And that's a good thing. It gives us purpose, and human beings need purpose to be happy."

"Do you think you could find *your* purpose here at the center?" he asked.

"Yes. I do. With the resources of Mr. Kamaras, there is an opportunity to impact the ability of the next generation to pursue *their* happiness. If we can't get a handle on environmental issues, we're dooming them to a very bleak future. I'm here because that is a purpose to which I am prepared to dedicate myself."

"I have to say this has been a fascinating discussion, Dr. Adams," said Richard as he leaned back in his chair.

"It has," she agreed.

"Before we conclude, do you have anything you'd like to ask me about the Center?"

"There is one thing," she said with momentary hesitation. "And please forgive me for asking."

"Of course. Anything."

"Am I here because of my skills, or because of my race?"

"What?" he asked, furrowing his brow.

"It's just that there *is* a lot of diversity here," she continued. "More than one could optimistically expect."

"Ah," smiled Richard. "I see what you mean. I am going to be honest with you."

"Please," she prompted.

"Part of the reason you are here—you and many of the others—is to ensure diversity."

She held his gaze without reaction and waited for him to say more.

"But not in the way you think," he continued. "There's not going to be any self-congratulatory photo ops showing the world how inclusive we are, or anything like that. Mr. Kamaras is much more pragmatic."

"How so?"

"This project is his top priority, and he's only interested in diversity to the extent it serves his goals here. Diversity yields better results, and we've done the math to prove it."

"The math?" she asked, raising an eyebrow.

"That's just a figure of speech," he clarified. "There's no *math* per se. It's actually hundreds of millions of computerized simulations that demonstrate better outcomes with a diverse team."

"I would very much like to know more about these simulations," she said with renewed enthusiasm. "The implications for minority opportunities outside of the Center could be significant."

"You'll learn more in due time," he assured. "But first, we need to work on the contract and get a non-disclosure agreement in place."

Chapter Six

Jayson had been unsuccessful in his attempts to book an immediate flight home, and briefly considered trying to get a hotel near the airport to distance himself from the center until he could escape the island for good. He realized the personal expense would be too much to bear, and decided instead to hide out in his room with his phone. As he read an article on the Pacific garbage gyre, a hit from Samaira finally appeared.

> *Still here?*
> *Want to talk?*

> Still here
> Meet at the bench?

> *On my way*

Jayson had mixed feelings. Although part of him wanted to see Samaira again, the other part was dreading having to explain what had happened in the interview. Ultimately, the part of him that found her more than just a little attractive emerged from the safety of his room and headed for the shoreline path. When he arrived at the bench where they first met, she was waiting for him.

"I was already walking back to the residence when I hit you," she explained.

"How'd it go?"

"Not bad," she shrugged, downplaying the experience. "Not so good for you, huh?"

"No," he admitted. "Not good at all."

"What happened?"

"He asked a lot of really personal questions and then insinuated, because I'm native, I might have a substance abuse problem."

"Yeah," she nodded. "He did the same kind of thing with me."

"What?"

"I was half-expecting him to offer me some watermelon and ask if he could touch my hair."

"Fucking racist prick."

"No. I don't think that's it."

"Huh? Then what the hell was that all about?"

"It's an interview technique designed to surreptitiously evaluate your temperament and see how you'll react to conflict. I didn't bite."

Jayson was agape.

"Son of a bitch."

"I take it you didn't react so well?"

"I told him to go fuck himself," he admitted.

"Ouch. That's a tough one to bounce back from," she sympathized.

"Not sure I really care about bouncing back," he shrugged. "I mean, what kind of person pulls shit like that?"

"Yeah. It wasn't exactly subtle, was it?"

"How was it so obvious to you? That it was some kind of game."

"I had an unfair advantage."

"What's that mean?" he asked, narrowing his eyes.

"I teach the technique in a workplace psychology class I give to HR students at the University of Georgia," she explained. "Although, if any of my students handed in an interview script as clumsy as Richard's, they'd get a C-minus, at best.

"That obvious, huh?"

"Sorry."

"Is that a normal thing? To piss people off in an interview?"

"Not really. It's usually just for high-stress jobs, or ones that put teams in prolonged isolation—like astronauts or arctic researchers. Maybe he read about it in some management magazine and decided to give it a try."

Jayson took a deep breath and shook his head. "Son of a bitch."

***

Richard was sitting at his desk, staring absent-mindedly out the window at a Navy cruiser passing behind the southern tip of Ford Island. Cal sat across the desk with Samaira's recruiter, waiting for him to process his thoughts so they could resume their deliberations.

"Let's deal with the easy one first, Denise," he said, turning back to his desk.

"Dr. Adams," replied the woman sitting next to Cal.

"She's rock solid," agreed Richard. "Where is she on acceptance?"

"According to the algorithms," said Cal, referring to his phone, "less than a one percent chance she won't be on board."

"Okay. Let's get started on the contract and the NDA right away," decided Richard.

"On it," assured Denise.

"As for that other shit show—"

"I know it looked bad," conceded Cal, "but it's a matter of offsetting factors."

"What factors offset being told to go fuck myself?"

"The algos still like him," assured Cal. "He's over ninety percent on acceptance, and we're predicting ninety-seven by Gamma. We might even use this incident to accelerate him."

"At least that's promising. No risks presented by the outburst? There's going to be some conflict, and we need him and the others under control."

"Overall, he's still showing as the go-along-to-get-along type. Besides, for compliance, it's more of an aggregate score we need to worry about. This is nothing."

Richard raised an eyebrow doubtfully, but said nothing.

"And the sample I took back at the first interview shows he's filling a critical gap in the DNA profiles," continued Cal. "His mitochondrial haplotype is the oldest North American one we've found among suitable candidates. He's got no corrective lenses, no teeth extractions or braces, no appendicitis, no significant risk of genetic disorder, etcetera, etcetera."

"What about his skills?"

"Usable, for sure. We just need to nudge him in a bit of a different direction."

"What are you saying, Cal? He's a go?"

"Let me ask a bit differently," he offered. "Do you trust the algorithms that built your fusion team?"

Richard studied him as he considered the information at hand.

"Fine. Pull the trigger," he said finally. "But you're the one who has to make up some bullshit story about how that interview wasn't a disaster."

"Yeah. That's no problem."

"So we're done identifying the Gamma recruits?" asked Richard.

"Yep. Looking good," assured Cal.

"No," protested Denise, "It's not looking good."

"What's the problem?" demanded Richard.

"Andrew Jorgensen," said Denise. "He's becoming increasingly isolated, and he's creeping people out. The women aren't comfortable with him."

"How is that even relevant?" asked Cal. "The profile is perfect."

"It's relevant," she insisted. "This isn't the Handmaid's Tale we're talking about here."

"I agree," said Richard. "This'll spread discord like cancer. Any indicators from the algos yet?"

"Acceptance has stalled out. Regressing a bit, even," cautioned Denise.

"Alright. Jorgensen is out," decided Richard. "I assume we have backups targeted and prepped?"

"Yeah. I'm on it," said Cal with a sigh.

"We only have a few months to get these kids committed," reminded Richard.

Chapter Seven

RUAN'S HUT, LIKE EVERYTHING in it, was made from materials he'd collected on the island. After a long enough period, it would all return to the earth as if it had never existed. It was a satisfying thought. At the end of this operation, like the others he'd carried out before it, all traces of his activity would disappear, and he'd vanish like a ghost.

His gear, however, was a different story. The metals, plastics, composites, and other advanced materials would linger for centuries. He'd cached that nearby under a few inches of soil in two hardened plastic cases. Per instructions, their location had been determined with precise reference to prominent landmarks.

Ruan unearthed the containers to ponder their contents and assess the likely utility of each item for his upcoming encounter. The M24 sniper rifle was oiled, clean, and useless. He'd long since run out of ammunition, but hadn't been able to overcome the compulsion to keep it in perfect condition. He doubted many Special Forces operatives could have just left it to rust, useless or not. The flare gun and two remaining flares went into his ruck, as did a pair of flashbangs and a handful of nylon ties. The Ka-Bar combat knife and P226 sidearm, loaded with its last seven rounds, would stay on him for easy access. He briefly considered a small, stainless steel cylinder, judging its weight before adding it to the supplies in his pack.

The last item, a self-illuminating tritium compass given to him by his wife just before the start of the final season of Survival Stories, occupied a special place. He flipped open the cover and read the words engraved to the right of the sight wire: '*May you always find your way home to me. Love, Lenora.*'

"Not fucking likely, is it?" he asked the device, snapping it closed before slipping it in his left breast pocket and fastening the button to keep it secure.

Along with his dried rations and a couple of liters of fresh water, the weight of his load was easily manageable and far less than he would have taken on a training mission into the South African bush. The major difference was the readily available clean water on the island. He never had to worry about carrying much. Satisfied, Ruan replaced the sealed containers and concealed them under a layer of dirt.

He started at dawn the next day, deciding on a route two kilometers inland running parallel to the shore. That way, he could stay well concealed in the dense trees, and avoid having to cross a few broad inlets that cut into the coastline. It was a trail he often traveled but had been careful not to wear in too obviously. He usually used it to get to the main north-south corridor of O'ahu when he was doing his regular recon tours of the north shore. Conveniently, it also passed near the north end of Pearl Harbor where his guests were lurking.

Extreme caution wasn't required until he got closer to making contact. There were no dangerous predators or poisonous snakes on the island. The most significant natural danger was the treacherous terrain of the mountains and parts of the shoreline. The path was relatively straightforward, aside from the dense vegetation that encroached on all sides. Even so, there was no reason to push hard and risk leaving himself exhausted and vulnerable at the end of his journey. He adopted a steady pace with regular stops for food, hydration, and rest.

By late afternoon, he was within two kilometers of Pearl and adjusted to a slower, stealthier approach. Although unlikely, it was possible an incursion was already underway, and he did not want to stumble upon the intruders accidentally. In a decade on the island, he had never been spotted—at least not by anyone who'd lived to tell about it—and he had no intention of allowing that to change now. '*Through Stealth, Our Strength*' had been the motto of One Reconnaissance Commando. Although that team had been disbanded before Ruan's time as a Recce, he'd adopted their maxim and made it his own.

To him, there was nothing excruciating about the final, two-hour slow advance to the nearby tall grass of the shoreline. It was just how these kinds of operations were done, and only the first test of his patience in what would likely be a days-long effort of repeatedly probing the shore and retreating into the jungle until he found the hidden campsite. He took out his binoculars and scanned the water's edge for signs of life.

To his surprise, it took only a few moments to locate his targets. They had left their canoes exposed on a beach on the south side of Ford Island and started a sizeable campfire that emitted a wispy line of smoke low into the sky. It was as if they wanted to be found. Diligently preparing to salt and dry their catch, the four men had made themselves apparent. All Ruan had to do was swim to the island and attack in the middle of the night. Still, if his instincts were right, and they were here as a provocation, it meant he must be missing something. They hadn't come all this way just to sacrifice themselves. He decided the best course of action was to watch and wait.

Ruan maintained his vigil for hours as the men cleaned and prepared their catch. They cut the larger fish into pieces and then laid everything out on stones around the fire before generously sprinkling it with salt. He was familiar with the process he'd seen carried out by the island's original inhabitants countless times.

It was nearly sunset when they finished, and they shifted their attention to preparing a meal. On a flat rock amid the low embers, they roasted a large amount of taro and several of the larger fresh fish they'd kept aside from their catch. It was a lot of food for the small party gathered around the fire. As they ate, they separated several portions of the meal and began wrapping them into individual banana leaf packets. Ruan counted them carefully; eight in total.

One fisherman gathered them into a crude satchel slung over his right shoulder and started walking northward away from the campsite, close enough to the shore for Ruan to follow his movements. Although sunlight was fading quickly, the moon and stars betrayed the dark figure picking his way through the trees. Every two-or-three hundred meters, he'd pop out near the shoreline grasses and stoop down momentarily before heading back into the cover of the denser vegetation.

He had to concede the brilliance of their plan. The fishermen hadn't just been running recon; they'd been advertising their presence and establishing a pattern of behavior to make sure they had his attention. Whether through direct experience or the accounts of the survivors, these new visitors understood if they went inland, they would never be seen alive again. The four men sitting around the fire were bait. Hidden among the grasses and trees of the shore, much like Ruan himself, were eight others watching for signs of an approach.

They had probably arrived in the early hours of the morning under cover of darkness and hidden their canoes from sight. Their mission, he surmised, was to assess the nature of the threat and ensure the survival of at least a few of them to return home with valuable intelligence. The only flaw in their plan was that it relied on them being stealthier and more patient than he was.

Rainfall usually happened overnight and was almost guaranteed every few days at this time of year. The darkness of a cloudy night and the sound of the rain would hide his arrival on Ford Island. All he had to do was wait for it. He chose a counterintuitive spot for the crossing nearer to their campsite and a longer swim than would be necessary from other, more direct approaches. It was likely the watchers would space themselves out a little farther apart where they deemed themselves less vulnerable. Satisfied with his plan, he settled in for the long task of surveilling the enemy's position and evaluating their defenses.

***

Ruan watched his visitors at various intervals, day and night, for several days before a cool wind picked up and a wall of clouds built against the peaks to the northeast. He knew by nightfall, the cloud cover would extend out into the Pacific Ocean, and pounding raindrops would make it impossible to discern his movements against the dark water of the lagoon. Once ashore, he'd be able to rely on the dense vegetation and the din of the storm to hide his activities.

The men keeping watch had been disciplined and hard to spot, and Ruan was thankful for the fishermen that had betrayed their positions. To make matters worse for the hapless sentries, the men providing their sustenance tracked the same path several times a day, essentially creating a map for Ruan to follow from one target to the next. The one advantage they still had was that he could not determine their cycles of alertness and sleep. They'd been too still and well-concealed for him to figure that out.

It didn't matter. In the early predawn hours of the next day, he would make the seven hundred meter crossing and engage them. He didn't want to wait any longer and risk the possibility they might just declare the island safe again, but it was unlikely they would rush to that assumption without a deeper incursion. Still, he weighed his desire for more intelligence against the possibility they might go home and return in more significant numbers. No, he determined. He'd rather not deal with that.

Hours later, already soaked from the rain, Ruan waded into the water under cover of darkness. He couldn't even see the outline of the nearby island, and knew that he, too, would be invisible from across the stretch of lagoon. He'd packed everything except his combat knife and compass safely in waterproof nylon bags in his ruck. Even with the dimly glowing compass to guide him, it was going to be challenging to maintain a perfect trajectory for his chosen landing spot. He had identified a pair of uniquely positioned, large rocks that he would seek on the other side to know exactly where he was relative to his first target.

He waded out into the shallow water for a hundred meters before the bottom dropped away, and he had to swim. He held the compass awkwardly in one hand, checking it every dozen strokes to make sure he was still on the correct heading. It was a tradeoff, but he'd rather take longer on the crossing than arrive on the other side only to realize he couldn't get his bearings in the darkness.

The sound of the rain pummeling the water all around him was disorienting as he continued steadily across the lagoon. Overloading one sense had the effect of diminishing the brain's ability to process information from the others, and required intense focus to overcome. Ruan had been trained to operate under duress, and so viewed the conditions as being overwhelmingly to his advantage versus the simple-minded savages he was stalking.

After less than an hour of slow swimming, he could touch the bottom with his feet once more. He kept his head barely above the water, crawling along the sand for the last few meters until he was confident he was below the field of vision of the nearest intruder. It was too dark to make out the landmarks by sight, and so he stumbled along the shoreline until he felt the first of the rocks he'd sighted earlier. Tracing the shape with his hands, he determined which of them he'd found, and quickly created a mental picture of where he was. He set his pack against the rock and retrieved his sidearm, holstering it at his right hip.

Working his way inland until he found the pathway worn by the fisherman, he planned to follow it north until it diverged toward the first lookout post. As he moved slowly forward, however, he realized the same dark skies and rain that had concealed his arrival were also making it impossible for him to find the path. He would need to rework his plan quickly and figure out how he would dispatch his targets before the first light of dawn left him vulnerable. He crouched down low behind a large tree and began thinking through alternate scenarios.

He had timed his arrival to catch the first guard unaware, and then ambush the fisherman making his usual rounds about thirty minutes later. He then planned to assume the fisherman's role so his next target would attribute his approach to the regular routine. Instead, he'd need to wait for the fisherman to pass and follow him to the first of the watchmen. After that, he wasn't yet sure, but taking on two targets at once was not part of the original plan.

Eventually, a globe of light dancing in the distance caught his attention. He realized if he could not see the path, it was unlikely anyone else could either. As a result, the approaching fisherman was making his rounds by torchlight. There wasn't much time to react to the unexpected development. The bobbing light approached the tree where Ruan was hiding and eventually gave evidence to the man holding it, illuminating his face in flickering light. His eyes were cast downward as he focused on keeping himself on the path.

As he passed, Ruan fell in silently behind him, synchronizing his footsteps to obscure the sound of his movements. Though not likely necessary amid the sound of the falling rain, it was habit nonetheless. He stayed in the torchbearer's shadow to avoid looking directly at the light and compromising his night vision. It also kept him hidden from view of anyone directly in front of them.

They reached the point where the path diverged and followed it towards the shore. The fisherman made a loud call like a bird and received an answer in-kind from ahead. A birdcall in the middle of the night while carrying a lit torch was unlikely an attempt at stealth. More likely, it was a way of identifying the approaching man as a friend. If this were Ruan's operation, the call would be different for every man along the way to prevent someone from learning the secret to infiltrating the route unchallenged. He would have to gamble their operational security wasn't as meticulous as his own.

Ruan crouched low and maintained his distance. He did not want to react until he could see both men clearly. Then it would be a matter of who had the best reaction time. The fisherman spoke a few words, and a whispered reply came from the shadows ahead. A glint of light caught his eye, and a stern, tattooed warrior became visible against a backdrop of vegetation. He held a short, fierce-looking spear in his right hand, its tip festooned with shark's teeth.

The torchlight had likely blinded the warrior, giving Ruan the opportunity to strike. He closed in behind the fisherman and drew his knife. With a swift thrust, he plunged the Ka-Bar through the back of his ribcage and directly into his heart. He threw the lifeless man down; the knife slicing out of him as he fell away. The torch hit the ground but somehow did not extinguish. In its struggling light, distorted shadows danced against the trees.

The startled warrior took a half step backward as Ruan lunged at him, buying him enough time and distance to swivel his spear in front of his body in self-defense. Though too slow to get it all the way around, he caught Ruan on the side under his left arm. The row of jagged shark teeth tore at Ruan's flesh as he extended his right arm to drive the knife into the warrior's gut. He landed on his knees as his wounded prey fell backward, clutching his stomach. Ruan stumbled forward and leaped on him, this time driving the knife into his heart. A last gasp of air escaped the warrior's lungs, and he went still.

Ruan grabbed the torch from the ground and reached for the stinging wound on his left side. He briefly examined the blood on his hand and decided it was not severe enough to need immediate tending. That was good. He couldn't afford to slow down if he had any chance of completing his mission by daybreak.

He knew he would need to keep the torch to have any chance of finding the other men. To get close, he'd need to fool them into believing he was an ally for as long as possible. He examined the dead fisherman and decided that, in stature, he was a close match. Ruan studied how his loincloth was wrapped before removing it from his body. He then stripped naked himself and put on the loincloth as well as he could manage, finally passing it through the belt loops on his holster before tying the two ends tightly together.

Skin and hair color were both still an issue. Ruan was well bronzed from years on the island, but he was still lighter than any of the natives—and the tan lines were all wrong. He scooped up handfuls of mud and rubbed them all over his body, face, and hair. It wasn't really a good match, but it might be close enough in the pale light of the torch. Even if his disguise bought him only a few tenths of a second, it could be enough to make a critical difference.

His weapons, too, were wrong for the new and unplanned tactics. The Ka-Bar was for close combat, and the Sig was too loud to be drowned out by anything but the most intense island weather—far worse than the current conditions. He glanced down at the dead warrior's spear. It was crude, but better suited to the distances in a face-to-face encounter. It also wouldn't seem as out-of-place as a stainless steel knife glinting in the torchlight.

Finally, there was his ruck. He debated the immediate utility of the contents, and wondered if he shouldn't just stash it with his clothes for later retrieval. He decided the risk of losing track of it was too much to offset any way in which it might compromise his disguise. In the faint, yellow light, the color of the dirty straps looked near enough to the mud smeared all over his body.

Satisfied with his preparations, he located the side trail by torchlight and followed it back to the fork, where it rejoined the main path. He counted two hundred paces, the distance he'd estimated between the first two posts during his recon, and started looking for the second side trail. It was easy to find where the grass was bent over from the repeated passages.

Ruan started towards the water, holding the torch slightly behind his head to obscure his features in a halo of light. He held the spear with the tip facing forward but unthreateningly low by his right thigh. Approaching the shore, he mimicked the birdcall he'd heard before and tensely waited for the countersign. To his relief, the echoing reply came from just a few meters ahead. It seemed they hadn't thought to have a unique call for each post after all—or they had, and he was walking into certain death.

He tightened his grip on the spear but did not dare cock his arm back for fear of betraying his intentions too soon. A shape emerged from the tall grass at the tree line and moved towards him. He issued what sounded like a hushed rebuke and pointed at the torch, perhaps unhappy to have his position revealed by such poor operational discipline. Ruan did not break stride. He closed the gap and motioned as if handing over the torch. His prey reached out and gasped in surprise as it briefly illuminated Ruan's face. It was too late. Ruan was already propelling the spear forward with a quick, underhand thrust. It pierced the warrior's gut at the base of his sternum; the placement ensuring he could manage no cry of warning to his brethren. The close combat was exhilarating. With growing excitement, Ruan hurried towards the next target.

At the next offshoot, he employed the same tactic of holding the torch behind to keep his features in shadow. He repeated the birdcall, but got no answer from the warrior. Perhaps he was on his designated sleep break. Ruan called again. Still no answer. Ahead of him, the hulking form of a man appeared in the pale, flickering light. He held his spear defensively in front of him and challenged Ruan with a few harsh-sounding words.

Ruan knew it was unlikely he could best the larger, younger man who was undoubtedly much more skilled with the short spear. As the warrior took a few cautious steps forward, Ruan made the quick decision to loft his weapon over his shoulder and launch it. The warrior turned his body and instinctively raised his arm to protect his head. The spear, not designed as a projectile weapon, made contact at a bad angle and glanced off his shoulder, leaving only a superficial cut.

Enraged, the warrior started forward again. Ruan backed away and caught his heel on a root. As he stumbled backward, he hurled the torch, desperate to slow his attacker and buy himself a few precious seconds. He crashed to the ground and quickly rolled one complete turn to the right. Fumbling for his sidearm, he managed to raise it just as the massive shadow appeared above him, back-lit by the torchlight. He squeezed the trigger, the momentary flash illuminating his attacker's harsh, tattooed features.

The weight of the warrior crashing down on him knocked the wind out of Ruan, and the flash from the muzzle left him unable to see anything but its blinding white imprint. It was stupid and undisciplined to forget to close his eyes when firing into the darkness. He struggled to extract himself from underneath the lifeless mass, all the while trying to blink away the muzzle blindness.

He sat catching his breath after his narrow escape while blackness slowly re-placed the fading imprint of the flash. The torch must have landed in pooling rainwater and gone out. Added to the fact the gunshot had surely alerted at least the closest of his targets that something was very wrong, it meant he would need a new plan to take care of the remaining eight people on the island.

Going forward blindly toward alerted prey was not an option. Ruan's only choice was to backtrack on the familiar part of the trail where he had already eliminated the threats. He calculated those remaining on the island would probably seek safety in numbers after hearing gunshots, and gather near their canoes on the beach where they had landed. There, they'd either try to make a stand or hastily retreat to sea.

He decided he would need to make his way as quickly as possible through the darkness to the campsite before they could escape. He fumbled his way forward in the blackness, straining to hear the waves against the shore to indicate he wasn't straying inland. It was no use. In all directions, all he could hear was the same monotonous tap-tap-tapping of raindrops splattering against the foliage.

Desperate for some way to speed his progress, Ruan remembered the flare gun in his ruck. He stopped to take it out and then loaded one of his two remaining flares. Shielding his eyes from the initial flash, he pointed the gun to the sky and pulled the trigger. He quickly stuffed it back and tossed the pack over one shoulder, not wanting to waste any of the precious few moments of light.

A path through the trees revealed itself under the white light of the towering flare. Ruan sprinted forward as he scanned the ground in front of him to stay on course. If he was lucky, he could cover a considerable distance in the thirty seconds, or so, before the light faded and he was fumbling in the dark again.

So focused was he on the ground immediately in front of him, he didn't notice until the last second he was not alone on the path. He saw the pair of stationary feet when they were only two meters away and glanced up just in time to see one of the fishermen standing transfixed in the pouring rain, staring up in terrified amazement at the flare. He only had a split second to turn his shoulder and drive it into the side of the distracted man's head. The popping sound, audible even above the din, left no doubt that he'd shattered the man's jaw with the impact. Ruan got up, rubbing his shoulder. It would be badly bruised, but otherwise, okay. The fisherman lay motionless and unconscious on the ground. Ruan dragged the limp body and leaned it up against the trunk of a nearby tree, cuffing his wrists around it with one of the nylon ties from his pack.

He stayed crouched by the unconscious man for several minutes to catch his breath and contemplate how to salvage a plan that was quickly unraveling. It was incredibly risky to push forward on the edge of control, but even more dangerous to stop and wait for daylight. The rain eased, and its disorienting noise faded to a light patter. If the clouds broke, perhaps he'd be able to see the path well enough by starlight to continue towards the camp. If the remaining warriors had made it back already and were standing watch, he'd also be an easier target. He decided the safer option was to use his last flare to light the path and distract his prey as he closed the remaining distance as quickly as possible. He'd then fumble the last few hundred meters in the dark as stealthily as he could manage.

Once more, Ruan took the flare gun from his ruck and briefly examined his last flare before loading it into the chamber. He shielded his eyes and fired into the sky. Wasting no time, he sprinted forward under the soaring white globe. He was careful to scan further into the distance this time, not wanting to run into anyone else along the way. The shadows of swaying tree branches danced in the uneven light, making it tricky to adjust to the terrain. He estimated he'd managed at least three hundred meters by the time the last of the light extinguished overhead. In darkness once more, he crouched down behind another large tree to catch his breath after the exertion of the full-on sprint.

As the pounding of his heart against the inside of his chest subsided, so too did the rain. Though a few drops still fell, the westward sky began to clear, allowing a handful of twinkling stars to show through scattered openings in the clouds. The water lapping at the shoreline to his left was now finally audible amid the diminishing rain, and Ruan used it to guide himself confidently yet slowly forward in the right direction. Before long, the dancing glow of a campfire became visible ahead. He crept forward even more slowly, scanning the vegetation in front of him for signs of watchers.

They were camped on the clear, sandy beach where Ruan had first spotted their fire days earlier. It was now sheltered under a hastily built bamboo structure to prevent it from being extinguished by the heavy rain. The two remaining fishermen and a pair of warriors were visible on the far side of the flickering yellow-orange flames. Though they spoke among themselves, their darting eyes never broke away from the perimeter of the campsite.

A rustle grew louder on the far side of the camp, and the men took a defensive posture with their spears. When a pair of their colleagues emerged from the tree line, they were visibly relieved, but held their stances as if expecting pursuers to burst forth at any moment. The new arrivals added to the excited chatter, pointing towards the sky where Ruan had fired off the last flare.

Moments later, another warrior—the final one, Ruan knew—stumbled from the jungle and fell to his knees in front of his colleagues. His chest was heaving from the extreme exertion of his frenzied retreat to camp. He spoke a few words and motioned to the canoes, igniting an intense exchange. Ruan imagined he was advocating for a hasty retreat, while his companions wanted to wait to see if anyone else would return.

The fishermen began edging towards the two smaller canoes still sitting exposed on the beach. The newly arrived warrior walked a few meters into the trees to Ruan's right and started hauling a bigger, hidden outrigger out into the open. Another warrior began yelling at him, pointing to the pathway.

While they argued, Ruan produced a flashbang from his ruck and pulled the safety pin. As he raised himself slowly to his knees, he pulled the primary pin and tossed the grenade into the center of the group. Immediately, he threw himself face down on the ground and clasped his hands over his ears. The violence of the concussive blast was slightly disorienting to Ruan, but devastating to the seven men who had instinctively focused on the strange object as it landed among them.

Ruan leaped to his feet and drew his sidearm as he strode into the campsite. Around him, the stunned men were fumbling in blindness and confusion. One by one, he approached the warriors and put a single bullet into each of their heads at close range. He then slipped back into the cover of the trees.

It only took a few minutes for the fishermen to regain their senses enough to find one another. They surveyed the horrifying scene around the campfire, and wasted no time dragging one of their small outriggers to the water. The first pink hints of sunrise illuminated the tops of the now sparse clouds, providing just enough light for them to navigate their way out of Pearl Harbor.

Ruan watched the dark shadow of their canoe disappear beyond the narrow inlet that would lead them back to the open ocean. The adrenaline high of the last few hours subsided, and he noticed the throbbing pain on his left side for the first time. He walked over to the fire to examine the wound in its dying light and nodded with satisfaction. Not a bad outcome at all when weighed against the damage he had inflicted on the intruders.

The two survivors never saw even a hint of their enemy, and would now report the demonic forces they had encountered to their brethren back home. It was unlikely anyone would return soon. There was only the unconscious man tied up on the trail left for him to deal with, and Ruan wanted to use the opportunity to do something dramatic to make sure they got the message they were not welcome to return. Nearly all of Ruan's ammunition was gone, and soon he would not have the resources to fend off more than a few invaders at a time.

Chapter Eight

JAYSON SAT ALONE ON the bed in his room, scrolling absently through his feed. After talking with Samaira and going for another walk around the point, he still couldn't shake his anger over the interview. Closing his eyes, he massaged the bridge of his nose between his thumb and forefinger to urge his thoughts into focus. The phone buzzed in his hand, another alert appearing at the top of the screen. This time, it was from Cal.

Got time to chat?

He ignored it and tapped a link to an article about microplastic concentrations in marine vertebrates from his feed. Ideally, he could duck Cal for the rest of his time at the center, but that wasn't realistic. Unless he still planned to pay for a flight home himself, he'd need Cal to either take him back to the jet at Wheeler or arrange a commercial flight. The phone buzzed again.

Need to go over the offer

Jayson parsed the message repeatedly to make sure he understood the implication. It was a simple enough statement, but so at odds with his expectations he assumed he was misreading it.

Offer?

To join the team

He snorted to himself. They really thought they could subject him to some bullshit psychological game, insult him, and then just pretend everything was okay?

Not sure this is right for me
Interview didn't go well

Just the opposite
Richard liked your passion

He tapped out a gut response and stared at it, his finger quivering over the send button.

Richard can fuck himself

"Shit," he sighed, shaking his head. Was pride even relevant in the face of a global crisis? He recalled Samaira's unspoken words on their walk the day before. *Suck it up, buttercup. There's work to be done.* He backspaced over the message and replaced it with something noncommittal he wouldn't end up regretting.

Tomorrow?

Tomorrow is good
Meet you in the caf for breakfast @8:00

***

Jayson sat across from Cal in the bright morning light of the cafeteria with a forkful of scrambled egg in one hand and a thick document in the other.

"That's a big contract," he observed, gauging its heft.

"That's the NDA—the nondisclosure agreement," clarified Cal. "The employment contract isn't as detailed."

"Why an NDA? I thought the whole point of this place was to share knowledge with the world about how to live sustainably."

"Oh, absolutely," agreed Cal. "We'll share the outcomes. It's the methods that need to be protected. You'll apply the same technology that makes Hitz-It.com the most highly valuated company on the planet to your work."

"Really? How does a social media company's technology apply to agriculture?"

"Sign the NDA and find out."

"What about Richard?"

"What about him?" asked Cal, furrowing his brow.

"I'd like an apology—and assurances this isn't going to be a hostile workplace."

Cal leaned back in his chair and regarded Jayson for a moment.

"Yeah. That shouldn't be a problem," he said finally.

Jayson nodded his appreciation and pushed his plate aside to give the document a cursory look-over. Turning to the last page, he looked up and locked eyes with Cal, searching for a sign he wasn't about to make a mistake. Cal handed him a pen.

Staring at the signature line, marked with a yellow sticky note, Jayson had a brief flashback of himself standing on a ten-meter diving board above the frigid, cloudy water of an old limestone quarry near his home that had been converted into a public swimming pool. The narrow ladder behind him was crowded with people waiting their turn. On the grass below, a group of bikini-clad girls from his school sat on beach towels, shielding their eyes from the sun to watch the antics of their pimpled-faced, testosterone-fueled classmates. Taking a deep breath, he signed the contract with the same sense of inevitability that had propelled him into the murky water.

"Great," said Cal as he took the document and slid another one into its place. "Just a couple more things to sign, and we can get you to work."

"Woah," protested Jayson. "I still have a month's worth of stuff to finish up on my thesis. And I gotta pack my stuff and move out of my apartment."

"I already spoke with your dean and faculty advisor. The Center is now officially providing a grant for your research, which will continue here at our facilities."

"How is that possible?"

"It's already two in the afternoon in Guelph," explained Cal. "Plenty of time to get things worked out."

"And my place?"

"We'll cover the remaining rent, and hire someone to pack up your stuff. Do you have anyone who can meet the landlord there with a key?"

The speed at which things were moving was disorienting. He'd assumed there'd be some time to see his family and wrap up a few things back home before relocating. Maybe his friends would even throw a party if he dropped a hint or two. Now it seemed as if the Center would not give him that opportunity.

"My dad has a key," he offered. "But what's the rush?"

"Many people think it's already too late to change course, Jayson. We're at a point of crisis where days matter."

"I guess," he allowed with a shrug.

"So it's settled," insisted Cal. "We'll get everything squared up back home, and get you working on saving the world."

Jayson sighed and sorted through the remaining documents before him. When he finished signing, Cal put the contracts into a folder and got up to leave.

"Perfect! Now, call your parents and reach out to anyone else you want to update. We'll meet up again in two hours in the plaza outside the main building to get you oriented."

"Uh, okay. See you in a bit."

Jayson shook his head and laughed to himself in disbelief. It was all so disorienting. Only two days prior, he'd arrived with no interest in the job. Now, he'd just signed a contract, and it seemed he would start without even going back home to say goodbye to friends and family in person. Surely signing the paperwork hadn't committed him to stay. He could talk to his parents and then tell Cal he really needed to go home for a couple of weeks before starting at the center.

He finished his breakfast alone while he contemplated what to tell his parents, and how to craft an excuse to go home that Cal wouldn't be able to deflect so easily. He took out his phone to compose a regular text message since neither of his parents used the Hitz-It messaging app.

> Got some news
> Video call in 30 mins?

He knew them well enough not to expect an immediate response, and opened Hitz-It to distract himself while he waited for a confirmation. He responded to several hitz before checking the latest headlines from his recommended articles. *'Sir David Attenborough says immediate action necessary to avert climate disaster.' 'Anton Kamaras implores fellow billionaires to focus on earth, not space.' 'Why technology alone cannot save the planet.'*

***

When Jayson arrived at the plaza, Cal, Samaira, and Richard were already there. Richard cleared his throat and shuffled awkwardly, glancing at the ground near his feet. Cal had promised an apology, but Richard seemed hesitant.

"Dr. Vandergroot," prompted Jayson. "I want to apologize for yesterday. I shouldn't have told you—I shouldn't have said what I said."

"No need to apologize, Jayson," he assured. "The interview was designed to antagonize. I should be the one apologizing for crossing a line." He glanced sideways at Cal and shook Jayson's hand as if to reinforce his sincerity.

"Thanks. I appreciate that."

"Not at all. Let's get you started on your work. I thought it would be nice to meet with our two newest team members out here to show off one of the advantages of working in Hawaii—the perfect year-round weather."

They looked around in admiring acceptance of his premise. Groups of chatting researchers occupied several tables scattered irregularly but neatly among the trees and pergolas. By all indications, the people working at the center were happy to be there.

"The first thing I want to talk about," continued Richard, "is the reason behind the NDA. To do your work here at the center, you will have access to the unique technology that makes Hitz-It.com special. It is crucial to us the nature of this technology remains hidden from our competitors."

"But the benefits we derive from its use will be publicly available and royalty-free," clarified Cal.

"Exactly," agreed Richard.

"Yesterday, you alluded to hundreds of millions of simulations," said Samaira. "Is that the technology you're talking about?"

"Anyone can do simulations," replied Richard, waving a hand dismissively. "What makes ours different are the machine learning algorithms continually refining the parameters and assumptions upon which the simulations are based with real-world, real-time data."

"Machine learning isn't exactly new," challenged Jayson.

"No, it's not," conceded Richard, "but none of it compares to what we're able to do."

"Like what?" asked Samaira.

"Our algorithms can frame problems in a way that allows us to exploit the full potential of quantum computing," explained Richard. "Quantum computing was my area of focus at the Naval Research Center, and one thing we learned was that, in many cases, it didn't offer any advantages over traditional computing. The trick was figuring out how to ask questions the right way."

"How does that make Anton Kamaras rich?" asked Jayson.

"Imagine you are a company with a product to sell."

"Okay."

"Instead of putting your ad campaign out into the real world and hoping for the best, you send it into a million simulations of the world first to see if it'll work consistently. If it doesn't, you tweak it and try again."

"That's just simulation, not machine learning," protested Jayson.

"So far, yes," agreed Richard. "Now imagine once your campaign *does* hit the real world, you're able to instantly identify, through reactions in social media, where the simulations deviated from reality."

"I then use that data to make the millions of simulated worlds more accurate, so my next campaign is even better," realized Jayson.

"Exactly. That's machine learning," said Richard. "And we can do it fast enough to allow companies to adjust their campaigns in real-time through our social media channels."

"That means they can iterate to a nearly perfect message almost instantly," said Samaira in amazement.

"I see you're already thinking of ways you could apply it," smiled Cal. "What about you, Jayson? Do you know what this has to do with you yet?"

"Not really," he admitted.

"That'll be clear soon enough. I'm going to take you to meet your team, and go over your objectives. Richard and Samaira are heading over to the guest researcher facilities where her office is set up."

"See you for lunch?" Jayson asked Samaira.

"Sure. Hit me later."

They split into pairs to continue with the individual orientation. Jayson and Cal made their way to the main building, and returned to the agricultural lab Jayson had seen before the interview the previous day. Three others were already there waiting when they arrived.

"Jayson Reilly, I'd like to introduce you to your teammates," said Cal.

"Hi there," he offered.

He only recognized one of the three from the cafeteria crowd, but couldn't remember her name.

"This is Aiden Watson," started Cal, gesturing to the tall, muscular man in the middle of the group. "He's the foreman for the agricultural crew in the fields. You'll be coordinating with him on what needs to get done out there."

"Welcome to the team, Jayson," said Aiden with a firm handshake. He looked to be in his mid-thirties; older than any of the others he'd met so far.

"Riyoko Kimura," he added, indicating the young woman on the left. "She's our nutritionist."

"Hi, Jayson. We were introduced in the cafeteria yesterday," she explained to Cal.

"And finally, Olena Voloshyn. She's in charge of lab operations."

"Very nice to meet you," she said with a polite nod.

"We've got a good start here in the lab, and we'll soon be ready to move things outside," continued Cal. "It's time to pick up our game."

"What's the plan?" asked Jayson.

"Our vision of a sustainable future includes community-based farming and local sourcing. It means reducing reliance on transportation, refrigeration, processing, and packaging of foods. It means no more chemical fertilizers and pesticides."

"I like the sound of that."

"And your challenge is to do it here, first," continued Cal. "We want all of the nutritional needs of the Center to be met by onsite sources—and we want it done in less than a year."

"Wow. That's an aggressive timeline."

"It is," agreed Cal. "But with the resources at your disposal, it should be possible."

"How do the algorithms and machine learning play into it?"

"We've established a baseline of the nutritional needs of the center, as well as some basic parameters about the yields and conditional preferences of various crops from around the world we're growing in the lab," explained Cal. "That gives us enough information to start running millions of parallel simulations of our food production."

"Are they accurate?"

"Not likely. At least not beyond a few weeks. To improve the models, you'll need to get the deviation data back into the system as quickly and accurately as possible. The impact of every soil augmentation, every change in precipitation, every insect infestation—you'll predict it all with the simulations, and then correct for real-world outcomes. Over time, the errors get smaller, and we can reliably predict our ability to support a growing staff years into the future."

"Now I understand why I'm here," smiled Jayson.

"Jayson's thesis work is on real-time agricultural data collection using connected sensors," explained Cal to the others.

"Imagine an entire farm as a single network with sensors monitoring soil conditions, rainfall, etcetera," added Jayson excitedly. "We can use the data to deliver exactly the right amount of irrigation and fertilizer to the precise locations that need it. We can reduce water and fuel usage considerably without impacting yields."

"Added to our technology," said Olena, "you can create a predictive model instead of the reactive one you envisioned."

"That's incredible," marveled Jayson. "I had no idea enough computing power to make that possible even existed."

"We've already had promising results applying the technique to medical research and drug development next door where Samaira is," assured Cal. "The potential applications are nearly limitless."

"So, where do we start?" asked Jayson, rubbing his hands together.

"Start planning the data acquisition network for the fields, and work with Olena to order any equipment you need," suggested Cal. "Aiden and his team can set everything up to your specs, and Riyoko is familiar with the simulation data model. She can help you design the interface to feed it—just like she does for her own research."

Jayson felt a rush of excitement as he processed everything he'd learned from Cal, and it became clear how much impact he could have on the world with access to the resources at the center. There were still a few pieces of the puzzle missing, but he was increasingly confident he was part of a very well-orchestrated effort to make a positive change.

"Andrew from IT is waiting in your office to get your accounts and access set up," said Cal, motioning to the far corner of the room. "Once you're in, I'll leave it to you and the team to manage your work and get things moving. Hit me if you have any questions."

"So that's it? The job starts now?"

"Congratulations, Jayson."

Cal nodded to the rest of the team and left, leaving Jayson to plan with his three new colleagues.

"Let's get together first thing after lunch to see where we are before we prioritize the next steps," he said, trying to sound confident.

He retreated to his new office to draw up a credible plan to demonstrate to his new team he knew what he was doing.

***

Samaira and Richard lingered outside to continue their discussion in the relative privacy of the courtyard. It was still midmorning, and most people were inside working. Those enjoying the fresh air, talking over cups of coffee in small groups around the periphery, were far enough away their conversations were not a distraction.

"I imagine you've already started considering the implications of our technology in a way Jayson may have missed," started Richard.

"I'm not sure about that," she replied modestly, "but I am pretty sure I have a general understanding of your intent."

"I'd love to hear that understanding," urged Richard.

"You're not just allowing advertisers to monitor people's reactions. You're allowing them to change their reactions and their behavior."

"Sure. That's what advertisers have always done," he countered. "They turn people who won't buy their products into people who will."

"But this is different. This is real-time manipulation of behaviors and opinions. Comparing this to a magazine ad or television commercial is like comparing a spear to a nuclear bomb."

"You are exactly right. And how do you like our chances in the fight against climate change if we're the ones using spears to fight off a comparative nuclear missile attack? Those who profit from pollution use every tool available to manipulate public opinion and fuel climate denial. We can't change that if we're not prepared to fight on equal footing—or better."

"You misunderstood me, Richard," she said with a smile. "I didn't mean that as a judgment. I understand it's my job to manipulate people. I just like to think I can do it for something a bit nobler than adding to the bottom line."

"So you don't have a problem with this? Ethically?"

"Not at all. We're just talking about tools here. Nothing else has changed. Human relationships and societies are based on the ability to influence the actions and perceptions of others. Look at it from another perspective," she suggested. "What's the difference between Jonas Salk and Joseph Mengele? Was it their medical knowledge? The tools available to them? Or was it what they pursued?"

"I would say it's obviously the latter," replied Richard.

"And I would agree. Tools aren't inherently ethical or unethical. What matters is how we use them."

"So the end justifies the means?"

"Too often, people take that to mean you can ignore the consequences as long as you get the result you want," she cautioned. "But if you fully weigh the good against the bad, then yes, the end justifies the means."

"I couldn't agree more," replied Richard. "Come on, let's get you started."

***

Jayson entered the spacious, glass-walled office and looked around with awe. It was much nicer than his basement cubbyhole at the university. Evidently, the people at the Center saw something in him if they were willing to let him run a project, and furnish him with such a high-end space.

"Not too shabby, huh?" observed the computer tech setting up Jayson's new laptop.

"Not bad at all."

"I'm Andrew," greeted the gangly redhead.

"I'm—"

"Jayson with a 'y,'" he interrupted. "Got it here on the work order. Can you go ahead and enter a new password for me?"

"Sure," replied Jayson, leaning over the seated tech to reach the keyboard.

He quickly entered a combination of characters and confirmed them.

"You really shouldn't do that," cautioned Andrew.

"Do what?"

"Use variations of the same password in multiple places."

"How do you know I do?"

"You typed in the first ten characters practically on auto-pilot and then pecked in the twenty-two at the end," he explained.

"Okay," replied Jayson, wrinkling his brow. "Noted."

"Just a few more minutes, and you should be all set to go. Cal had me go over some of your research papers to make sure we had the software you needed. If I missed anything, just let me know."

"Thanks," said Jayson. "What about hardware specs?"

"Overkill," assured Andrew. "The quantum stack handles most of the heavy crunching, anyway."

"Right. I just didn't recognize the brand, and wondered what I was getting."

"This thing?" he asked with an exaggerated swing of his arm.

The back of his hand caught the top of the screen and knocked the laptop off the desk. It hit the tiled floor with a loud clatter.

"Shit!" said Jayson, putting his hands to his head.

"Fuck, fuck, fuck!" exclaimed Andrew. "Richard is going to fire my ass—unless I tell him you did it."

"What? Me?" What the hell is wrong with you?"

"You've gotta take the fall for me, man. I'm getting fired this time, for sure."

"Listen, I can't help you with that. How bad is it?"

Andrew started laughing as he reached down to retrieve the laptop and then tossed it unceremoniously onto the desk.

"That never gets old," he said, shaking his head.

"What?"

"It's our own design. Everything is solid-state and built to survive the apocalypse. We can update and repair it modularly, but really it's just meant to keep on working."

"Jesus Christ. That was *not* funny."

Sorry, man but that will *always* be funny. Don't feel bad. I get all the noobs with that one."

Andrew continued pecking away intermittently at the keyboard, working his way through several dialog boxes before pushing away from the desk and rising from the chair.

"All set, chief," he announced before quickly realizing his mistake. "Uh, that wasn't a racial thing. I just call people that sometimes."

"No worries. I didn't even notice," lied Jayson.

Andrew nodded toward Jayson's teammates in the lab and changed the subject.

"So, have you figured out which one you'd rather do?"

"Huh?"

"Olena or Riyoko?"

"Uh, I don't know," replied Jayson, raising an eyebrow.

"Good choice. Both together," said Andrew with a wink.

"No," protested Jayson, "I didn't—"

"Aiden?" interrupted Andrew.

"That's not what I meant."

"It's all cool, man," assured Andrew. "We don't judge here. I can totally see that being your thing."

"What I mean is I don't spend my time considering which of my colleagues I'd 'do.'"

"Sure, man. Keep telling yourself that. If you need anything else—hardware, software, whatever—just hit me. I've already added myself to your contacts."

Andrew gave a mock salute, turned on his heel, and left the room. As he passed behind Olena and Riyoko on the way out of the lab, he turned back and winked at Jayson while making a grabbing motion towards their backsides.

***

The small conference room on the second floor of the center's guest researcher building overlooked the harbor and nearby docks. Samaira stood by the windows and watched as workers lashed the last section of Fusion B onto the deck of a cargo ship. Following several hours of effort, all eight sections were now in place and secured for transport.

As the crew checked the load one last time, an enormous helicopter thundered in from across Ford Island Channel from Pearl Harbor-Hickam and touched down on the empty concrete pad where Fusion B had stood only two days before.

The roar of the engines subsided as it throttled down to an idle. Samaira was watching the spectacle with interest when Richard walked into the conference room with another young researcher in tow.

"Dr. Samaira Adams," he started, "I'd like you to meet Kailani Kahue, from the University of Hawaii."

Samaira took her extended hand.

"Nice to meet you, Kailani. That's a beautiful name."

"Thank you," she blushed.

"Kailani is working on an exciting project in paleolinguistics. Mr. Kamaras was so intrigued, he felt compelled to support it."

"Really? You've piqued my curiosity."

"My thesis advisor has been reconstructing a proto-Polynesian language by comparing the modern offshoots," she explained. "I'm pursuing a computational approach to accelerating and validating the development of the vocabulary and pronunciation models."

"So you're re-creating a dead language?"

"Technically, we call it a theoretical language."

"What's the difference?"

"We have proof that dead languages really existed. With proto-Polynesian, we're pretty sure it existed, but there's no direct proof since nobody ever wrote it down."

"What's the value in recreating a language that's never been written and has no artifacts to decipher?"

"It's a part of my heritage," explained Kailani. "It gives me pride to know I might learn to express myself in the words of my ancestors."

"Of course. I get it," nodded Samaira. "Sorry if that question sounded insensitive."

"Not at all," smiled Kailani.

"And Mr. Kamaras has his own reasons to support this as well," added Richard. "This is a unique kind of problem for our algorithms to tackle, and a great way to test their adaptability."

"What do you mean?" asked Samaira.

"There's no way to give real-time feedback on the outcomes of recreating a language nobody uses. We have to find other ways to enable the machine learning to improve our understanding of proto-Polynesian."

"That makes sense. So how do you do it?"

"One approach," explained Richard, "is to look at patterns of development in other related languages that are better documented—Latin and the Romance languages, for example. Using what we learn, we can try to re-develop the modern offshoots of proto-Polynesian from their theoretical origin."

"That is an interesting approach."

"If we can successfully derive the modern languages from our theoretical one, that means our theoretical one is likely accurate," added Kailani.

"Kailani has spent a lot of time learning to frame problems for the quantum stack, and has volunteered to get you familiar with the interface," explained Richard. "I have to leave to coordinate some things at another site, so I'll be leaving you in her capable hands for the rest of the day."

"We'll get on just fine," assured Samaira.

"Andrew from IT should be here in a few minutes with your new laptop. He'll take you to your office and set up your account access. Just hold tight here for a bit."

After Richard left the room, Kailani sighed and dropped her shoulders.

"Is everything okay?" asked Samaira. "I'm happy to wait if you have something you need to do first."

"No. It's nothing to do with you," assured Kailani. "It's Andrew. He's a creep."

"I can deal with him on my own. Why don't you come by after he's gone?"

"No," insisted Kailani with a resigned smile, "I can't do that to you."

"Honestly," confided Samaira, "situations like this are kind of fun for me. I'll be fine."

"Really?"

"Really," she insisted, holding up her phone. "Hit me, and I'll get in touch with you when it's safe."

Kailani tapped her phone against Samaira's and shrugged.

"If you insist."

Chapter Nine

OUTSIDE THE CENTER, AT the former location of Fusion B next to the docks, Richard stepped aboard the waiting Navy CH-53E Super Stallion heavy-lift helicopter and donned a flight helmet.

"I appreciate the ride, guys," he said into the built-in microphone.

"No problem," came the choppy reply. "We're going the same way."

The pilot eased the massive machine into the air and turned southward, following the harbor inlet out to sea. He stayed low over the water to keep clear of the flight paths in and out of Daniel K. Inouye International Airport. From there, the helicopter banked left, taking its passenger and crew eastward along the coastline of O'ahu. They passed Honolulu Harbor, Waikiki Beach, and the massive, extinct coastline volcano, Diamond Head. Just past Maunalua Bay, after only about twenty minutes in the air, they touched down on a flat, grassy plain among the gentle slopes of Pai'Olu'Olu Point. Usually part of a publicly accessible natural area, a razor-wire-topped fence running along the western ridge temporarily blocked it off.

The pilot powered down to wait for the offshore arrival of the cargo ship carrying the dismantled pieces of Fusion B. Richard jumped from the helicopter and walked over to inspect the concrete pad that would soon be the new site of the center's modular test facility. A group of men in hard hats and bright orange vests examined the site plans while arguing with another man wearing a cheap white dress shirt and tie.

"Hey guys, what's going on?" he greeted.

"Don's bitching we didn't get approval on the base prep before we poured the pad," explained a worker."

"What's the problem this time?" he asked the man in the cheap shirt, pulling him aside.

"You can't pour a pad for this kind of load without an inspection on the base," he complained. "We have to make sure it's going to be safe."

"We're putting a billion dollars of technology on this thing, Don. You think we're not making sure it'll hold up?"

"It doesn't matter if you're sure. I need to be sure, Richard. Those are the rules."

"Don't you ever get tired of this bullshit?"

"What are you talking about?" asked Don with a sneer.

"It's always the same thing. You come around to one of our sites to bitch about something, I call your boss, and he tells you to fuck off."

Don turned red, but did not respond.

"How about this time," continued Richard, "we just skip straight to the part where you fuck off?"

"Go to hell, Richard," spat Don.

"It's nothing personal, Don. I just don't have any time for your bullshit today."

The inspector shook his head and turned away, heading for the snaking dirt trail leading back up the broken asphalt road on the other side of the fence where he'd parked his truck.

"Good to go, boys," called Richard to the assembled crew as he strode past the empty pad towards the temporary office structure and living quarters dropped next to it piece-by-piece by the Super Stallion the week prior.

A disheveled man in a crumpled, expensive-looking suit sat in the waiting area just beyond the outer door.

"I've been waiting here for hours," he complained as Richard entered.

"My apologies," replied Richard, "but I doubt you have many people vying for your time right now."

"Depends if you include reporters. Got lots of *them* trying to talk to me."

"That's a great suit, by the way," said Richard.

"Vestiges of a previous life," explained the Special Forces operator-turned-B-list celebrity. "Are we here to talk about my suit, or do you have something more interesting in mind?"

***

Samaira and Kailani watched the helicopter disappear into the distance as they chatted and waited for the creepy computer tech to arrive.

"Looks like Richard has a busy day," observed Samaira. "Is he always running around like that?"

"Lately, yes," replied Kailani. "He's been a lot more tense for the last few months, and hasn't been coming around to get updates on the research as often."

"He's involved in the research directly?"

"Like I said, not as much anymore. At first, he used to show the new researchers how to work with the interface and set problems up for the stack. He even came up with a few great ideas, like reconstructing modern languages to validate proto-Polynesian. Now, he's passed training duties on to those of us with a bit more experience."

"How long have you been here?"

"Almost a year."

"You were among the first, then?"

"No," recalled Kailani, "some of the biomedical researchers were here before me. In fact, half of them have already finished whatever they were doing and cycled out."

"And new ones arrived with new research projects?"

"Yeah. I'm pretty thankful for that. The newer crowd is a lot younger and more friendly."

A knock at the open door concluded their conversation.

"I hope I'm interrupting something, ladies," greeted Andrew, raising his eyebrows suggestively. "I'm happy to stand here and watch until you're done."

Kailani rolled her eyes.

"Hit me when you're ready," she said to Samaira and walked out of the conference room without a word to Andrew.

"I guess it's just you and me now," he observed.

"Nice to meet you," she said, brushing off the insinuation. "I'm Samaira."

"Yes. Dr. Adams from Atlanta, Georgia. I have your requisition here."

"It's nice you've done your homework. I wish I could say I've done the same."

"I'm Andrew Jorgensen, your friendly neighborhood IT guy. You can hit me any time—for anything."

"Where are you from, Andrew?"

"Minnesota," he replied, exaggerating the 'o' sound. "My accent usually gives me away."

"Mine too," she sympathized. "What are we doing today?"

"I'm here to show you to your office and get you set up on your laptop. After that? Who knows?" he said with a shrug.

"Alright. Lead the way."

She motioned towards the door, and he led her out into the main hallway.

"To the right, back where you got off the elevator, you'll find restrooms and a lounge with coffee, snacks, and drinks," he explained. "The doors on the other side of the elevators lead to the biomedical research facilities, but you need special badge permissions to get in there."

"Sounds mysterious. Do you have access to that?"

"Me? No way. They're super paranoid about contamination. People only go in and out once a day because the entry and exit procedures take so long. There's a dedicated IT guy who stays in there with them all the time."

"Yikes. Sounds like a prison."

"Yeah. You'd think that based on how some of them act."

They followed the corridor away from the elevators past several bright, open offices occupied by diligently working researchers and technicians.

"Your badge will get you anywhere on this side of the second floor," explained Andrew. "This is where all of the arts and humanities researchers are—basically anything that doesn't relate to science and engineering."

"Where does the science and engineering work take place?"

"Guest researchers in those fields are located here on the main floor, and everyone else is in the main building next door. You're kind of an anomaly."

"How's that?"

"You're the only full-time staff member I know of that does the fluffy stuff. The rest are pretty practical."

"Fluffy stuff?"

"No offense," clarified Andrew, "I just mean that you don't make stuff you can touch, or eat, or use to power an aircraft carrier. It's mostly guest researchers doing stuff like that."

"I see," she laughed. "I never heard it categorized like that before."

"Anyway, take it as a compliment that you're over here," said Andrew.

"Why's that?"

"This is where they put the hot chicks."

They arrived at a glass office door marked 'Organizational Behavior,' and Andrew motioned for Samaira to enter ahead of him. It was smaller than the other offices, but still large enough for three or four desks. Presently, there was only one desk and two chairs positioned to take advantage of the view offered by the floor-to-ceiling windows.

"This is yours," he announced. "Have a seat."

"It's lovely. Thank you."

"Don't thank me," he said as he pulled the laptop from under his arm and approached the desk. "I'm just her to give you this."

Andrew pretended to trip over some nonexistent obstacle and let the laptop slip from his hands with an embellished look of terror. It clattered across the floor and stopped at Samaira's feet.

"Shit! Richard said he was going to fire me if that happened again. We'll have to tell him you did it."

"Why would you do that, Andrew?"

"Because he won't fire you. You're new and pretty. You'll be fine."

"I mean, why would you play such a mean-spirited joke on someone you just met?"

"But the laptop—"

"We both know the laptop is either fake or fine, Andrew. The only question is why you did it."

"It was just a joke," he admitted, his face turning bright red.

"Then it was a mean joke," she reproached. "Does anyone other than you actually laugh when you do that?"

"Whatever," he said. "It was just supposed to be a little fun."

"And what about all of the sexual innuendo? Is that supposed to be fun, too?"

"I get it. You don't appreciate my humor," he said with defeat as he retrieved the laptop from the floor. "Not everyone does."

"I'm not even convinced you appreciate it, Andrew. Do you think you're being funny?"

"Listen, can we drop this? Then you never have to talk to me unless you have a tech issue."

"Would that be easier? If I don't speak to you again?"

"You think I'm an asshole, so yeah. Probably."

"I didn't say that. Do you think you're an asshole?"

"What?"

"Do you like yourself, Andrew?"

"Now you're just being bitchy," he said, furrowing his brow.

"I'm not," she insisted. "I'm just trying to understand you."

He stared at her, narrowing an eye.

"The real you," she clarified. "Not the made-up jerk who alienates everyone he works with."

"Maybe you wouldn't like the real me either."

"Why not?"

"Because I'm not very interesting."

"Can I let you in on a secret? The key to being liked isn't about how interesting you are."

"It's not?"

"No. It's about making those around you feel like *they're* interesting."

"Have you met the people around here? That's one hell of a tall order."

"Oh, that's good," she laughed. "Finally, a joke that's really funny."

Andrew's face cracked into a broad smile, and they both started laughing.

"You really had me going," he said with a grin when he finally regained his composure.

"No, no, no," she warned, waving a finger at him. "I'm not letting you off that easy. You were real there for a moment. Can you stay real for me?"

His smile vanished, and he was suddenly serious.

"I don't know."

"It's not always easy," she allowed. "You don't have to do it all at once. How about one hour a day?"

"What do you mean?"

"Meet me for lunch," she said. "One hour every day. Just you and me."

"Seriously?"

"Yes. Seriously. But only if you agree to be yourself," she cautioned.

"I can do that," he said with as much confidence as circumstances allowed.

"I can see this is a hard conversation for you," she said. "Let's leave it there for today."

"Yeah. Sure," he agreed.

"Now, get me into this laptop and say something inappropriate before you have an aneurysm."

They both started laughing again, but with genuine ease and relief that the tension between them had evaporated.

Chapter Ten

THE TRIAL OF RUAN Van Zijl, also known as Ron Van Zeal, was a media circus. Before his wife's death and his subsequent arrest for the murder of a random couple from Oxnard, he barely registered as a celebrity at all; enjoying a degree of anonymity, despite his modestly successful television career. The breathless reporting of his tragic loss and details of the murder, from the discovery of the brutalized bodies to his dramatic acquittal, had propelled him to a level of fame that he'd neither imagined nor wanted.

The first reports of his wife's accident had been relegated to the back pages of trashy tabloid magazines. She'd been on a hard ride in the mountains north of Malibu, training for the Bayshore Triathlon, when she lost control of her bike, falling down a steep hillside and into the trees along Piuma Road. The tragic story took on a life of its own on social media, first as genuine messages of condolence from Ruan's social media followers, then as fodder for conspiracy theorists and trolls.

Photos of the accident scene emerged, supposedly leaked by an anonymous police whistleblower, showing evidence of a coverup. Yellow scuff marks on Lenora's bike and some of the injuries on her left leg were inconsistent with the official story. Time-stamped photos taken by security cameras at some luxury estates dotting the sparsely populated road revealed a yellow Lamborghini Urus taking longer than usual to descend the hill. They also seemed to show fresh damage to the front fascia when it reached Malibu Canyon Road.

As if the yellow Urus wasn't unique enough on its own, internet researchers known only by their whimsical user names revealed one had recently undergone bodywork repairs consistent with the damage shown in the grainy photos. It belonged to musician and producer Ray Kamakawiwoʻole. A well-known Hawaiian sovereignty activist, he'd risen to prominence bringing native and other marginalized voices to the mainstream. Poor Ray was bewildered when he suddenly became the target of a sustained barrage of online threats and abuse.

Soon, the mainstream media latched onto the popularity of the manufactured mystery surrounding Lenora Van Zijl's death. There were daily television news updates as the nation fixated once more on the fate of a pretty, white blonde. It probably didn't hurt that most of the publicly available photos and footage featured her in tight spandex or a skimpy swimsuit during one of her many competitions.

Despite investigators' insistence there was no evidence at all linking Ray Kamakawiwoʻole to Lenora's death, the cable news channels included the suspicions against him in their extensive coverage, and a growing number of people suspected a coverup. Among them was Ruan, desperately trying to find meaning in his sudden loss.

When reports surfaced police were investigating the discovery of two bodies at Ray Kamakawiwoʻole's Oxnard home, the media conducted their own ad hoc trial, and found Ruan guilty of murder before there was even enough evidence for a judge to issue an arrest warrant. When the arrest finally came, the cameras were waiting, and his perp walk headlined global news coverage.

The frenzy only intensified as the televised trial garnered ratings a hundred times greater than the *Survival Stories* series had ever managed. Dozens of online celebrity watchers live-blogged about every gruesome detail of the crime scene and each new piece of evidence. Sentiment gradually shifted inexplicably towards Ray being an innocent victim instead of a heartless killer who'd gotten what he deserved.

Every day after court adjourned, reporters stood on the steps of the courthouse to regurgitate the damning evidence that would lead to likely conviction. On the cable news shows, perfectly coifed anchors convened panels of paid experts to discuss how Ruan's background made him a perfect killer, and how it was almost certain the jury would find him guilty.

Trial watchers were incredulous when the defense presented evidence they said corroborated his alibi beyond the shadow of a doubt. It was proof, they claimed, that Ruan was hundreds of miles away at the time of the murders. The jury agreed. He left the courthouse innocent in the eyes of the law, but guilty in the court of public opinion. Surely he had orchestrated the plot, opined the experts and online amateurs alike, even if he didn't carry it out himself. As a result, the media continued to hound him wherever he went.

The call from Richard months later had been a welcome distraction for Ruan. It offered an opportunity for some much-needed income and, more importantly, a chance to get him out of his self-imposed home imprisonment. That they'd whisked him away secretly in the early morning hours, evading the ever-present reporters, was an added bonus. A private jet took him from Hollywood Burbank Airport to Wheeler Army Airfield on O'ahu, where a waiting helicopter carried him on the last leg of the journey to the temporary office and living quarters at the Beta site where he had waited alone inside for his host to arrive.

***

"I have to admit this is not quite what I was expecting when I chose my outfit," said Ruan. "I feel a bit overdressed."

"What were you expecting?" asked Richard.

"I thought a man like Anton Kamaras would have a nicer facility."

"He does, actually. But you won't see it. Besides, that suit has seen better days—and so have you."

Ruan examined his wrinkled suit, rubbing at an unidentifiable stain on the right sleeve.

"Yeah," he realized. "And I guess we wouldn't want to tarnish his reputation by association."

"You're an innocent man, Mr. Van Zijl. How could you possibly tarnish his reputation?"

"According to a jury of my peers, at least. And I suppose I have you to thank for that?"

"Your lawyer requested the geotag data, and we were happy to comply," shrugged Richard.

"There's that," said Ruan. "But after you called me, I also did a little digging into that gas station outside of Henderson."

"The one with the high-resolution video of you filling up your car."

"It turns out," he continued, "the company that handles their security surveillance manages everything using Hitz-It.com cloud services."

"That is an interesting coincidence."

"A coincidence for which I was very grateful—at first."

"At first?"

"And then I started to think that if you could fake my alibi, then maybe you could have faked a few other things, too. You want to hear another interesting coincidence?"

Richard raised an eyebrow expectantly, waiting for Ruan to continue.

"It turns out the security cameras that caught that fancy, yellow SUV on Piuma road also use the Hitz-It cloud data services."

"As do over three-quarters of all commercial and residential security providers," replied Richard with a dismissive wave of his hand. "Is there a specific question you want to ask me?"

Ruan narrowed his eyes and calmly evaluated the physicist.

"Did you have my wife killed?" he demanded.

"Jesus Christ! We had nothing to do with that."

Though he was prepared to fake indignance as needed, his reaction to the startling question was genuine. Ruan had been among hundreds of potential candidates identified by the algorithms, but the circumstances of his wife's death were merely a fortunate coincidence. With the unrelated discovery of the Hawaiian activist needing a timely car repair, the algos reacted like a slot machine lining up a row of bright, red cherries, and decided Ruan was their man.

"Maybe not," allowed Ruan with a barely perceptible shrug, "but there's sure-as-shit something fishy going on here, because we both know I was nowhere near Henderson."

"We did you a favor," insisted Richard.

"And why the fuck did I need a favor in the first place?" he demanded, slamming a fist on the desk. "Do you think I'm an idiot?"

"There's no need to be confrontational," assured Richard as he reached slowly into his desk. "You're here for an opportunity."

"Yeah. An opportunity to snap your fucking pencil neck."

"Let's not be hasty," cautioned Richard, as he produced a gun from the drawer. He held it as casually as he could manage, pointing it at the ground to avoid further unnecessary escalation.

Ruan snorted and rolled his eyes.

"You're holding that thing like it's going to bite you. Besides, no matter which one of us ends up dead, it's a win for me."

"Is that what Lenora would want?"

"Leave her out of this," he spat.

"Tell me, Ruan, how did a mercenary like you end up with her, anyway?"

"I was never a mercenary. I was a private security contractor working for legitimate governments in actions that were sanctioned by the United Nations."

"My apologies," said Richard. "I'm sure you're very proud of what you've done. Did you ever tell her what you got up to in these sanctioned actions of yours?"

"No," he said simply.

"I doubt she'd have been with you if you had."

"She wasn't like me," acknowledged Ruan with a slow nod. "But I was trying to be more like her. I was trying to be a better person."

"Until you gutted a man's wife right in front of him, you mean?"

"Don't let my appearance fool you," he cautioned. "I'll have you by the throat before you can fire a single shot. I know what you did to me."

"I did you a favor. I'm the good guy here."

Ruan snorted again.

"I wonder if Kamakawi—or whatever the fuck his name was—would agree with that," he asked.

"He and his wife dug their own graves when they decided to flee the scene."

"There was no evidence of that. It was all bullshit—just like my alibi."

"You believe there was no coverup? That a rich, connected producer didn't use his influence to whitewash the whole thing?"

Ruan studied him silently for several seconds.

"If it was anyone else lying dead in that gorge, he probably would have gotten away with it, too," continued Richard. "He fucked with the wrong guy and paid the price."

"What do you want from me?" asked Ruan finally.

"Simply secure and defend an objective—some property—for Mr. Kamaras."

"Why me?"

"He's a fan of your work, and he'd like to help you out of your current circumstances."

"Well, isn't that charitable," snorted Ruan. "I assume the pay is good?"

"That's where we run into a bit of difficulty, I'm afraid," replied Richard.

"You expect me to believe you're on a budget?"

"It's not that. It's just that money won't do you much good where we'd be sending you."

"Not much of a negotiator, are you?"

"Let me try again. How would you like to go where nobody knows about your past, and you can escape any kind of scrutiny for the rest of your life? We'll give you complete, autonomous reign over your own private paradise."

"Okay," he asked, narrowing his eyes. "What's the catch?"

"There's no coming back. It's a one-way ticket."

"And how do I get paid if money has no value?"

"What we can offer has no price," said Richard.

"Spell it out," demanded Ruan.

"You'll vanish. Disappear without a trace and become a legend—like D. B. Cooper."

"You're still not selling this very well."

"There's more," assured Richard. "We'll use social media to make sure the truth about your wife's death comes out. The entire world will learn how the system failed you, and you had to take matters into your own hands. Maybe you'll even get a movie about your life and disappearance. I like Leonardo DiCaprio for the starring role."

"His accent is shit," complained Ruan. "And I'm better looking—on a good day."

"So we have a deal? Aside from DiCaprio, of course."

Ruan stared at Richard for several moments, silently evaluating him.

"How do I know I can trust you to uphold your end of the deal?" he asked finally.

"Your disappearance starts today," explained Richard. "There's no record of your trip here, and no witnesses we don't control. There's a month of training and prep for you to do here before you go, and you'll see our operation to rehabilitate your image bear fruit before you're deployed."

"Okay," agreed Ruan with a shrug. "This is starting to sound a little better. Let's talk details."

Chapter Eleven

A LIFETIME OF PERFECTING the art of procrastination had prepared Jayson for the abrupt start to his duties at the Center. Cramming for exams and starting assignments the day before they were due, he'd managed to convince himself, were all part of his formula for success. After staring at a blank screen in his new office for nearly half an hour, paralyzed with fear he'd fail to demonstrate his competence, he'd put together a convincing, high-level briefing that seemed to resonate with his new team. They were ready to support his plan to transition the operation outdoors for a larger-scale test and development phase. Now, at the end of his first day, he was eager to catch up with Samaira. He tried to tell himself it was to see how her first day had gone, but he knew it was mostly to gush about his own success.

As he passed through the sliding glass doors at the front of the building, he saw her standing next to a Prius in the circular driveway of the main building, talking to an elderly woman. She noticed him and waved, excusing herself from the conversation to come over and greet him.

"How was your day?" she asked.

"Great! How about yours?"

"Very interesting," she said, raising one eyebrow.

"Who's that you were talking to?"

"Check out the vanity plates and see if you can tell me."

He took a moment to decipher it phonetically.

"Love doctor Jimi? Who is love doctor Jimi?"

"Remember the physicist who left the party on Sunday evening?"

"Yeah?"

"Luping said his mom picks him up," she continued.

"That was Dr. Akindele's mother? I thought they were kidding about that."

"Apparently not."

"I don't get the vanity plates, though. He doesn't seem like the type who would call himself 'love doctor.'"

"They're her plates. At least I hope they are," clarified Samaira. "I guess it's her way of saying she loves her son?"

"I'm gonna guess English is not her first language? That's all kinds of wrong. Why Jimi, though?"

"Jimi is short for Olujimi. Dr. Olujimi Akindele."

"That's a mouthful. I can see why he goes by Jimi."

"He doesn't. She warned me she's the only one who gets away with it."

"Noted," said Jayson. "From what I have seen, I'm just going to avoid talking to him altogether."

"Yeah. Probably the safest bet. He's probably not too fond of the plates either—but I got the sense she enjoys pushing his buttons."

"So, what'd she want?"

"I got the feeling she was trying to pick me up—for him, I mean."

"The love doctor is single? Who'd have guessed?" laughed Jayson. "You'd better move in quick before someone snatches him up."

"I don't get the feeling there's a lot of competition, but I'll find out more on my first date," said Samaira with a sly smile.

"Date?"

"Just with her," she laughed. "She's invited me for tea on Sunday afternoon."

Jayson rolled his eyes.

"By the way," he said, "I wanted to apologize for not hitting you at lunch. I was busy with something."

"No problem. Me too."

"Let's sync up and head to lunch together when we can," he suggested.

"Sorry, I can't. I kind of made a commitment to someone else."

"Who?" asked Jayson, hoping he didn't sound jealous.

"Andrew. The IT guy."

"Are you kidding me? That guy is a total incel. He's a weirdo, Samaira."

"Maybe," she allowed, "but there's something interesting there. I'm going to make him a bit of a side project."

"So, you're setting up a free counseling service?"

"Nothing like that. It's hard to explain."

"Give it a try," he urged." I'm listening."

"People like Andrew create disharmony. In my profession, that's a blaring siren, and I can't just ignore it."

"Can't you tell Richard he creeps you out and get him fired, or something?"

"That's always a possibility," she admitted, "but I prefer not to treat people as disposable. To me, it's a last resort."

"Of course," he conceded. "You're right."

He was in awe of Samaira. From the moment they'd met, she'd been friendly, upbeat, and level-headed with everyone. She never joined in when the group shared gossip or negative thoughts, and she seemed to connect with anyone—Richard, creepy Andrew, and Dr. Akindele's mother. Even Jayson felt more at ease with her than he did with his oldest friends and his own family. He wondered if she might charm even the aloof physicist himself. Probably not, he imagined. Whatever gifts she had, surely they had limits.

***

Olujimi means 'God gave me this' in Yoruba, the language of over thirty million West Africans. Jimi's mother often wondered what she had done to deserve such a cursed gift from God. Even as an infant, he exhibited signs something about him was different. He avoided eye contact, and didn't react to his mother's attempts to bond with him with baby-talk and games of peekaboo.

As a toddler, he regarded other children as elements of his surroundings rather than living beings like himself. He would prod, bite, and push them, studying their reactions with curiosity rather than empathy. The other parents, tired of the continual abuse, eventually avoided Jimi and his mother altogether. Despite her efforts to shepherd him into friendships, none of them lasted long, and he didn't even seem to notice. The genius that accompanied his curse became more pronounced with time, and it was apparent he could not maintain relationships with his peers because he didn't have any.

Despite his evident brilliance, young Jimi was helpless in many ways. He relied on his mother to organize and direct every aspect of his life, and it became her full-time job to guide his path. Choosing his schools and courses, managing his enrollment, applying for scholarships—it all fell to her—and she was determined if his life could not be normal, it would at least be consequential.

So outstanding were his achievements in theoretical physics, into which she had guided him, that upon completion of his doctorate at Cambridge University, they offered him a tenured position as a professor with no teaching duties. His only responsibility was to continue his theoretical work to support the university's efforts to advance the field of quantum supercomputing. His mother shed tears of joy, knowing she had secured a future for her strange little gift from God.

She'd chosen a pathway to an academic career deliberately, feeling he had the best chance of success in a comfortable, familiar environment isolated from the pressures of the corporate world. And so, she reacted with doubt when contacted by a recruiter for a nascent social media company called Hitz-It.com.

The company spared no expense in recruiting her as a proxy for her son. They flew her to their headquarters in Silicon Valley to show her the facility where her son would play a critical role in their efforts to transform quantum computing from theory to reality. They listened intently to her concerns, and addressed the list of environmental requirements she presented. Finally, they placed a stock certificate and an enormous check in front of her as a proposed signing bonus. Only the technicality of telling her son where to sign remained. She accepted the offer on his behalf, and Jimi was going to the United States.

Initially, the quantum computing program leader and former navy researcher, Dr. Richard Vandergroot, was excited by the arrival of a new colleague. It didn't take long for his enthusiasm to fade as the peculiarities of Dr. Akindele's personality caused friction with others on the team. The older physicist was envious of the newcomer's brilliance, and enraged by the condescension with which he explained his ideas.

As irksome as his behavior was, it was undeniable the arrogant young physicist's contributions were essential to the breakthrough that eventually made Anton

Kamaras the richest man in the world. Jimi's mathematics demonstrated a practical path to a quantum computing system the company's computer and software engineers brought to life in the form of the proprietary Hitz-It.com quantum stack.

While others celebrated Jimi's revolutionary interpretations of quantum physics, he seemed frustrated by his own achievement and refused to move on. Without a word, late one afternoon, he walked into Richard's office and wiped his portable whiteboard clean before rolling it towards the door.

"What the hell are you doing?" asked Dr. Vandergroot, throwing his hands in the air.

"Did you need this?"

"Well, no," admitted Richard with a frown, "but it's still mine. It'd be nice if you asked."

"Can I borrow your whiteboard, please, Richard?" he asked sarcastically.

"Yes, Jimi. Go ahead."

Akindele crossed his arms and glared silently.

"Yes, Dr. Akindele," sighed Richard, correcting the apparently grievous slight.

A couple of hours later, after he thought everyone else had gone home, Richard left his office and was surprised to see the lights on behind the frosted glass of the largest of the department's conference rooms. He poked his head in and found Dr. Akindele, his brow furrowed in thought, pondering a half-dozen appropriated whiteboards.

"You okay?" asked Richard with little genuine concern.

"The solution isn't right," he said, shaking his head.

"What do you mean? It's perfect. The engineers have confirmed everything with the prototype."

"But it's ugly, Richard. Mathematics is meant to be a thing of elegance and symmetry."

It was the kind of qualitative observation that annoyed Richard greatly. Math was math. It either worked, or it didn't.

"Is that what you're obsessing about in here?" he laughed.

"I don't expect you to understand. You're like a man with a candle exploring a dark cave, only able to consider one small section at a time."

'*Fuck you,*' thought Richard to himself with a snort. He never got used to being spoken to like he had some sort of pitiable mental impairment.

"Try me," he urged.

"Something is wrong with how we are modeling the superposition. It feels incomplete."

"You're right, doctor. I don't get it," said Richard, shaking his head. "Try not to go any crazier than you already are trying to figure it out."

With that, Richard closed the door and left.

He couldn't imagine what was troubling his colleague. Superposition was an established and well-understood phenomenon in the world of physics, even if the general public still struggled with the concept. Perhaps it was an overstatement, realized Richard, that it was *well* understood among physicists, but it was, at the very least, accepted without controversy.

Einstein famously hated the idea of superposition—the idea something could be in two contradictory states simultaneously—dubbing it 'too spooky' to be real. His onetime friend, Erwin Schrodinger, took his own contempt for the concept one step further, illustrating the implications with a gruesome thought experiment.

It was easy to accept the strange theory as it applied to particles so small they'd never be seen. Schrodinger's idea was to tie it to something tangible so the strangeness could not be ignored. He imagined a closed box containing a single radioactive atom. It would have a fifty percent chance of decaying and emitting detectible radiation during its half-life. Then, Schrodinger placed in his imaginary box a radiation detector attached to a mechanism that would break open a container of cyanide gas with a small steel hammer if the atom decayed. The final addition to the box was a healthy, living cat.

As long as the box remained closed—the inner workings unexamined from the outside—quantum theory stated the atom had both decayed and not decayed. It was in two contradictory states at the same time. Of course, this meant the radiation was both undetected and detected, the cyanide was both safely encapsulated and released, and the cat was simultaneously alive and dead. Only upon opening the inside of the box to examination did the superposition collapse, and a single, definitive state emerge. It was easy to understand why both Schrodinger and Einstein found the notion unsettling.

Whatever problems Akindele had with superposition, it was unlikely he'd be able to cast doubt where even Einstein had failed to do so. Richard was happy to let him take all the time he needed to make a fool of himself.

He smiled with amusement the following morning when a requisition for a dozen more whiteboards landed on his desk. He signed it eagerly and even put a rush on the delivery, anxious to see his arrogant colleague burn himself out over the weekend chasing his tail while the rest of the team enjoyed some well-deserved rest. They were rolling past his office towards the conference room by the end of the day.

On his way to the elevator after work, he poked his head in to see how things were going. The room reeked of body odor. Empty cola cans and half-eaten boxes of takeout spilled over the side of the receptacle by the door. Richard could hear the squeak of a dry erase marker coming from somewhere within the maze of whiteboards. He smirked to himself before retreating to the lobby undetected.

Throughout the weekend, Richard's thoughts turned to Akindele, toiling away with futility in the tenth-floor conference room. With the physics side of the quantum computing research winding down, maybe he'd take some time to humor the humorless asshole and see how long he could keep him going. Ideally, he could get Akindele to submit something embarrassing for peer review and open him to wider ridicule.

He arrived at work earlier than usual Monday morning, excited by the prospect of reviewing his colleague's progress. Both the mess and the stench in the room were worse than they'd been the previous Friday afternoon. Akindele must have chased the cleaning staff out of the room to rid himself of distraction, realized Richard as he began wandering the maze and examining the whiteboards.

"Richard! I asked you a question."

"What?"

He looked toward the sound of the sudden intrusion. It was Rebecca Steinman, the new superstar executive who'd appeared out of nowhere to begin an impressive ascent through the Hitz-It organizational hierarchy.

"What the hell is going on in here? And what's that smell?"

"I—uh."

Richard glanced at the clock on the digital presentation display on the wall by the entrance. He'd been in the room for over three hours.

"I doubt he has the capacity to explain what's going on here," announced Dr. Akindele as he appeared in the doorway.

Looking fresh and alert, evidently, he'd gone home for a shower and some sleep.

"No. I get it—I think," said Richard, shaking his head a couple of times.

He'd lost track of time as bemusement transformed first to confusion and then to wonder. For the moment, there was no space among his thoughts to accommodate his antipathy for his colleague. He'd completely misunderstood Akindele's concern with the superposition model and was overwhelmed by what now revealed itself on the whiteboards.

"Someone want to clue me in?" asked Rebecca, raising an eyebrow at Richard.

"The cat is both alive *and* dead—and remains that way even after observation," he replied as though staring past her at some distant object. "Superposition does not collapse."

"Very good, Richard," Akindele nodded approvingly. "You might be a physicist after all."

"What cat? What is going on?" demanded Rebecca.

"How were we so stupid?" asked Richard, ignoring her.

"Indeed," agreed Akindele. "To believe we could change the nature of reality itself simply by observing it is the ultimate arrogance. We have no such power. Observation only reveals in which reality we find ourselves."

"If you two assholes keep talking like I'm not here," warned Rebecca, "I'm going to lodge my right shoe about ten inches up someone's ass."

Akindele gagged in revulsion at what he viewed as an unladylike and unnecessarily graphic comment.

"Forgive us, Ms. Steinman," said Richard, snapping out of his trance. "What was the question?"

"What is going on here?"

"Dr. Akindele has reinvented physics," he said with reluctant admiration. "He's reinvented the universe."

"Are you sure?" she asked, surveying the room. "It smells like he and his colleagues have been playing Dungeons and Dragons in here all weekend. What did he do, exactly?"

Richard took a moment to consider how best to frame a response that didn't require more than a superficial understanding of physics.

"You know our quantum computer uses qubits instead of bits for its calculations."

"Of course," she confirmed, tapping her foot impatiently.

"The bits used by regular computers have two possible values—one or zero," he continued. "Our qubits have a third value. Besides one *or* zero, they can be simultaneously one *and* zero. When something is in two contradictory states simultaneously, we call that a state of superposition."

"I don't exactly know what that means," admitted Rebecca, "but I've heard all of this before."

"They might not admit it, but most physicists can't tell you exactly what it means, either."

"So, how do we know it's really happening?"

"Because it works," shrugged Richard. "It works mathematically and experimentally."

"I'm hopeless at math. More of a practical person," she confessed. "Tell me about the experiments that prove it's real."

"I'm going to dumb it down a bit," he said with a gulp. "No offense."

"Go ahead," she urged, showing no sign she'd taken the comment personally.

"Okay. We know matter behaves noticeably as both a particle and a wave at small scales. One way we've proven this is by firing a beam of electrons at a barrier with two tiny slits in it. The electrons going through both slits and striking the detection plate on the other side of the barrier demonstrate a classic wave interference pattern."

Rebecca gave no sign she wasn't following, so Richard continued.

"There's nothing strange about those results when you're firing a steady beam of electrons at the slits. The strange part happens when you fire the electrons one at a time. They still create an interference pattern on the detector, even when there are no other electrons to interfere with."

"What does that mean?"

"Just like the dual nature of the third state of our qubit," offered Dr. Akindele, "it means the individual electrons have gone through both slits simultaneously—in a state of superposition."

"This isn't anything new, mind you," interjected Richard. "This experiment was first done over a hundred years ago."

"So why all of the excitement today?"

"Because Dr. Akindele has proven superposition isn't a paradox. No qubits or electrons are ever in two states at once. Both states exist simultaneously but exclusively in separate realities."

Rebecca eyed Richard dubiously before turning her attention to Akindele.

"If I understand Dr. Vandergroot correctly, he's telling me you have proven the existence of parallel universes."

"I don't like that terminology," said Akindele with a sneer. "It's been turned into a vulgarity by talentless science fiction writers and Hollywood hacks."

"But that *is* what you're saying, right?"

"Basically, yes," said Richard. "What's different here is how he's shown that these alternate realities can, and do, interact with one another."

"At a subatomic level," cautioned Akindele, "and only briefly."

"I didn't see anything in your work imposing those limitations," frowned Richard.

"Not explicitly—but the energy requirements for larger scales would make it impractical."

"I guess that's not really the point," conceded Richard.

"What is the point, then?" asked Rebecca.

"We need to publish," replied Richard. "We owe it to the world to get this out to have it peer reviewed as quickly as possible."

"We owe the world nothing," said Rebecca with sudden aggression, raising a finger to Richard's face. "This stays here until we can figure out if it has any commercial value."

"What?" protested Richard in a rare defense of his colleague. "You can't suppress Dr. Akindele's work."

"It's not his work. All of this," she said, gesturing to the whiteboards, "belongs to Hitz-It.com. Read your fucking contracts."

Rebecca pulled out her phone and quickly made a call.

"Dianne, I need you to get locks put on the large conference room on the tenth floor."

Richard looked at Dr. Akindele in disbelief.

"Screw it," she reconsidered. "Cut all access to the tenth floor for everyone but Dr. Akindele and me. And get security to clear everyone else out immediately."

Chapter Twelve

RICHARD'S RESENTMENT TOWARDS HIS younger, brighter colleague, already considerable, had exploded to a new level on the day he was unceremoniously ushered from his office with a box of belongings and given a small cubicle next to the accounting department on the ninth floor. After he and the other scientists working on the quantum computing team slowly wrapped up their theoretical work and handed everything over to the engineers, he feared his journey at Hitz-It.com was coming to an end. He blamed Akindele for not standing up for him that day in the conference room. He could have insisted Richard would be a valuable contributor to the new project. Instead, he took it all for himself.

When Richard learned he wouldn't be leaving the company, but would instead oversee a new venture to support sustainability research, he was both puzzled and relieved. It had nothing to do with his expertise, but the title of managing director represented a considerable promotion. Once Kamaras revealed the true nature of the Center's mission, he understood why he had been chosen. Providing for Akindele's needs would require someone who could speak his language. The role of managing director also meant he was technically Dr. Akindele's boss, and he reveled in the idea of regaining control over his former subordinate.

The org chart, however, turned out to be a poor reflection of the actual power dynamic between the two, and they continued to prod and jab back-and-forth in their efforts to assert dominance. On the day the cargo ship carrying the two massive capacitor networks arrived off the shore of Pai'Olu'Olu Point on the southeast side of O'ahu, Dr. Akindele had the upper hand.

"How did you imagine your monstrosities would get from the ship up to the Beta site?" he asked with a laugh.

"I haven't worked that out yet."

"Perhaps you should have worked that out during the design phase—as I did."

"We're a little past that now, Jimi."

"If only there was some way to subdivide a structure into manageable pieces," he continued, ignoring the use of his hated nickname. "Like a modular approach of some kind."

"Yeah, I get it. This isn't going to be a problem," assured Richard.

"Tick-tock, Richard," said Dr. Akindele, tapping his wrist. "Fusion B is ready and waiting for your capacitors, and, by my calculations, we have just twelve days to the Beta window."

"I said it wouldn't be a problem, and it won't."

Richard left the temporary office structure at the Beta site and boarded a waiting helicopter. This one, owned by Hitz-It.com, was much smaller than the one that had placed the modular components of Fusion B into place. Even the Super Stallion couldn't help him with the capacitor networks. They were at least two tons over the maximum capacity of the Navy's most capable heavy-lift helicopter. When he got back to his office, he'd need to find a high-rise construction company that wanted to make an obscene amount of money in a very short time.

Too many things were happening simultaneously, and Richard found it hard to stay on top of them all. When he landed back at the center, another cargo ship was just arriving at the docks, and workers were already removing covers from the equipment lashed to the deck for unloading. The ship carried a dozen identical, massive, arched structures ringed with cable bundles and lined with wire coils. They were fastened onto frames designed to cradle their curved shape and keep them stable during transport. Richard had no choice but to trust everything at the docks was under control so he could focus on fixing his screw-up with the capacitor network.

He rushed from the helicopter directly to his office in the main building and started making calls, knowing it would be a serious challenge to get the capacitor networks into place in time. There was no way to drive a traditional rough terrain crane into place on the isolated point where it could reach the anchored Taiwanese cargo ship.

Not being an expert, he imagined they'd have to use the Super Stallion to move in pieces of a stationary crane, and assemble it onsite. In fact, because of the overall distance from the deep water offshore and the pads where the capacitors would sit, they'd likely need to set up two. He didn't know if that was even possible in less than two weeks, but it would have to be. Richard was determined he would not be the reason for the Beta to fail. He couldn't bear the idea of meeting Anton Kamaras, alongside the smug freak, and having to explain why they needed a massive rework of their carefully developed plans.

He reached out to several construction companies on the island and learned the largest of their cranes were already committed. Few people were interested in breaking existing agreements to secure such a short job, even at double or triple the standard rates. Sensing his desperation, one of the mid-sized, family-owned companies finally agreed to meet Richard at the site if he would sign a six-month contract and pay the delay penalties on any impacted projects. He agreed immediately, adding his own condition they would send an engineer and project manager to meet him on site later the same day.

Satisfied that he at least had a plan, Richard breathed a sigh of relief and pulled out his phone to hit Cal.

Need you to handle the plan with Aiden

What's wrong?

Nothing
Have to go to Beta

Ok
No problem

Richard grabbed his laptop and sprinted back to the helicopter for yet another trip to the Beta site on the opposite side of Honolulu.

***

When Cal arrived at Richard's office, Aiden was pacing impatiently in the outer room.

"Sorry to keep you waiting, Aiden. Richard just asked me to cover, so I rushed right over."

"He's not coming?" asked Aiden with a frown.

"Listen, I know I'm not one of you Navy guys, but I'm going to have to do for now."

The former SEAL followed Cal into Richard's office and sat down.

"It's fine," assured Aiden. "It's just he usually likes to have his fingers in the details."

"Yeah. A bit of a micromanager," agreed Cal. "But I can brief you on this."

"Changes?"

"No. Just some groundwork for Gamma. How's our mercenary doing for Beta prep, by the way?"

"Independent security contractor," corrected Aiden. "Really hates being called a merc."

"Better than murderous psychopath."

"Yeah. We don't talk about that. We've done a bunch of flyovers of the island, and he went over the archeological maps."

"What about objectives?"

"We've been covering that too," assured Aiden.

"How's the mental conditioning going?"

"He was a bit of a sociopath to begin with, so getting him over the line hasn't been hard."

"You any closer to finalizing the gear?"

"Yeah. Almost there. The one-eighty kilo limit makes things a bit tricky, and he's a pretty beefy guy, too."

"Bring him down a few pounds?"

"For sure," agreed Aiden, "but there's only so much we can do. He should be down to ninety kilos by next week."

"Not bad. That'll leave us another ninety kilos—about a hundred and ninety pounds—for gear."

"That gets eaten up fast," cautioned Aiden. "It's not as much as it sounds. We've reconstructed as much of the gear as we can with lighter components, but I still wish we could give him another fifty pounds."

"Ron Van Zeal, the famous survivalist? He should be asking for less, not more. Just give him a penknife and a shoelace, and he should be fine," joked Cal.

"I wouldn't bet against him. He might have faked a few things on the show, but he is definitely the real deal. Those Recces don't fuck around."

"Yeah. I heard he threatened to kill Richard."

"Can't blame him. We fucked him pretty bad."

"That's for sure. Compared to him, you're going on a vacation," said Cal. "Actually, more like a honeymoon."

"How's that?" asked Aiden, regarding Cal through a narrowed an eye.

"You know we need you to keep things on the rails, right?"

"Yeah."

"One of the recruits, Samaira Adams," continued Cal, "is a bit of a freethinker. We're afraid she might improvise a little too much."

"Then get someone else."

"It's not that easy. She's got what we need, and there isn't time to find another match."

"What do you want me to do?"

"Get close to her," said Cal. "Really close."

"I'm a charming guy, but I can't make any guarantees," protested Aiden.

"Don't worry. We started prepping her to be receptive to an older white man," assured Cal. "We just need to create a backstory for you that aligns with her predispositions and the suggestions we've been implanting."

"And that'll work?"

"It worked with our mercenary, didn't it?"

"Fair enough. So who am I?"

"Definitely not a Navy SEAL. Small town, Midwest, raised by a single mom. Stuff to make you seem vulnerable, but strong."

"Nice. How do we do that?"

"It's not hard. The algos will guide us based on what we already know about her."

"I always wanted a puppy as a kid. Can I have one in my backstory?" he joked.

"Sure. As long as it's a manly, likable breed. No poodles or pit bulls, or anything like that. I can give you a Lab."

"Maybe it's a Lab puppy with a sympathetic limp?" added Aiden with a laugh.

"One of those doggie wheelchairs would be better if we're trying to tug at the heartstrings," suggested Cal.

"That's probably taking it a bit too far."

"Shoot for the moon," laughed Cal.

"Alright. Send me the details of the backstory so I can work on it. Anything else I need to know?"

"Jayson's getting pretty attached to her, so we'll need to monitor his reactions. We can do some stuff to push him away if we need to. I suggest you start spending a bit more time with him after hours to use the friendship as a pretext for meeting Samaira."

"Sounds good. Anything else?"

"How's the farm doing?"

"Not bad. Everything has taken root and seems to be producing well."

"Does Jayson know what he's doing?"

"Yeah. He seems to know his stuff. I think we'll be good there."

"Fantastic. Don't want anyone starving to death."

"I'm not worried about that at all," assured Aiden. "Listen, I should head back out to the fields so nobody wonders where I am again. Been spending a lot of time with Van Zijl lately."

"Yep," agreed Cal. "We're good. Keep me up to date on the Samaira situation so I can adapt the model and see how we're doing."

"You got it," replied Aiden as he stood to leave.

Chapter Thirteen

RICHARD HAD GROWN IMPATIENT waiting for the engineer and project manager from the construction company to arrive, and hiked up to the road at the top of the ridge to meet them. The panoramic view of the Southeast corner of the island was spectacular. In the distance, he could even see the verdant mountains of Moloka'i beyond its nearer, more barren landscapes.

The sound of a pickup truck approaching drew his attention back to the immediate concern. A man and woman that looked to be in their mid-thirties jumped from the cab and greeted him.

"Are you Richard?" asked the woman.

"Yes. That's me."

"I'm Michelle, and this is my brother David. Our dad sent us over to see how we could help you."

David took Richard's hand and gave it a vigorous shake. Michelle's grip was even tighter, and she scrutinized him as she shook his hand.

"This is a good spot to get an overview of what we're up against," explained Richard. "Out there—on the deck of that cargo ship—are two twenty-ton containers that need to get over to those concrete pads. And it has to be done in ten days."

"How'd you get the rest of that stuff up here?" asked Michelle.

"Helicopter."

"That's way too big for a helicopter," she objected.

"It's modular."

"Smart. So do the same thing," suggested David. "Take some stuff out of the containers and bring it up in manageable loads by helicopter."

"Can't do that," explained Richard. "It's one solid piece of equipment. That's why you're here."

"I can tell you right now it's not getting done in ten days," said Michelle. "It'll take more than a month just for them to deny us a permit to build the crane base in a nature area."

"I'll have your permit ready tomorrow," assured Richard. "How long does it take to do the rest?"

"Can that ship get any closer?" asked David.

"There's a spot right below that cliff," indicated Richard, "where there's a flat outcrop to set up a crane, and the water's deep enough to get about one hundred and fifty feet from shore."

"That's good. What about that helicopter? You still have it?"

"If you need it, yes. It's all yours."

"This road is a bit dodgy for hauling in anything substantial," continued David. "But I saw a big parking lot where we could stage things a half-mile back."

"How long?" interrupted Richard. "There's no point talking logistics before I know the answer to that."

"Two days to prepare the base," replied Michelle. "Two more for the concrete to cure enough."

"Usually one day to set up the crane, but in this terrain? It's going to be two," added David.

"That's six days," said Richard with relief.

"But that only gets us halfway, by my estimate," cautioned David. "Then we've got to move the crane and do it all again."

"Another six days is too long."

"It's not double the time," assured Michelle. "The second base will be prepped and cured by the time the first lift is done, so we can take four days out of the equation there."

"Yeah," agreed David. "Two or three days max to move the crane after the first lift. That puts us at nine, and we're doing the final lift into place on day ten."

"That's cutting it too close," said Richard, shaking his head.

"You're the one who said ten days," complained Michelle.

Richard ignored her.

"What about bringing in a second crane and setting it up at the same time as the first one?"

"Even if we had another one available, we don't have a big enough crew to handle two simultaneous builds like that," said Michelle, shaking her head.

"We know what we're doing," assured David. "If you really can get a permit by tomorrow, we'll have those containers in place in ten days."

With twelve days to the Beta window, there was no room for error. Unfortunately, Richard couldn't think of any better options than the one presented by the experienced siblings.

"I'll meet you in that parking lot back there at eight tomorrow morning with a permit and a helicopter," promised Richard. "Do not let me down."

***

Richard was waiting in the far section of the Hanauma Bay parking lot when a flatbed truck loaded with equipment pulled in. Behind it followed the crew in two king cab pickups. David got out of the lead pickup and walked over to greet Richard.

"Here's your permit," said Richard.

"That's impressive. We can't get that kind of turnaround for paving a driveway, let alone tearing up part of a nature preserve."

"We've made commitments to restore the area and invest in its long-term protection."

"Sure," said David. "I bet you've invested in something. We've been doing this long enough to know how things get done, and not to ask questions about it."

"Then let's get moving," suggested Richard.

"That our helicopter?" asked David, pointing at the Super Stallion.

"Yep. That's it. With a Navy loadmaster and crew included for as long as you need them."

"Well, that changes the schedule a bit."

"How?" demanded Richard, furrowing his brow.

"Don't worry," assured David. "It's good news. With that monster, we can do a lot more preassembly here in the parking lot and take at least a day off the entire project."

Richard breathed a sigh of relief. An extra day to double-and-triple-check the installation was welcome news. David returned to the second pickup to give some instructions to the crew inside. When he finished, they left the parking lot and drove up towards the ridge.

"The first crane base is in a tricky spot," he explained, walking back to Richard. "They're going to set up all of the harnesses and safety lines while we prepare the first load of equipment to send down by chopper. If everything goes to plan, we should have the concrete truck rolling up to the parking lot by midafternoon today."

"Sounds good."

"If it's okay with you," he continued, "we'd rather use our own guy to helicopter concrete into the forms. Our crew already knows how to work with him."

"No problem for me. Whatever you need to do to get it done. I'll be spending the week onsite in the temporary office so you can come and find me if you need anything at all."

"Appreciate it, Richard."

The two men shook hands once again, and David went over to the flatbed to supervise the preparation of the first load of equipment. Richard headed back to the Beta site to gloat to Dr. Akindele that he had found a solution to the capacitor problem.

***

By the end of the fourth full day of construction, things were progressing to plan. As required, the first crane base had cured for a full forty-eight hours, and the crew had finished pouring the concrete for the second base midway between the shore and the final resting place for the capacitor networks. After cleaning up for the day, the exhausted workers had made their way back up to their trucks and gone home for the evening. The only ones left at the Beta site were Richard and Ruan, going over more mission details.

"You got your second shot today?" asked Richard.

"Yes," confirmed Ruan. "They stuck me first thing this morning."

"Perfect. You should be good before you leave, but I would wait at least a couple more weeks to be sure."

"Understood."

"You want to go over the preparation process again?"

"No. I've got it memorized," assured Ruan.

"Tell me," urged Richard.

"I know how to prepare the stuff, Richard. If you don't already trust me, it's too late to do anything about it now."

"Fine. What *do* we need to go over, then?"

"Nothing," asserted Ruan. "I know what to do."

"You're running out of time for questions," warned Richard. "If you need any clarity, you need to ask soon, because there's no contact after Beta."

"No questions about what's expected of me, but I'm still not clear on how any of this is possible."

"What do you know about quantum physics?"

"Same as I know about ballet. Nothing. And I'm fine keeping it that way."

"Well, then there's not much hope of explaining it to you."

"Give me the meathead version."

"Alright," started Richard. "Imagine you and a friend in separate cars are on a highway from New York to Los Angeles. It diverges into two separate routes, and you each decide to go a different way. His route turns out to be fairly direct, while yours is more scenic."

"Okay," nodded Ruan.

"Somewhere around Wichita, the highways cross over one another," said Richard, crossing his outstretched arms to demonstrate. "We have a machine to create an offramp to the other highway so you can join your friend."

"But he's miles ahead by now."

"Or to say it another way," offered Richard, "You're at a point where he was in the past."

"Alright," allowed Ruan. "What about that SEAL I met? And you? You're all supposed to be further down the road than me."

"After you merge onto the other highway, it becomes the scenic route, while ours becomes more direct."

"Just my fucking luck," snorted Ruan.

"He and I will join your route at different points ahead of you."

"How does the machine work?" asked Ruan. "The one that builds the on-ramps."

"That's harder to explain—"

A knock at the door interrupted them, and David McCullough walked in without waiting for an invitation.

"David," said Richard with a start, "what are you doing here?"

"You said I should come and find you any time."

"Yes, of course. What do you need?"

David didn't immediately reply, and kept glancing back and forth between Richard and Ruan.

"You're Ron Van Zeal!" he said finally. "The survival guy."

"I get that all the time," deflected Ruan.

"David McCullough," he said, extending his hand. "I'm a huge fan."

"Nice to meet you, David."

"What the hell are you doing here?"

"Mr. Van Zijl is interviewing for a job as our head of security at this site," interrupted Richard.

"Talk about overkill," said David.

"My options are limited," explained Ruan.

"Yeah. Sorry you had to go through that."

"I appreciate you saying so."

"And now there's all that stuff about how that producer left your wife to die, and the cops covered it up. What a bunch of slimeballs."

"You're following that?" asked Ruan with surprise.

"Hell, everyone is. It's blowing up."

Ruan glanced at Richard with an approving nod.

"We believe in Mr. Van Zijl as well, David. So we're offering him a way to make a living while his reputation recovers."

"I have to admit, when nobody could find you to comment on the story, I just assumed the worst," said David. "Glad to see you're okay."

"What brings you by, David?" asked Richard, changing the subject.

"I just wanted you to know I'm here to test the first pad. If everything turns out like it should, we'll be erecting the crane tomorrow."

"That's great news."

"We spent part of today pre-assembling it into larger sections to take advantage of that behemoth the Navy lent you. I think there's a good chance we could finish the first lift the day after tomorrow."

"Well, let's get these tests going, then," urged Richard.

"Sure thing. I'll let you know the results before I leave."

"Actually, we'd love to come and check it out with you," said Richard, glancing at Ruan as he stood from his chair.

"Sure," agreed David. "Follow me."

The site for the crane base was a large, flat outcropping at the bottom of a cliff just east of the small plateau where they'd established the Beta site. It was a short, mostly flat walk for the three men, and it took only a few minutes to get there. David's team had erected a safety barrier at the edge, and installed a ladder for easy access to the outcrop thirty feet below. The top of the ladder was anchored securely into the rock to prevent it from toppling.

"After you, Richard," offered David.

"I'm petrified of heights," replied Richard. "I'll watch from up here."

"I'm game," announced Ruan. "Want me to carry any of your gear?"

"I've got it," assured David as he yanked on the straps of his pack to demonstrate it was secure.

Ruan swung onto the ladder and began quickly descending. David got on a little more gingerly and took a few steps down before looking back up at Richard with a huge smile.

"This is so cool," he said. "It's like I'm in my own survival story with Ron Van Zeal."

He followed Ruan down the ladder and dismounted at the bottom, right next to the concrete pad. Standing next to Ruan, he took off his pack and brought out the equipment for the first test.

"What does that do?" asked Ruan.

"It's an abrasion resistance tester to verify the surface material has fully hardened. I hook it up to this controller, and it spins an abrasive pad against the concrete."

Ruan watched with interest as David ran through his test procedures and recorded the results. After packing the machine away, he took out a small steel cylinder with a pin protruding from one end. It had a number scale engraved on the side.

"What's this one?" asked Ruan.

"It's called a rebound hammer, and it's for testing hardness below the surface."

David pushed it down against the surface and listened for a faint knocking noise. He noted the number indicated on the side and repeated the procedure in several locations.

"That's it?" asked Ruan.

"Yep. That's it."

"What's next?"

"I write down the numbers and initial them to show they're all good. We can get started putting up the crane tomorrow."

"That's really cool. Thanks for showing me."

"My pleasure," replied David as he finished some notations and packed everything away for the ascent.

Ruan looked reluctantly to the top of the ladder. Richard met his gaze and frowned, shaking his head before turning away and vanishing from sight beyond the edge of the cliff. As David took hold of the ladder, Ruan kicked the side of his right knee. David screamed out in pain and buckled towards the concrete pad, narrowly missing the corner with his head.

"What the fuck, man?" he yelled. "You almost broke my skull!"

"Sorry I have to do this," sighed Ruan.

David's eyes widened in terror as Ruan grabbed him by the head and slammed his right temple into the corner of the pad. A pool of blood slowly engulfed his upper body as he twitched violently for a few moments before going still.

Ruan looked around for something that could easily explain the terrible accident at the crane pad. He surveyed the outcrop and noticed a significant amount of guano had accumulated along the edge where it overhung the ocean. He collected some of the freshest globs in one hand until he felt like there was enough to serve his purpose. After pressing some of it onto the tread of David's right boot, he smeared the rest onto the second rung of the ladder. Keeping his dirty hand free to avoid contaminating the rest of the rungs, he climbed back up to join Richard.

"The tests were good," he said. "They're in his backpack."

"Does it look like an accident?"

Ruan held up his dirty hand.

"Slipped on bird shit," he explained with a frown.

"Hell of a way to go," lamented Richard. "You have to disappear until Beta so we don't have to go through this again."

"No problem. I'm good at that," he replied with a shrug.

Chapter Fourteen

THE NEXT MORNING, RICHARD emerged from the temporary quarters to a flurry of activity. Emergency vehicles lined the roadway above the site, and an air medical services helicopter was just touching down. He walked over to an assembled crowd of people on the cliff overlooking the crane pad, trying to show the appropriate mix of bewilderment and concern.

"Officer?" he started. "What's going on?"

"Sorry, sir, you're going to have to stop right there."

"I'm in charge of the site. I need to know what's going on."

"There's been an accident, sir."

"Oh my God! Is it serious?"

He tried to say it just as he had perfected it in front of the mirror.

"Yes, sir. A man is dead. Did you just arrive?"

"No. I've been here all night—in the living quarters."

"Did you notice Mr. McCullough at all yesterday evening?"

"David? Is—is it David down there?"

"I can't say anything about that, sir. Did you see anyone yesterday evening?"

"I came out to check on progress as the crew was getting ready to leave—around four o'clock. I didn't see anyone after that."

"Do you normally stay all night?"

"When I work late, yes. I've been doing a lot of that lately."

The distant sound of screaming interrupted the interrogation.

"David! David!"

His sister, Michelle, ran down the path toward the scene, flanked by two more men from the crew. She arrived out of breath with tears streaming down her face. Richard winced. He didn't expect to feel the pang of regret triggered by the appearance of David's mourning sister.

"Oh God," she panted, "Is it true? Is it David?"

"Ma'am, can you come with me, please?" asked the officer. He turned to escort her over to the ladder, leaving Richard and the crew behind.

Among those in the crowd at the top of the cliff was Don Lee, the local inspector with whom Richard had already had multiple run-ins. He approached with a disapproving look.

"This is bad, Richard," he said, shaking his head. "This is what happens when you cut corners on safety."

"Are you kidding me, Don? A man is dead, and you're using it to get to me?"

"Just calling it like I see it."

"You're telling me these guys here—and the McCulloughs—don't know what they're doing?" he said, pointing to the crew standing next to him.

They regarded the inspector with angry looks.

"No. Not at all," he replied. "This is a reflection of your operation."

"This is our work," shot back one of the crew, "and it's exactly the fuckin' way it's supposed to be."

"Even so, I'm shutting you down."

"Listen here, you little shit," replied Richard. "You can't do that unless there's a permit issue."

"I can't," admitted Don, "but OSHA can. I told them I was concerned about your cavalier approach to permits and procedures. They've got someone on the way now to make sure you get checked out properly for once."

"Until now, I've just been fucking around with you, Don," warned Richard. "If we get shut down, things are going to get much worse."

"Are you threatening me, Richard?"

"Fucking right I am."

With that, he turned and walked back to his temporary office to make some calls.

***

The fallout of David's necessary death was spiraling out of Richard's control. Undermining Don by the usual means wasn't a problem, but shortcutting the OSHA investigation was a more significant challenge. The lead inspector turned out to be an absolute Pitbull, doubtlessly spurred on by Don's warnings. She'd shut down all work at the site and sent everyone who wasn't involved in recovery and investigation home. Even worse, she'd refused to give a timeline for allowing work to continue. The extra day David had gifted him by pre-assembling much of the crane was already gone, and things were getting tight again. Richard had no choice but to make a phone call that would show he had things somewhat less than fully under control.

"Admiral, thanks for taking my call."

"By the sound of things, I didn't have much choice, Richard. What's going on?"

"The Beta is in jeopardy, sir."

"I gathered that much," replied Admiral Daniels curtly. "What's the issue?"

"I've got OSHA crawling up my ass, and they've shut everything down."

"And you need me to sort this out?"

"Anton's name isn't doing the trick. We need something more official."

"I'll take care of it, Richard. Just make sure we get our Beta done."

"Yes, sir."

He hung up the phone, relieved to have solved the problem, but annoyed he hadn't been able to manage it on his own. To make matters worse, the morning of firefighting had forced him to skip a couple of meetings, and ignore his emails and hits. He started triaging his overdue tasks and responding to messages requiring immediate attention. Midway through composing a status update for Rebecca, there was a knock on his door.

"Come in."

"Mr. Vandergroot?" greeted the OSHA inspector.

Under normal circumstances, he'd have corrected the omission of his proper title, but now was not the time to quibble. He decided simply to appease her while Admiral Daniels worked on the problem from his end.

"Please, call me Richard."

"Mr. Vandergroot," she continued, "we've reached a conclusion on the death of Mr. McCullough."

"And?"

"Accidental. Looks like he slipped on—on something."

"That's terrible," replied Richard with as much feigned sympathy as he felt appropriate under the circumstances. "So no safety issues?"

"Nothing we've seen so far. The ladder and the barriers were all good."

"When can we start work again?"

"Some other concerns have been raised," she said vaguely. "We'd like to keep things shut down for a bit while we look around and interview some of your contractors."

"I'll support you in any way I can."

"I understand you've been working with some Navy personnel as well?"

"Yes. That's correct."

"I'd like to make sure they're available to interview."

"I can't help you there, but I can point you to their commanding officer."

"That'll do. Thanks. I'd also like to interview you a little more formally."

"More formally?"

"On the record," she clarified.

"No problem. I can set aside some time for you tomorrow afternoon," he promised.

"I'd prefer something sooner if—"

A buzz from her phone interrupted the inspector mid-sentence.

"Excuse me," she said. "I need to take this."

Richard looked at his own phone to check the time. Fourteen minutes had passed since he concluded his call with the admiral, and he listened for a sign the two calls were related.

"Yes. I'm here now," he heard her respond to an unheard question.

"Accidental, yes," she continued before another brief pause.

"There are a few more things I need to look—"

The pause was longer this time, and she furrowed her brow.

"But I have a great deal of latitude in these situations to—"

Again, she was interrupted before she could complete her statement.

"Alright. Understood," she said with a frown, and ended the call.

"Everything okay?" asked Richard with feigned concern.

"I guess I should have been expecting that," she said. "From what I heard, you're not really accountable for anything you do on this island."

"I am held to the highest account for *everything* I do," assured Richard. "And the implications of what I do reach *far* beyond what you and that other fucking weasel can appreciate."

"That was a quick change in attitude," she remarked.

"There's no longer a need to pretend that you have any influence over what's going to happen here."

"I guess not," she conceded. "You're up and running again, asshole."

Richard let her have the parting shot, saying nothing as he leaned back in his chair with a grin and watched her leave.

Chapter Fifteen

JAYSON AND SAMAIRA WERE settling into the routine of life at the Center for Sustainability Research. Though rarely planned, they occasionally met at breakfast, but did not see each other again until after work. Samaira had her lunch with Andrew while Jayson spent more time with his immediate team—especially Aiden. In the evening, they continued meeting with everyone at sunset before dining together. Aiden and Olena were becoming regulars at dinner as well.

News of the troubling accident at the Beta site had not found its way to the hitzlists of the team members assembled in the cafeteria that evening, so the after-dinner conversation centered on other trending topics instead. The algorithms gave one topic in particular an artificial boost to insert it into their collective consciousness.

"Check this out," said Aiden as he glanced up from his phone. "Younger millennials unlikely to have children, citing environmental anxiety. Is that true?"

"Don't ask me, old man. I'm Gen Z," replied Jayson with a laugh.

"Watch out, kid. Not that long ago, I was the young guy in my crowd. It changes faster than you think," retorted Aiden.

"I want to have kids," said Hitarthi, "but it doesn't seem fair to bring them into the mess we're making."

"I'm the same way," added Luping.

"I know it's selfish," admitted Kailani, "but I still want kids someday—even though I know things will be hard for them."

"I'm an older millennial than most of you. Okay, probably all of you," said Aiden with a laugh, "and even a lot of my friends back home aren't having kids."

"What about you?" Samaira asked him.

"I have to admit I'm torn," replied Aiden. "I've always seen myself as a father—teaching my kids how to play baseball and ride a bike. You know, stuff like that."

"But you're not sure?"

"It's like Kailani said," he continued. "I feel like it's selfish to do it just for me, and ignore what they might have to face after I'm gone. It's why I'm here at the center. If there's any hope at all we can make a better world for our kids, I want to be part of it."

"That is so sweet," said Kailani. "Who would have thought a big, tough-looking guy like you could be such a softie?"

Aiden blushed and laughed aloud.

"Promise not to tell anyone? I've got a reputation to protect."

"How about you, Samaira?" asked Jayson. "Do you want kids?"

"For the longest time, I didn't think so," she said. "Lately, I've felt more like I could miss out on something if I don't. But just like you guys, I realize what they'd face, and I feel guilty for even considering it."

It was the most revealing thing Jayson had ever heard her say. Aiden reached across the table and placed a hand over hers. She met his gaze with surprise but didn't pull away.

"Let's make this opportunity mean something, then," he said.

There was an awkward silence for a few moments, and Samaira looked down at Aiden's hand.

"I'm sorry," he said, quickly pulling back.

"That's alright. I understand why you're passionate about this. It's why I'm here, too."

Samaira's gentle response diffused the momentary tension, and the others expressed their support to Aiden, who was clearly emotional about the topic.

"I don't think I've hit you yet, Samaira," said Aiden.

"No. I don't think you have," she replied, holding her phone up.

They tapped their phones together, and Samaira glanced down at the new profile displayed in front of her.

"Oh! That's such a cute dog! How old were you in that picture?"

"Uh, probably twelve?" he guessed.

"What's that?" she asked, turning the screen to him and pointing.

He hesitated for a moment, biting his lip.

"That's one of those doggie wheelchairs. Basically, just a pair of wheels you strap around them if they don't have use of their back legs."

"That poor thing. What happened to him?"

"Her. She was like that when I got her," said Aiden. "We were pretty poor growing up and couldn't afford a nice purebred lab like that one. A neighbor—he was a breeder—had a litter with one disabled pup. He was going to put her down, so I begged my mother to let me have her instead."

The girls at the table melted, and Aiden, suddenly looking very upset, stood up. "Excuse me. I need to go."

Everyone watched with sympathy as he hurried from the cafeteria. Once out of sight, he pulled out his phone to hit Cal.

Can't fucking believe you

What?

Wheelchair dog
Asshole
That was a joke

Algos loved it

Shoulda told me
Almost lost my shit

K
No more surprises

***

The McCullough crew took an extra full day off for the funeral of the beloved oldest son of their company founder. Richard didn't dare complain and rationalized there was still enough margin to complete the lift because of the accelerated schedule. He even went to the funeral himself to announce that once completed, the updated natural area on Pai'Olu'Olu point would include a new feature called the McCullough Memorial Overlook at the cliff-side location where David had lost his life. It was Mr. Kamaras, he told the grief-stricken family, who had insisted they honor the man who had committed to helping them out of a tough situation. So touched was the family by the gesture they decided meeting David's last commitment was a fitting way to honor his passing.

The next day, the crew was hard at work, and by sunset, the capacitor networks were resting in a temporary location halfway between the departing Taiwanese cargo ship and their final resting place a few hundred meters from Fusion B. Thirty-six hours before Beta, they were finally in place, and the Fusion team was coupling the heavy gauge cables as the Navy crew lifted the final section of the McCullough's crane away.

The USS Ronald Reagan had also arrived with the rest of its carrier group and positioned itself in the deep water just off the point. Crew members were hauling the thick, heavy cable from the Reagan up the cliff with ropes so the carrier's reactors could feed the power-hungry apparatus hidden inside the unassuming, windowless structure.

"Thank you for not ruining my Beta, Richard," said Dr. Akindele as the two stood together, watching techs performing the diagnostic testing of the capacitor controllers and connections.

"Nice of you to say, Jimi," he replied with a sneer.

"Or maybe I should say thank you for not ruining my Beta *yet*—since there is no way to test a full discharge cycle."

"It's going to work," promised Richard.

"We shall see, Richard. We shall see."

Dr. Akindele left him alone to watch over the rest of the preparations and system checks.

***

On the day of the Beta window, the VIPs who had attended Alpha reassembled in the control room—including Rebecca Steinman and Admiral Daniels. The Admiral had also invited a new guest to attend. Captain Raul Ibarra, a distinguished Navy submariner, was in charge of the contracts for developing the new Columbia class of ballistic missile submarines slated to replace the aging Ohio class. He'd been briefed on the success of Alpha and wanted to witness Beta for himself.

The star of the show was the other addition to the guest list for Beta. Ruan Van Zijl stood in the test chamber surrounded by techs, fitting him with instrumentation and double-checking his gear. He wore a full pack strapped to his back, and two large, hardened plastic cases were stacked next to him.

"So, he's really doing it," marveled Captain Ibarra, looking down into the chamber.

"He's shown no hesitation whatsoever since we came to an understanding," confirmed Richard.

"How did you manage that?"

"It was a long process," explained Richard. "First, we had to identify potential candidates based on their predispositions so we'd have something to work with."

"How do you do that?"

"Nearly half the world voluntarily shares with us every aspect of what they think and do. It really isn't hard to find a pool of candidates when you've got three billion people to choose from."

"Fair enough," allowed the Captain. "What next?"

"We search for things we can use as leverage to influence them. Depending on their personalities and what we learn, there's a wide range of possibilities. We can narrow down the pool very quickly by running and refining the simulated responses to different manipulation strategies."

"And for him," asked Ibarra, nodding towards the chamber, "the opportunity you exploited was the death of his wife?"

"A fortunate accident," admitted Richard. "The algorithms pounced as soon as the possibilities became clear."

"That doesn't sound like much to work with."

"It was enough to build a strategy. Then, we essentially programmed him to hit Kamakawiwoʻole and his wife. The news he read, the media he consumed, the way our bots reacted to his posts—it was all orchestrated to get the results we needed. The algos even predicted the time of death within a few hours."

"Shit, that's scary. I still don't understand how you convinced him that Kamakawiwoʻole really did it."

"That was the easy part. He wanted to believe it because it meant he may still be worthy of his wife. Part of him knows it's bullshit, but he voluntarily represses that."

"What's the strategy for the Gamma recruits? How are you getting them to buy in?"

"That's a slightly different approach. We identified people with the skills and traits we needed, and then looked for those predisposed to climate anxiety. After that, we cranked it up to eleven. It honestly wasn't that hard to do. Any kid with half a brain should be terrified of what they might be facing."

"No shit," agreed Captain Ibarra.

"It's the next part that's the key. Right now, we're building them up to believe they'll make a difference—giving them a light at the end of the tunnel. At just the right time, we'll snuff it out."

"Jesus Christ. That's cruel."

"Maybe so," agreed Richard, "but the simulations show it's necessary. After we dash all hope, we open up another door and invite them to walk through it."

"And they don't suspect anything?"

"Like our mercenary here, they don't want to believe anything different from what we've told them. They willfully ignore evidence that doesn't support the narrative they've accepted, and attach extra significance to evidence that does."

"Just like that?" asked Ibarra doubtfully, snapping his fingers.

"We all do it to one degree or another every day. It's in our nature, and remarkably easy to reinforce through psychological conditioning."

The captain considered everything Richard had just told him and then eyed the physicist through narrowed eyes.

"Did you manipulate me into being part of this?"

"You were identified with the help of our platform," allowed Richard. "But, unlike our Gamma recruits, we've shown you the full picture."

"You have," agreed Ibarra.

"And how do you feel about your involvement?"

"Honestly? I'd prefer to be part of Epsilon."

"Without Delta, there is no Epsilon."

"Understood," conceded Ibarra. "And I *do* appreciate how lucky I am to be involved at all."

"I know you do, Captain," assured Richard. "Please excuse me for a moment. I need to verify a few things before we get started."

"Of course." The captain rejoined Admiral Daniels and Rebecca as Richard left to check on the preparations.

A new equipment configuration in the chamber accommodated the needs of Beta. The pedestal where the sample had been resting during Alpha was gone, and in its place was a ten-meter-long elevated walkway with a gentle ramp at the far end. The walkway was about a half-meter off the ground and two meters wide. It terminated at the twin-ringed apparatus.

A tech walked in, pulling a two-wheeled bamboo cart that looked a bit like a rickshaw. Even the enormous wheels were made of natural materials, and the entire structure was bound using plant fibers. The juxtaposition of the simple device against the high-tech surroundings was striking. A colleague helped him lift the two large cases and fasten them on the cart while another went over some final details with Ruan.

"We're about five minutes out, Mr. Van Zijl. You want to do a last run-through of the procedure?"

"Yeah. Let's do it," replied Ruan nervously.

"You'll grab the cart and walk it up to the top of the ramp," started the tech. "Then, keep an eye on the color of the walkway LEDs."

"Yep. Got it."

"Five seconds before go, they'll turn red and start moving towards the aperture at a steady rate. That's the speed you're going to need to maintain."

Ruan nodded.

"When the lights go green, step on top of them and keep following. Both you and the cart need to stay inside the green zone. If you start to get ahead or fall behind, don't worry. We'll give you some guidance over the intercom."

"What kind of drop should I expect at the end?"

"Nothing noticeable. We should be lined up pretty good."

"Am I going to materialize inside of a tree, or something?"

"No," laughed the tech. "We chose this location partly for its stability. I can assure you, this place hasn't changed much for a very long time."

One of the techs in the control room addressed the chamber over the intercom. "Let's clear non-essential personnel from the chamber, please. We're going to start the sequence in sixty seconds."

The tech working with Ruan clapped him on the shoulder.

"You'll be fine," he assured. "Just stay in the green zone."

Ruan nodded again and watched as everyone else proceeded to the exit and left him alone in the chamber.

"Initiating power sequence," came the announcement from overhead.

A hum filled the room, and the floor began to vibrate as the inner rings of the apparatus started their slow acceleration in opposite directions. Ruan took a deep breath and lifted the handle of the two-wheeled cart from the floor, trailing it behind him as he approached the ramp. Once at the top, he stood and waited for the signal to go.

Admiral Daniels, watching from above, learned from his earlier rebuke, and knew better than to ask Dr. Akindele questions during Beta. Instead, he turned to Richard, who had rejoined the assembled group of VIPs.

"What's the transfer rate this time around?"

"About sixty kilos per second," replied Richard.

"How does that compare to Alpha?"

"The theoretical limit for Alpha was around half a kilo per second, but we limited it to a tenth of that to stay on the safe side."

"That's impressive scaling. Do we expect the trend to continue as expected?"

"Everything has matched predictions so far," assured Richard, "so we should be good."

"Superposition achieved," announced a control tech.

Richard and the admiral stopped talking and looked down at the apparatus. The rail-mounted ring began moving toward its stationary counterpart, causing their concentric, translucent waves to interfere. After a few seconds, the standing wave pattern emerged from the chaos.

In front of Ruan, the rows of lights on the walkway turned red in a steady succession, advancing towards the rings. He counted slowly to five and stepped forward just as the lights beneath his foot turned green. Walking at the steady pace indicated by the changing colors in front of him, Ruan kept himself and the makeshift rickshaw in the middle of the advancing green zone.

"Target waveform is locked," confirmed the control tech.

Ruan focused on the lights in front of him and followed them to the end of the walkway. He stepped through the first ring and into the standing wave without hesitation. Flashes of light pulsed from the center for three full seconds while first Ruan, and then the trailing cart, vanished into the aperture.

Everyone held their breath as they waited for Dr. Akindele to speak.

"Complete mass entanglement with resultant waveform confirmed," he said simply.

A round of subdued applause rose from the assembled team and their awestruck guests.

Chapter Sixteen

NOHEA WAS HAVING THE strangest dream. Wandering the forest alone in the dark, he was searching for something. He couldn't remember what. Then, the night sky exploded, and for a few moments, he could see all around him like it was midday. Well, not exactly like midday. A glowing white orb traced low across the sky, and the shadows of the trees danced strangely in its flickering light.

A dark form rose from the ground and was upon him without warning. He tried to run away, but his legs felt heavy and lifeless, as so often happened in his dreams. He plodded forward slowly, and only with great effort. Finally reaching the shore, he resolved to escape whatever followed him by canoe. His arms failed, just as his legs had, leaving him unable to paddle away from his shadowy pursuer.

As he transitioned slowly to wakefulness, Nohea took comfort in the dawning awareness that the paralysis would soon pass, and he'd be able to move again. But something was wrong. His head and face hurt terribly, and he couldn't see anything more than a hint of daylight. Though he was able to shift his legs around and bend his knees, his arms were immobile—held fast behind him. He realized with a start that he'd was blindfolded and tied up against a tree.

His brain worked frantically to retrieve his most recent memories. He was on an island in the middle of a lagoon on O'ahu with his fellow fisherman and their hidden protectors when something happened. What was it? He'd left the comfort of the campfire to check on Ahe, who was taking longer than usual to return from his rounds. But then what? His dream, he realized. It wasn't all a dream. The ball of white fire in the sky, the dark shape in the corner of his eye appearing suddenly from nowhere—that was all real, but he could recall nothing more.

He remained as still as possible, listening for the voices or movements of his captors. The only sounds came from the nearby gentle waves lapping at the shore, and the birds calling to one another in the branches above him. Perhaps his colleagues were similarly restrained nearby, waiting silently for something to happen. He whispered a few words to see if anyone would respond.

As soon as he moved his mouth, intense pain seared across the lower right part of his face and jaw, doubling him forward as far as his restraints would allow. It felt like a dozen giant centipedes had bitten him in the face. He panted heavily, trying to recover from the shock as his eyes welled up with tears. One or two even made it past the blindfold and rolled down his cheek.

A rustling noise to his left startled him, and he held his breath—willing himself into invisibility. It was futile, he realized. He'd been caught by the evil he was sent to provoke. His heartbeat echoed so loudly in his ears, Nohea was convinced anyone within a couple of arms' lengths of him would be able to hear it. The rustling got closer, stopping immediately beside him, and he could feel a looming presence. He cowered in terror, waiting for the evil to reveal itself as either natural or supernatural—as human or demon.

Nohea started as an unexpected splash of liquid fell on his head and trickled down his face. It was water. Perhaps it wasn't a demon after all. He slowly parted his lips as far as he could before the pain became too much, and then tilted his head back. A slow, steady stream rewarded him, and he gulped it down.

"Masalo," offered Nohea gratefully when his thirst was quenched.

The word emerged strangely from his shattered mouth, sounding more like 'uh-thalo,' but he imagined his intention was clear enough. His captor offered no response, and Nohea strained to listen as his footsteps faded into the sound of gently breaking waves.

The cool, refreshing water helped lift some of the fog from Nohea's thoughts, and spurred his mind to action. Deprived of sight, he employed his other senses to discover what he could about his circumstances. The smells were familiar, but something was out of place. He guessed he was still in the camp because he could smell the smoke from the fire and the lingering scent of their dried catch. What was the other smell? He knew it from somewhere. He realized it was the rotten, sour smell of volcanic effluent. Was that the magic he'd witnessed? Had his attacker somehow harnessed the power of Pele?

He tried once again to listen for clues. Besides the sounds of water and wildlife, he could hear his captor laboring at some unknown task. There was a pattern to his work; the faint sound of something heavy being dragged across the sand, followed by muted grunts.

Tied, immobile to a tree, there was a limit to how much he could learn, but he urged himself to focus. His legs, from the knees down, were getting warmer. He was partially in the sun. The camp was on the east side of the tiny island-within-an-island, so he realized it must be midmorning.

He tugged on his arms to get a sense of how firmly he was tied. There was no give at all in his restraints, and they felt strange against his wrists; smooth, not fibrous like the rope he was used to. Maneuvering his arms around, he could tell whatever manner of cordage bound him in place had an edge to it, as though the profile was flat instead of round. Perhaps a minor detail, Nohea found it oddly discomforting.

Among the other smells, he noticed something was cooking over the remains of the fire. While he was hungry, Nohea dreaded the thought of trying to chew anything. It was sure to be an impossibly painful ordeal, but he would have to eat something, eventually. The smell of food faded, and, realizing his captor would offer nothing, he drifted into an uneasy sleep.

Another splash of water jolted him to alertness, and he took several seconds to reacquaint himself with his circumstances before once more opening his mouth to accept a drink. When he was finished, his captor released the restraint behind his back with one quick movement, allowing his arms to flop to his sides. He exhaled with relief and briefly rubbed his aching shoulders. The reprieve was far too short, and he was hauled to his feet. He heard first one, then another series of rapid clicks, like an abbreviated conversation between a pair of cicadas. In an instant, the cold, smooth restraints secured his wrists behind his back once more.

Guided roughly by unseen hands, Nohea struggled to stay upright. When his feet sank into cool, wet sand, he realized with terror he was being forced into the water. He dropped to his knees and resisted going any farther, sure he was about to be drowned. His captor pulled him up and shoved him forward until he was nearly knee-deep in the lagoon. He toppled forward with a final shove from behind and winced in preparation for a face-first impact with the water. Instead, he tumbled into a waiting outrigger. Was he to be set free?

Thoughts of freedom quickly vanished as a horrifying stench overwhelmed him. He thrashed his feet frantically, trying to find some grip against the slick bottom of the canoe so he could prop himself up and distance his face from the source of the awful smell. Once more, his captor yanked him upright and tossed him onto one of the seats.

Still, the smell was overwhelming, and Nohea thought he might have heard his heretofore silent companion retching before wading quickly away. The sound, the rocking motion, and above all, the reeking contents of the outrigger now covering his body were too much. His stomach spasmed uncontrollably, and he vomited. Without regard for his injury, the involuntary process forced his jaw wide open, triggering a pain so intense he could see it in the form of a blinding white flash. Then, there was nothing.

***

Though he'd regained his senses, he could see nothing but blackness. There was not even a hint of light filtering through his blindfold, and Nohea realized it must be nighttime. He tilted his head back and opened his nostrils to the steady breeze of fresh sea air, giving him some relief from the stench still surrounding him. Ahead, he heard the steady rhythm of a paddle hitting the water. Judging the sound to be maybe five or six arms' lengths away, he realized he was being towed across the open water.

His circumstances were bewildering. Why was he still alive? Why was his captor transporting him across open water? What was the source of the horrible smell? He feared he knew the answer to the last question, and shivered with revulsion as his feet squished about in the mess in the bottom of the canoe. He tried to ignore it and to focus instead on deducing as much as possible about his captor's intent.

The breeze was coming from ahead and a bit to his left. If he really was out in the open water, he was likely traveling toward sunrise—traveling towards his home on Moloka'i. For a moment, he was hopeful it meant he would soon see his family.

His eyes widened with dread behind his blindfold as the implication became clear. His wordless companion—the inhuman creature that had effortlessly bested the most potent warriors in the kingdom of Maui—was also going to his home.

The steady sound of paddling stopped, and Nohea held his breath in anticipation. After a moment, he heard the splashing of the paddle approaching him, followed by a bump as the other outrigger came alongside. He leaned his head back expectantly and was rewarded once more with a stream of fresh water. When he'd had his fill, his companion paddled away, and they resumed their journey.

Exhausted and hungry, Nohea drifted in and out of awareness to the constant, rhythmic splash of the paddle. Occasionally, his head would droop too far forward, jarring him awake. The pattern repeated countless times before hints of the sunrise ahead filtered through his blindfold, confirming they were headed for Moloka'i. He prayed to his family god to deliver him safely and protect his loved ones from harm.

Soon, the familiar sound of sand scuffing the bottom of the outrigger told him they had arrived at a beach. His silent companion waded through the water toward him and tugged the bow of his canoe ashore, and then quickly vanished again. A few moments later, he returned, offering another drink along with some food he'd pulverized into a soft paste. Nohea took it gratefully, moving his jaw as little as possible as his captor gently thumbed it into the left side of his barely opened mouth. He recognized the familiar taste of uala and fish.

The small display of humanity gave the fisherman hope that perhaps he could reason with his abductor. He fought through the pain to apologize and beg forgiveness for his trespass, offering assurances he would warn his brethren against ever returning. There was no response. Nohea's shoulders sank in dismay.

He knew they must be in some kind of sheltered area along the shore because there was only a minimal breeze to combat the heat of the climbing sun, and the smell emanating from all around was worsening. Beyond that, there was nothing he could deduce. The lack of interaction from his captor was maddening, and he wracked his brain trying to imagine why they'd stopped. Then, intermittent snoring sounded above the surf, providing an answer. Sleeping? Did this mean his captor was something mortal? He had no experience to draw from to answer the question, but allowed himself at least some comfort at the thought.

***

Nohea had not slept nearly as well as his mysterious companion. His pleas to be temporarily unsecured from the canoe had gone unanswered, and he'd been forced to relieve himself where he sat. The inhumanity erased whatever goodwill he thought might be developing after he'd had a meal. Though he'd been able to find moments of uneasy sleep, he'd spent most of the day awake and uncomfortable in the filth that surrounded him, waiting for his captor to waken. The flecks of sunlight filtering through his blindfold gave way to the orange glow of twilight before he heard any signs of movement. Once more, invisible hands offered Nohea some food and water before pushing his outrigger back into the water. The sound of paddling resumed, and he felt a lurch as the rope connecting the two canoes went taut, pulling him forward.

It seemed the journey was underway, but they stopped again after only a few strokes, drifting and bobbing in the water. His captor jumped into the water with a splash and waded back towards Nohea, perhaps to offer another drink. The fisherman leaned his head back expectantly, but instead of a stream of cool water, he felt a sharp sting in his left shoulder. He yelped in surprise, regretting it immediately as his jaw erupted in fiery pain.

It took some time for him to recover and refocus on his surroundings. The sound of the surf to his left made it clear they were following the southern shore of Moloka'i. Knowing his own village was among those they'd eventually encounter just past the crook in the shoreline marking the island's midpoint, the hairs on Nohea's neck pricked with dread. He feared the day's sleep had been in preparation for a night of murder, and wondered if he'd been brought along to bear witness to the consequences of the violation of O'ahu.

The desperate fisherman prayed for countless hours as they continued steadily along the coast, repeatedly begging his 'aumakua—his family god—to manifest as a shark and kill his tormentor before any harm could come to his loved ones. The night air felt unseasonably cold, and Nohea shivered uncontrollably. It was a sign, he hoped, that his prayers had been answered, and some great force was gathering, changing the very composition of the air as it prepared to deliver him from the silent evil.

The paddling ceased, and once more, he heard the scuffing sound of his canoe being dragged onto the beach. His captor offered another drink before unexpectedly cutting the restraints binding his hands behind his back. No prompt or instruction was offered to explain the meaning of this welcome, yet unsettling, development.

He waited a few moments before tentatively reaching for his blindfold. A smack across the side of his head warned him against it, and he pulled his arms quickly to his lap in a show of compliance. They were aching—probably from being tied in the same uncomfortable position for so long, he thought. But the rest of his muscles were starting to hurt, too, and he couldn't stop shivering.

Nohea waited silently for a sign of what his captor expected of him, but none came. Instead, he heard a grunt punctuated by the splash of the other canoe sliding back into the water. Then he listened as the sound of labored paddling faded in the direction from which they had come. It was a baffling development. Had his 'aumakua intervened to gain his freedom and ensure the safety of his family?

When he was sure he no longer heard anything but the waves and nocturnal insects, Nohea reached slowly for the blindfold again, wincing in expectation of another corrective blow to the head. None came. He blinked a few times and looked around to get his bearings, but the light of the stars and moon was too dim for him to recognize where he was. As he shifted in his seat, his foot slipped on the canoe's slick bottom.

He'd almost forgotten the mess at his feet and the horrible smell, having grown used to it during his long captivity. He closed his eyes momentarily to steel himself against what he might find in the bottom of his canoe. Something glinted in the moonlight, and he leaned in for a closer look. His eyes widening in sudden terror, Nohea jolted upright and stumbled frantically from the outrigger, tripping over the boom and landing on the wet sand.

Chapter Seventeen

Outside of Fusion B, Richard stood surveying the damage to the smoldering capacitor network. While it was clear it would never function again, at least the fire suppression system had worked as intended, limiting the fire to the reinforced container. Rebecca Steinman, Admiral Daniels, and Captain Ibarra approached.

"You slipped out quickly," observed Rebecca.

"Yeah," said Richard. "I just wanted to check out the capacitor situation to see if we needed to replace any of the couplings for Gamma."

"Dr. Akindele went over all of the post-event diagnostics with us," said the Admiral. "He confirmed everything went as expected, and Beta was a success."

"It was never in doubt," assured Richard.

"That's not exactly true, though, is it?" demanded Rebecca, placing her hands on her hips.

"If it was never in doubt, I wouldn't have had to call in a favor to get that OSHA bitch off your back," added the Admiral.

"I can't foresee everything, sir," protested Richard. "How was I supposed to know some klutz was going to get himself killed on our construction site?"

"It should never have been a construction site in the first place," countered Rebecca. "This was a sloppy operation, and you got lucky. I don't want to see logistics for an event coming down to the wire like this again."

"Understood."

"It's not like we can redo these things, Richard," added the Admiral. "The window is the window, and we need to be ready for it."

"Despite what Jimi might say, I *do* understand how this all works," said Richard.

"I know, Richard, but I've been speaking with Captain Ibarra, and we'd be a lot more comfortable if we could see some more thought going into the Delta planning."

"How do you mean?"

"We want to see a full digital validation of the assembly and setup of the equipment. The scale is so much bigger than Beta. If we made this by the skin of our teeth, it raises real concerns for the people taking risks."

"We don't have the information for that," protested Richard. "We have the apparatus data, but we don't know anything about the Columbia class aside from the overall dimensions and weight."

"I can get you the details," offered Captain Ibarra.

"How?" asked Richard, furrowing his brow.

"It's my program. I'll just ask the guys at Electric Boat in Connecticut for the digital mockup of the prototype configuration."

"Under what pretext, Raul?" asked Daniels. "That's going to raise flags."

"I'll tell 'em we're simulating some underwater blast percussion models, and want to see what they'll do to our new sub."

"It won't fly. There are too many connections between our researchers and the General Dynamics team. Somebody's going to figure out it's bullshit, and try to find out what's going on."

"It doesn't have to be bullshit, sir," said Ibarra. "Just commission a research team to do some blast simulations. It's the perfect cover."

The admiral considered the suggestion for a moment. "That's brilliant, Raul."

"It could work," added Richard.

"I'm not looking for your input right now, Richard," cautioned Daniels. "You've got some work to do to regain my full trust."

"Yes, sir."

"Right now, I'm looking at a giant smoking bomb you're planning to put on the deck of one of my carriers," he added, pointing to the damaged capacitor. "Why don't you start by figuring out how you're going to make me feel better about that?"

"Yes, sir," replied Richard.

Rebecca regarded him through narrowed eyes.

"We'll speak later," she promised. "I'm going to fly Admiral Daniels and Captain Ibarra back to Pearl. I assume you can find your own way to the Center?"

"Of course, Rebecca. See you there this afternoon."

Rebecca escorted the two men to a waiting helicopter, leaving Richard to catch a ride with the other departing members of the fusion team.

***

Richard arrived late for the biweekly Center for Sustainability Research team meeting in the amphitheater looking irritated. Parth was presenting advancements in his efforts to reduce the carbon footprint of producing Luping's energy-storing concrete.

"As you know," explained Parth with a series of graphs displayed on the interactive wall behind him, "concrete production represents nearly ten percent of global carbon dioxide emissions. Through testing, Dr. Zhang and I have confirmed we can replace up to fifty percent of the limestone with fly ash leftover from coal-fired power production without compromising strength and durability. Fifty percent less limestone equates to fifty percent less carbon dioxide."

"How does that help if you have to burn coal to make it?" asked Herman Dietrich, an electrical engineer with a thick German accent.

"We don't," replied Parth. "There's enough of it already lying around to supply the world's needs for a hundred years. We'd be mining a known pollutant, and actually cleaning up the places where it's been dumped."

"And there is no impact to the energy storage capacity," added Luping from the audience.

"What Dr. Zhang and I would like to propose is that we now move forward with our architecture team to compete for a few small-scale, local design contracts. The solar and geothermal teams are ready to support with their own breakthroughs to make the greenest building on the planet right here on O'ahu," he said excitedly. "It will be our first foray into the outside world to show them what Mr. Kamaras is funding."

153

He tapped an image of a futuristic-looking building on the interactive wall, and it expanded to fill the screen. Rotating slowly, callouts and graphs on the three-dimensional model highlighted the advanced features and their benefits. The sound of light applause filled the room.

"I'm not too excited about the prospect of mining fly ash," said Richard, silencing the murmurs among the assembled teams. "The optics aren't good, and it could reduce the urgency around replacing coal power at a global level."

"That's just a matter of controlling perceptions," offered Samaira. "We can handle that pretty easily."

"Maybe so," allowed Richard, "but I'd prefer to see an approach that doesn't rely on us using other people's garbage."

"Reusing garbage is a cornerstone of sustainability," protested Parth.

"Let's go back to the drawing board on carbon-friendly concrete with a clean slate approach. Assume you have no piles of fly ash to work with and show me what you come up with."

"I guess we can do that," said Parth with a frown.

"And Parth," continued Richard. "I don't want to hear anything about taking our work out into the real world without it going through me first. Mr. Kamaras has been very clear he wants total control over how we introduce our concepts to the world."

"Understood," he confirmed before leaving the podium with his shoulders slumped.

Jayson was next on the agenda with updates on the progress of the sustainable agriculture team. He brought up his presentation material on the interactive wall and looked around to ensure he had everyone's focus before starting.

"You've probably noticed we've got a lot of new plants moved out into the fields over the last two weeks, and we've been able to introduce some more variety into the cafeteria rotation. Our focus since the last update has been establishing the legumes and getting the soil conditions zeroed-in based on what the models have been telling us. If the yield predictions are correct, we'll be able to phase out all external sources by the end of October."

He surveyed the crowd for signs that people were engaged, but noticed many were zoning out or whispering among themselves. Competing for attention against exciting, high-tech breakthroughs while armed only with vegetables wasn't easy.

"We've prepped the soil in this location," he indicated on the display, "to introduce a variety of tubers. The pH and salinity are optimal, and the simulations have provided a roadmap for the types, amounts, and frequency of soil augmentations to provide the best results. Again, we're targeting October for discontinuing outside sources."

Though Samaira was smiling and listening politely, more and more of the others were focusing on their phones or having sidebar conversations.

"There were indications last week we might have a sasquatch infestation in the sweet corn," Jayson continued, "but it turned out to be Aiden working without his shirt on."

Samaira laughed, and a few others glanced up with quizzical looks.

"Is this a joke to you, Jayson?" demanded Richard from the back of the room.

"I'm just trying to see if anyone's actually listening," he explained.

"If you want us to be interested, then how about showing us some meaningful information?"

"What do you mean?"

"What's been your environmental impact so far? How's it going to develop over time?"

"I'm focused on maximizing yields—per your directions," reminded Jayson.

"What do yields matter if we don't know how they cover our needs? You're working with a nutritionist, and we haven't seen how you plan to close the gap between what we're growing and what we actually need to stay healthy. How do you even know how much of what crop to grow? I haven't seen that anywhere."

"I just asked the cafeteria manager what she typically orders."

"Jesus Christ. How is that scientific? Use the team, Jayson. We need meal plans and associated yields to meet our needs, not just guesses from the lunch lady."

"Yes, sir," he replied.

"I've seen enough from you today. Who's next?" he demanded.

"I am," replied Hitarthi meekly as she stood up and approached the podium, trying to conceal a look of dread.

***

"That was interesting," said Jayson after the meeting was over.

"He came in angry and needing to assert authority," assured Samaira. "Nothing to do with your work."

"I don't know what he expected," continued Jayson. "I haven't seen him since the day we started working. All I've had to go on was what he told me then."

"He's been rushing around looking pretty stressed. I get the feeling things aren't going well."

"For him, or for the Center?"

"I don't know. I'm going to feel him out a bit to see what's going on."

***

After finishing work for the day, Samaira stopped by the main building to see if she could catch Richard in his office. She was surprised to find Aiden there, reviewing something on Richard's laptop. They both glanced up as she walked into the outer office. Richard said something and folded his screen down as Aiden stood up and gave him a slight nod before turning smartly to leave the room.

"Hi Aiden," she greeted. "I hope I didn't make you cut something short."

"We were just finishing up," he assured. "Look, I was hoping to run into you today."

"What's up?"

"I was wondering if you'd be interested in heading into Honolulu with me for dinner tonight—just the two of us."

"I'd like that," she replied. "What time?"

"I'll hit you around six? We'll grab one of the loaner cars and watch the sunset from somewhere nicer for a change, and then get some dinner."

"Sounds good. See you then."

As Aiden left, Samaira knocked gently on the glass door of Richard's inner office. He motioned for her to come in.

"Hi, Richard. I'm sorry to drop by unannounced."

"No need to apologize. I just asked Aiden to come up here to discuss the work in the fields and get a different perspective. Jayson's presentation today had me a bit worried."

"Feeling better now?"

"One hundred percent. Aiden completely backed him up."

"That's good."

"Listen," he continued. "I'd appreciate it if you could keep it to yourself that I called him up here to check on Jayson. I don't want to create any tension on the team."

"Of course not," she assured him.

"Now, what can I do for you?"

"I heard what you said to Parth about running things by you."

"Yes?"

"And I have an initiative I'd like to get started on as soon as possible."

"Mr. Kamaras wants control over any publicity," he reminded her.

"What I'm proposing would be a lot less public than what Parth had in mind. Midterm elections are going to be here before we realize it, and I'd like to start building up positivity around some green-minded candidates before the primaries."

"No. It's too soon," he replied immediately.

"A legislative approach would be an enormous multiplier for our efforts," she appealed.

"Any significant change to the balance of power could have unintended consequences for other aspects of the plan. I'd need to run it up the ladder."

"This is a terrible way to run things, Richard."

He was stunned by the pronouncement.

"Pardon me?"

"You hired me for my expertise in establishing behaviors and motivating people," she reminded him. "And I can tell you right now, you're in danger of demotivating your own team."

"What do you mean?" he demanded.

"Everyone here is committed to the cause, and understands the urgency of our mission."

"Yes?"

"But we don't have any vision or strategy defined. On the one hand, people have freedom to explore ideas here, but on the other, they don't know where it's going. Parth showed some initiative, and you shot him down. Didn't you notice how defeated he looked? And poor Jayson," she continued. "He's got very little to guide his efforts, and you ripped into him for trying to work it out on his own."

"That's temporary," assured Richard. "They'll understand soon enough."

"It's already too late for 'soon enough.' Show us a vision, Richard. Show us how we'll make a difference."

"I'll be straight with you, Samaira," he said, leaning in towards her. "We haven't worked all of that out yet. We're running millions and millions of simulations on how we bring all of the efforts here together, and we could not converge on a consistent, positive outcome."

"What does that mean?"

"It means we might already be out of time."

"There must be a way," she insisted.

"It's the permafrost methane feedback loop," he explained. "We don't think we can stop it. We haven't shared the plan because we don't have one yet."

"Oh my God. What do we do?"

"Don't give up. Not yet."

"You have to let the others know."

"Mr. Kamaras will address all of you himself once we're certain. A teleconference is scheduled in two weeks, but please keep this between us for now."

"I will," she promised.

"Have a nice evening, Samaira."

She left Richard's office and wandered to the elevator, trembling in shock.

Chapter Eighteen

A SENSE OF EXCITEMENT rippled through the center when Richard announced Anton Kamaras would address the team in the amphitheater via videoconference. The first-of-a-kind communication was a sure sign of a major inflection point and, hopefully, an indication the world would soon experience the direct benefits of their work.

In the days leading to the event, dinner conversation among the young researchers was dominated by speculation about the next phase. They shared increasingly grandiose fantasies of how Kamaras intended to introduce their efforts to the world and start implementing their new ideas and technology.

Jayson noticed Samaira wasn't contributing to the gossip. In a way, it was perfectly in line with her character—just as she'd avoided speculating about Dr. Akindele's psychological diagnosis on the night of the Fusion Team celebration. This was different. She'd always been engaged and present in their mealtime conversations, but now she seemed distant and withdrawn. It was especially noticeable when juxtaposed against the general mood of anticipation among the rest of the team.

When the day of the announcement finally arrived, the excitement had reached a crescendo. It was hard to describe. The nearest experience Jayson could recall was the celebration that took over downtown Toronto when the Raptors won their first NBA championship. Although nobody at the center was flipping over police cars or high-fiving random strangers, the shared sense of being part of something incredible was the same. Every time he made eye contact with someone, they both knew instantly what the other was thinking.

Jayson arrived a few minutes before the scheduled starting time to find Samaira in the seat next to Aiden, leaning up against him. He thought he should be jealous, but instead felt concerned for his friend. He gave Aiden a nod as he sat next to them, and smiled at Samaira. She smiled back halfheartedly.

Richard walked solemnly up to the podium and greeted his gathered researchers.

"Good morning," he said. "Thank you all for coming to the teleconference today to hear from the Center for Sustainability Research founder and benefactor, Anton Kamaras."

The Interactive wall blinked to life amid applause, displaying a live video feed of Kamaras seated at a spartan desk in front of a large window. Visible through the glass was a sizeable, tree-lined lake. It was rainy and presumably cold wherever he was calling from, as he wore a heavy wool sweater. Somberly, he motioned for silence.

"Ordinarily," he started, "I'm a fan of a big production. I'd like to be introduced to you today with grandiose music and a light show—and to be in a mood to accept your generous applause. However, it's not that kind of day."

The mood in the room transformed from excitement to apprehension in an instant. Jayson looked worriedly at his companions. Aiden offered a weak shrug, and Samaira, still focused on the video feed, betrayed nothing by way of reaction.

"Let me get right to the point," continued Kamaras. "Our ambitions for a drastic course correction on climate change cannot be realized with the solutions we're developing here. Even our most optimistic models predict billions around the globe will die over the next few decades as a direct result of climate change. I know that sounds pessimistic to an extreme, but the accelerating feedback loop of methane and carbon dioxide release from arctic permafrost cannot be stopped. Intense heatwaves, crippling cold spells, severe storms, and droughts. These are the things awaiting humanity because of our astounding hubris."

Murmurs filled the amphitheater.

"Jesus Christ," whispered Jayson.

"This does not mean we're giving up," added Kamaras. "But it does mean we need to shift our focus. Our mission will become one of triage and treatment rather than prevention. We will need to lay the foundation for a centuries-long recovery effort to restore the planet to a state that will permit humanity to continue its journey forward. We are considering several extreme alternatives to the present course, and will put forward a plan very soon. In the meantime, please continue with your excellent work and try not to lose hope. Thank you."

Kamaras vanished after his short, direct message without offering an opportunity for questions. Richard reappeared at the podium amid the rising, anxious whispers, which quickly abated as he started speaking.

"I know this news probably comes as a shock to most of you," he said. "Please keep in mind it does not mark an end to our journey—just a change of direction. You can expect a plan with clear targets and objectives in the coming weeks as we continue our simulations to determine the most effective course of action. If you have anything you'd like to ask, I will do my best to answer."

"What does this mean for our current research?" asked Parth

"That'll depend on what you're doing, and how it fits into the new triage model. It's too soon to answer that for your work specifically."

"Is there going to be any kind of press release or public announcement of these new findings?" called out Jayson.

"I don't know that yet either. It will depend on whether the simulations show it would be helpful to our efforts or not. In the meantime, we ask that you not share what you've learned today with any friends or family. We don't want to cause any panic."

"People should know," insisted Jayson.

"Why?" interjected Samaira. "They've been hearing it for years, and it hasn't changed a thing. The anti-science propaganda has people so numb to the truth I doubt the news would even register."

She was the last person from whom he expected such stark negativity. The enormity of what they'd just learned took hold of him. Things would get a lot worse—for generations, probably—before they got better. If Samaira couldn't rise to meet the challenge, who could?

At the conclusion of Richard's unhelpful question-and-answer session, the researchers filed out of the auditorium mostly in a state of quiet reflection—as if leaving the funeral of a close friend who had died too young. Some went back to work, while others decided to call it an early day and hit a nearby bar in Waipahu.

Aiden, Samaira, and Jayson were among those who decided they needed a drink more than they needed the distraction of work.

***

Late morning was not usually a busy time for the small bar tucked between a beauty salon and a cell phone store in a nondescript strip mall on Leonui Street, northwest of Waipi'O Point. When more than a dozen people from the Center showed up, there was enough space to accommodate them all at a group of tables along the back wall. Several gathered in a corner booth meant for fewer than the number of people now squeezed onto its crescent-shaped seat.

"I guess we're going to need a new name for the Center for Sustainability Research," observed Parth.

"How about the center for being totally screwed?" suggested Jayson.

"Center for people who fucking told you so?" offered Aiden.

"What about you, Samaira?" asked Jayson. "Any suggestions?"

"Sorry. I'm not really on the right wavelength for this."

"You're processing all of this pretty quickly," observed Hitarthi.

"She already knew," realized Jayson. "She's been weird for at least a week now."

"I did," she admitted.

"Why didn't you tell us?" asked Jayson.

"Because it wasn't one hundred percent certain yet—and Richard asked me not to say anything."

"When did you talk to him about it?"

"The day of the last review. I went to his office to ask him why we hadn't seen a proper plan yet, and he told me they weren't even sure what to plan for."

"Preventive action versus treatment?"

"May as well be palliative care, at this point," interjected Parth with a snort. "Anyone else here support euthanizing the patient?"

"I don't know about that. I'm just looking forward to some self-medication," said Aiden as the bartender arrived with two pitchers of a local ale.

"I'll drink to that," agreed Herman.

162

"Herman the German wants some beer?" asked Aiden with mock surprise. "Who'd have thought?"

Everyone laughed, and even Samaira cracked a bit of a smile.

"Seriously, though, what are we going to do?" asked Hitarthi.

"Kamaras was pretty clear this fight's not over," Aiden reminded them. "I'm willing to wait a bit longer to hear more about the 'extreme measures' he's working on. I mean, what other options do any of us have? Curl up in a ball and wait to die?"

There were nods of acceptance around the table, and nobody volunteered an alternate viewpoint. The only immediate question that needed answering was how many more pitchers they'd be ordering as the first two started looking dangerously empty.

***

After dinner that evening, Richard gathered Aiden and the recruiters in his office for a status update. He was eager to review the early data and get firsthand accounts of how the Gamma recruits were reacting to the carefully timed revelation from Anton Kamaras.

"How are the early indicators looking?" he asked no one in particular.

"Good so far," said Denise, "but it's too early to have enough data points to establish a clear trend."

"I'm worried about Adams," admitted Cal.

"What are you seeing?"

"The depression is deeper and sooner than predicted. I think the early reveal might have been a mistake."

"I called an audible," explained Richard. "I had to react and offer her something significant."

"Maybe there'd be nothing to react to if you weren't such a dick in that team review," said Cal.

Richard shot him an angry look.

"I was just trying to keep them motivated."

Cal raised an eyebrow doubtfully but decided not to challenge his boss further.

"The models say our chances are better if we keep them somewhere between denial and acceptance," reminded Denise.

"But it doesn't need to be all of them," replied Richard. "Reaching a critical level of momentum will overcome any lingering reluctance—which is where you come in, Aiden."

"Yep," he agreed. "You just tell me when to pull the trigger."

"It'll have to be soon after we brief them on Gamma. If we get everyone to make the commitment to each other—before they have too much time to really think it over—then we've probably got them. It'll be your job to initiate that. For now, just keep Samaira in a holding pattern while the others wrap their heads around everything."

Chapter Nineteen

RUAN HAD RAISED ONE end of his outrigger onto a large rock on the sheltered beach near the unpopulated southwest tip of Moloka'i to create a shady spot where he could spend the day. He'd underestimated the difficulty of towing his captive all the way from Pearl Harbor against the prevailing current. Exhausted, he lay panting on the bare sand, forcing himself to hydrate and take in protein.

As he drank, his fingers explored the cut on his side where the warrior had caught him with the shark-tooth spear during their clash on Ford Island. The area was sore and swollen. He squeezed it between his thumb and forefinger, and examined the resulting mix of blood and pus. With nothing to treat the infection, he'd have to rely on his body to fight it off.

It had been nearly twenty-four hours since he'd left Oahu, and he still faced a dangerous, final leg back to his home at Diamond Head. There was no way he'd make it without sleep. He did his best to get comfortable and then passed out, just as he had under similar circumstances many years earlier during Recce selection. This time, it was his hands rather than his feet, covered with sores and blisters.

Hours later, he woke to a tickling sensation on the side of his ribcage and was startled to full alertness by flies feasting on the ooze draining from his wound. Disgusted, he leaped to his feet and waded out into the water to wash himself off. The sting of the saltwater was a relief compared to the lingering sensation of crawling insects.

It was late afternoon, and Ruan imagined his former captive must now be among friends and family, unknowingly infecting them with a pathogen that would condemn most of them to death. There was no other choice, he rationalized. With diminishing supplies and an aging body, there was no way he'd be able to continue fighting off incursions. He had to do something that would take on a life beyond his own and mark O'ahu as forever cursed.

Perhaps with luck, the disease would spread all the way to Maui and Lanai—maybe even as far as the Big Island. Along with it would spread the tale of the terrifying encounter on Ford Island, as relayed by the fishermen he'd allowed to escape the day before, and confirmed by his captive in the hours remaining before he was too weak to communicate. They'd embellish it with whatever meaning they eventually derived from the canoe in which he had returned, filled with the severed heads of warriors lying in a bed of their own putrefying entrails. Ruan himself had no particular message in mind when fashioning the grisly scene, but was confident the primitive minds of the natives would invent a suitably terrifying narrative.

Whatever was happening with his former captive was now beyond Ruan's control, and it was time to focus on getting back alive. An inventory of his food and water rations left him confident he'd planned his supplies correctly. The only obstacles to success would be the water conditions and exhaustion, with his stamina undoubtedly taxed further by his injury. Relieved of the burden of the second canoe dragging through the water behind him, he was hopeful he could make it home by daybreak.

As he reluctantly pushed off, Ruan promised himself it would be the last time he ventured out onto the open water. Taking the compass from his breast pocket, he read the message next to the sight wire. '*May you always find your way home to me. Love, Lenora.*' He shook his head. What had been meant as a message of love now seemed like a taunt. Still, he would need it to bring him back to a home of sorts. Soon it would be too dark to see the distant peak of Diamond Head.

***

Ruan pushed through increasing pain and discomfort throughout the night and arrived on Waikiki beach a little after sunrise. It took longer than he'd hoped due to his quickly vanishing strength and a repeated need to stop and vomit over the side of the canoe. Despite finally being out of the water and lying in the warm sun, he was shivering uncontrollably. Soberly, he acknowledged his worsening symptoms pointed to acute septic shock.

He struggled to put on his rucksack, determined he would somehow make it back to his hut to stow his gear, and then ascend one final time to his favorite place on the island; his ocean lookout at the peak of the crater wall. He knew it was irrational, but having a mission upon which he could focus his thoughts gave him a degree of comfort despite the knowledge he would soon be dead from the infection spreading through his body.

The climb up the outside of the crater was dangerous under ideal circumstances, but Ruan had done a considerable amount of work to make it easier for himself. At a low spot on the north side of the crater wall, where he came and went from his hidden campsite, he'd made a discrete pathway taking advantage of some natural step-shaped features in the volcanic rock. Typically, the one-and-a-half kilometers from the beach to where the path started was an easy fifteen-minute jog. From there to his hut inside the crater usually took another thirty minutes. Battling sickness and fatigue, it took him nearly four hours to make the same trip after the arduous journey from Moloka'i.

He uncovered the plastic containers hidden near his hut and opened them for a final survey. Sliding his holster and K-bar sheath off his belt, he placed them in the container with the other weapons. His belt and ruck went into the other container with his personal supplies, clothing, and two worn-out pairs of boots he kept in case he got desperate enough to need them again. After a moment of consideration, he closed both containers and covered them.

The trail to the summit appeared to have doubled in elevation from his perspective at the bottom. There was no practical reason to subject himself to the climb, but he nonetheless felt compelled to do so. He believed he would find some solace at the summit in his final hours, and seeking that solace provided a welcome distraction. Ruan was determined to make it one more time or expel his last breath in the effort.

With each step, pain radiated through his body. Reaching for the rungs of his makeshift ladders in the steep sections was especially excruciating due to the wound on his side. As he progressed farther up, he had lapses of awareness and could not remember climbing parts of the trail. He briefly forgot where he was and what he was doing.

At other times, he would hallucinate he was climbing the path to Devil's Peak behind his childhood home in the Rondebosch suburb of Cape Town. Lenora was there, too, wasn't she? She climbed with ease, urging him forward before disappearing over some rock or ledge above him, only to reappear further ahead, and always out of reach.

Ruan reached the summit with little recollection of the climb, and no idea how long it had taken. He was vaguely aware the sun was getting low but not yet taking on the orange tint of sunset. Below him, the sprawling city of Cape Town sparkled like a jewel against a backdrop of iridescent ocean—or maybe it was Honolulu. He no longer had any sense of place or time as he sat on his familiar perch and watched one image blur into the next.

Suddenly, Lenora was sitting next to him, sharing the breathtaking view. The sunlight glinting off the waves looked like a swirling sea of beautiful sapphires, and it filled him with a euphoric sense of peaceful awe.

"I knew you'd be here," he said with a smile.

She frowned, her face quivering as a single tear rolled down her cheek.

"But I'm not here," she replied, shaking her head.

"Yes, you are. And we can be together now."

"I can't be with you, Ruan. Everything good about you died with me."

"I don't understand."

"Yes," she insisted, as she disintegrated into a fog, "you do."

He collapsed backward, dislodging the compass he'd forgotten to remove from his breast pocket as he hit the ground with a thud. It slid down his shoulder, coming to rest by the side of his head.

The glittering sapphires in his mind slowly transformed into the flickering campfire of the fishermen on Ford Island. He saw the men gathered around it—talking and laughing. His former captive turned towards him as his face slowly transformed into the grotesque, misshapen mess it had become after their collision. He smiled at Ruan and then began laughing maniacally with one side of his lower jaw unhinged and flapping around loosely. Everything started to spin, and Ruan had the sensation he was falling into the blackness of his former prisoner's deformed, gaping maw. He screamed as he tried frantically to claw his way out. From below rose the stench of rot. With no strength left to fight, Ruan tumbled into the putrid darkness.

Chapter Twenty

It was a challenge for the Center for Sustainability Research team to stay focused on their work with Kamaras's unsettling revelation dealing such a devastating blow to what had been a sense of growing optimism. To Jayson, it seemed as if he was just going through the motions of work while his mind was elsewhere. Interactions with his immediate team and the larger group at dinner were subdued, and the conversations had morbid, fatalistic undertones.

Even news from outside the center and the posts from Jayson's friends and family seemed to have taken on a darker tone. He briefly considered packing up his things and heading home to find some comfort in familiar surroundings. The thing preventing him from doing so were those few words from Kamaras he was still clinging to for some degree of hope: '*we are considering several extreme alternatives to the present course.*' It was silly to expect Kamaras would somehow be able to wave a magic wand and fix everything, but at least it was something to hold on to.

Another meeting was already on the schedule and just a couple of days away. He imagined Kamaras announcing increasingly fantastical scenarios that would save the world. Maybe he'd arranged an alliance of billionaires to pour all of their resources into a new carbon capture technology. Maybe he'd gone to the United Nations and finally convinced the world's governments it was now time to work together to stave off disaster. Maybe he'd made contact with a super-advanced race of alien beings that could move the earth's orbit just enough to buy them some more time. He shook his head and snorted at the absurd, desperation-fueled imaginings.

***

Increasingly isolated from the team, Andrew looked forward to his lunches with Samaira more than any other part of his daily routine. Even though she'd been a bit distracted for weeks, it was still better than eating alone in his office and pretending it didn't bother him. Often, they'd grab their food from the cafeteria and walk to a bench on the trail or find a spot in the courtyard where they could be alone to talk without distraction.

Hearing the crunch of footsteps on the fine gravel path, Andrew looked up with a smile as Samaira approached.

"How's your day going?" she asked.

"Pretty good. What about you?"

"Good," replied Samaira with a shrug.

"Is everything okay? You seem a bit down lately."

"I'm fine," she insisted.

"Is it me? I know you've been spending a lot of time with Aiden lately," he said, cocking his head. "Would you rather be having lunch with him?"

"No. I like our time together."

"Okay," he allowed.

"How long have you known Aiden?" she asked.

"I don't really know him at all. We've barely ever spoken."

"How long has he been here?"

"I don't know. I'm pretty sure I've seen him around since I got here, so that's gotta be at least a year. Why?"

"No reason. I was just wondering."

"Haven't you asked him that question?"

"I have," she admitted.

"Uh oh. Trouble in paradise? You know I could offer you a shoulder to cry on—or some other part of my anatomy, if it would help."

"Andrew," she cautioned, narrowing an eye.

"Sorry. I didn't mean it. Old habits."

"Anyway, it's nothing," she continued, brushing off his momentary regression.

"Is he upset you're spending time with me?"

"He's never even mentioned it, to be honest."

"Is that weird? That he wouldn't be concerned about you hanging out with other guys?"

"I'd call it pretty healthy behavior."

"I thought women didn't like it when men don't act all jealous and angry."

"Some women, maybe. You don't need anyone who's going to play games like that with you, Andrew."

"Listen, I can't afford to be picky," he said with a laugh. "I need to take what I can get."

"What you need is to learn not to sell yourself short."

Andrew paused and exhaled deeply.

"Thank you, Samaira—for being my friend."

"I feel the same way, Andrew."

"I don't understand why. I mean, why would you give an asshole like me the time of day to begin with?"

"I wouldn't. There's no point wasting even a moment of your life dealing with an asshole, if you can avoid it," she laughed. "But I can tell the difference between a real asshole and somebody who just needs a little help finding themselves."

"Thanks," he replied with a blush. "That means a lot to me."

"You've made good progress, and we should start getting you reconnected with the rest of the group soon," suggested Samaira.

"I'm not sure we need to bother with that."

"Why not? Aren't you ready to rehabilitate your image?"

"It's not that I don't want to. More like I won't have an opportunity."

"What am I missing?"

"For the last month, I've been training a new guy on our proprietary systems and solid-state hardware. I get the feeling he's my replacement."

"Really? Has Richard said anything to you?"

"Nothing specific. Just that he'll be taking on a new project that's launching soon."

"What's his name?"

"Matteus. Matteus Christensen. Danish guy—and a redhead, too. Maybe they're hoping they can swap me out without anyone noticing," he laughed.

"I think I've seen him at a meeting recently."

"That's the other thing that has me thinking I'm on the way out. I didn't get invited to the last all-hands, and I'm not on the list for the one on Friday either."

"I hope that's not true, Andrew."

"Maybe it's for the best. It'll give me a chance to start fresh with a new group of people."

"A fresh start is nice sometimes," she admitted, "but I'd miss you."

"Yeah. Me too," he replied.

***

Andrew's replacement was already seated in the second row of the amphitheater when Jayson arrived for the second all-hands meeting. Walking past, he had to look twice. The new IT guy and his gangly predecessor easily passed for brothers. He dismissed it as an interesting coincidence and made his way to the seat Samaira was saving in the front row next to her and Aiden. She was still stuck gloomily to his side.

As the start time approached, Jayson glanced back and was surprised to see a different composition of attendees than the last meeting. In addition to the regular team members, many of the guest researchers and a handful of very fit and serious-looking young men and women he'd never seen before were occupying seats towards the back.

Richard walked onto the dais, past two empty chairs and a small table, and stepped up to the podium to address the anxious audience.

"Good afternoon, everyone," he started. "I know it's been a tough couple of weeks, and I want to start by thanking all of you for carrying on so diligently. I assure you, we've been working just as hard to determine the best course of action to ensure the continuity of humanity. We now know the only way to move forward is to take a few steps back."

Confused murmurs rose from the audience.

"Before I continue," he cautioned, "I must insist on absolute secrecy. We cannot be successful without it. Although I suspect if you tried to tell anyone what you're about to learn, you'd be locked up for a psychiatric evaluation."

He chuckled at his own joke. It seemed grotesquely out-of-place amid the seriousness of the situation, and Jayson wondered if he might be cracking under pressure.

"I'd like to introduce you to my co-presenters today. The first is Dr. Olujimi Akindele, the leader of the Fusion team."

Akindele emerged onto the dais and walked uncomfortably towards the chairs. He turned and made a gesture of acknowledgment before sitting down. The attendees were unsure how to react. There was some light, hesitant applause as they collectively wondered what was appropriate under the circumstances. Richard clapped his hands a few times to provide encouragement.

"Second," he continued, "is Admiral Spencer Daniels of the United States Navy."

There was more buy-in on the applause for the admiral as Richard smiled and gave him a salute. Aiden reflexively pushed back into his seat and straightened his back.

"Many years ago, when I was a naval researcher, I had the pleasure of meeting Admiral Daniels on several occasions," he said vaguely. "Back then, he was still Commander Daniels."

After a smart nod to the crowd, the admiral sat down next to Akindele.

"After the navy, when I came to work for Mr. Kamaras, I had the enormous privilege of meeting one of the greatest minds in the world of modern physics. Dr. Akindele and I collaborated to create the quantum computing capabilities that propelled Hitz-It.com to the forefront of social media, and made it the most valuable company in the history of the world. In pursuit of that technology, Dr. Akindele went down a rabbit hole."

Richard paused and glanced over at the physicist to emphasize the next point.

"And just like Alice, down that rabbit hole, he found a looking glass."

Jayson thought he saw Dr. Akindele roll his eyes as he stood up to approach the podium. Richard stepped back and applauded. By now, the audience was sensing a change in mood, and clapped along with more enthusiasm.

"Thank you, Richard," started Dr. Akindele. "Today, I want to explore with you some implications of quantum theory we have recently confirmed experimentally. Those of you who are familiar with quantum mechanics will appreciate this discussion on multiple additional levels."

Jayson looked around to see how others were reacting. Parth shook his head slightly and shrugged. He was one of the sharpest in the group, and if he was already confused, realized Jayson, the rest of them didn't have a chance.

"Quantum computing exploits the phenomenon of superposition," he continued. "In traditional computing, we deal with bits that are either one or zero. In quantum computing, superposition allows us to use qubits to exploit a third state—simultaneous values of both one and zero. Adding this third state—this third dimension—exponentially increases the computational power at our disposal."

Jayson had read about bits and qubits on Wikipedia after the conversation with Richard on his first day of work. So far, he was following.

"How do we resolve a single answer from this third state of superposition?" asked the physicist rhetorically. "It's simple. We resolve both states simultaneously in separate realities—one where the value is zero and the other where the value is one. Some people have viewed these other realities as being somehow theoretical. We have deduced mathematically, and proven through experimentation, they are not. They are as real as our own—and we have learned how to interact with them."

Dr. Akindele paused as if waiting for some reaction or acknowledgment from the team. Given the stakes, he had their undivided attention, if not their complete understanding, and it became clear he would have to explain further before getting the response he was hoping for.

"We have been able to interact with a minimally divergent reality that intersects our own at several temporally mismatched convergences. Furthermore, we have been successful in our attempts to induce a superposition in that reality to create a new one of our own making."

Some scattered whispers flitted among the crowd, but nothing was approaching the epiphany the physicist was still expecting. He sighed almost imperceptibly and began speaking again.

"Most importantly, we have been successful in disentangling matter from our own reality and re-entangling it with the new one."

Apparently convinced he'd made his point, Dr. Akindele folded his arms across his chest, seemingly determined not to speak again until someone provided a sign they were following his cryptic lecture. Luping was the first to make a target of herself.

"Are you—," she hesitated. "Are you talking about some kind of interdimensional time travel?"

The physicist snorted, shaking his head slowly as he looked to the floor in dismay.

"How did you get something so ridiculous from what I described? Do you imagine yourself in some sort of children's comic book? Superposition implies the continual decomposition of an overarching space-time field into a nearly infinite number of subfields that allow all possibilities to exist. I never said anything about alternate dimensions."

"Obviously, when you put it that way, it makes perfect sense," whispered Jayson to nobody in particular.

Aiden chuckled under his breath.

"Do you have an observation you'd like to share?" asked Dr. Akindele with a sharp glance.

"Uh, sure," replied Jayson. "This all seems pretty clear—from a theoretical sense, I mean. Maybe you can talk us through how it applies to us practically?"

"Of course," he replied, raising an eyebrow skeptically. "We have an upcoming window of convergence with our minimally divergent reality during which we will transfer a significant amount of mass to a point in the timeline before large-scale population growth and industrialization can impact the environment."

"So I was right about the time travel?" interjected Luping.

Akindele threw his hands in the air.

"I can't do this anymore, Richard. You are uniquely skilled to bring this down to the level required for them to understand."

He returned to his place next to the admiral and slumped down into the chair, defeated. Richard returned to the podium to address Luping's question.

"Very close, Dr. Zhang, but not exactly correct. Time travel, as you understand it, remains an impossibility according to the laws of physics."

"Then how do we get to another time?"

"Let's start with the basics. We know everything in the universe travels through space-time at the same speed—the speed of light."

"I'm traveling at the speed of light?" she asked, furrowing her brow.

"Through space? No," said Richard as he lofted his index finger. "Through space-time? Yes. That's why time travels more slowly for objects as they move faster—so their speed in space-time remains the same."

"I didn't realize time travels slower for things that move faster."

"It's at the core of relativity, Dr. Zhang. And something we've known for more than a hundred years."

Luping turned red with embarrassment, and Jayson was thankful she was the one asking supposedly stupid questions—because he didn't know the answers either.

"It's understandable you're not aware, Dr. Zhang," said Richard, softening his tone. "It has no impact on day-to-day life because nothing around us moves fast enough to make a noticeable difference. I've prepared a simplified visual to help explain how this concept makes our mission possible."

The lights dimmed, and he pushed a button on the lectern, bringing the interactive wall to life. An enormous pale, blue torus filled the entire display.

"This donut shape represents an extreme simplification of the overarching space-time field that Dr.Akindele mentioned earlier."

Akindele, sitting next to Admiral Daniels, cleared his throat, and Richard sighed almost imperceptibly.

"We're calling the model Akindele Space-Time—AST," he added reluctantly.

A single white dot trailing a fading tail like a comet traced a path around the outside of the torus.

"This dot represents the space-time field of our own reality traveling through AST. It has branched off into new realities countless times."

Other dots emerged from the first, which diverged further until hundreds of white comets were racing around the donut's surface. Some maintained a more-or-less circular path, while others corkscrewed their way around the torus.

"Just like everything in our reality travels through space-time at the same speed, these parallel realities travel through AST at the same speed. You'll notice they're all progressing around the torus at the same rate."

The dots were dense enough to create the clear impression of a perfectly circular band going around the torus at a constant speed.

"Some of these paths are straightforward," added Richard as he walked up to the display and pointed at a dot tracing a roughly circular path. "While others are not. The more the pathway corkscrews around the torus, the faster it has to move in space to keep up with the others."

It was clear to everyone watching the dots following the longer paths had to move much quicker to maintain their place in the glowing ring circling the donut, keeping up with those taking a more direct route.

"And since these realities are moving faster in space," continued Richard with a smile, "what does that mean, Dr. Zhang?"

"They travel more slowly through time to maintain a constant speed through Akindele Space-Time?"

"Correct!" he said triumphantly. "See? This isn't so hard."

Richard tapped on the wall to pause the simulation, pointing at two nearly superimposed dots.

"When a reality converges with our own, we have a way to transfer the entanglement of matter from one reality to another."

"Not all of us have a STEM background," complained a frustrated voice from the center row. It was Melinda Littleton, an expert in early childhood learning and development. "What is entanglement?"

"There are practically an infinite number of realities occupying AST," explained Richard. "Think of entanglement as a kind of unique signature that binds us to ours. We've learned how to modify that signature at the moment of convergence to bind matter and energy to a different reality."

"How does the transfer of entanglement work?" asked Herman, crossing his arms.

Richard recycled the ridiculously simplified analogy that had resonated with his mercenary.

JAMES PELKMANS

"If you imagine the realities as separate highways, we're just creating the on-ramp where they cross over," he explained, putting his palms together in front of him and then quickly pulling one hand to the side to represent taking the exit. "The process is too technically heavy to go into details here, but one of the engineers from Dr. Akindele's team will gladly cover it with anyone who's interested."

Akindele dropped his face into his hands and moaned audibly. Unable to stomach Richard's somewhat flawed explanations, he stood and left the room.

"Jimi gets carsick just talking about driving," explained Richard as the door closed behind the exasperated physicist. "That's why his mother has to take him everywhere."

His weak joke derived more laughter than it should have, as everyone desperately needed an outlet for the tension they'd been carrying for weeks. After the laughter subsided, there was more chatter in the room. Richard's explanations made the implication for the team much clearer—and very concerning.

"Are you really talking about sending us to another place at another time?" asked Kailani in disbelief.

"Essentially, yes," admitted Richard. "We have determined through countless simulations it is the most likely way to secure the future of humanity."

"So we just go there, start mingling with the locals and try to prevent them from industrializing?" asked Jayson. "Then what? We die in primitive squalor? That doesn't sound like much of a plan."

"You won't be in any position to directly impact the development of the planet," conceded Richard. "You'll be confined to O'ahu—and maybe some of the surrounding islands—with the limited amount of technology we can give you. You'll have some power generation, computing capabilities, and the capacity to grow wonderful food and produce essential medicines. All the while, you'll be breathing the freshest air you've ever experienced, and drinking water free of microplastics for the first time in your lives."

"But what's the point if we're not going to have any impact on development and industrialization?" countered Hitarthi.

"I didn't say you wouldn't have an impact," explained Richard. "I said no *direct* impact. Your descendants will do the heavy work of saving the world as their society flourishes and their influence spreads."

"How are our descendants even going to know what to do?" challenged Parth.

"You'll take with you the totality of humanity's current knowledge and establish a social system to maintain and grow that knowledge across generations."

"If I know anything about kids," continued Parth, "it's that we don't really care what our parents want. I give it two generations at most before *our* kids discover weed and start wasting their days at the beach trying to get laid."

That got him a few laughs and even more nods of agreement. Samaira, who'd been quietly listening to the discussions, finally joined in.

"Not if we do it right," she said.

It was the first remotely positive reaction to the idea. Everyone turned toward her and waited for elaboration.

"We establish a culture that values the environment above all else. We instill an indelible connection to the planet, and a sense of stewardship that is core to who we are. We make it the mission of an entire civilization to secure a healthy environment in which it can thrive indefinitely."

"And this, ladies and gentlemen," said Richard, "is why we're so happy to have Dr. Adams with us."

"How can we be sure it'll work?" asked Herman.

"We're doing the simulations," assured Richard, "and they're converging."

"So you've spent the last two weeks playing 'The Sims' using us as characters?" asked Parth.

"If you want to be cynical, I suppose you could say it that way."

At that moment, Aiden stood up and surveyed his colleagues around the room before addressing Richard directly.

"I'm in," he said simply.

Jayson looked up at him with surprise.

"Really?"

"Why not? What other option do we have? If I stay here, this is the end of my family line. I'm not bringing kids into this mess. I know there are uncertainties involved, but it beats the hell out of the certainty we face if we don't do this. There is no future here. If there's even a slight chance we can do what Samaira said, we might give our children—and their children, and so on—a chance to reach the stars. That's the closest thing any of us can ever get to achieving immortality."

Nobody offered a counterpoint to Aiden's seemingly impromptu speech, and the sounds of side conversations rose once more from the audience. It was Kailani who quieted them with the next obvious question.

"Why is the admiral here?"

"Good question, Kailani," said Richard. "I'm going to let Admiral Daniels address that himself."

The admiral approached the podium and took a few moments to look around the room as if assessing one of his crews.

"I've known Richard for a long time," he started. "If anyone else had approached me with the details of this operation, I would have dismissed them as a lunatic. But I trust him—and the more we spoke, the more I realized what he was saying made sense. He and Mr. Kamaras convinced me I had a duty to humanity to ensure your success in any way I could. When he told me about some of the potential danger you could face, I offered to help."

"What kind of danger are we talking about?" demanded Herman.

"When you arrive, there could be a small number of local inhabitants who will be confused and upset by your sudden appearance among them. I'm providing a small team of brave volunteers who will keep you safe."

"Inhabitants? When are we arriving?" asked Kailani.

Admiral Daniels looked to Richard for guidance.

"We've calculated 1174 A.D.," replied Richard.

"There will be thousands of local inhabitants," asserted Kailani. "I've studied the history."

Jayson started shaking his head. "No way. I'm not going to be part of any genocide."

"Absolutely not," agreed the admiral. "The role of our volunteers will be to provide initial security until you can reach some sort of détente—an agreement of peaceful coexistence."

"Isn't there a chance for an awful lot of bloodshed before we can figure things out?"

Richard intervened on the admiral's behalf to ease Jayson's concern.

"We've done extensive archeological studies and believe the conventionally accepted timeline for the inhabitation of O'ahu is inaccurate. We're confident if it's inhabited at all, it will only be a few small coastal fishing communities," said Richard. "This is also where Kailani's research comes into play. Her work on reconstructing proto-Polynesian should allow you to establish communication. We'd be sending you with at least some of the computing capacity you have here, so the algorithms will quickly correct for any inaccuracies in the initial translations."

"I'm not comfortable collaborating with the military," said Kailani flatly in response to the invocation of her name.

"Government corruption has been a major part of the problem in dealing with the environment," added Parth. "This whole thing sounds a lot less appealing if they're running the show."

"I couldn't agree more," laughed Admiral Daniels. "What's your name, young man?"

"Parth."

"Let me assure you, Parth," he continued. "Despite assumptions you might make about me, I am a man of science. My involvement with Richard was in his capacity as a naval researcher, not a soldier. The anti-science movement infecting our country and infiltrating our government is one reason we're in this mess, and I'm just as sickened by it as you are. These men and women assembled behind you are not just brawn. They are engineers, microbiologists, medics, and other scientists, who only enlisted to take advantage of the GI Bill and better their minds. We have hand-picked them for their trust in science, not for their bloodlust."

"That may be," allowed Parth, "but by involving the government, you've tainted this whole thing in a way that makes it hard to trust."

"You want to talk about trust?" asked Admiral Daniels. "Then let me demonstrate my trust in the brilliant minds assembled in this room by exposing my own vulnerability. Neither the United States government nor the Navy knows the details of what I'm supporting here. As far as they know, I'm using their resources to help Mr. Kamaras develop fusion reactors we can use in our fleet. If they knew the truth, I would be immediately court-martialed and imprisoned for the rest of my life. I take this risk because I see no other option."

"What's in it for you? Why take that risk at all?"

"There is something in it for the admiral, myself, and Mr. Kamaras," interjected Richard. "And there's something more in it for you as well."

He paused dramatically to allow the words to sink in, and for the room to fall silent.

"Relative to us, time in the parallel reality we are tracking is now moving much more quickly. Additional convergences will offer an opportunity to transfer significantly more mass as the time delta decreases. As it approaches zero, a select group of like-minded individuals—including the admiral, Mr. Kamaras, and the rest of the Center staff—will arrive in the alternate equivalent of the modern world you have created."

"I get how that works out well for you," said Parth, "but what do we get out of it?"

"The parents and siblings of everyone here, along with their immediate families, will be invited to accompany us. Once there, they will meet with your descendants at a family reunion hundreds of years in the making. You'd be making this brave sacrifice not only for your own children, but also for the families you leave behind."

Aiden, still standing, raised his voice above the growing chatter.

"Even with the risks, I'm thankful for the chance—any chance—at a future. I'm doing this."

"I admit," added Samaira, "I find the opportunity for an environmental and societal reset hard to resist. We can do more lasting good than we could ever achieve against the noise of misinformation and propaganda we face here."

Jayson looked at both of them in disbelief.

"Seriously?"

Samaira rose to her feet next to Aiden and took aim at Richard.

"But I still have one issue gnawing at me and I need you to address it."

"Of course, Dr. Adams. Please share your concern."

"The fake fusion research, Kailani's work on proto-Polynesian, Jayson figuring out how to feed us self-sufficiently—this all tells me it was never a 'plan B.' This was 'plan A' all along."

Richard laughed.

"It's a pretty extreme 'plan A' even for someone as eccentric as Mr. Kamaras. You have to understand his mind does not work like yours. For him, there is no plan A or B—only a single, well-orchestrated plan to account for innumerable contingencies. You'll recall in his brief announcement, Mr. Kamaras mentioned several extreme alternatives could still yield hope."

"Like what?" prompted Parth.

"Your initial understanding of our goal—fixing the planet—was always the primary one. The extreme alternatives being investigated in parallel included putting you all in a sealed biodome or an orbital space station to await earth's natural recovery. We considered starting a generations-long inter-planetary mission to find new, habitable worlds. We even briefly studied cryogenically freezing all of you—and Mr. Kamaras—to be woken in the future when the environment recovers."

"I find it hard to believe traveling to a parallel universe was the least crazy idea," replied Parth.

"Mr. Kamaras doesn't think in subjective terms like that. He compared the alternatives by only a single, objective measure."

"And what's that?"

"Probability of success. Even after millions of simulations, most alternatives showed a near-zero percent chance of working. Once the experimental results proved Dr. Akindele's theories correct, the simulations showed a greater than eighty percent chance you'll be able to re-direct the development of the world—if you follow the plan exactly."

"I like those odds," said Aiden.

"And remember all of us, including Mr. Kamaras, are taking the same leap of faith into the unknown. Admittedly, you have the harder task, but you also have the most to gain."

"How's that?" asked Jayson.

"Mr. Kamaras is obscenely wealthy and will live in comfort for the rest of his life, no matter what happens to the environment. The admiral and I are considerably older than all of you, and we're unlikely to live long enough to face the direst consequences of climate change. You would all be dealing with constant war and unrest as nations battle for control of whatever clean water and arable land is left."

The final thought from Richard left his audience in contemplative silence.

"I'm sorry," he continued. "This was meant to be an exciting announcement, and I shouldn't be bringing you down like that. Let's focus instead on the exciting new possibilities that lay before us. I've planned with the admiral for him and his team to join us in a celebration this evening. After 7:00 PM, the cafeteria will be restricted only to those with direct knowledge of our new mission so you'll be able to speak freely and get to know each other better. We'll reassemble here in a couple of days for another briefing, where you'll be able to ask more questions."

"One last thing before we adjourn," interjected Admiral Daniels. "One hundred percent operational security from this point forward is essential. Leaks of any kind will jeopardize the entire mission—not to mention my status as a free man."

The audience acknowledged him with nods as they rose from their seats, and the isolated pockets of chatter rose to a cacophony. The teams filed out of the room, talking excitedly among themselves in small groups as they left. Admiral Daniels pulled Richard aside.

"Are you sure we can accommodate all their families for Epsilon? I've got a growing list of people I need to take care of."

"You really think they're invited?" snorted Richard. "Just another piece of the story to keep them on board. The next few days are going to be the critical tipping point, and we need to pull out all the stops to make sure they tip the right way."

"And the ones that don't?"

"Let's hope we don't have to worry about that."

Chapter Twenty-One

JAYSON WEDGED HIS WAY between Samaira and Aiden as they filed out of the auditorium.

"So you guys are really down for this?"

"Definitely," said Aiden without hesitation.

"I think so, yeah," added Samaira. "You're not?"

"I didn't say I'm not. I just need more time to think about it. This is kind of out of left field."

"I already figured it was going to be something like this," said Samaira.

"You already figured the solution to climate change would be interdimensional time travel?" asked Jayson.

"That's not what this is," started Aiden before Jayson cut him off.

"Yeah, I heard what Akindele said. I'm not too worried about pedantics at the moment."

The trio emerged into the foyer where Parth, Hitarthi, and Luping were waiting for them before Jayson could ask Samaira to explain what she meant.

"What did you guys think of that?" asked Parth.

"It sounds pretty crazy to me," admitted Jayson, "but these two seem onboard."

"Yeah," said Parth. "I'm thinking I am too."

"Really?"

"It's not the most appealing thing that's ever been put in front of me," he allowed. "But it beats the hell out of the alternative."

"What about you guys?"

"Not sure," said Hitarthi. "I don't think it's fully sunk in yet."

"I'm leaning towards yes, I think," added Luping.

"I'm going to take a walk to clear my head," declared Jayson. "I feel like I'm watching all of this happen from outside of my own body, you know?"

"I know the feeling," assured Samaira. "I think a walk will do you good."

"I want to catch up with some of the others to see where their heads are," said Parth. "Want to join me?"

Aiden looked at Samaira, who shrugged and then nodded in affirmation.

"Yeah. Alright."

"Me too," added Luping.

"I'm going back to my room," said Hitarthi. "I need some time to think."

"I'll walk you back on my way out to the point," offered Jayson.

She accepted with a weak nod, and they headed outside together.

Hitarthi was quiet for the short walk back to the residence. Jayson didn't mind, or even notice, for that matter. He was in his own world of contemplation, trying to absorb the implications of the briefing. When they reached the back entrance of the residence by the expansive windows of the first-floor gymnasium and pool area, she paused and looked at him.

"It's not just me, is it?" she asked. "I mean, this is nuts, right?"

"Totally nuts," he agreed.

"Why is everyone taking it in stride?"

"You don't look a gift horse in the mouth, I guess."

"I've heard that before. What does it even mean?"

"I don't know the literal meaning, but basically, it means you don't ask too many questions when someone's handing you an unexpected gift."

"I guess," she replied with a frown.

"Listen, do you want to come with me for a walk around the point? It might do you some good."

"No, thanks. I really just need to be alone right now."

"Okay. No worries. I'll see you at the thing tonight."

As Hitarthi made her way inside, Jayson continued down the path towards the benches where he'd first met Samaira months earlier. In some ways, it felt so much more recent. At the same time, it felt like something that might have happened years ago. He shook off the strange feeling—a superposition of perception, he realized with amusement—and picked up the pace to get his blood flowing.

***

The evening celebration turned out to be a much more elaborate affair than the team expected. An army of workers from a local event planning company had completely transformed the cafeteria. Numbered, round tables with tablecloths and fancy place settings replaced the usual configuration. Outside of the main doors, a table filled with pre-made takeout options was set up for the Center staff not invited to the event.

Jayson arrived a bit after seven, coincidentally at the same time as Parth and Luping. Several others were already there, taking advantage of the open bar and hors d'oeuvres offered ahead of the meal.

"Wow. Fancy," observed Jayson.

"Where's the music coming from?" asked Luping.

"There," said Parth, pointing to the far side of the room where a temporary platform had been erected, and an unusual string quartet was playing Mozart.

"That's amazing," remarked Luping.

"That's creepy as hell," countered Jayson.

Four vaguely humanoid robots exhibiting flawless form were seated on minimalist stools playing their instruments.

"I think it's beautiful," she insisted.

They spotted Samaira and Aiden mingling with a few of the new team members introduced by Admiral Daniels earlier in the day, and wandered over to meet them.

"Hey!" greeted Aiden enthusiastically as they approached. "Come and meet the latest arrivals. Josh Talbot, Lisa Washington, and Martina de la Cruz—meet Jayson Reilly, Parth Ravinderan, and Luping Zhang."

"Impressive memory," remarked Josh.

"Let's see if I can keep it going. Josh and Martina were both combat medics and are now doctors. Lisa is a mechanical engineer."

"I'm still technically a resident," corrected Josh, "but close enough."

"Parth is a civil engineer, Luping is a materials scientist, and Jayson is—"

"A farmer," he interrupted, thrusting out his hand.

"The most important one of us all, then," remarked Josh.

"Couldn't do it without my trusty farmhand," he said with a wink.

Aiden laughed.

"I *am* pretty good with a wheelbarrow."

"Has anyone seen Hitarthi yet?" asked Samaira. "She seemed a little shaken up earlier."

"She'll be fine," assured Jayson. "Just said she needed a bit of time by herself."

"Okay," she said doubtfully.

On the other side of the room, Richard was enjoying a glass of champagne with Admiral Daniels when Denise rushed up to him. The worried recruiter held up her phone for him to see.

"We could have an issue," she warned.

"Excuse me, admiral." He pulled Denise aside. "What's going on?"

"Hitarthi is reaching out. She tried to call her mother and then sent out a few texts."

"That's not unusual under the circumstances."

"She's not stable. I'm afraid she could let something slip."

"Nothing actually got out, though, right?"

"We intercepted the call and sent it to a spoofed voicemail. She's saying she needs advice, and asked her to call back."

"The texts?"

"We've got a bot responding. It'll try some probing to see what we can coax her into revealing."

"Okay. Make sure she doesn't leave, though. Camp out by the cars in case she gets the idea to go somewhere."

"Everything okay, Richard?" asked the admiral as Denise scurried away.

"Overreaction," he assured. "But we're on top of it, just in case."

Waiters entered the room with trays of champagne and encouraged everyone to take a fresh glass to take part in a toast. After they'd made their rounds and vanished, a screen on the wall by the robotic quartet flickered to life. Anton Kamaras appeared before them, holding a glass of his own.

"Ladies and gentlemen," he started. "It's nice to see you all again under happier circumstances. I imagine it's been quite an interesting day for you, just as it's been an interesting week for me."

There were some laughs and light applause.

"The fourteenth Dalai Lama once said," he continued, "'to remain indifferent to the challenges we face is indefensible. If the goal is noble, whether or not it is realized within our lifetime is largely irrelevant.'"

He paused briefly to let the quote sink in among his audience.

"What we must do, therefore, is to strive, and persevere, and never give up. I can't express how happy it's made me to present you with new hope, and an opportunity to meet our noble goal. Tonight is a celebration of that hope."

The audience met his moving remarks with loud, enthusiastic cheers. Over a few disorienting weeks, the atmosphere at the center had cycled through hope, despair, shock, and finally, relief. The contagious excitement enabled by that welcome relief had Jayson clapping along with just as much enthusiasm as the others despite some lingering doubts.

"Thank you so much for that," continued Kamaras as the applause died down. "Thank you. I hope you've been enjoying my string quartet this evening. Every aspect of their performance has been iterated to perfection by our algorithms using recordings from countless performances of the works of history's greatest composers. You won't find a more flawless human performance anywhere in the world. After seeing what they could do, I decided to find out if I could use the algorithms to teach them to compose their own music."

He paused for dramatic effect.

"And indeed, they can. They can compose the most objectively soulless, stiff, and unmoving melodies you can imagine. They're here tonight as an illustration of both the wonders and limits of technology. On your journey, we'll provide you with as many marvels of technology as we can. But never forget *you* will reimagine what the world will be. You will compose the score of humanity. When your families, colleagues, and I arrive in the reality you've created for us, we will experience the symphony your efforts have become."

He raised his glass to the camera on the other end of the connection.

"I offer this toast, inadequate as it is, in honor of the great things you will do."

Immediately after taking a sip, the screen went dark, and Kamaras was gone. Richard stepped onto the platform amid the applause to address the team.

"I hope you were all as moved by Mr. Kamaras's words as I was. It's impossible to express the enormity of what you are undertaking, but he did it as well as anyone could. For this evening's gathering, we're going to have a little fun and get you to mingle with some of those you may not have met yet. You will each receive a hit with a table number and a conversation prompt based on how your complementary skills will work together to create a better society. Please have a seat at your assigned table as quickly as possible when you get the hit. Dinner service will begin shortly."

Immediately, phones started vibrating, and everyone checked their Hitz-It apps. Jayson read his message aloud.

"Table four. Livable cities. Seems kind of the opposite of agriculture."

"Same one for me," said Parth.

"Me too," added Luping.

"Makes sense for a civil engineer and building materials scientist," said Jayson. "Let's see where I fit in."

"Table two," said Samaira. "Contact with established cultures."

"Me too," added Aiden.

"Okay. Now I know this is just random," complained Jayson with a laugh.

"They need me for my charm," laughed Aiden.

"Table five—infrastructure and systems," interjected Lisa.

"I guess we'll talk to you guys later," said Josh. "Table one is effective healthcare with limited resources."

Several other topics were proposed for various tables around the room where people were gathering. Kailani was already sitting down and chatting with one of Admiral Daniels' recruits at table two when Aiden and Samaira arrived to take their seats.

"This is Ted Park," she said as they sat down. "He's a sociologist. These are my friends Samaira and Aiden."

"Nice to meet you," he said. "What are your specializations?"

"Organizational psychology," replied Samaira.

"Great! We'll have a lot to talk about, I imagine. What about you, Aiden?"

"Agricultural operations," he shrugged. "Guess they had nowhere else to put me."

"I don't know about that," replied Ted. "Food has enormous significance, and is a language all of its own. The sharing of food with strangers has ritualistic importance across many cultures."

"If you say so."

Riyoko joined Jayson, Luping, and Parth, a guest researcher, and one of the admiral's recruits at table four. Jayson had met the guest researcher, Serge Goudreau, several times in the cafeteria, but had never spoken with him about his work. The admiral's recruit introduced herself as Jen, and described her expertise as logistics and supply. Jayson consciously focused on her eyes to avoid making her feel uncomfortable. She obviously spent a lot of time at the gym, and looked like she could probably body-slam Aiden if he pissed her off enough. He found her mix of strength and delicate femininity intriguing and more than a little attractive, and wondered what she would think of his physique. He took care of himself, but didn't dedicate nearly as much time to it as she obviously did.

Already familiar with Serge's work, Parth was the first to address the table's designated topic of conversation.

"What's new in the world of urban planning, Serge?"

"Everything, it would seem," he replied in his Parisian accent. "It is not often I would have the chance to start with carte blanche—a blank slate."

"What's your background, Serge?" asked Jayson.

"I started as a research and development intern at Dassault Systemes, supporting their Virtual Singapore project. I enjoyed it so much I switched from computer science to urban planning. Now I'm working towards my master's degree."

"I guess the master's is off the table now, huh?"

"It's not really relevant anymore," he shrugged.

"I guess not," conceded Jayson. "What's Virtual Singapore?"

"It's awesome," interjected Parth.

"So, basically, we modeled the entire city of Singapore," explained Serge. "Not just physically, but also the processes and the daily activities of the people. We added real-time monitoring of air quality, noise pollution, traffic flows, power demand, and so on."

"Sounds cool, but why?"

"Singapore has not much room left to grow. Every urban planning decision must be the right one, because the stakes for them are very high. Modeling and simulating the impacts of all proposed development is the only way for them to grow sustainably."

"Sustainably?" challenged Jayson, narrowing his eyes.

"In their context, the word does not mean the same as it does for us here," admitted Serge. "But we can apply the lessons to suit our own goals, as well. We can model the growth of our society to verify the impact our choices might have hundreds of years into the future."

"I find it hard to believe we can model an entire civilization that far into the future," said Jayson.

"We can do Singapore now with conventional computing," explained Serge. "I am interfacing the Dassault Systemes platform with our quantum capabilities to do unimaginable things. For example, I can help Parth decide how the water supply, sewers, roads, and utilities should evolve, so we don't make mistakes that have to be fixed in a hundred years. I can tell Luping how much power we'll need to store in her special concrete in different seasons for every year far into the future as the society grows."

"All that stuff sounds great, but it won't come to fruition until years after we're already dead," lamented Jayson. "I assume we'll be living in mud huts for the rest of our lives."

"If we stay or go, it doesn't matter," observed Jen. "Either way, our generation is being asked to make sacrifices."

"Screwed by the boomers," said Jayson shaking his head.

"Screwed by human nature, I would say," corrected Serge. "The generation responsible is only an accident of time."

"So we're just unlucky to be born when we were?"

"Exactly this," he confirmed with a shrug.

"As interesting as all this is, I can't help but think I'm at the wrong table," observed Jayson.

"Far from it," objected Jen. "In the navy, it's my job to get stuff where it needs to be. If that means burning ten thousand kilos of avgas and loading up a dozen diesel trucks, nobody batts an eye. In peacetime, what do you think I ship more than anything else besides fuel?"

"Food," realized Jayson.

"You got it. For me, the goal of this project is to minimize the need for logistics infrastructure like roads. That means working with people like you and Serge."

"To do what?"

"To do our best to make me unemployed so I can sit on the beach and work on my tan," she said with a laugh. "Put the food among the people where they need it, so I don't have to figure out how to move it. Rooftop gardens, vertical farming, urban cooperative gardens, whatever. You're the expert on this stuff."

"You're more than just a pretty face," blurted Jayson, immediately regretting it as he cringed to himself.

"I try to keep people off balance," she replied, unfazed.

"I keep overlooking the fact that we're starting from scratch," he continued, grateful his remark seemed to have gone unnoticed. "We can establish the concept that being responsible for at least some of your own food production is normal. We can also prevent the weird urban versus rural political divide we're dealing with now if we reduce the physical divide."

"This makes sense to me, too," added Serge. "An urban planner should look for ways to leave nature untouched instead of trying to develop it. We should be partners, Jayson, to bring some of the farm into the city, and reimagine our surroundings as a beautiful, green oasis."

There was less agreement emerging at table two, where Kailani and Ted were at an impasse regarding the best way to integrate into their new world. Kailani insisted her linguistic skills could facilitate rapid assimilation of the local tribes they might encounter. Ted thought the technological and theological divide between them would quickly turn into a source of violent conflict. It was better, he asserted, to establish friendly yet distant relations with them.

"You don't think it will arouse even more suspicion and animosity if we just show up among them and shut them out?" demanded Kailani.

"Maybe at first," conceded Ted, "but they'll learn to live with our presence."

"Wouldn't it be better to have them celebrating our presence?"

"Not if those celebrations involve us as human sacrifice."

"Why are you automatically assuming they're going to be savages?"

Aiden narrowed his eyes at Ted from across the table.

"I'm sorry," he relented. "I'm showing prejudice here. Our best approach is to adapt to what we find, and shoot for the best possible outcome. We're in this together, and we'll need to decide together."

"Agreed," said Kailani as she leaned out of her aggressive posture and exhaled.

Most of the other conversations throughout the room progressed congenially, punctuated by the arrival of various courses and expertly paired wines. By the time the waiters were clearing the dessert plates and offering coffee, any of the tension the team members might have felt heading into the evening had melted away. The earnest exchanges with the new arrivals allayed the fears they might be uneducated grunts who would undermine the peaceful nature of the mission.

Jayson, especially, felt a lot better. Meeting Jen and connecting with Serge had erased all remaining doubt. He was going to take the leap.

***

Though still home to some of its former staff, the Fusion A building was much less populated since being left behind when Fusion B was disassembled and shipped halfway across the island. For that reason, and because it was access controlled, a select group of Gamma recruits chose one of its small conference rooms as the location for a post-celebration debrief.

Aiden was late. He'd walked Samaira to her room and stayed talking with her in the hallway for nearly twenty minutes, obtusely deflecting her obvious advances before she gave up and turned in. After that, he took his time walking the path towards his rendezvous, not wanting to appear in a rush to be somewhere. When he finally arrived in the conference room, Ted Park snapped smartly to his feet and saluted.

"What the fuck are you doing, Park?" he asked, shaking his head.

"Sorry, sir. I mean, sorry, Aiden."

"Lift your shirt, Park."

"Come on," he pleaded.

"Lift your fucking shirt, Park. I told you we were going to do this as a reminder if anyone slipped up."

Ted sighed and raised his shirt, holding the bottom all the way up to his armpits with both hands. The rest of the admiral's recruits lined up in front of him. Most were chuckling and shaking their heads. Josh stepped up first. He raised his right hand back above his head as far as he could reach and delivered an open-handed slap across Ted's bare stomach.

He winced in pain. "I'm going to remember that windup, asshole."

"Remember it all you want. I'm not going to fuck up and give you a chance to do anything about it," he replied with a laugh.

Martina went next, but didn't put as much into it as Josh had.

"I appreciate it, de la Cruz," said Ted.

Next, Jen stepped up with a wide grin.

"Ready for me, Park?"

"Fuck me," lamented Ted. "Always gotta prove you can hang with the big boys, don't you?"

Her hand landed with a loud smack, and Park winced again, shaking his head.

"The rest of you fuckers better remember I just ate," he warned. "Someone's gonna get puked on."

"Worth it," confirmed his next punisher with a sadistic smile.

In all, eleven blows landed on Ted's stomach to remind him of the operational security protocols. When it was over, he gingerly lowered his shirt over the welts that were already forming.

"Alright, sit down," offered Aiden. "Great work tonight, and very disarming, for the most part. You got a little aggressive with Kailani, Park."

"Sorry about that. I just want to make sure they don't go in there expecting to get all friendly."

"It doesn't matter what they expect. Let them think whatever feels good for now. No matter what, we're going to make sure things stay frosty with the natives," he assured. "Properly provoked, they won't leave us many options."

"Understood."

"Otherwise," continued Aiden, "great stuff. They're accepting you like colleagues, and the initial suspicion is diffusing."

"If that's the goal, why even mention our background at all?" asked Martina.

"You'll be the only ones armed, and they'd naturally question that. We've established the expectation by getting it out of the way early. They'll accept your authority when it comes to matters of security."

"Any other concerns or observations to share?" asked Olena, who was leaning against the back wall, farthest from the door.

Silent head shaking was the only reply.

"How was Jayson?" asked Aiden.

"He was trying hard not to be obvious," replied Jen with a smile, "but I've caught his interest."

"Excellent. Richard said any hesitation would be subconsciously linked to Samaira's unavailability. I doubt he's thinking about her right now."

"Why me?" she asked.

"Are you complaining?"

"No. He's cute enough," she allowed. "Just wondering."

"Private browsing does not exactly live up to its name. We know more than we want to about some of these recruits," he replied with a sly smile. "Don't be afraid to flex those muscles and get a bit aggressive with him."

"What do you know about Josh?" asked Ted. "I owe him some payback."

"He knows I'm upset your mom isn't coming," shot Josh.

"Ouch, Park. I bet that burns worse than the pink belly," laughed Jen.

"Adding it to the list," assured Park. "Revenge is a dish best served cold."

"Revenge is a dish best served pink," corrected Josh as he poked Ted playfully in the stomach.

"I can't believe you imbeciles managed such good behavior tonight," marveled Olena, shaking her head. "Let's see if we can hold our shit together for just a few more weeks, alright?"

"Yes, ma'am," said Park, catching himself as he was about to salute.

Olena glared as he and the others filed out. Only Aiden remained behind.

"Lighten up a little," he said. "They did pretty well."

"They're not taking this seriously enough."

"If they're too serious, they won't be able to connect with the other recruits."

"And if they connect too well, they won't be able to do what's necessary when the time comes."

"*If* the time comes," cautioned Aiden.

"Hmph," she snorted.

"We're all committed to this just as much as you are, Olena."

"Are you?" she questioned. "My parents grew up in the shadow of Chernobyl. They were only children when they were forced to flee."

"I didn't know that."

"But fleeing wasn't enough. My mother died when I was still in diapers, and my father wasted away slowly for years right in front of my eyes. I've seen firsthand what humanity's filth can do."

"I'm sorry."

"Don't be sorry. Just do your job."

Chapter Twenty-Two

THOUGH IT WAS FALL, the Center for Sustainability Research had a spring break vibe the next day. Outside of the residence building, a dump truck had deposited a load of pristine, white sand onto a pair of large tarps to set up for a day of beach volleyball. Beer and wine coolers were set out alongside various finger foods under a large tent, and people were helping themselves despite that it was not yet noon.

At a nearby temporary stage, technicians performed a soundcheck to prepare for an evening of live entertainment. The theme was retro, and the Center had booked performers like Earth, Wind, & Fire and Abba tribute band Björn Again to provide the campy entertainment.

The Gamma recruits were under strict orders to have fun and forget about the mission for the weekend. The event was open to all Center staff, and they were to avoid discussing anything that might compromise operational security. Jayson felt a sense of importance mingling among those with no idea what was really going on. He was like a spy on a top-secret, life-and-death mission only a select few of those around him understood. Like James Bond, he was saving them all from certain doom without them even realizing it.

"Jayson," called out a voice from the crowd. It was Jen.

"Hi, Jen. Good morning."

"Nothing like beer for brunch," she said as she raised her bottle and clinked it against his.

"Not a wine cooler kind of girl, huh?"

"Nope. Not at all," she confirmed.

"Looking forward to the show today?"

"I am. Even though it's supposed to be kind of funny and cheesy, I have to admit I really love Abba."

"Really? Did you inherit that from your parents?"

"No," she laughed. "They hate 'em. They grew up on grunge, and I had to listen to that depressing crap too much as a kid. I think I like Abba just to piss them off."

"That's the common goal of all teenagers, I guess."

"You sign up yet? For the volleyball?"

"No. I'm not that great at it."

"That doesn't matter," she insisted. "It's just for fun."

"I don't—"

"Come on," she urged, "Let's do it together."

"Sure. Why not?"

She took him by the hand and led him toward the courts.

***

In his office, Richard was conducting a review with Cal and Denise to get an update on the latest data from their recruits.

"What do we have since last night?"

"A lot of good news and some not-so-good news," replied Cal.

"Let's go with the good news first," sighed Richard.

"Hits among the recruits are significantly more positive," he said. "Internet searches are trending towards things like survival tactics, self-sustained living, and the history of the islands. For the most part, they're preparing to go."

"And the bad news?"

"Hitarthi," he replied flatly. "She's freaking out."

Richard looked at Denise, but she wasn't paying attention. Instead, she was glued to her phone.

"That's not an analysis," he complained. "I need details."

"Mainly still reaching out to her mother—but also a few friends in the mix now. We've got bots responding in place of all of them."

"Any risk she'll figure it out?"

"The bots are good. Mannerisms, vernacular, everything—but it's only a matter of time before she wonders why they all keep deferring voice and video calls."

"We can't fake that in real-time?"

"Still experimental. It's too risky," he explained. "And to make things worse, she's been looking at flights."

"Shit."

"Not only looking," interrupted Denise. "She just booked."

"When?"

"Today. Departing in a couple of hours for LAX."

"She must have already packed," he realized. "We don't have much time."

He grabbed his phone from the desk and made a call.

***

Hitarthi emerged from her room after nearly a day of self-imposed isolation with a small carry-on bag. The only contact she'd had with her teammates were a few brief exchanges via the Hitz-It app assuring them she was okay. The distraction of the events outside, she hoped, would allow her to slip away unnoticed. She wasn't ready to talk to anyone at the Center, and desperately wanted an outside perspective. She knew she'd have to be creative to get one without revealing too much, but she could figure that out on the fly. Whatever the risks, she needed something familiar to ground her thoughts.

As she passed through the lobby, Olena was just reaching the bottom of the spiral staircase that led up to the cafeteria.

"Good morning, Hitarthi. How are you?" she asked with a warm smile.

"Fine, Olena. How about you?"

"Going somewhere?"

"Just a quick trip home," she explained.

"I didn't know you were going anywhere."

"I haven't said anything because I didn't want anyone to get worried. I'll be back before anyone even notices I'm gone."

"Need a ride to the airport?"

"I don't want to trouble you. I'll just take one of the pool cars."

"It's no trouble," insisted Olena. "I'm heading to Honolulu right now on an errand."

"An errand? You'll miss all the excitement here."

"It's only quick. I just need to get something."

"What?"

"It's embarrassing," said Olena, glancing at the ground.

Hitarthi smiled for the first time that morning.

"Now you *have* to tell me."

"I'm going to a thrift shop to see if I can get some funky seventies clothes to wear tonight. It's just a fun little gag to go along with the music."

"That's cute, Olena. I'm sorry I'm going to miss it."

"Don't worry," she assured. "I'll post some videos. Let's get out of here, so you don't miss your flight, and I don't miss the chance to embarrass myself."

As they walked out the door, Olena glanced around to see if anyone noticed them leaving together.

***

Jayson turned out to be better at beach volleyball than he'd let on. He knew the rules, could get the ball mostly where he wanted it, and rarely missed a serve even though he could only deliver them underhand. Jen, on the other hand, was incredible. From the moment she slipped off her t-shirt and track shorts to reveal her impressive, muscular form in a sports bikini, it was clear she was there to win.

He deferred to her superior knowledge of the game, following directions as Jen guided his positioning, and called out where she needed him to put the ball. They dispatched their rivals one after the other in the round-robin style tournament and, after a close call in the semi-finals against Josh and Kailani, cruised to victory in the last game. When it was over, she gave him a high-five and embraced him.

"Aren't you glad you decided to play?" she asked as she let go and gave him a playful slap across the butt.

"That was incredible!" he said, beaming. "You're incredible."

She squeezed his hand and smiled modestly. "I might have played semi-professionally for a while, but don't tell anyone."

"You're lucky my partner bailed on me," said Aiden as he approached to congratulate them. "We'd have kicked your asses."

"Samaira's not your partner?" asked Jayson.

"Told me it wasn't her thing. I was supposed to play with Olena."

"She's here now," said Jayson, pointing at Aiden's AWOL teammate standing next to the open trunk of the car she'd borrowed from the fleet.

"I need help with something, Aiden," she called. "It's too much for me to do alone."

He walked over and looked into the trunk to find the back seats were down, and there was a large bundle rolled up in a blanket taking up most of the room.

"What's this?" he asked with alarm.

"You'll see. Help me lift it out."

"Are you crazy? Not here."

"I'm not stupid, Aiden. Just grab one end and help me carry it over by the volleyball courts."

Glancing at her doubtfully, he grabbed one end and pulled.

"Jesus Christ," he said with relief upon realizing it was lighter than he expected.

They carried it over to where the others were gathered and dropped it on the ground.

"I have a surprise," announced Olena.

"What is it?" asked Kailani, rubbing her hands together with excitement.

"Costumes for tonight," she announced triumphantly as she unrolled the bundle to reveal an extensive collection of vintage seventies clothing.

"Oh my God! Where did you get all that?" asked Jen.

"I went to a couple of thrift stores to get something for myself and decided to buy every piece of seventies stuff they had. I cleared them out."

"That must have cost you a fortune," realized Kailani.

"No problem. I put it all on credit," laughed Olena. "I'd love to see them try to collect where I'm going."

Everyone crowded around to see what they could find in their respective sizes—or close enough for just one night. Aiden stepped away and pulled Olena aside.

"Brilliant idea," he marveled. "How did you come up with this?"

"I didn't," she admitted. "Denise has been running some options on how to fine-tune the event for maximum impact. The algorithms came up with this one."

"They scare the hell out of me sometimes," he replied, shaking his head. "Almost makes me grateful to have the chance to step back from all this so-called progress."

"I know what you mean."

"How'd it go with Hitarthi? Everything good?"

"Won't be a problem," replied Olena absently, without taking her eyes off the group of laughing researchers and navy recruits sorting through the piles of old clothing.

***

The party that evening could only be described as wild; at least relative to the ordinarily restrained and professional behavior of the young scientists who'd been burdened with the herculean and unfair task of fixing what others before them had broken. It was an opportunity to let go of their concerns, for at least a little while, with the aid of copious alcohol.

Earth, Wind, and Fire put on an incredible show. Their practice of continually cycling in young talent provided an opportunity for the aging original members to keep up the energy of the performance. They happily paced themselves and allowed a new generation to take most of the spotlight in front of the dancing crowd. Boogie Wonderland, Sing a Song, and September—even though the songs were hits decades before anyone in the audience had been born, the young revelers grooved as if they knew every one of them.

Björn Again had evolved from its original form into a franchise of several different Abba tribute groups touring under the same name. Careful quality control ensured fans could expect a similar, high-quality experience no matter which one of the band's incarnations was performing. The antiseptic practices of big business behind the routine were the furthest things from even the most cynical of minds among the crowd. The closing act was energetic and flawless—and everyone loved it.

Jayson had found an undersized, long white jacket and a comically short pair of matching bell-bottom pants to complement the evening's seventies theme. A sequined fedora with a feather in it topped off his ridiculous ensemble. He didn't feel at all out of place, as others had gone for equally outlandish looks.

Jen had opted for a leopard print halter-top and a pair of hot pants that looked as though they might burst apart under pressure from her bulging quadriceps. As they bounced up and down in unison to the chorus of Waterloo, Jayson tuned out the jostling crowd and focused only on her. Her flirtatious behavior had been evolving throughout the day, and she now clung to him tightly as they danced. He was finding it impossible to hide his growing interest, and knew that she must be able to feel it as she pressed against him.

"I'd really like to see your room," she yelled in his ear over the din of the music.

"It's just like all the others, I assume," he replied.

She wordlessly cocked her head to the side and raised an eyebrow.

"Oh," he realized. "Yeah, of course."

She grabbed his hand and pulled him through the crowd, towards the residence building. Jayson glanced back to see if anyone was watching them leave but wasn't sure if he was hoping to slip away unnoticed or not. Either way, it seemed everyone was having too much fun to care. He rummaged through his pockets for the keycard with his free hand as they hurried into the building, not wanting to waste time trying to find it when they got to his room.

Reaching the door, he quickly unlocked it, and Jen pushed him aggressively over the threshold towards the bed. She was already kissing him passionately as they collapsed down onto the pillows together and started fumbling to remove each other's clothes.

Chapter Twenty-Three

SUNDAY WAS A RECOVERY day, and an opportunity for rest or quiet contemplation. While a crew of laborers dismantled the stage and cleaned up the mess, Jayson spent most of the morning locked away in his room with Jen, ignoring all attempts at intrusion from the outside world arriving as vibrations emanating from his phone. He didn't know how the others had decided to spend their last carefree day for the foreseeable future, but was confident it couldn't be as perfect as his.

Monday morning brought a renewed focus on the mission, and everyone gathered once again in the auditorium to get their orders. Though it had only been a few days since they'd learned of the mind-bending plan for a global reset, it no longer seemed crazy or risky. It was simply their new reality.

Once again, Richard addressed the assembled recruits from the podium.

"I trust you all had a great weekend?" he asked with a smile. "We thought it would be fun to allow you to spend some time with your new family and blow off steam after a few very disorienting weeks. Judging by some of the videos you posted, I'd say we were right."

His observation was met by laughter and even a loud 'woo' of concurrence from one of the navy recruits.

"Now we get to work," he continued. "No more parties and no more weekends off. We've got less than a month to redirect all of our energy toward the new mission. Today, I'll be outlining the overall plan and assigning responsibilities. Any questions?"

Nothing but a few silent head shakes. Richard accessed a digitally generated, three-dimensional model of what O'ahu would have looked like before the arrival of humans, and displayed it on the interactive wall behind him. He tapped on Pai'Olu'Olu Point, east of Honolulu, to initiate a dramatic zoom-in.

"This is where you'll arrive on O'ahu. It's not the most conveniently located place with respect to terrain and resources, and it's certainly not somewhere you'll want to stay for very long. We've chosen it because it is well concealed and unlikely to be populated. Here, you'll set up a temporary camp where you'll wait for Admiral Daniels' team to scout the area and secure resources."

"Will I go with the scouts to assist with contact?" asked Kailani.

"No. There is to be no contact on the scouting missions—just observation. A team of three will always stay with the main group to provide security. Three additional teams will scout primary and secondary campsites close to fresh water and abundant fishing. They'll report back to get consensus on where and when to move the camp, and how to handle any local populations."

"Shouldn't we decide now where to establish ourselves?" asked Serge. "This way, I can plan our layout and growth while I still have more computing power."

"Agreed," replied Richard. "The goal is ultimately to get to Honolulu and build a civilization centered on the natural harbor. You may need to get there incrementally, depending on what you find when you arrive."

He tapped on the wall to zoom out and then focused on Honolulu Harbor.

"Honolulu will be pretty established already," protested Kailani. "The first settlements date back to at least a century before our arrival."

"As I said, we think those estimates are off considerably in our favor," assured Richard. "Let's move on to the preparations. We're limited to ninety-five hundred kilograms, including all of you. That might sound like a lot, but I think you'll find it will get spoken for quickly. I need you to compile lists of what'll be nice to have to do your work versus what is absolutely essential. Carefully document the mass and be prepared to defend your choices."

The team began looking around at one another uncomfortably as they digested the implications. They'd be competing with one another for a share of a limited amount of supplies they could bring.

"Want to bring extra food and fresh water just to be safe for the first few days? That could cost you critical equipment used to make antibiotics," explained Richard. "Make good choices."

"I guess I'm not getting a tractor, am I?" asked Jayson.

"No," agreed Richard, "but you can bring more things by being creative. For example, take the handles off your tools and make new ones from bamboo when you arrive."

The researchers nodded at the wisdom of his example.

"Jayson and Riyoko—you'll spend the next weeks planning how to feed everyone in the short and long term. Farzin Khan from the admiral's team will join you for his expertise in fishing methods and aquaculture."

Farzin waved at Jayson from across the room to identify himself.

"Parth, Luping, and Serge—get started on planning the setup for Honolulu."

"What about Hitarthi?" asked Samaira.

"What about her?"

"Where is she?"

"I assume you've been in contact with her, Samaira. She informed me she needs time to process things and still hasn't decided if she'll join you for the mission. For now, we'll make do without her. I need you to get started on defining the aspects of a sustainable culture that will work towards our goals for generations."

"Already working on it," she assured him.

Richard continued calling out names and detailing the responsibilities that would keep the recruits busy for the remaining weeks leading up to the start of the mission. He also explained they'd continue to meet every Monday morning to discuss progress, share their equipment lists, and debate the mass allocations. Once the assignments were complete, he drew in a deep breath and exhaled before continuing.

"You might find the next subject a bit uncomfortable," he warned, "but you are all smart people, and I'm sure you understand some of the unspoken insinuations of your mission. At some point, your culture will establish contact with the rest of the world to help them maintain the health of the global environment. There is an enormous amount of work to do ahead of that to ensure you're secure enough to defend against potential threats. The multi-generational timeline of development we've established for your civilization will require a significant population to stay on track."

Some people started squirming awkwardly in their seats as Richard looked around. A single cough from somewhere near the middle of the room punctuated the silence.

"Forty people—twenty men and twenty women—are establishing a new society. Obviously, that implies a level of planned procreation and population growth. With a targeted average of one percent annual growth, there will be over fifteen thousand of your descendants by the time they're ready to make contact and change the course of the industrial revolution."

"What exactly do you mean by planned procreation?" asked Kailani, narrowing her eyes.

"There's preferable timing and frequency of reproduction to achieve the required growth rate, and to allow for an effective early childhood education experience for the first couple of generations."

"To what degree are things planned?" demanded Samaira. "Is there any level of choice involved?"

"Let me be clear," he stated, raising a finger to emphasize his point. "You will all make your own decisions on this matter. I only ask that you look at the models and run some simulations to consider the impacts your choices will have on subsequent generations. We've gone to great lengths to ensure we're providing you with enough genetic diversity and healthy stock to make your civilization viable."

"I wouldn't have guessed you were such a romantic," quipped Jayson.

"Alright. Enough of that," cautioned Richard over the resulting laughter. "Let's all pretend we've moved beyond a high school mentality here. We'll stop for now, and reconvene next week to see how things look with your plans and equipment lists. Reach out if you have questions."

As the team filed out of the room, the women gravitated towards one another as if they instinctively understood they had a shared concern to discuss. Olena led them outside and assertively shooed a few people away from the corner of the courtyard farthest from the buildings so they could have some privacy.

"I can't be the only one feeling uncomfortable," she started.

"Not with the mission," clarified Kailani. "It's the idea of reducing us down to breeding pairs. I know I said I wanted kids, but this just isn't, I don't know—"

"Romantic?" offered Olena.

"Yeah. It creeps me out to think they've been simulating our reproduction."

"Just the results, I hope," replied Olena with a laugh. "I don't think they've been simulating the actual act."

"What about you, Samaira?" asked Riyoko.

"I think nature takes its course, and these kinds of things just work themselves out," she replied with a shrug.

"That's easy for you to say. You've already found someone perfect."

"Maybe," she replied with a coy smile. "It's too soon to say for sure."

"The way I look at it," said Olena, "there's an awful lot of to swipe right for in this crowd. It's definitely an above-average dating pool."

"I have to give you that," agreed Riyoko.

"And, look at the bright side," added Kailani. "At least Andrew's not coming."

***

Aiden had convinced the men, too, that they should take some time to talk about the meeting. He sent them to the cafeteria lanai, which was deserted in the midafternoon hours between late lunch and early dinner, with the promise he'd make it worth their while. True to his word, he arrived soon after with two cases of beer.

"Where did you get those?" probed Herman.

"I snuck into the kitchen and grabbed them from the cooler. I figured they'd have something left from the party."

"Do you think that was a good idea?" asked Parth.

"I don't think there's any danger of getting fired at this point. Who wants one?"

Hands shot up around the group of tables they'd pulled together to accommodate everyone. Herman raised his thumb and index finger, the German sign for 'two, please.'

"What are you going to do when you don't have beer anymore, Herman?" asked Jayson.

"We will have beer," he said, nodding confidently. "You will bring barley and hops, and I will bring the very best German ale yeast."

"Deal," agreed Jayson immediately.

"I bet the women aren't drinking beer right now," laughed Parth.

"Their loss," said Aiden.

"Why do you think they wanted to talk without us?" asked Matteus.

"Because they're talking *about* us," said Aiden.

"I don't see the big deal," said Parth.

"Really?"

"Yeah. I mean, it's just part of what has to be done—part of the mission."

"Some advice from someone a bit older and maybe even a bit wiser," announced Aiden to the group. "Don't get relationship counseling from Parth."

Everyone laughed.

"You mean you don't agree?" persisted Parth.

"Even if I did, I'd never be stupid enough to say it out loud."

"There's nothing wrong with being pragmatic."

"I don't know what that word means, but in this context, I have to assume it's a synonym for virgin," quipped Aiden, evoking another round of laughter.

"Fine, Romeo. Tell me where I'm wrong."

"I don't even know where to start. First of all, referring to procreation as part of a mission isn't the surest way into a woman's heart. If you want my advice, they're not going to accept our situation as an excuse for skipping the romance. Pick flowers, write poems, and tell them they're pretty. That's the extent of my wisdom on the subject—and it's all you really need."

"I'm not trying to sound like Samaira here," added Jayson, "but this isn't just a mission. It's not something that's going to end, and allow us to move on with our lives."

"Completely agree," said Serge. "This mission will *be* our lives—and the lives of our children. We must take time to find beauty. We must laugh and love as we work, or we are no longer human."

"That's how you do it, Parth," said Aiden. "Frenchie here is definitely getting himself laid."

Chapter Twenty-Four

THE FOLLOWING WEEK, AS the team continued their efforts to pare down their equipment lists, Richard announced a schedule of practice runs for the event. All of their movements needed to be choreographed with precision, he had explained, to keep the mass transfer rates within range and ensure everyone made it through during the brief window.

The Center facilities team had sectioned off a corner of the warehouse by the docks with office dividers and turned it into a mockup of the Fusion B test chamber. When the team arrived for their first run-through, they found Richard and Dr. Akindele waiting for them in front of a whiteboard.

"Welcome to what we call the test chamber," greeted Richard. "Or at least an adequate representation for our purposes. Dr. Akindele is going to start us off with some numbers."

"Hello, everyone," started Akindele. Our window for the transfer is approximately two minutes and thirty-three seconds."

He wrote it on the whiteboard in large black letters and underlined it twice.

"You must get yourselves and your equipment through the portal within that window. If you go too slowly, some of you will be left behind. If you go too quickly, we will not be able to transfer all of the mass as it passes through. This would be very bad for your equipment, and even worse for you," he said dryly. "To make this work, you will need to maintain a consistent pace of approximately one-point-five meters per second."

He wrote the number on the whiteboard, as if it was somehow relatable, and underlined it as Richard stepped forward to speak.

"That's a pretty normal walking pace," he added. "But you will need to maintain that while wearing a pack, pushing a cart, or perhaps carrying something in your arms."

"Or what? We kill ourselves?" asked Herman.

"It's not as hard as it sounds," assured Richard. "We've covered our walkway in an array of LEDs that change color and keep the pace for you. You just need to get close to the person in front of you and keep pace with the lights."

"How, exactly, do we do that?" asked Riyoko.

"Practice. That's what you'll do for a little while today and a few more times before you go. We'll start with a low-tech overview on the whiteboard."

Richard sketched out a rectangle representing the room and added the apparatus and walkway. He filled the rest of the space in the room with a broad, s-shaped pathway.

"We'll stage all of you and the carts along this path here," he explained. "First through will be two members of the security team carrying only their weapons and a backpack each. Due to the remote location, this is really just an overabundance of caution, and not because of likely danger."

He then indicated the blank space on the opposite side of the portal and drew a large rectangle.

"This is where you will arrive. We've constructed a platform to represent the assembly area for the dry run. After the first two go through and secure the area, the rest of the admiral's recruits will follow, each pushing a cart with approximately two hundred and fifty kilos on it. As soon as they pass through, they'll place their carts aside and go back to help the next arrivals move out of the way."

Richard drew a crude-looking arrangement of rectangles to represent the placement of the carts.

"The rest of the team will go next, either pushing the remaining carts or carrying some odds-and-ends in boxes or hardened cases. Who's ready to give it a try?" he asked, rubbing his hands together enthusiastically.

"Let's do it," replied Aiden.

"Okay. Ted and Jen—you're up first. Grab the pack with your name on it from against the wall. We've made some assumptions about how much everyone could carry, and created a mock load for you to try out today."

Responding immediately to his order, they grabbed their packs and headed for the ramp.

"You may as well go to the top to make sure we have lots of room for everyone," advised Richard. "Now, I need two volunteers to help pull the carts up the ramp in case people need a bit of a boost."

Aiden raised his hand. "I'll do it."

"Me too," added Samaira quickly, following Aiden to the line of packs against the wall.

"Are you sure you're up for it?" asked Richard.

"We'll find out," she said confidently as she grabbed the pack with her name on it and walked over to the ramp with Aiden.

"Okay. As soon as Jen and Ted start walking, you two will go and stand on either side at the top of the ramp to help get the carts up. They each have two small handles on the front of the frame for you to grab onto."

They nodded in unison.

"Security team," continued Richard. "Grab your packs and a cart and line up."

The carts were more modern-looking carbon fiber versions of the large-wheeled rickshaw Ruan had taken with him earlier. It took the security team a while to get organized and in place because the carts were already preloaded with sandbags to simulate the weight of the equipment they'd be carrying.

"Next, I'm going to need ten volunteers from among the rest of you to handle the remaining carts. I'm not looking for anyone to be a hero, so let's base it on strength."

The remaining twenty-six recruits sized each other up.

"I'll get one," volunteered Herman.

"Me too," added Jayson.

A few more volunteers, all men, claimed a cart and joined Herman and Jayson in preparation to join the growing line.

"There's no rule saying it can only be men," prompted Richard. "If you think you can handle a cart, go get one."

Kailani, Zaina, and the early childhood education specialist, Melinda Littleton, stepped forward. Perhaps shamed by their own gender bias, two more of the men

219

claimed their packs and the last two carts before joining the end of the growing line.

"Everyone else—grab your packs and a box to carry and get in line. After a few practice runs, we'll note who thinks they can take a bit more and who wants to take a bit less."

After everyone took their positions in the snaking line leading to the walkway, there were still two boxes left.

"What about those?" asked Parth from his place at the end of the queue.

"That's why we're doing a dry run," explained Richard. "Those two are for Aiden and Samaira. Once the carts are on the walkway, they'll need to go back and get those before joining the back of the line."

"I don't want to risk jostling or bumping anyone on the way down," said Aiden. "Can we just have someone hand them to us where we are?"

"For today's runs, I'll handle that," said Richard. "But we'll need to come up with a better way."

"We'll need a platform or pedestal of some kind," suggested Dr. Akindele.

"Okay with you if we add that detail next time?" asked Richard.

Aiden nodded.

"Then let's give this a try," he urged. "We'll start with a countdown, and then the green lights will start moving down the walkway at one-point-five meters per second. Remember to keep pace as best you can."

Richard pulled a remote control device from his pocket and pressed a large green button. The lights on the walkway turned red, and, almost immediately, a soft, robotic-sounding female voice started counting down from five.

At zero, Ted and Jen stepped onto the emerging green zone of moving lights, and walked steadily toward the aperture of the mocked-up apparatus. The next navy recruit was already pushing her cart up the ramp. Aiden and Samaira went to help, but it was unnecessary. She made it up with ease.

"Close the gap as quickly as you can and then keep pace," encouraged Richard from beside them.

By the time the third cart reached the top of the ramp, the first recruits were already on the other side of the portal, sweeping their eyes and weapons across an imaginary landscape. Quickly, they changed their focus to ushering through the new arrivals and guiding their carts out of the way.

The dry run was progressing smoothly until the last of the security team was up the ramp, and the rest of the recruits began their efforts. Herman underestimated the weight of his load and wasn't leaning into it enough. Halfway up the ramp, he lost speed and almost came to a complete stop before Aiden and Samaira caught the handles at the front and gave him a pull. Once at the top, he had to scramble to close the gap, and then underestimated the force needed to slow down; bumping his cart against the man ahead of him.

"Sorry," he called out as he adjusted his distance and pace.

Jayson and the following recruits had similar issues, and all needed help getting to the top of the ramp. As a result, a growing gap appeared between subsequent carts as each one arrived on the walkway. Richard called a stop to the first practice run to avoid having anyone lose control and possibly end up injured attempting to close the gap too quickly.

"Alright. Let's call that a pretty good first try," he called out as he pressed the red button on the remote and the green lights went dark. "Get back in the line, and we'll talk through where things are going off track."

Richard waited patiently for everyone to return to their starting positions before continuing.

"The first dozen went fine, but then we ran into compounding problems getting up the ramp. Any suggestions?"

"You've got all the people without carts at the end of the line," observed Jen. "They should be able to get up easier, so we should intersperse them to minimize the gaps."

"Leave it to our logistics expert," said Richard with a smile. "Let's rearrange and try again."

The second attempt went much more smoothly. The recruits were accustomed to the weight of their loads, and instinctively adopted a short running start up the ramp for momentum. Aiden and Samaira established a better rhythm for pulling the carts from the top. It helped to have an extra couple of seconds to prepare for the next one, with the spacing between them now offset by the rearrangement suggested by Jen. Despite some frantic catch-up for the final cart, all of the recruits made it through before the strip of green lights turned red.

"They were impressive, Richard," allowed Dr. Akindele. "That was very consistent through the aperture."

"Not bad at all," he agreed.

"If they can get just a little better, and the loads are balanced perfectly, I can give you another nine hundred kilos by reducing the safety margin on the transfer rate."

"That's great news. I'll let them know at the next review to keep up the motivation to practice."

Richard rubbed his hands together excitedly and congratulated the team for their solid second effort.

"That was fantastic! Everyone made it through in one piece, and with all the equipment intact. Let's do it two more times today, and then we're back the day after tomorrow to try again."

They lined up for the third attempt without complaint to perfect the critical ritual that would launch their journey into a new world.

***

After a few days of practice sessions interspersed with their regular work, the team could execute the transfer procedure flawlessly. Serge even used his internship experience to write an algorithm for the Dassault modeling software to iteratively simulate and improve the weight distribution of loads among the packs and carts. So impressed was Dr. Akindele by the results of the team's collective efforts, he allowed an extra thousand kilos of load from his safety margin to allow for a few more luxuries.

Jayson decided to bring along a few live hens and a rooster to provide a bit more variety in their protein sources. Zaina El Masri, an electro-mechanical engineer recruited from the American University of Beirut, quickly convinced everyone that a couple of extra pumps and motors, combined with additional wiring and tubing, could free the team of some of the more menial tasks associated with their basic daily needs. Dr. Ezra Kitzinger, the obstetrician, decided on a few sets of guitar strings and tuning pegs along with some small hand tools so he could make his own acoustic guitar in his downtime. Surprisingly, nobody argued he was being too indulgent.

The unexpected weight bonus, though minor, put everyone in a good mood, and eased some of the natural tension that built up as the mission approached. They finalized the equipment list, and much of the gear was already onsite at Pai'Olu'Olu Point being secured to the carts precisely as determined by Serge's optimization algorithm. There was very little preparation work left, and the team spent most of the remaining time reviewing models and contingencies.

One afternoon, with only a few days remaining until the transfer, Richard assembled the team in the auditorium one last time before they'd be shuttling over to the Point.

"There is one more task that remains," he announced to the team. "I know all of you will want to say some kind of goodbye to your loved ones. Of course, it remains critical you not divulge the exact nature of your mission. We've prepared a cover story that explains you have all volunteered to be part of an ecological bio-dome experiment that requires you to be without external contact."

There were some expressions of concern as the young team members whispered among themselves at the news they'd need to lie to their families.

"At the same time," he continued, "we recognize eventually, they will need to know the truth so we can prepare them to join us on the voyage to see what you have created. I need you to create personalized videos to explain, in your own words, what you are doing. Send those to me when they're ready, so I can share them at the right time."

He delivered his lie coldly and convincingly. The video messages were part of yet another psychological game to commit them to the mission and reduce the likelihood of last-minute doubts. The oblivious team left the auditorium with excited thoughts of how they might explain their noble sacrifice. They imagined the strange mix of pride, sorrow, and appreciation their families would feel upon learning what their brave children had done. Richard felt not even the slightest pangs of guilt knowing he would delete the videos after he received them.

Chapter Twenty-Five

THE TRAGICALLY HIP PROVIDED the soundtrack of Canada for a generation, releasing more than a dozen albums since their 1987 self-titled debut. For decades, their songs had featured prominently at the top of Canadian charts alongside hits from the best-known international artists from the United States, Europe, and Australia. Like their more famous contemporaries, they could sell out any venue in the country. However, the uniquely Canadian flavor of their songs meant they had limited international success, and it's unlikely they'd have wanted it any other way.

Jayson's father was a fan of the band, and had the framed t-shirts hanging in his basement workshop to chronicle the many concerts he'd attended. He'd often recounted to his young son the story of meeting the band backstage in a tiny theater in Boulder, Colorado, at the height of their fame—a feat that would have been impossible at one of their sold-out shows in Toronto.

On May 24, 2016, the nation was stunned by the announcement charismatic lead singer Gord Downie had terminal brain cancer. The unofficial poet laureate of Canada was dying. For the next week, the band's music played in Jayson's Brantford, Ontario, home every evening, and his father's eyes were covered with a permanent glossy film.

The band announced a farewell tour that would start in Victoria, British Columbia, and move eastward to conclude where it had all started; their historic hometown of Kingston, Ontario, with its centuries-old buildings and stone-cobbled streets. Tickets for the tour were impossible to get, and Jayson's father, like millions of others, settled for watching the nationally televised concert at home with his family.

Across the country, Canadians gathered in front of their televisions as the band took stage for the final time, with Gord dressed head-to-toe in sparkling silver. In true Hip fashion, they opened with a song about hockey and followed it with a collection of their most memorable tributes to Canadian icons, landmarks, and culture. At times both jubilant and heartbroken, the crowd sang along with every one of them.

With the eyes of a nation fixed on the bittersweet spectacle, Gord could have used the opportunity to draw focus to anything he wanted. He could have implored the government to fund more cancer research, or plugged some greatest hits album. Instead, he made it his final public act to call on Prime Minister Justin Trudeau to finally uncover and address the abuses First Nations peoples had been subjected to for generations. Trudeau was there in person, prominently positioned in the audience, when Gord —half promising and half hoping—assured the crowd they were in good hands, and that the Prime Minister 'cares about the people way up north we were trained our entire lives to ignore.'

The entire performance had been moving, but Jayson noticed both of his parents broke down and cried as the Hip's front man continued his plea on behalf of natives, and the Prime Minister fought to hold back tears of his own. Even as the concert continued, taking on a more uplifting tone, his parents had seemed unable to shake the powerful words. Tears streamed down their faces, and Jayson sensed something more was going on.

Although he knew he was native, and had been adopted as an infant, Jayson knew nothing about his birth parents, and had been told that nobody was sure who they were or where they were from. On the evening of the farewell concert, two weeks after his eighteenth birthday, he learned the truth. His birth parents were from the tiny James Bay community of Fort Albany, in Northern Ontario, where the Catholic Church, with tacit permission from the government, had subjected his ancestors to generations of emotional, physical, and sexual abuse as part of what could only be described as a cultural genocide.

His parents recounted what they'd been told. His birth mother had become frantic when she found out she was pregnant, insisting on hiding herself away from the community and swearing Jayson's biological father to secrecy on the matter. Following the dangerous home birth, she became increasingly guilt-ridden and despondent. Even though the St. Anne's Residential School where she'd been abused had long since closed, in her mind, she was convinced she had given the church another victim in the person of her newborn son.

She pleaded with her partner to give Jayson up for adoption and make sure he ended up as far away from Fort Albany as possible, and resolved to turn the baby over to Child Welfare Services the next day. When Jayson's biological father awoke the following day, she was gone—leaving him to put Jayson up for adoption on his own.

At the same time, the Reillys, unable to have biological children of their own, were seeking to adopt through the public process and learned of Jayson through their caseworker. The open process allowed contact with the biological father, and they discovered the tragic circumstances of the adoption directly from him through a series of phone calls.

They grew to like him and, though not required by law, agreed to provide him with regular updates on Jayson's progress after the adoption. It turned out not to be necessary for long. A few months after Jayson moved in with his new parents, his biological father had shot himself in the head. Shortly after, a note of apology arrived with a plea to isolate Jayson from the burdens of his past so he could enjoy a normal future. They'd honored that request for eighteen years before finally unburdening themselves against the juxtaposed background of cheering fans demonstrating their love and appreciation for everything Gord and the rest of the Tragically Hip had given the nation.

***

Dozens of fires darkened the skies of Western Canada in the months after Jayson's arrival on O'ahu. It wasn't all due to an early start to forest fire season, though that had been an issue as well. Enraged arsonists were setting fire to Catholic churches across the west as authorities announced seemingly daily discoveries of unmarked mass graves at churches and former residential schools. Investigators had uncovered more than a thousand bodies in total, and the cultural genocide of First Nations peoples was looking more and more like a literal one. Across the country, communities wrestled with decisions to scale back or cancel Canada Day festivities, as they considered that perhaps it should be a year of reflection rather than celebration.

Jayson had spoken with his parents several times since starting at the Center for Sustainability Research, and the heartbreaking events dominating the news back home were always the focus of his father's heated tirades. Far from mellowing with age, he'd become increasingly angry and strident in his political and religious rantings.

Stridency seemed to be an epidemic spreading worldwide as social media divided people into camps, and pitted them against one another in online battles of words and wit. Jayson's father was not immune. It showed in their final phone call before the mission.

"Hey, dad, how are things going?"

"Not bad, Jayson. Nice to hear from you. How are things at work?"

"Great. Things are going well at the Center, and I couldn't ask for better weather."

"Summer's been shit here this year," complained his father. "When it's not raining, it's too hot to do anything outside."

"That sucks. I hope you guys are finding stuff to do."

"Did you hear two more churches got lit up in B.C. last week?" he asked, changing topics abruptly.

"I haven't really been following for the last month. That's awful."

"What do they expect? You know the Pope isn't even coming to apologize in person for these residential school massacres?"

"That doesn't really excuse arson, dad," replied Jayson.

"Like hell it doesn't. I hope churches keep burning to the ground until he gets his ass on a plane and begs tribal leaders for forgiveness—from his knees."

"Jesus Christ, dad. That's a bit of an extreme view—and not really helpful."

"I guess not," conceded the self-described recovering Catholic. "I'm just so pissed off by this whole thing."

"Is it worse because of me?"

"I'm sure it makes a difference, but I'd like to think I'm the kind of person who'd be pissed off by it regardless."

"Being pissed off doesn't do you any good. Can I make a recommendation?"

"Shoot."

"I know I work for Anton Kamaras, but you really need to spend less time on Hitz-It. You'd be a lot happier."

"Someone's gotta counter all the bullshit out there," he protested.

"It's a losing battle, and completely irrelevant. You're most likely just fighting with bots, trolls, or paid provocateurs. You're going to have a heart attack for nothing."

Jayson's dad softened his tone, sensing his son wasn't in the mood to humor a rant.

"What about you? Anything exciting happening in your life? Girlfriend?"

"Maybe," he said evasively. "Actually, there's this big project I'm going to be starting soon. Kind of a biodome thing that'll have me incommunicado for a bit."

"Really? What's it all about?"

"We're keeping the details pretty tight until it's over. I hope you understand."

"Of course," he allowed. "But at least tell me if you think you guys have figured something out for all this climate chaos."

"I really think we have, dad," he replied earnestly. "I can hardly wait to tell you all about it when I can."

"I'm proud of you, Jayson. I always knew you'd do something special."

Jayson thought he heard his father's voice crack, and he felt tears welling up in his own eyes.

"Thanks, dad. Put mom back on for a minute? I want to let her know we won't have a chance to talk again for a while."

***

Samaira, too, had called her parents and was satisfied that she'd done an okay job of hiding her emotions. It was a thin line to walk—trying to say an adequate final goodbye without making it sound like one. She also set aside time for a last lunch with Andrew. Heavy rain constrained the outdoor options, but they found a private spot in the covered area of the lanai. Most of their colleagues chose not to brave the unseasonably cool weather, opting instead to eat inside.

"So you're still here, it seems," she observed with a smile.

"Yeah. I guess so. Richard swears they still need me around here."

"I'm glad to hear it."

"I do feel a bit like an outsider now," he admitted. "I know a lot is going on, but nobody's talking."

"I'm sorry I can't say more right now," said Samaira.

"Don't worry. I get it," he assured.

"You've been a great friend, Andrew." Samaira hesitated for a moment before continuing. "I don't want to put you in an uncomfortable situation, but I need to ask you for a favor."

"Anything you need."

She produced a sealed envelope and placed it on the table.

"I need you to take this note and promise me you won't open it until Friday."

"Okay," he agreed. "Then what do I do?"

"Whatever you decide is right."

"Very mysterious," he replied, furrowing his brow. "And a little concerning. Is everything okay?"

"Absolutely," she assured him. "Please don't tell anyone, though. It's our secret."

"You can count on me."

"I know I can, Andrew. That's what I love about you."

She leaned over the table and gave him a kiss on the cheek.

***

With their goodbyes complete and their video messages uploaded to the system, a sense of calm resolve settled over the team. The day before the big event, they prepared themselves and packed the few personal items allowed within the mass limit before assembling at the concrete base of Fusion B now serving as a landing pad.

A steady stream of Navy helicopters arrived from across the harbor to ferry small groups of people over to the temporary living quarters at Pai'Olu'Olu Point for one final night of sleep in the only reality they'd ever known. The operation had been underway for just over two-and-a-half hours when the last helicopter, a VH-3D Sea King, departed the remote site after dropping off a load of recruits.

It was the first time they'd seen Fusion B in months, and the building held a new significance they hadn't appreciated when they'd watched it being dismantled and shipped away earlier that year. Richard took them inside to see the *actual* test chamber for the first time. Completely enclosed, it felt smaller than the mockup separated from the rest of the warehouse space by cubicle dividers.

Fully packed carts and stacks of containers with names on them lined the long wall opposite the raised walkway. The only things not yet secured and ready to go were Jayson's hens and rooster. They were outside in a temporary enclosure, obliviously scratching at the ground in search of food. His cart was now last in line, so the live animals could be secured to the load as late as possible to minimize any distraction their protestations might cause.

Through the windows above them, the team could see a few techs wandering around in the control room preparing for the next morning's event. Otherwise, the place was eerily still.

"It's kind of jarring to see the portal thingy without a walkway coming out of the back of it," observed Jayson. "Any chance we can see it working before we go?"

"It doesn't work like that," reminded Richard. "The windows arrive at set times, and they're too rare to waste."

"Yeah. Okay."

"I hope you're not getting cold feet."

"Nothing serious," he assured. "Kind of like when you decide to go skydiving. Just because you're committed, it doesn't mean you're not still shitting your pants the whole ride up."

"Ever done it?" asked Richard.

"Just once," admitted Jayson. "And that was enough."

"Perfect. You've only got to do this once, too," he said with a laugh. "But in all seriousness, if anyone needs a bit of valium, we can give you a small amount without impacting your ability to get through. Just something to consider if you're feeling nervous."

People nodded, but nobody made a request. Jayson decided it would be a game-time decision for him.

"If you have any questions or concerns," continued Richard, "now is the time to address them."

But there was nothing else to talk about. They stood in contemplative silence, taking in the details of the last piece of their world they would ever experience.

Chapter Twenty-Six

For obvious reasons, the Gamma recruits had never heard themselves referred to as such. Understanding they were Gamma would beg questions relating to Beta that were better left unanswered. Early the next morning, hours before sunrise, most recruits were too tired or distracted with their own thoughts to notice as two techs complained at the breakfast buffet about the ungodly hour of the Gamma window.

Jayson was thankful the transfer was so early in the morning. Getting up, having some food, and verifying the contents of his pack accounted for most of his time. He wouldn't have to spend his day waiting for something to happen while getting increasingly nervous the whole time. In fact, he barely had time to process anything before he found himself in the chamber arranging his cart into place at the end of the snaking line behind his colleagues. Despite the close quarters, everyone seemed isolated in their own world of thought, and there was very little chatter to compete with the clucking of the chickens being loaded onto his cart.

Above them, the control room was buzzing with activity, and there were far more techs than the previous day, along with others who appeared to be observers. Among them, Jayson recognized Admiral Daniels. He was standing with a woman Jayson had seen before and a man in a Navy uniform he had not. They surveyed the scene below somberly, as if feeling the same mix of anxiety and excitement as the recruits who were about to step into the unknown.

A few techs wandered the test chamber, double-checking the loads on the carts and offering last-minute adjustments to the fit of people's backpacks. Another tech lifted boxes marked with Aiden and Samaira's names onto the pedestals on either side of the top of the ramp to the elevated walkway. Amid the excitement, Jayson felt the sudden need to urinate. He'd been advised to use the bathroom before leaving, and had done so several times. It was just nerves, he realized, pushing the discomfort to the back of his mind.

Over the loudspeaker, someone directed the techs to leave the room in preparation for the power sequence. Then, Richard addressed the team from his position in the control room above.

"Okay, everybody. This is it. Just a few more minutes, and we're going to do everything as perfectly as we did in practice. I'll be here giving you guidance the whole time."

The recruits shifted around nervously, fidgeting with their straps and buckles or offering themselves whispered incantations for courage. Jayson stared at his feet, unconsciously gripping and releasing the handles of his cart while he tried vainly not to think about what was happening.

A growing hum filled the room and seemed to be coming from everywhere. Jayson started feeling like he might throw up. The sensation quickly passed when movement from the inner rings on the two-piece apparatus caught his attention. They started spinning in opposite directions. The mockup hadn't done that—nor had it emitted mesmerizing, glowing wave interference patterns like the ones now dancing in front of him. Once they appeared to have reached full speed, another noise—like the whine of a servo motor—accompanied the slight axial movement of the nearest ring.

"Here we go," came Richard's encouraging voice over the loudspeaker.

It was immediately followed by the countdown's soft, now familiar voice. At zero, Ted's foot fell onto the first emerging row of green lights, and he advanced forward. Jen trailed immediately after, followed by the security team members pushing their carts at a perfectly consistent pace. Aiden and Samaira didn't bother trying to help. The fit, well-trained soldiers had everything under control. There were a few gasps of surprise as the standing wave emerged, swallowing Ted in a flash of light. Unfazed, the team continued steadily, their advance punctuated by additional flashes as each one vanished in succession.

Aiden and Samaira readied themselves for action and reached down in unison as Herman, the first researcher, pushed his load onto the ramp. The well-choreographed effort to bring him to the top went just as perfectly as it had in recent practices. He was immediately behind the cart in front and keeping pace. Samaira and Aiden readied themselves for the next cart as Luping passed by carrying a hardened plastic box. Once more, it went exactly as planned.

The snaking queue advanced steadily forward as Richard cheered them enthusiastically from above. The researchers displayed bravery and resolve equal to that of the security team, walking steadfastly into the portal; just as they had in countless rehearsals.

Finally, it was Jayson's turn to mount the ramp with his load of equipment and comically clucking chickens. Aiden and Samaira grabbed the supplemental handles and assisted him to the top. The spacing was perfect, as was his pace. He felt a strange detachment that allowed him to keep moving forward without fear or reluctance.

Samaira and Aiden both turned to retrieve their cargo—hardened cases sitting on the pedestals behind them. Then, they faced one another at the far end of the raised platform, and Samaira offered a gentle smile. Aiden nodded back and waited for her to fall in behind Jayson. She didn't. She stood, transfixed, looking into his eyes.

"Samaira," he urged. "Go!"

Richard chimed in from overhead. "Go! Go! Go!"

Jayson turned around to see what was causing the commotion just as Samaira nodded at Aiden and took a step towards him. Instead of turning down the ramp, she lunged at him, using all of her strength to push the container in her hands against him. Taken by surprise, he lost his balance and fell backward, landing seated on the pedestal. She took another step towards him and pushed her foot against the plastic container he was still trying desperately to hold on to. Aiden, the box, and the pedestal crashed to the concrete floor beside the walkway.

"What the hell are you doing?" yelled Jayson.

"Just turn around and go!" she called as she raced up from behind to close the gap.

Jayson stared at her in bewilderment.

"Go! Just fucking go!" she commanded again.

He'd never seen her in such a frenzied state, and certainly never heard her curse before. Whatever was happening, there was no time to process it, and he instinctively submitted to his trust in her. He turned around and sped up just enough to close the gap in front of him before resuming the proper pace and vanishing into a flash of light.

"No, no, no!" screamed Richard over the loudspeaker. "What the fuck?"

Aiden had landed on his backpack, cushioning the fall and allowing him to react quickly to the unexpected attack. He leaped to his feet and grabbed the plastic box from the floor. Tucking it under his left arm, he bypassed the ramp and jumped straight back onto the platform.

"Get in there!" ordered Richard.

Aiden got to his feet and started running full speed towards the aperture. The lights beneath his feet were red, but the moving green zone ahead was within reach. Samaira, glancing backward, resisted the urge to speed away from him. She adjusted pace and disappeared just as Aiden arrived at the portal entrance with the very last row of green lights. A final flash erupted from the portal as he vanished. The waves dissipated, and the humming stopped. There was a slight noise from the decelerating rings as a light mist fell slowly to the ground.

***

While the test chamber reverted to a state of calm silence, the same could not be said for the control room. Chaos erupted as it became clear things had not gone to plan. Technicians called out to one another for numbers and status, and Dr. Akindele was tapping furiously on his keyboard as he examined the information on the monitor in front of him.

"What in God's name did we just witness, Richard?" demanded Rebecca Steinman.

"I don't know," he replied, "but it looks like he made it through."

"How do we get confirmation on that?" demanded Admiral Daniels.

"Jimi!" called Richard. "What the hell happened?"

"I won't answer to that—"

"Nobody fucking cares, Jimi. Just tell us he made it through."

"We're still compiling the numbers, Richard. Be patient."

"What the fuck was she thinking?" Richard demanded of nobody in particular.

"You're the one who's supposed to know the answer to that, aren't you?" reminded Rebecca.

"We knew she might be a wildcard, but Aiden had her under control."

"Evidently not."

"Well, he's going to be pissed now," assured Richard. "He'll deal with her."

"If he made it," she qualified.

"He's not here. Where the fuck else would he be?"

"Analysis is complete," called Dr. Akindele without looking up from his screen.

"Well?" demanded Richard.

"We have a discrepancy in the mass transfer. Fifteen hundred thousandths of a percent short of completion."

"Give us numbers that make sense, Jimi."

"Approximately one hundred and fifty grams—for those of us with an understanding of third-grade mathematics."

Richard breathed a sigh of relief.

"That's nothing."

"Evenly distributed across the transfer? Yes, it could be inconsequential," agreed Akindele. "Unfortunately, it was not."

"What are you saying?"

"The loss occurred entirely in the final few tenths of a second."

"Bring up the replay," demanded Richard. "I want to see it in slow motion."

Rebecca, Admiral Daniels, and Captain Ibarra followed Richard to a large monitor mounted to the back wall of the control room. Dr. Akindele queued up the replay and walked over to join them. He tapped the screen to start the playback and slowed it down to just a few frames per second as Aiden rushed up behind Samaira. Then, he pulled up a second window and placed it beside the video.

"This red line," explained Akindele, "is the maximum mass transfer rate. These overlaid bars represent the actual rate, synchronized to the video."

The bars approached but did not exceed the limit line as Samaira vanished. Two frames later, Aiden broke the aperture plane as the transfer rate shot higher and immediately hit the limit line.

"Now we are exceeding the maximum. During these few frames, we did not transfer all of the mass passing through."

"Rewind a few frames and slow it down," demanded Rebecca.

Akindele dragged the indicator on the play bar back a tiny amount and lowered the playback speed. They examined every movement as Aiden entered the portal.

"There," said Daniels as he pointed to the box tucked under Aiden's left arm. "He's pulling it forward as part of his running motion."

"The angle is wrong," complained Richard. "Get us the side view so we can see what's happening here."

Akindele toggled to a camera view ninety degrees to the walkway, directly in line with the aperture.

"Shit," observed Richard. "See how he's leaning in and pulling the package forward as he enters?"

"I see it," confirmed Rebecca. "His head is going through just as he pulls the box forward—and that's where we max out on the rate."

"So we're losing what here? A quarter of a pound?" asked Daniels. "That's not much."

"If I were to remove a quarter of a pound randomly from your head, I don't think you'd say it wasn't much," chided Akindele.

"There's the package too," protested the admiral. "Some of the loss is coming from there, right?"

The others were less optimistic.

"Play it all the way through," directed Rebecca.

They continued through the final tenth of a second at slow speed and watched in horror as two distinct clouds of mist formed around the box and Aiden's vanishing head.

"Assuming that mist is what I think it is," prefaced Ibarra, "I'd say his head is accounting for at least a third of the loss."

"Looks about right," agreed Richard with dismay. "Any chance he's okay?"

"I am not a biologist," replied Akindele, "but I doubt he's feeling well right now."

Richard looked down at the floor and exhaled deeply. "Jesus Christ."

"The admiral and I are going to give Anton an update on the situation," advised Rebecca. "Don't go far."

***

The pale, cranberry predawn light slowly eased the veil of darkness from Pai'Olu'Olu Point. Standing alone outside of Fusion B, watching wisps of smoke rise from the second destroyed capacitor, Richard wondered what his recruits might be doing now. He laughed to himself at the abstract nature of 'now.' Relative to his own timeline, they'd already been dead for nearly a thousand years. Deep in thought, he didn't notice Dr. Akindele approaching.

"It's been quite an interesting morning, Richard," he observed.

Startled, Richard turned around to issue a warning.

"I'm not in the mood to talk to you, Jimi."

Akindele smiled.

"I've realized I should not be so upset when you call me Jimi. I should embrace it."

"Why?"

"Because it's all you have, Richard. Calling me Jimi when you know I hate it is the only thing you have over me."

"Fuck off."

"I think you mean to say 'fuck off, Jimi.' Use the name all you want, Richard. You have my permission."

He glared at the arrogant physicist, but said nothing.

"We should leave these capacitors here as a kind of modern art installation when all of this is converted back to parkland," continued Akindele. "Abject Failure, by Dr. Richard Vandergroot. It has a nice ring to it, no?"

"Fuck off—and don't make me say it again."

"I think I will," he agreed. "It's time for me to focus on Delta now. I wonder if you'll be doing the same."

Akindele walked back to Fusion B, leaving Richard to stew. His opportunity for further reflection didn't last long. Shortly after Akindele parted, Rebecca called out as she approached with the admiral.

"I have excellent news from Anton," she said with a smile. "You're getting a promotion, Richard."

"What?"

"You're in charge of Delta."

"I'm already in charge of Delta," he replied.

"Let me rephrase," she offered. "You're leading Delta—alongside Captain Ibarra."

"What?" he demanded again.

"You lost control of Samaira, and we have no idea how that's going to play out. All we know for sure is that it will play out over a few hundred years, and we'll need to get back on course. That's your job now."

"Aiden wasn't the only one," protested Richard. "We've got the admiral's entire team and Olena to keep things on track."

"We've lost confidence in the plan, Richard. You've been barely hanging on for a couple of months now—and today, you dropped the ball."

"I can't do Delta," he protested. "I'm confirmed for Epsilon."

"It's decided. You're Delta, or you're nothing."

Richard closed his eyes and frowned. He knew there was no point in appealing to Rebecca. Kamaras was his only hope.

***

On the other side of Honolulu, the same pale morning light filtered into Andrew's room through the east-facing windows. Ordinarily, it would have been too early for him to get up, but he'd set his alarm early in anticipation of reading Samaira's letter before breakfast. He'd briefly considered opening it immediately after their lunch together, but couldn't bring himself to break her trust.

His phone buzzed and blared a short, repeated melody from the table across the room, where he placed it every night to foil his habit of hitting the snooze option a half-dozen times before finally getting up. That wasn't a risk under the current circumstances. He got up quickly and canceled the alarm before eagerly tearing open the envelope he'd left propped up against the table lamp. He took out a neatly folded piece of lined paper and was surprised to see a handwritten note. Almost nobody did that anymore—at least nobody under the age of fifty. Eagerly, he started reading.

He had to stop and re-read sections of the note multiple times to make sure he understood it. When he finished, he reread the whole thing from start to finish and then sat for several minutes in dazed contemplation. It wasn't until his second alarm went off that he shook off his paralysis and decided what to do.

Andrew silenced his phone and walked into the bathroom. Glancing up from the note, he surveyed himself in the mirror as if asking his reflection what to do. If he showed it to Richard, he'd undoubtedly be rewarded for his loyalty. Or would he be silenced for knowing too much? At least now he understood why it was handwritten. Samaira couldn't risk having any electronic echoes of the message discovered on the system, and depending on what he was going to do, Andrew couldn't keep any evidence, either. His reflection made a decision and nodded back at him with resolve. He tore the letter into pieces, tossed them into the toilet, and flushed.

Chapter Twenty-Seven

HAD ANYONE BEEN ON the volcanic promontory at the southeast tip of O'ahu at 8:17 AM, on April 26, 1174, of the yet-to-be-invented Gregorian calendar, they'd have thought they were witnessing the arrival of gods. Ted Park and Jen Jefferson emerged into the newly divergent reality in a flash of blueish-white light and immediately sidestepped a few meters apart before sweeping their weapons across opposing one-hundred-and-eighty-degree arcs to verify the area was secure.

As they scanned for threats, the first of the equipment-laden carts materialized on the grassy clearing, with Josh pushing it along steadily. He counted off the paces to get clear of those arriving behind him.

"We've got some shrubs here on the left," he called out to de la Cruz behind him. "Add another ten paces before you push off to the side."

"Got it," she confirmed before relaying the message back.

Josh parked his load and hurried back to update the new arrivals on the obstacles, and redirect them as necessary.

"Get back here to take the carts from the geeks when they start coming out," he directed the team. "Jen, Park—keep 'em out of the way. I don't want anyone getting run over."

When Herman arrived, two security team members grabbed his cart by the front handles, and Jen pulled him off to the side.

"Some unexpected obstacles," she explained. "Stay out of the way while we get everything clear."

"Yeah," nodded Herman, as he looked around in amazement.

Luping was next through, carrying a plastic container. Park took hold of her backpack straps and gently pulled her aside.

"Keep going a few paces and make some room," directed Ted.

The arrivals continued steadily, and the security team kept the carts arranged as neatly as the scattered shrubs would allow. To either side of the flashing portal of light, boxes and backpacks piled up amid a growing crowd of disoriented researchers.

When Jayson arrived with the final cart, he was looking back over his shoulder instead of straight ahead. Even as he felt someone pull the cart away from him and Jen tugged him gently aside, he kept staring back—oblivious of her instructions. Next, Samaira emerged with a look of terror on her face. Before Park could pull her aside, Aiden crashed through the portal and knocked her over.

"Fuck," yelled Park. "Careful, man!"

Aiden jumped to his feet and started yelling. There were no discernable words—just horrible, guttural screaming. He walked around aimlessly, flailing his arms and knocking people to the ground. Rivulets of blood began running from his eyes, nose, and ears. The sight and sound were horrifying; like he was suffering some kind of demonic possession.

Members of the security team rushed forward to contain him, but their attempts only seemed to enrage him further. Finally, three of them managed to entrap him in a bear hug to stop the flailing, but his screams continued unabated—punctuated only by brief pauses as he caught his breath.

"Medic! We need a fucking medic!" screamed Park.

Josh and Martina were already running toward the disturbing scene.

"Get him on the ground," ordered Martina.

Careful not to let him escape, they lowered Aiden down, pinning his shoulders and legs. He started convulsing, and pinkish foam streamed from the corners of his mouth.

"He's seizing," yelled Josh. "Somebody find the fucking medical supplies and get me some diazepam!"

"Do we even have any?" asked Martina frantically.

Josh didn't answer. The convulsions stopped, and Aiden lay motionless on the ground. Those restraining him sensed the struggle was over and released their hold.

"He's gone," said Josh in disbelief.

Olena stared down in silence, her mouth agape.

"What the fuck just happened?" demanded Ted.

Samaira had sought out Jayson during the short period of chaos and stood beside him. She squeezed his hand tightly.

"I think he tripped," she offered weakly. "I heard him cursing behind me, and he was on the ground when I looked back."

"How could a trip cause this?" wondered Josh aloud.

"I don't know," said Samaira, as she started crying. "He yelled at me to turn around and keep going. So I did. I don't know what happened after that."

Jayson said nothing. He was replaying the scene in his mind while listening to Samaira's explanation. Nothing made sense. He knew she was lying, but was convinced her tears were real. It was all too much to process. He resolved to say nothing about the incident until he had a chance to talk to her alone.

***

Olena paced backed-and-forth in a state of agitation, rebuffing any attempt to offer comfort. Josh had pulled a tarp from a cart and enlisted a few others to help him carry Aiden's body off to the side of the clearing and cover it until they decided what to do. In contrast to the shocked researchers, the former Navy recruits could compartmentalize—silently mourning their colleague while maintaining their focus on the mission. Jen kept the team on task while Josh inspected the body.

"Top priorities are recon and securing a source of fresh water," she reminded them. "We all have our assignments."

"Aiden just died," protested Kailani. "Shouldn't we do something?"

"We will," assured Jen. "But if we don't stay focused, he won't be the only one dying. The security team will divide up to do our recon, and Park will stay here with de la Cruz to make sure you're safe."

"And what about Aiden?"

245

"Jayson. Get a couple of shovels and find someone to help you dig a grave. We'll say a few words for him tonight, and then move out in the morning. The rest of you can set up camp."

She called on the security team to form up into their recon groups, signaling there would be no further debate. Jayson went to find the cart with his tools, and Samaira followed a few paces behind to steal some time with him apart from the others.

"I need to talk to you, Jayson," she said in a hushed voice.

He ignored her until they were among the carts, out of earshot, before turning around to respond.

"I saw everything, Samaira," he started.

Tears streamed down her face as she tried to speak.

"I killed him, Jayson. I—I murdered him," she stuttered.

"Yeah, I know. But why?"

"I wasn't trying to hurt him. I just wanted him to miss the window. Why did he have to get back up so fast?"

"Why the hell would you want him to miss the window? I don't get it."

"Because he lied, Jayson. He wasn't who he said he was."

"What are you talking about?" he demanded.

"There's more going on here than we know—and he was part of it."

"What do you mean?"

"I don't know, exactly," she admitted. "But whatever is happening is not good."

They paused as Zaina approached to grab a couple of lightweight tents and some rations from the cart next to them.

"I'm sorry about Aiden," she said to Samaira. "I know you two were close."

Samaira wiped away a tear.

"Thanks."

"You're going to have to explain this to me," said Jayson as Zaina walked away.

"The whole thing has been weird from the beginning," she explained. "Everything we've been told, all the information we've been fed—it's all been aimed at manipulating us. I thought I was too smart to fall for any of it, and just wanted to see where it was going. Then Aiden happened."

"What do you mean, 'Aiden happened?'"

"He was perfect. Everything was perfect—like he was tailor-made for me."

"And that's a bad thing?"

"It's because he *was* tailor-made for me. He was as much of a lie as everything else."

"He seemed fine to me."

"It was little things. The day Richard was berating you in front of everyone at the review, I went to his office. Aiden was there and—," she paused. "It's hard to explain."

"Did he do something? Say something?"

"When he left, he kind of saluted Richard without actually doing it. I know that doesn't make sense."

"Not really," agreed Jayson.

"It was his body language," she continued. "It had every aspect of being dismissed by a superior officer except the actual salute."

"It's gotta be more than that."

"The same thing happened when Admiral Daniels came on stage the day they told us about the plan."

"I was right there with you. If Aiden saluted, I'd have noticed."

"I know it sounds crazy, Jayson, but you have to trust me. I know how to read people."

"You killed someone based on their body language? Jesus Christ!"

"I didn't mean to kill him, Jayson. This is tearing me up."

He could see by the desperation in her eyes she was earnest.

"I believe you. That you didn't mean to hurt him, I mean."

"I need you to trust me," she pleaded. "I was trying to do the right thing."

"If you thought we were being lied to, then why did you stay at the Center? Why not just leave?"

"Hitarthi," she answered simply.

"What about her?"

"At first, I stuck around just to see if I could figure out the truth and then tell the rest of you what was going on."

"What's that got to do with Hitarthi?"

"I think something terrible happened to her when she backed out."

"She's fine. We had a group hit going, and everything."

"We were talking to a bot."

"Come on," he pleaded. "Now you're sounding paranoid. This is nuts."

"I know I'm right," she insisted. "If I tried to back out or warn anyone, we could all be dead right now."

"Listen, Samaira, this has been a really weird couple of months. I get it if you're a bit messed up. So am I."

"Please!" she whispered as more people approached for supplies to set up camp. "I need you right now."

"You have me. I'm here," he promised. "I'm just asking you to calm down a bit and take some time to think through this. You're not making any sense, and I'm worried about you. You're the last person I expected to see break down like this."

She closed her eyes and began sobbing again. Parth and Luping set down the boxes they were carrying to embrace her.

"We're going to be okay," promised Luping. "I'm so sorry about Aiden."

Jayson felt the need to distance himself from her, and used the distraction as an opportunity to retrieve a shovel. He'd used some of the extra weight allotment to put a carbon fiber handle on one of them instead of just bringing the heads. It was a last-minute decision that was now paying off, although in an admittedly grim and unexpected way.

Without another word to Samaira, he walked off to find an appropriate place at the perimeter of the clearing to dig a shallow grave for Aiden. Jayson couldn't shake his doubts about her mental state. What if she'd decided *he* was the one acting strange instead of Aiden? Would he be the one lying dead on the ground? What if she was having doubts about him now? What was she capable of? Watching over her while doing his job at the same time was going to be difficult, and he wrestled with the idea of telling someone he could trust that Samaira was losing it.

He found a spot that seemed promising, and absent-mindedly drove the shovelhead into the ground a few times to gauge the softness of the soil. He had no idea what made for a good gravesite, but imagined himself as good a choice as anyone for the job. Jen approached at a light jog just as he began digging in earnest.

"Hey, Jayson. You got this? I'm about to head out on recon."

"Yeah," he said. "I'm good."

"I saw you talking with Samaira," she added. "Is everything okay?"

"Not really. She's pretty messed up."

"Yeah. I can imagine. You think she'll be alright?"

"I hope so."

"It's hard for all of us," she sympathized. "I can't imagine how much worse it is for her."

It was true, he realized, that Aiden's death was going to impact everyone. He decided not to further burden Jen with his concerns about Samaira. If she continued to spiral, he'd re-evaluate the need to seek guidance from the rest of the team.

"We should be fine here," he asserted. "Go find us some water. And if you find anything that looks edible, bring it back here so I can take a look at it before you decide to take a bite."

"You got it," she assured him before jogging back to her recon team.

***

After setting up a basic camp, there wasn't much for the recruits to do. Some passed the time talking quietly in small groups while others wandered the small, secure area on the point. As advised by the security team, they were careful not to crest any of the surrounding ridges to potentially expose their position to native inhabitants. Samaira had isolated herself in a tent, and the others eventually decided to leave her alone after repeated inquires had been met by gentle assurances she just needed some time by herself.

The recon teams regrouped around mid-afternoon, as planned, on the beach at Hanauma Bay, where they could debrief privately among themselves before returning to camp. The last team to arrive, led by former Petty Officer Third Class Isiah O'Neal, had the job of probing the beaches and inlets to the west for signs of inhabitants.

"What's the word, O'Neal?" asked Josh.

"Not a thing from here to Diamond Head."

"You got that far?"

"Didn't make it all the way, but close enough to know there's nobody between here and there."

"Any sign there *were* any people?"

"Humans have definitely worked the big fishpond," said Farzin Khan, the aquaculture expert. "It's nothing like the modern version, but there've been some manmade improvizations there."

"How long ago?"

He shook his head. "Hard to say, but nothing recent."

"What about you guys?" asked O'Neal.

"We did five or six clicks up the coast and climbed to the top of Makapu'U point to get a look down at Waimanalo. Nobody there—and no sign there ever was."

"Jen?"

"We checked out four of the nearby valleys. No signs of inhabitants," she confirmed.

"Water?"

"Lots of it. We're packing as much as we can, and picked up some stuff that looks edible, too."

"Your boyfriend is going to be happy about that," laughed Josh.

"Screw you, asshole," she replied with a sarcastic smile.

"You guys ever meet Van Zijl?" asked O'Neal.

"Not me," answered Josh.

The others shook their heads as well.

"He must have been one bad-ass motherfucker," said O'Neal with admiration. "We should have found something by now."

"It's definitely looking good," agreed Josh. "If it's like this all the way to Honolulu, it's safe to say we can move phase two up by at least a year."

"Hell yeah! Looks like I don't have to worry about losing my sea legs," said O'Neal, rubbing his hands together.

"Don't get too carried away," cautioned Jen. "It's a big island."

"No sweat. We'll have it covered in no time," he assured.

***

The recon teams returned to camp to find everyone in a somber mood. The tragic, horrifying events of that morning, followed by a long period of inaction, were having a predictable impact on everyone. Hearing that they'd be able to pack up and start moving the following day was a welcome relief. They could say goodbye to Aiden, and then leave behind the landscape that would forever remind them of his anguished screams.

A short, moving funeral ceremony started as the sun touched the top of the ridge just west of the grassy clearing. Six security team members served as pallbearers, carrying the tarpaulin-wrapped body to the grave Jayson had prepared. He, Olena, and Samaira all offered a few words of remembrance.

When there were no words left to say, most of the team drifted back over to the collection of tents to prepare for dinner. Those closest to Aiden stayed behind to watch as the pallbearers unwrapped his body and removed his boots and outer layer of clothing before lowering him gently into the grave by his arms and legs. There was an unspoken understanding the clothing and tarp were too valuable to leave behind. Aiden would have forgiven the desecration, and accepted the need to balance their sorrow with such practicality. For Jayson and Samaira, the thought of watching him disappear under a pile of dirt was too much. Of the researchers, only Olena remained behind to bear witness.

Shortly after the final orange glimmer of sunset faded from the sky, Jen approached Jayson as he sat illuminated by the flickering light of a camp stove.

"I have something that might cheer you up," she said with a smile.

"What's that?"

She proudly produced a few coconuts and some sweet potatoes for him to examine.

"You didn't find any signs of inhabitants?" he asked.

"No. Why?"

"These are uala tubers."

"So?"

"They're common on the O'ahu we knew, but they're not native."

"Hmm. Maybe we have to rethink that."

"Maybe," he allowed, wrinkling his brow.

"The real question is; how do they taste?"

"Only one way to find out," he declared with a smile. "Did you bring back any extra water?"

"Lots. It's not going to be an issue," she assured.

"All right, then. Let's cook these up," he replied.

Happy for the distraction, Jayson went to find a pot as Jen pulled out her knife and started peeling. After a while, a small crowd gathered to watch them prepare the sweet potatoes and offer their services to test the island's first native meal.

Chapter Twenty-Eight

WHILE THE ISOLATED CLEARING was a safe place to arrive on the island, it was not an ideal place to stay. There was no easy access to fresh water or to the bounty of the sea, and they were exposed to the elements on all sides. Their plan was to set up a temporary settlement somewhere closer to Honolulu harbor, where they could take advantage of natural shelter and gradually convert it into something permanent.

After learning the true nature of their mission while still at the Center, Serge and Parth had started modeling their city and its sources of food and water for several centuries into the future. They resolved to establish settlements on the slopes of craters and mountains to minimize the waste of arable land and avoid the potentially devastating impact of a tsunami. There were no reliable historical records, and they believed being on the low ground closer to shore was too great a risk.

The core of their civilization would be Punchbowl Crater; an extinct volcano just a couple of kilometers inland from the natural harbor. The outer-facing slopes would serve as a place to build housing for the first several generations, while the inside of the bowl could secure their priceless technology and critical supplies.

Moving the team and all of their equipment from the rocky point to their new home took almost three full weeks of steady effort. The large-wheeled carts were unloaded and repacked with half their original cargo to make the twenty-kilometer trek across the uneven ground easier. The majority of the team then shared the burden of pushing and pulling the loads overland while two of the admiral's team members stayed behind to guard the supplies left behind for a second trip.

Though difficult, the journey was also one of beauty and wonder. Every morning, scouts moved out ahead of the steadily advancing column of people and equipment to survey potential barriers along the route and look for signs of inhabitants. Those following behind passed the time noting familiar landmarks and marveling at the unspoiled surroundings. The air seemed sweeter and fresher, and the natural beauty far surpassed modern O'ahu.

When their path allowed them a view of the open ocean, they caught occasional glimpses of humpback whales coming up for air and sometimes playfully breaching above the surface of the water. The carefree creatures had yet to experience the pursuit of relentless whalers or the perpetual, deafening noise of maritime traffic. Onshore, the background noise of civilization was notable for its absence.

Close to sundown every day—or a little earlier, if the trek had been particularly brutal—the recruits set up their small tents and gathered around a campfire for an evening meal with friendly conversation. Exhausted from the daily efforts, they never lasted long into the night before going to their tents to rest up for another day of exertion.

When they finally reached their destination at the southern base of Punchbowl Crater, the scouts continued pushing westward, exploring the shoreline around Pearl Harbor and as far as Ewa Beach. Still, they found nothing significant to report. A small team remained at the crater with minimal security to survey the land and begin setting up a more permanent camp while the rest returned to Pai'Olu'Olu Point with empty carts to gather up the equipment and personnel they'd left behind.

When everything was finally consolidated into one location, the security teams organized to do a full sweep of the coastline and low plains to see if there was anything they'd missed. Three groups fanned out across the island while the rest continued establishing the nascent city of Honolulu. There was some discussion of naming their new home in honor of their fallen comrade, but they chose instead to bestow the name Aiden Point upon the place where they'd buried him. The returning scouts confirmed the Island was a blank slate with no residents to object to the name.

Soon after arriving, Zaina began overseeing the first wind turbine installation high on the crater rim above them to take advantage of the steady, unobstructed trade winds. The highest priority for Parth was establishing water and sewer infra-structure to unburden the team of the time-consuming tasks of maintaining water supplies and sanitation. Jayson, naturally, spent his time establishing crops on the flat, fertile land on either side of the nearby Nu'uanu Stream he'd cleared with a series of controlled fires. The team had modest enough needs for the time being to allow for manual irrigation, but eventually, they'd need to develop a better system, and the stream would serve as a perfect source.

With everyone seemingly focused on the essential elements of civilization, there was a great deal of surprise among the scientists when Josh announced the security team had resolved to build a ship a full year ahead of the agreed schedule so they could assess the threat from neighboring islands. Going off-island to secure mineral resources would eventually become necessary, but it seemed premature when there was still so much foundational work to do. A dozen sets of strong hands diverted to another task would be a blow to their efforts to build a city.

Despite several attempts to negotiate shared priorities, the security team began felling large koa trees from the mountainside to the north before hauling them to the harbor. There, they insisted on setting up the second of their two wind turbines to power the tools they needed to work the trees into timbers. Instead of one team with one set of priorities, it became increasingly clear there were two separate teams on the island.

The exception was Farzin Khan. Among the admiral's recruits, he alone seemed focused on efforts for the greater good. Initially, he'd spent many hours a day casting his nets in the harbor to catch enough food for everyone. After a month, and with help from Riyoko, he'd been able to build up enough of a stockpile of dry fish so he could invest time in finding a more efficient way to provide for the team.

He turned his attention to a large inlet to the east, on the far side of Diamond Head. With a bit of effort, he hoped to turn it into a productive fishpond that would require less sustained effort than his daily net fishing. He and Riyoko packed a cart with tools, supplies, and a small tent before heading off together with a promise to report on the project's viability as soon as possible.

***

They centered the settlement at Punchbowl Crater on a large, flat area at the base of the southern slope. Though trees obscured the sightline to Honolulu Harbor itself, the elevation was high enough to offer a view of the ocean just beyond. On the site, a large, tree-lined, cobblestone plaza full of flower gardens, tables, and benches, dominated by an ornate fountain, would eventually serve as a sanctuary, and place to enjoy a cup of coffee or a meal. Two months after their arrival, it was still just a campsite; a steadily evolving mix of scattered lightweight tents and semi-permanent wooden structures.

The largest of these structures, covered with a patchwork of tarpaulins, served as a communal dining room and evening gathering place where people came to chat, play cards, or crowd in around a tablet screen to watch some of the innumerable movies and television shows in their archives. Jayson and Herman had finished eating dinner there one evening and were sketching out how they might rig up a makeshift brewery using surplus medical and cooking equipment to supplement the natural resources of the island. Next to them, a small group played a homemade version of Monopoly featuring hand-carved pieces and properties modeled after Serge's future vision of Honolulu.

Things had been strange between Samaira and Jayson since their arrival. Though still friendly with one another, the mutual trust they'd shared was damaged, and their interactions had become more superficial. Of course, everyone recognized the difference in Samaira—but to them, it was easily explained by Aiden's gruesome death. Jayson alone carried the burden of understanding the deeper tragedy. As with most of his burdens, he coped by ignoring it. As he sat reading an article on fermenting, Samaira plopped down next to Herman and examined the drawing on his tablet.

"What are you guys working on?" she asked.

"We're trying to figure out the best way to brew up a batch of ale with the equipment and resources we have here," explained Herman.

"It's mostly him," clarified Jayson. "I'm just here for optics. If it's a bad sign to drink alone, what does it say about someone who designs an entire brewery by himself?"

"How are you doing, Samaira?" asked Herman. "Are you sleeping any better?"

"I'm getting there," she said unconvincingly. "I just came over to talk to Jayson for a minute. Do you mind me interrupting?"

"Not at all. I'll leave you two alone."

"No need. I think I'd rather go for a walk. How about you, Jayson?"

"Yeah. Alright," he agreed.

They stepped outside with time to enjoy the last minutes of daylight, walking the now well-worn path towards the harbor.

"So, how are you really sleeping?" he asked.

"Not great," she admitted. "You?"

"Fine. Good enough."

"How are things going with Jen?"

"It's been cooling off since we got here. She spends most of her time working on the boat, and I hardly ever see her," he lamented, pointing down to the harbor where work lights were flickering to life.

The work on the ship usually extended a couple of hours past sundown and only concluded when the dying shoreline winds and spent batteries meant there was no more power for the lights and tools.

"I'm not surprised things have been cooling off," said Samaira.

"Thanks for the confidence boost," he replied with a snort.

"I didn't mean that, Jayson. I mean the whole thing was pretty convenient in the first place."

"What are you talking about?"

"You had doubts about the mission, and then suddenly she's all over you."

"Were you jealous?"

"Of course not," she replied. "I had Aiden."

"But did you? Really? I mean, that's when you were acting all weird and started having doubts about him."

"I'm just saying it was convenient you suddenly had more of a reason to say yes to the mission."

"You're seeing what you want to see. You're still trying to make it okay—what happened to Aiden."

"It's never going to be okay, Jayson," she retorted. "No matter what's really going on, I didn't mean to hurt him."

"I'm sorry. That came out wrong. What I meant to say is you're still trying to be right."

"I am right," she insisted. "And the only reason you don't see it is because you don't want to."

"What are you talking about?"

"If something's going on, it means you have to deal with it. You're a lot happier pretending it doesn't exist, so you don't have to do anything at all."

"Or maybe you're paranoid. Did you consider that?"

"Yes. A lot," she admitted. "Every night when I close my eyes and watch him die again, I wonder if I was being crazy. Then, I go through everything in my mind and come back to the same conclusion. Something bad is going on, and he was part of it."

"Jesus Christ."

"Answer a question for me, Jayson. Honestly."

"Okay."

"If you had to describe the perfect woman from your fantasies, what would she look like? What would she be like?"

"That's a bit more personal than I was expecting."

"Okay," she conceded. "You don't have to tell me. Just be honest with yourself."

"Alright," he allowed.

"What happens when the door closes and you're alone with her? What does she do to you? What does she let you do to her?"

"Jesus, Samaira."

"I don't need you to tell me," she reminded him. "Just think about the things you've always wanted but would never ask for. Is that what Jen gave you?"

"Why? Is that what Aiden gave you?" he shot back to avoid answering.

"I'm kicking myself for not seeing it right away," she said. "I thought I was a step ahead of them the whole time, and they got me with some bullshit about a little boy who saved a disabled puppy. I was so mad and hurt. The worst part was that I had to keep playing along."

"So, if it really was all just a bunch of bullshit, then why are we here?"

"I told you before—I don't know yet," admitted Samaira, "but I'm going to find out, and I need your help."

"Jesus Christ," he lamented again.

"Doesn't this concern you even a little bit?" she asked as she motioned to the construction scene in front of them. "That's got to be at least a hundred feet long. A bit much for checking out nearby islands, don't you think?"

"It's a bit of overkill, maybe."

"The trade and transport we have in our plan don't require anything of that size for another century. How do you explain it?"

"I haven't thought much about it," he admitted.

"Their plan is not the same as ours, Jayson. Can you at least admit that?"

"Yeah," he agreed.

"All I'm asking you to do is look for things that don't seem right, and have a critical mind."

He looked at the ground and exhaled.

"What is it?" she asked.

"There is one thing that seems strange."

"What?" she demanded.

"The uala—the sweet potatoes. They shouldn't have been here before inhabitation."

"Could they have gotten here some other way?"

"Maybe," he said with a shrug. "But on the way here, I saw a patch that looked like it had been cultivated at some point. It seemed too—regular."

"So you're saying we're not the first ones here?"

"It doesn't look like it to me."

"And you figured this out by looking at some potatoes?"

"I know it seems stupid, but yeah."

"It doesn't seem stupid at all," replied Samaira. "This is your area of expertise, so I trust you. I wish you'd have the same faith in me."

"I'm sorry, Samaira. It's not as easy as that."

"Why not?"

"Potatoes are tangible. Your gut feeling isn't."

"Just because you can't read body language, it doesn't mean it's not real," she protested.

"I guess so," he allowed. "It's just always been such a mystery to me. It's hard to imagine you can get anything reliable out of it."

"I can prove it."

"How?"

"Just now, we were talking about Jen—and what went on behind closed doors," she started.

"Yeah?"

"I can tell by how you reacted that I was right. It was a little too perfect, and you'd rather not talk about what you guys did."

"You're right. I'd rather not talk about it," he confirmed.

"Just like I'm right about Aiden," she continued. "And just like I knew Richard was telling half-truths every time he opened his mouth."

Jayson was silent for a while. The last of the sunlight faded from the sky as they watched the admiral's recruits continue their efforts under the illumination of work lights set on bamboo poles. Their project wasn't obviously a ship yet, but the dimensions were revealing themselves to be on a scale larger than he'd imagined.

"It's getting dark," he said finally. "We should head back."

"What's bothering you, Jayson?"

"If we really are here because of a lie," he hesitated, "it means I've thrown my life away before it even started."

"Look up at that sky," she countered. "Have you ever seen anything like it?"

"I never even imagined anything like it," he replied.

He marveled at the jagged, purple-white ribbon of the Milky Way fringed by bright, irregular bands of orange and yellow light. On either side, stars too numerous to count filled the sky.

"We were manipulated into coming here by a lie," she conceded, "but I wouldn't go back even if I could."

"It is beautiful," he agreed. "Beyond what I'd hoped for."

"It doesn't have to be a waste of our lives," she implored. "If they can change the rules on us, we can do the same to them."

"You seem to forget who has the guns."

"I'm not talking about taking them on directly, or anything stupid like that."

"Then what?"

"I don't know, but we have time on our side to figure it out. We need to tell people what's going on, and then figure out what to do together."

"*We* don't even know what's going on," he protested. "It's too soon. If time is really on our side, there's no need to rush into making everyone think we're crazy."

"You're right," she agreed. "I'm just glad to have you back."

"I'm not there yet," he warned. "I've got to let all of this sink in."

Chapter Twenty-Nine

WITH THEIR DAYS OCCUPIED by efforts to build a new civilization from nothing, the weeks and months passed quickly for the recruits. Although the work was hard, it was gratifying to lay the foundations of an enduring legacy. The knowledge the families they left behind would one day walk among their works fueled their dedication to the efforts and made them seem less burdensome. Though some were skilled in trades, it was the first real exposure to sustained manual labor for many. For them, the calluses, scrapes, blisters, and bruises they now earned daily were a source of great pride.

They envisioned a grand capitol building dominating the north side of the plaza, flanked by two-and-three-story buildings, with shops and restaurants at street level and apartments above. It would be a center of commerce and government for their civilization, much like the Forum of ancient Rome. On either side of the capitol, twin staircases would lead to the hillside neighborhoods ringing the outside of the crater wall. After converging below the rim, they would crest the peak to reveal a hidden, verdant oasis of parks and gardens on the university grounds. The home of their secret technology, it would be off-limits to all but their most trusted allies.

Dreams of the future aside, the recruits focused on what they could do with the technology and workforce at hand. Concrete of lime, volcanic ash, and aggregates formed the hillside foundations and lower portions of the walls of the primary structures. They made the upper part of the walls and the roof trusses from koa wood, as would be the case for several generations before they could produce stronger concrete at scale.

They prioritized the construction of a medical clinic where the capitol would one day loom impressively over the plaza, and complemented it with a large common building on the south side to serve as both a cafeteria and a meeting place. Communal bathrooms with running water were also essential for public health, and the plumbing to support them was nearly complete along the plaza's eastern edge. The infrastructure plan allowed for future private bathrooms and running water in the residences, but that would have to wait to find its way to the top of the list.

In an effort to alleviate the growing resentment towards the security team and speed up the development of the community, Josh had instructed them to provide a steady supply of koa lumber to the Punchbowl building site while felling trees for their ship. Though not ideal from the perspective of the rest of the recruits, it helped keep relations between the two groups civil, and sped the construction of the main buildings at least somewhat. The efforts of Farzin Khan to develop the fishpond, providing a steady flow of much-needed protein, continued to be the strongest bond preventing the recruits from devolving into two completely separate factions.

Jayson's fields were already supplementing Farzin's efforts by providing an impressive variety of vegetables for the team, and the fruit trees that would provide longer-term payoff were doing well. Much to the delight of the others, he also established some coffee and cacao at the nearby Kaaikahi spring. Although the elevation probably wasn't perfect, it was the best he could do for the time being without it becoming too much of a distraction at the expense of his other crops.

He wasn't completely alone in his efforts. From the start, Olena had made sure he had help when he needed it by splitting her time between the farm and construction work. Having been greatly affected by the death of Aiden, she appreciated the relative solitude of agriculture. More recently, Samaira offered regular help with watering, weeding, and harvesting. She spent her days occupied by manual labor, and her sleepless nights working on cultural models and simulations to uncover how best to provide the guardrails that would keep their society on track. She desperately wanted to simulate surreptitious methods to thwart Kamaras's secret plans, but she was still missing too many pieces of the puzzle and feared the resulting data trail could betray her suspicions.

The security team offered no helpful insight into their motives beyond a standard response they could accelerate access to mineral resources and that it was prudent to be able to assess and deter nearby threats. The nature of those threats—ones that apparently could not be deterred by a dozen trained soldiers with automatic weapons—was not something they disclosed. With the hull construction complete, part of the team worked on scraping and sealing the seams with coconut husk cordage and waterproof resin derived from eucalyptus trees. Others moved on to laying the decking.

***

As gratifying as it was to bring their settlement to life, the most exciting news arrived in the form of a different kind of creation. Not unexpectedly, Riyoko announced she was pregnant. She and Farzin had been splitting their time between Honolulu and the fishpond, often spending several nights a week away together. Their small campsite on the far side of Diamond Head had become a second home, and a romantic hideaway where they could enjoy one another's company.

Dr. Kitzinger, the obstetrician, and Melinda Littleton, the childhood development and education specialist, were especially excited. On the evening of the announcement, they gathered in enthusiastic conversation with the rest of the team in the quickly evolving communal building.

"Have you thought of any names yet?" asked Melinda.

"We haven't thought of a girl's name yet, but Farzin likes Aiden for a boy."

"We'll know soon if you need a girl's name," said Dr. Kitzinger. "There's a portable ultrasound among the equipment we brought along."

"That's a relief," replied Riyoko. "It's a bit nerve-wracking to know I'll be going through this without being able to go to a hospital."

"We've equipped ourselves with the priority of safely delivering healthy babies," he assured with a smile.

"I'm not trying to pressure anyone," hinted Melinda to the others, "but I hope my first class will have more than one student."

There were some chuckles and awkward glances around the room.

"Listen, Riyoko," started the doctor with a more serious tone. "I want you to start taking some precautions—just to be on the safe side. I know I don't need to tell you anything about nutrition, but I'd like you to consider staying closer to the clinic when Farzin is at the fishpond."

"Is that really necessary?" she asked.

"Not necessary," he conceded, "but I want to be close by if anything happens—or even if you just have a few doubts and want to talk."

"I think I'd rather stay with my routine for as long as possible. It'll help me not to overthink things and go crazy."

"Our network doesn't cover you over there. If something happens, it could take a long time for me to find out."

"We could extend the network," offered Matteus. "We brought enough line-of-sight equipment to cover most of the south coast. That way, she could hit you any time she wants to talk about something."

Dr. Kitzinger considered it for a moment.

"It's not too much effort?"

"No more than a day to hike up to the peak at Diamond Head and install it," he assured. "Then it connects with our main network here via the relay up top. It's something we want to do eventually, anyway."

"I'll give you a hand," offered Jayson. "I'd love to see what kind of stuff is growing over there."

"Sure. It'll be nice to have some company," agreed Matteus.

"I really appreciate it, guys," said Riyoko. "I'm not ready to be treated like I'm made of glass."

"And I appreciate the opportunity to do something techy for a change," laughed Matteus. "It'll give my hands a chance to recover from the blisters."

***

Two days later, with gear and supplies in their packs, Jayson and Matteus set out for Diamond Head. Without heavily laden carts to manage, it would be considerably easier than their trek across the island six months earlier, when they'd made their way from the isolated point to Honolulu Harbor. Through their biweekly trips, Farzin and Riyoko had worn an easy-to-follow path from Punchbowl to the fishpond, passing within a kilometer of Diamond Head. They'd stay on it as long as possible before diverging southward into the dense vegetation towards the slopes of the massive extinct volcano.

The night before, at dinner, they'd done a review of a three-dimensional map on one of the nearly indestructible solid-state laptops provided among the gear. In the absence of the modern-day paths, they felt the easiest thing to do would be to climb the lower northern side and then perhaps follow the rim around to the highest peak. If that turned out to be more treacherous than it appeared on the map, they could always descend the relatively gentle inner slopes and try the approach from a different angle. The lack of an exact plan didn't bother either of them. They viewed it as an opportunity for adventure rather than a task to be executed as efficiently as possible.

Two hours into the hike, they passed an offshoot of the trail leading towards Waikiki Beach, where some of their more adventurous colleagues had taught themselves to surf. Shortly beyond that, at the point closest to Diamond Head, the pair broke from the trail into the denser trees and vegetation. They used a compass to stay on a southerly heading, hacking away at head-level vines and branches to create visual markers to follow home later that day. The trail-breaking effort was exhausting. It wasn't long before they opted to break for lunch in the shade of a kukui tree, and Jayson decided to learn more about his quiet colleague.

"This is kind of mind-blowing, isn't it?" he asked, looking around.

"It is," agreed Matteus. "I often dream none of this is real, and I'm sure I'll wake up back at the Center."

"And when you don't? Are you disappointed?"

"There were times during the first few months when I was," he admitted. "But now that I'm used to it, I'm grateful."

"Is there anything you miss?"

"Besides being able to talk to my family? I would say it's the food."

"Me too," agreed Jayson. "I've never been a big fan of seafood."

"The variety from the farm has helped a lot lately," said Matteus.

"And we'll be able to rotate some chicken onto the menu soon," replied Jayson.

"That'll be nice."

"What food do you miss the most?"

"Frikadeller. Danish meatballs," he said. "You?"

"Cheese. Any kind of cheese would be a godsend."

"Too bad you can't milk the chickens," laughed Matteus.

"I'm desperate enough that I might just try. Anything else you miss besides food?"

"Anonymity," he replied after a moment of consideration.

"What do you mean?"

"Sometimes I would just sit out at some café by myself and watch the people passing by. I would imagine what their lives were like, where they were going, that sort of thing. Here I know who everyone is and exactly what their lives are like."

"Hmm. I never thought of that."

"It's not the most important thing. Just something I miss."

"Would you go back if you could?"

Matteus took a deep breath and exhaled before answering.

"No. The future here may be uncertain, but it's better than having no future at all."

"Yeah. Same here," agreed Jayson, before changing the subject. "Figure we can get this thing set up today?"

"I hope so. If we finish early enough, we might even get back to camp before dark."

"You think so?"

"If we keep moving, yeah." Matteus stood up and grabbed his pack. Slinging it over his shoulder, he started up the crater wall. "Let's go."

Though the outside of the crater was steep, the small trees and shrubs that blanketed the slope made the climb relatively easy. They hauled themselves up using the limbs and branches for leverage. At the summit of the lower northern edge, they paused to survey the journey ahead.

"The rim looks pretty dodgy from here," observed Jayson.

"Yeah," replied Matteus. "It looked easier on the screen."

"Seems like a pretty easy stroll to the base of the southern wall if we go through the crater."

"And then what?"

"We find a way up once we get there."

"Alright," agreed Matteus. "Let's do it."

They ambled down the gentler inside slopes of the crater to the plateau below, and crossed over to the southern side in under fifteen minutes. The vegetation was low and sparse, offering no significant obstacle to their progress.

"It doesn't look too bad if we approach from the east," offered Matteus when they arrived at the base.

Jayson nodded in contemplation—as if he had some kind of relevant experience to validate the observation.

"Yeah. It looks pretty good to me."

They started up the slope, picking their way carefully forward in a more-or-less direct path to the summit. Twenty minutes into the climb, they found themselves hemmed in by bare walls a bit too steep to attempt comfortably without climbing gear. After backtracking, they tried an arcing approach—bringing them further around to the south. Although nearly as steep, this time, the walls were dotted with enough firmly rooted shrubs to allow them to pull themselves up.

They crested the ridge about a hundred meters short of the peak and took in the view.

"Unbelievable," remarked Matteus.

"Yep," agreed Jayson, huffing from the exertion of the climb. "It sure is."

"The rest of the way looks pretty straightforward, as long as we're careful with our footing."

"Seems easy enough. Just need a minute to catch my breath."

They advanced carefully along the ridgeline, finally arriving at the highest point of the crater wall. There they stood in silent awe, taking in the panoramic view of unspoiled beauty. It was a clear day, and Moloka'i was visible in the distance.

"Look! Over there!" exclaimed Jayson, breaking the silence.

Matteus spun around to see where he was pointing. They had arrived at the island near the end of the humpback whale migration season and were witnessing the beginning of another. Not far offshore, a steady series of spouts erupted from the water. So numerous were the whales, there was hardly a minute when a geyser of moist air wasn't erupting from some place or another within the pod.

Distracted by the surrounding beauty, the two men seemed for a while to forget the purpose of their hike. Matteus was the first to return his thoughts to the task at hand, prompting Jayson out of his reverie.

"We should get started if we want to make sure we're not trying to climb down in the dark."

"Yeah," agreed Jayson. "That doesn't sound like fun."

They both set down their packs and started pulling out equipment.

"How does this work?" asked Jayson.

"Line-of-sight is the easiest way to span large distances in a network when you don't have wires or satellites," explained Matteus. "As the name implies, the relays just need to see one another. Then they can provide a signal to any laptops and tablets with a clear view of the relay locations."

"Cool. So Riyoko will be able to video chat with Dr. Kitzinger?"

"Exactly. We just need to set this up where it can see the other relay at the top of Punchbowl, and the fishpond."

"This spot definitely works," observed Jayson with a glance in both directions. "What's next?"

"We'll need to make a few holes. A one-inch diameter for the post and three half-inch diameter for the tension wire lags."

Matteus used some small stones to mark the location of the holes, while Jayson readied the battery-powered drill and appropriate bits. He started on the center hole first.

"How deep?"

"Let's do about six inches for the center and three inches for the others."

Jayson made quick work of the holes in the soft, volcanic rock while Matteus assembled the equipment and fastened sections of hollow titanium rod for the central post. When erected, the relay was about level with Matteus' eyes. Just above, oriented in a southerly direction, sat a small solar panel. Both were wired to a battery pack seated at the base. Next, he screwed three titanium lags into the remaining holes, and attached them to the central pole with lightweight monofilament wire to steady the assembly against the wind.

"There we go," he asserted with satisfaction after fine-tuning the tension in each wire.

"That's it?" asked Jayson.

"We still need to test the signal and establish the network connection. Sometimes that's the hard part."

"Just sometimes?"

"It's all up to the will of the tech gods."

He started fiddling with the device, becoming increasingly concerned as it failed to come to life. Double-checking each connection and referring to a diagram on his tablet, he came to a realization and shook his head.

"Shit."

"What's wrong?"

"I'm an idiot. That's what's wrong," said Matteus. "I should have charged the battery before we left so we could connect right away. We'll need to let the solar panel do its thing for a while."

"How long?"

"A couple of hours at the most. Sorry."

"No need to be sorry," assured Jayson. "There are worse places to be stuck."

"Yeah," agreed Matteus with a laugh. "I suppose there are."

"Snack?" suggested Jayson.

"What do you have?"

"The usual," he said with a frown, "but I'm working on it. We're going to have trail mix with nuts, dried fruit, and dark chocolate someday."

"And bits of dried fish thrown in, no doubt," said Matteus.

"You're Scandinavian. Gross seafood should be right up your alley."

"You're thinking of lutefisk. Norwegians eat that shit, not Danes."

"Okay, then. No fish of any kind in the trail mix."

"Agreed. And yes, I'll take a snack while we're waiting."

They picked away at their meals, wandering the ridge to admire the varying perspectives on the landscape below. A nearby secondary peak, a bit lower than where they'd installed the network equipment, offered a large, flat area to rest comfortably while they passed the time.

"This might be my new favorite place on the island," said Jayson as they sat down together.

"It's peaceful," agreed Matteus. "Watching the waves without hearing them is putting me in a kind of trance. Like meditation."

"Ever thought of learning to surf?" asked Jayson as he watched a perfect wave breaking silently off the shoreline of Waikiki beach below them.

Matteus didn't answer. Something jutting from the ground under his right palm had caught his attention.

"What the hell?" he said as he picked up a small, irregular object and dusted it off.

"What's that?" asked Jayson.

"I don't know," replied Matteus as he continued cleaning it.

Removing the layer of dust and dirt revealed it to be a metallic, olive green object with engraved lettering.

"Model 3H Cammenga," he read. "Compass, magnetic."

"What?" wondered Jayson, furrowing his brow.

"There's something on the other side, too. Controlled disposal required. Do not open—and there's a radiation symbol below that."

"On a compass? Why? And how did it get here?"

"No idea. Maybe someone from the security team was up here and dropped it?"

Matteus slid open the latch, which offered considerable resistance because of its state, and opened it to reveal the compass face.

"It works. But it looks like it's been here a while. Maybe this was part of the security team sweep when we first arrived."

"Maybe," allowed Matteus as he slipped it into his pocket. "We can ask them when we get back."

"Yeah," said Jayson doubtfully.

"Let's see if the battery's got enough power to establish the connection so we can get down before it gets dangerous."

They stood and returned carefully along the ridge to the relay. There, Matteus was able to draw enough power to initiate the connection and use his tablet to verify it was on the network.

"We're on," he announced. "Riyoko should be able to connect with anyone back at Punchbowl."

He pulled the compass out of his pocket and held it out in front of his raised tablet.

"What are you doing?" asked Jayson.

"Going to post a picture of this to a group hit to see who lost it."

"No!" exclaimed Jayson with more intensity than he intended.

Matteus regarded him with puzzlement.

"What's wrong?"

"Don't do that yet, please."

"Why not?"

"It's hard to explain," replied Jayson.

"Try me."

Jayson took a moment to consider his options before relenting. He and Samaira would eventually need to trust someone, and Matteus, with his knowledge of the systems, would be a potent ally—if he wasn't a wolf in sheep's clothing.

"We think there might be more going on here than we realize—Samaira and me."

"No shit," replied Matteus. "The security team went off to start their own private party almost as soon as we got here."

"And why do you think they did that?"

"I have no idea," he admitted. "You guys?"

"No," conceded Jayson. "But if it was anything we'd be okay with, I assume it wouldn't be such a secret."

"So why not just ask? Why not confront them?"

"Because whatever it is, Samaira is convinced it's important enough to kill for."

"What? Why?"

"She thinks they killed Hitarthi because she tried to get out, and says we were communicating with a bot before we left."

Jayson explained Samaira's reasoning in detail as Matteus listened intently.

"And Aiden?" he asked. "Was he killed too?"

"It's definitely part of the story," replied Jayson. "Samaira's going to need to tell you more about that."

"How does the compass play into it?"

"I'm not sure it does. Things about the island make me think we're not the first ones here. The compass could prove it."

"Gamma," said Matteus with sudden realization.

"What?"

"The morning we left—at breakfast—I heard someone refer to the operation as Gamma."

"What does that mean?"

"It's the third letter of the Greek alphabet," explained Matteus. "It implies the existence of an Alpha and Beta."

"Shit," said Jayson. "ETA to Beta site. I heard the helicopter pilot say that on the trip over to the point. What do you think it means?"

"I know what it means for software development," replied Matteus, "but I don't know that it's relevant here."

"What's that?"

"Well, Alpha proves out the code before you get any actual end-users. Beta is the first time you try it out for real with a limited audience."

"So maybe the description fits. I mean, it's no secret they're sending people after us—so why not before, too?"

"If that's the case, why not tell us? Make us feel better about not being guinea pigs?"

"I have a bad feeling I know the answer to that," replied Jayson. "It's because we wouldn't approve of the mission."

"What are you thinking?"

"Remember how Kailani was convinced there should be native settlements here by now?"

"Oh shit," realized Matteus.

"Are we done here? Can we still make it back to Punchbowl before it gets too dark?"

"Still three hours to sunset," said Matteus with a glance at the clock on his tablet. "We should make it if we push harder than we did this morning, but it'll be close."

"I'm fine with that," confirmed Jayson. "Let's get moving. We can stop for the night somewhere along the way if we need to."

Chapter Thirty

TOURISTS DISCOVERED THE BODY washed ashore at Kahala Beach park early that morning. According to the coroner, the cause of death was accidental drowning. It wasn't too hard for police to piece together what had happened once they found the identification among the personal effects tucked into a waterproof fanny pack around the victim's waist. Credit card records showed Hitarthi Srinivasan had rented a sea kayak from a place at a nearby marina, and her last social media post had shown her standing next to it with a huge smile on her face. Another visitor to the island had either overestimated her own skill or underestimated the danger of heading out alone on the deceptively calm-looking water.

Days earlier, Andrew had bought a burner phone and created a fake Hitz-It account to verify one of the most disturbing assertions Samaira had made in her note. Posing as a friend from school, he reached out to Hitarthi to see if she wanted to catch up. Her vague yet affirming responses to their fictional relationship confirmed a horrifying truth—her account had been taken over by a bot.

Once a day, he left the Center grounds and drove until he was confident he was pinging a cell tower far from their reach. It was the only time he ever powered on the burner to converse with the bot or type Hitarthi's name into a search engine. Finally, he got the news he was dreading. She was dead.

After reading the note from Samaira, he'd been able to surreptitiously recover the deleted videos meant to inform the families of the Gamma recruits of the true nature of their sacrifice. He hadn't watched them all, but he'd seen enough to understand Samaira was telling the truth. Despite the unnerving discovery, he held out hope she was wrong about Hitarthi and the lengths to which Kamaras would go to protect his secrets. Unfortunately, the news reports proved she wasn't.

Running, he realized, was probably a mistake. There wasn't likely a place on the planet beyond Kamaras's reach. If the highest levels of the navy were among his secret allies, then surely the local police—or anyone else he might turn to—could be part of the conspiracy as well. There was another reason not to run. Samaira had expressed her resolve to overcome whatever plans Kamaras might have, and implored Andrew to look for opportunities to help.

When Richard requested to meet with him late in the afternoon after the police had discovered the body, Andrew couldn't help but feel distressed. Perhaps he hadn't been careful enough covering his tracks, and they were onto him. He wiped his sweaty palms on his shirt and exhaled deeply as the elevator doors shut behind him for the ascent to the top floor. A benefit of always looking nervous and uncomfortable, he realized, was that perhaps Richard wouldn't be able to sense his heightened agitation.

Arriving in the outer office, he found his boss sitting alone, drumming his fingers on his desk as he stared at his laptop monitor. Andrew knocked gently on the glass door of the inner office to get his attention. Richard looked up and waved him inside.

"You wanted to see me, sir?"

"Yes, Andrew," he confirmed. "There's been so much going on I haven't had time to talk about your change of plans."

"Change of plans?"

"I know you were disappointed when Matteus started taking over some of your duties. The truth is, we realized you're too valuable for what we had planned originally."

"And what was that?"

"Of course, you realize a large part of the team has now departed to take part in an important experiment, correct?"

"It's pretty hard to miss. Being ferried off in helicopters was pretty dramatic—but the fact all of their network traffic is gone is what has me most curious. What's going on?"

"They've finally got their chance to do something about our mission here at the Center," replied Richard. "And soon, it will be your turn."

"What do you mean?" asked Andrew.

"You're going to look over their data personally to validate the results. I need someone familiar with the systems who knows how to deal with a lot of data."

"So I'm going to see them? Samaira and the others?" he asked.

"Not exactly. But you will see all of the data that she and the others have been generating. We have to do it subtly to avoid contaminating the process."

"How much data are we talking about?"

"Pick a reasonable number and multiply it by a thousand," he said with a smile.

"Uh, okay. I'm also going to need a list of the hardware they've got. If it's all our stuff, I can pretty much back-door any of it without anyone noticing."

"I'll send you the list," confirmed Richard. "Thanks for coming by."

Andrew took the hint and rose with a nod.

"Any time, sir," he replied, and quickly left.

He fought the urge to run as he headed down the corridor to the elevator. Pressing the button, he realized he was concentrating so hard on looking composed he'd forgotten to breathe. He took a few deep, calming breaths and stepped into the elevator, hoping he could make it back to his office without hyperventilating.

Samaira had asked him to look for opportunities to help, and now it seemed it might come sooner than he'd hoped. He'd imagined himself arriving in the beautiful, clean, new world described by the recruits in their videos after having helped somehow clandestinely overcome whatever Kamaras had planned for them. Now he would be part of some sooner intermediate effort to make sure Kamaras got exactly what he wanted. Something must have tipped Samaira's hand if Richard was so concerned about getting into their systems and finding out what she and the others were doing. There was little choice, Andrew realized, other than to go along with Richard's plan to wait for his chance.

***

Jayson and Matteus arrived back at Punchbowl after sunset. A cloudless night, the moon and stars provided more than enough light to allow them to safely complete the last part of their journey along the well-worn path. Most of the researchers were finished eating, and had settled into their regular routine of winding down with conversation, games, and other forms of distraction when the pair entered the common building. They weren't alone in arriving late. With the last of their battery power spent, some security team members were just getting seated with heaping plates of food.

Samaira and Kailani, empty plates pushed aside, were at one of the rough-hewn tables in the quickly evolving building having a quiet conversation. Jayson and Matteus joined them.

"That was a long trip," observed Samaira with a smile.

She'd slowly started regaining her usual disposition after the traumatic arrival, and ensuing period of intense guilt.

"And eventful," replied Jayson.

"Do tell," she invited, raising her eyebrows.

He glanced at Kailani, deciding on the spot she was the least likely of anyone to be a potential Aiden—a hidden agent of Kamaras.

"Matteus found something interesting," he said in a hushed voice.

"What is it?"

"A compass. It was at the top of Diamond Head."

Matteus retrieved it from his pocket and placed it on the table.

"It looks like it's been there a long time," he elaborated. "The latch is really stiff."

"A long time? Like, longer than us?" asked Samaira.

"We can't be sure," replied Jayson.

"What's going on?" interjected Kailani.

Jayson looked at Samaira with a deferential shrug.

"We've sensed for a while there's more going on than we know," she explained. "We just don't know *what*."

"What's that compass got to do with it?"

"No idea," admitted Jayson.

"Let me look it up," suggested Matteus. "We basically brought all of the data on the planet with us when we came here."

He took out his tablet and entered the model number into the Hitz-It search engine.

"Here we go. This is it—the Cammenga Tritium Compass."

Matteus placed the tablet on the table and spun it to face Samaira. She quickly scanned the description, scrolling down the page.

"Okay. Decaying tritium illuminates the compass without batteries for twelve to fifteen years. Does it still glow?"

"I'm not sure. It's too bright in here to tell," said Matteus.

He tried cupping it in his hands to block out the light, but too much was still getting in.

"Let's go outside and see," suggested Kailani.

Jayson glanced up nervously at the table of dining security team members.

"Yeah. Nothing suspicious about all of us whispering and slinking outside together," he said. "Give it to me. I'll go out and take a look."

He pocketed the compass and walked casually outside and around a corner into the shadow of the moonlight. There, against the side of the building, he took it out and flipped the latch. The sound of approaching footsteps echoed in the plaza, freezing him in place before he could open it fully. He expected to hear the footfalls disappear into the common building, but they stopped right behind him.

"What are you doing, Jayson?"

It was Jen. His heart raced with sudden panic.

"Nothing," he replied, his voice cracking.

"Really? What are you holding onto there?"

"My dick," he tried in desperation. "I'm taking a piss."

"Haven't seen that in a while," she said playfully as she leaned over his shoulder. He shoved the compass quickly down the front of his pants.

"I can't do it with you watching," he complained.

"You shouldn't be doing it here at all," she admonished, pointing at a building less than two hundred meters away on the adjacent side of the plaza. "The latrine is right there."

"You're right. I'm being lazy."

"And kind of gross."

"Yeah. And kind of gross," he agreed as he turned to face her.

"Listen. We should catch up sometime," she said.

"Uh, yeah. We should."

For what seemed like a minute, but was probably only a few seconds, she regarded him in silence.

"Alright then. I'm going to get some dinner before there's nothing left," she said finally.

"Okay. See you later."

His heart was pounding in his chest, and he felt like he was going to be sick. He couldn't understand how anyone could be an undercover agent; living every moment the way he'd just lived the last two minutes. At least she'd given him a good idea. In one of the bathroom's private stalls, he'd have complete darkness, and a lot more privacy to examine the compass.

Minutes later, he returned to the table in the corner where the others were waiting.

"That took a long time," remarked Matteus, reaching out for the compass.

"I don't think you want it now," cautioned Jayson.

"Why not?"

"Jen almost caught me with it. I had to stuff it in my pants."

"Jesus Christ," said Matteus, withdrawing his hand with an exaggerated look of disgust.

"Can we get to the important part, please?" implored Samaira.

Jayson shook his head and frowned.

"Nothing. Completely dark."

"Maybe someone on the security team just brought an old compass," offered Kailani.

"If these things have expiry dates, it must be marked somewhere," realized Samaira.

"Let me check," offered Matteus, returning to the tablet.

He typed in the search term and navigated a few pages before finding it.

"The manufacture date can be found on the inside of the compass cover next to the sight wire," he read verbatim. "Here's a picture of what it looks like."

Jayson opened the compass and oriented it the same way as the picture on the tablet. A thin layer of dirt obscured the surface on either side of the sight wire slot.

He stuck a finger behind the bottom of his t-shirt and used the fabric to clean the spot where the date should be.

"January 2017," he said with dismay. "It should still be lit up pretty brightly."

"What does that mean?" asked Kailani.

"It means our mission isn't the first one," said Matteus.

"It also means they didn't want us to know about the first mission," added Jayson.

"Why not?"

"Because we wouldn't approve of the objective," said Samaira.

Jayson nodded in solemn agreement.

"Exactly."

"Oh my God!" realized Kailani. "No wonder there was nobody here. They murdered them!"

"Keep your voice down!" whispered Jayson.

"We should go over there and tell them the game is over," she replied, rising from her stool.

"No!" hissed Jayson, grabbing her by the shoulder to restrain her. "They have the guns and the training. They decide the rules of the game."

"And they're dangerous, Kailani," added Samaira. "We have to be careful."

"So, tell me what we're going to do," she demanded. "There's no way we can let this go."

"We won't," promised Jayson. "But let's be smart about it."

"How?"

"We learn as much as we can, gather our allies, and wait for our opportunities," declared Samaira.

Kailani, still scowling in the direction of the security team, nodded grudgingly.

"Matteus," continued Samaira, "see what you can find snooping through the system."

"Sure," he agreed immediately. He'd gone even paler than usual as he digested the meaning of his accidental discovery.

"I think we need to cut this short," said Jayson nervously. "We've been here a long time conducting a pretty serious-looking debate. This isn't exactly a private place to talk."

"Any ideas on a better place?" asked Kailani.

"I think it's time to work on an irrigation system for the fields. I could use some help tomorrow."

"I'll be there," assured Matteus.

"Me too," agreed Kailani.

Samaira nodded, and Jayson returned the compass to his pocket, having implicitly declared ownership through the now intimate nature of his relationship with it.

***

The following morning, armed with picks and shovels, they headed upstream of the fields toward the small pool at the base of Kapena Falls.

"I found something else last night," whispered Jayson as soon as they cleared the settlement.

"What is it?" asked Matteus.

"Another inscription on the other side of the sight wire. It says, 'May you always find your way home to me. Love, Lenora.'"

"What do you make of that?" asked Kailani.

"Not a clue," admitted Jayson.

"Holy shit!" said Matteus, stopping in his tracks. "Are you sure it says Lenora?"

"Yeah. Why?"

"Just before we left, there were a bunch of stories about the disappearance of Ron Van Zeal—the survivalist."

"Is that the guy who drinks his own piss?" asked Jayson.

"Oh my God!" said Kailani with a look of revulsion. "That's disgusting."

"I didn't say it wasn't," shrugged Jayson. "Just looking for some context here."

"No." replied Matteus, "You're thinking of that British SAS guy. This one's South African."

"How many of these stupid shows are there?"

"Can we get to the point?" pleaded Kailani.

"Sorry," said Jayson.

"Anyway," said Matteus, undeterred, "it was a huge story. This Van Zeal guy's wife, Lenora, was killed in an accident. When police didn't charge the suspects, they turned up dead. Not just dead, but totally brutalized. You guys never heard about this?"

"Celebrity gossip isn't really my thing," said Samaira.

Kailani was shaking her head, and Jayson shrugged.

"Somehow, he gets acquitted," continued Matteus. "But everyone knows he did it—or at least he made it happen."

"What's this got to do with the compass?"

"Lenora isn't that common a name, is it? And Van Zeal disappeared not long before we did."

Jayson regarded Matteus with skepticism.

"I've gotten used to accepting some pretty incredible shit over the last year, but I have to draw the line somewhere. You *really* think Anton Kamaras hired a B-list celebrity survivalist to clear Oahu of its native inhabitants for his time-traveling scientists?"

"That is one hell of a Madlib," offered Samaira without a hint of a smile.

"It doesn't matter who it was," said Kailani, raising her arms in frustration as she started walking again.

The others followed.

"Did you find anything in the system last night, Matteus?" asked Samaira.

"Yes. Quite a lot, actually. Andrew showed me some backdoors he programmed into the bridge to the quantum OS."

"That fits," observed Jayson. "Andrew couldn't do something clever without bragging about it."

"I was able to get into the security team manifest to see what they brought," continued Matteus.

"Weapons?" asked Kailani.

"Not as much as I expected. I mean, for sure, they brought enough to fight a small war—automatic weapons, sniper rifles, handguns, handheld surface-to-surface missiles, and all of that."

"What else?"

"Lots of stuff for the ship. Titanium fasteners, sections of carbon-fiber mast, resin and hardener to assemble them, sails, various titanium or composite brackets and fittings, and so on."

"Why would they be so secretive about that?" wondered Kailani.

"I'm not sure."

"Whatever the reason," declared Samaira, "it's not an accident. I'm sure they've simulated our reaction to different approaches, and figured this was the best way to get what they want."

"Are we so predictable?" asked Jayson. "Do you think they already know everything we're thinking?"

"They don't know about the compass," reminded Matteus. "All it takes is one bad variable to throw off the most carefully designed simulation."

"What else did you find?" asked Samaira.

"Not much else. There are two boxes of stuff labeled 'Scylla' and two more labeled 'Charybdis.' Another couple of larger containers are listed as 'Imperial Jade.' They must all be code for something."

"Anything else?"

"Nothing that jumped out as being odd or significant on the manifest, but there is some segregated data I can't access. It's encrypted at the file level—not the system level. Otherwise, I'd be able to read it no problem."

"Who *can* read it?"

"There's no way to know. Whoever knows the password, I guess," said Matteus. "But there is something odd with the user groups that control access to the file system itself."

"What?" demanded Jayson.

"Everyone here has a unique user name that's allocated to a user group. The names are first initial, followed by last name—up to eight characters. There's forty of us here. Uh, thirty-nine," he realized. "Sorry, Samaira."

"Don't worry about it," she assured him. "Keep going."

"There are forty-two user names—two of which look like random alphanumeric codes assigned to the security team group."

"What does that mean?" asked Jayson.

"I can't be sure, but I think it means a couple of our fellow researchers are not who they appear to be."

"Who?"

"I don't know. Only one account has been active since we arrived—and only sporadically."

"Oh, thank God," said Samaira, exhaling deeply.

"Huh? You think it's a good thing we can't trust each other?"

"Sorry. No, of course not. I was just relieved to hear only one account has been active."

"Why?"

Samaira looked at Jayson and raised an eyebrow. He shrugged in reply, indicating the decision of whether or not to elaborate was hers alone. She took a deep breath."

"I think I know why only one of the accounts has been active."

She told the story of her evolving suspicions about Aiden and the dark secret behind Hitarthi's disappearance that prevented her from warning any of the others. They listened with rapt attention, pausing in their work, as she explained her reasoning.

"I guess, in a way, we're kind of lucky with what happened to Aiden," said Kailani.

Samaira, already emotional from recounting the story, began to cry.

"I'm sorry, Samaira. I didn't mean to sound callous. I know he meant a lot to you."

"It's not that," she managed between sobs. "It wasn't luck. I killed him."

She recounted the moment-by-moment events on the elevated walkway on the morning of their departure—how she'd planned what to do and came to the last-minute decision to go forward with it. Finally, she explained how it had all gone terribly wrong when Aiden managed to get back up and make a run for the portal. By the end of her story, she was shaking and sobbing uncontrollably.

"You must think I'm a monster," she concluded.

Kailani dropped her shovel and embraced her.

"You're a hero, Samaira."

"What?"

"We might not know everything," she continued, "but there's no way to deny what they've done here. I knew it should have been populated with a thriving culture when we arrived, but there's nothing. They were wiped out to make room for us."

"I agree," said Jayson. "There was a culture here before us. The signs are subtle, but they're there."

"This might be a different reality, but those were still my people," said Kailani with a sneer. "If Aiden knew they were being murdered, then I'm glad he's dead."

"The worst part is that it might not be over," added Jayson. "I've been thinking about it all night. Why the ship? Why the secrecy? Are they planning to attack the other islands, too?"

"We have to stop them!" realized Kailani.

"How?" asked Matteus.

"If we act rashly, we can't save anyone," cautioned Samaira. "We don't even know who we can trust among our friends."

"Agreed," said Jayson. "We need to figure that out first."

Chapter Thirty-One

Months passed on the island as the two teams continued their disparate efforts. A secret plot to expand the resistance moved slowly forward at the same time. Samaira had devised a series of clever and intricate engagements among the co-conspirators and the rest of the research team, allowing them to seek out allies without exposing their purpose. It was a lengthy process, but necessary for their protection.

Samaira carefully studied the evolution of the interactions to determine when it was safe to bring someone new into the fold. So far, they'd expanded their faction to include Luping, Parth, and Serge. It didn't mean the rest were suspect, just the level of certainty was less than she was comfortable with.

Critically, no aspect of their conspiracy was written down or communicated by unsecured means. The few things they documented, they hid away and encrypted on the system. Matteus had arranged an elaborate security scheme that perhaps even Andrew couldn't untangle, let alone the security team. Nothing in their behavior or system usage showed they had the ability or inclination to root out suspicious files.

What they lacked in computer knowledge, they more than made up for in their shipbuilding skills. The carbon fiber mast was in place, the decking and cabin complete, and it seemed the ship would soon be ready to sail. It was impossible to accept their skill in creating something so impressive in such a short period was accidental. Whatever they were—doctors, engineers, etcetera—they'd also been well trained in the art of shipbuilding.

As the ship neared completion, Kailani became increasingly disheartened. She was desperate for an opportunity to set back their progress, but none materialized. She'd gone as far as suggesting she might sneak out in the middle of the night to set the whole thing on fire. Alarmed, Jayson and Samaira forced her to promise she wouldn't. It was too risky.

To placate Kailani, Samaira agreed to a more aggressive approach in identifying who might be a spy for the security team. She called a team meeting to discuss the establishment of a culture that would outlive them indefinitely. While it was important work that needed attention, the true purpose was to discover if anyone would try to steer them in a direction more sympathetic to the goals of the security team.

She rearranged some tables and benches in the now completed common building to facilitate a discussion, and scheduled it for a time in the late afternoon when members of the security team were least likely to attend. It wasn't likely they would, anyway. They'd long since given up any pretense of participation with the larger community.

Riyoko wasn't in attendance either. Although her closeness with Aiden and her relationship with Farzin made her a person of interest, she wouldn't have come alone. Samaira deliberately chose a day when she'd be at the fishpond. Nevertheless, attendance was robust. All of the expected invitees were there.

"I know you're all familiar with my research on establishing culture," she started after everyone settled down, "but the last time we spoke about it as a group, it was in a very different context. We all had to change our thinking when Richard revealed the true nature of our mission. For most of you, things got a lot harder. I wouldn't say they got easier for me, but the possibilities expanded immensely. We have an opportunity to create a mindset and a way of life for the entire world—not just for ourselves—and we have hundreds of years to do it."

She paused to look for signs of concern, and draw out questions and comments. If none came, her confidants would carry the conversation and eventually say something provocative to induce a reaction in their mole.

"I assume we're not starting with a blank slate here," said Dr. Kitzinger. "What have you come up with so far?"

"I think the objective is obvious," she said. "We want to create a world where development doesn't come at the cost of the environment, so humanity can sustain a high quality of life, in balance with nature, indefinitely. What isn't as obvious is how to get there."

"Surely you have some ideas," he insisted.

"I do," she assured. "But I don't want to eliminate any good ideas by biasing you with my thoughts. We have to get this right—and get started soon, so our ideologies can be adopted into those developing all over the world."

"Creation myths are a foundational element of all cultures," suggested Luping. "Maybe we need to start by considering our own."

"Agreed," said Samaira. "Some aspects of creation myths are nearly universal. We should think about how we can design something with the broadest possible appeal."

"Can't we just tell the truth?" asked Herman. "It would explain our technology and give our warnings about the future more credibility."

"I have thought of that. The risk is the world would see us as invaders, and it could turn everyone against us."

"I don't even think anyone could understand the truth, Herman," added Parth. "I mean, we went through it, and we still don't understand."

"I agree some pieces of the truth could be helpful," said Samaira, "but we need commonality with existing belief systems so what we're offering doesn't seem too alien. Look at the way Christianity spread among the pagans of Europe. Early Christians blended their theology with Pagan holidays and traditions to make it more appealing."

"I have to admit I don't know a lot about Christian traditions," said Parth. "And with such a diverse team, I'm probably not the only one."

"Sure. Take Easter, for example," continued Samaira. "The name comes from Eostre, the goddess of spring. In pagan mythology, she transforms a bird into a rabbit that lays eggs. That's why egg hunts and bunnies are associated with the most important Christian holiday, and just one example of how pagan traditions were co-opted to make Christianity more appealing."

"So we need to do the same thing?" asked Herman.

"I think it would be the most effective way," replied Samaira. "We should consider which beliefs of existing cultures are compatible with our goals, and use the commonality to slowly absorb them—just like the early Christians did."

Sitting next to Dr. Kitzinger, Melinda Littleton looked about nervously before contributing her own thoughts.

"Christianity is already established now in Europe, and we know there is an appetite for it in many other places—even here in Hawai'i. Why not use it as the basis for our culture?"

Kailani's face went red, but she had the sense to stay quiet. She knew she would undermine the intent of the meeting by going off on a rant about colonialism and forced conversion. Jayson noticed her squirming next to him and squeezed her hand in support.

Dr. Kitzinger gave Melinda a sideways glance and frowned.

"There's a lot of questionable history around the so-called 'appetite' for Christianity. Besides, how could an island in the middle of the Pacific—thousands of miles from Jerusalem—have any influence over the development of Christian theology?"

Melinda seemed offended in a way that suggested the two had more than just a casual relationship.

"We could say Jesus was here among us, too—after the resurrection—preaching the sacred duty to keep God's creation clean and beautiful for all of His children," she offered.

"So we're basically Mormons, then? Is that what you're suggesting?" he asked.

"Interdimensional Mormons from the future," added Parth with a laugh.

Even though things were quickly going off the rails, Jayson couldn't help laughing out loud at the mental image of a pair of young men in shirtsleeves and ties stalking the sidewalks of some suburban neighborhood on futuristic hoverbikes. In fact, most of the people in the room were laughing. Melinda and Samaira were notable exceptions. Samaira shot an accusing glance at Parth, who looked sheepishly at the ground in recognition he wasn't helping. Melinda stood up and stomped towards the door with Dr. Kitzinger in pursuit, likely aware their budding relationship was in trouble thanks to his part in subjecting her to such ridicule.

"I think we should do a test by trying to integrate with the natives on nearby islands," called Kailani over the noise of the quickly devolving meeting.

Everyone was immediately silent. Melinda and Dr. Kitzinger froze near the entrance and looked back at her.

"After all, we have a nearly completed ship down at the harbor."

"It's not our ship," said Olena.

"The hell it isn't," replied Kailani, taking a more aggressive approach than agreed. "The work we've done to provide food and shelter benefits everyone—so should the work done on that ship. We should all have a say in how it gets used."

Nobody spoke immediately, but it was clear from the nods around the room Kailani was expressing a widely shared frustration.

"You're right," relented Olena immediately. "I hadn't thought of it that way."

"I like your suggestion, Kailani," said Samaira. "Back at the Center, I could test my theories on a small audience using Hitz-It, and then fine-tune them in real-time based on the reactions. Here, I can only simulate using models developed from modern culture. It's a big risk to rely on them exclusively."

"What are you saying?" asked Olena, furrowing her brow.

"I'm saying we need a test case where we can perfect our methods of influence. The nearby islands are an obvious choice."

"The plan calls for isolation for generations until we're well established and secure. What you're suggesting is too dangerous."

"Perhaps," allowed Samaira. "Either way, we need to consider how we want to define ourselves and how we intend to spread our influence. Let's take the idea of immediate contact off the table for now."

Olena seemed satisfied with the answer, but her posture was stiff and closed. Though the exchange had not been sufficiently damning to expose her definitively as a mole for the security team, it certainly warranted increased scrutiny. Satisfied they'd achieved what they wanted, the co-conspirators backed away from the more provocative suggestions. Instead, they focused on the more fundamental question of the sorts of beliefs they needed to pass down to their children.

***

They avoided gathering too often as an exclusive group so they wouldn't inadvertently isolate themselves from the rest of their colleagues, or arouse suspicion. Following the meeting, Kailani, Matteus, and Serge dined among a group including Zaina, Olena, and a few others. Jayson, Samaira, Luping, and Parth joined Dr. Kitzinger and Melinda. There was still some tension between the two of them, but they seemed to be working it out.

"I'm sorry about earlier, Melinda," started Samaira. "I hope you didn't feel singled out."

"It's not your fault. Maybe the idea was a bit stupid."

"It wasn't stupid," interjected Dr. Kitzinger. "I was stupid."

"Me too," added Parth. "Sorry."

"I think it was very creative," assured Samaira. "It's exactly the kind of idea we can turn into something brilliant."

"I overreacted, though," added the doctor contritely. "It's just—things tend not to work out well for my people when Christians get too excited. The idea of reinforcing their ideology got me a bit defensive."

"Same here," agreed Jayson.

"I grew up in a religious household," explained Melinda. "I'm not a believer myself anymore, but I still find a lot of comfort in the rituals."

"That's normal," said Samaira, "and perfectly understandable. We need to replicate that comfort in our own rituals."

"It's not just Christians, by the way," continued Dr. Kitzinger, sticking to the previous topic. "Muslims, Sikhs, Hindus, and Jews are just as capable of violent zealotry. There's even such a thing as militant Buddhists, for God's sake, if you can imagine such an oxymoron."

"Religion is not the problem," insisted Samaira.

"Then what is?"

"It's us. People. We're the problem."

"What makes you say that?"

"Look at it this way," she explained. "We evolved from primates over millions of years—changing bit-by-bit into what we are now—all while surrounded by dangerous predators and enemies. Then, in a relative instant, we're living in skyscrapers in big cities, launching people into orbit, and doing whatever it was that Dr. Akindele did to get us here. Our mentality hasn't had time to catch up with our technology, and we're now the evolutionary equivalent of an orangutan brandishing a machine gun."

"I never thought of it that way," said the doctor.

"We can't be surprised by the mess we've made of our world with war, genocide, corruption, and the destruction of the environment," she continued. "It would be like bringing a bunch of wild monkeys in tuxedos to a dinner party and then acting surprised when they start throwing feces all over the place."

"Ouch," he remarked, taken aback. "It sounds like you hold humanity in quite a bit of contempt."

"Not at all," she insisted. "In fact, it's quite the opposite."

"How so?"

"If we were created by God, in His image, and what we've done to each other and the planet is the best we can do, then we should be truly ashamed of ourselves. If, on the other hand, we found our way out of the trees to get where we are, then humanity is a marvel."

"A marvel, perhaps, but one that's doomed to self-destruct, if I understand what you're saying."

"Not necessarily," countered Samaira. "Imagine if we could accept being human comes with certain primitive baggage that will undermine us if we're not careful. Our blind spot is only a blind spot if we fail to recognize it. Embracing our falli-bility, second-guessing ourselves, inviting and applauding criticism—these things need to be engrained in our culture if we're to have any hope of getting it right this time. We can't have a world where any critical self-evaluation of humanity is seen as an affront to God's order."

Dr. Kitzinger nodded in contemplation.

"So no religion, then?" asked Melinda.

"We shouldn't count it out," cautioned Samaira. "Religion gives humanity many important things. We just can't afford to embrace a theology that elevates our importance above the well-being of the planet."

"This is heavy dinner conversation," interjected Jayson.

"You're right," agreed Samaira. "I've just been spending so much time thinking about all of this. It feels good to get it out there to face some critical examination."

"I found it very thought-provoking. A nice change of pace from idle chitchat," added Dr. Kitzinger.

An awkward silence followed, and Jayson immediately regretted interrupting the flow of conversation.

"Luping has some news that might interest you as well, doctor," prompted Parth, sensing an opportunity to change the subject.

She blushed and grinned widely.

"What is it?" asked Jayson.

"I'm pregnant. I think."

"Mazel tov!" congratulated the doctor, raising his aluminum cup. "Come and see me tomorrow, and we can be sure."

"That's great news," added Samaira. "Congratulations."

"Thanks," replied Luping quietly, embarrassed by the sudden attention.

"And congratulations to you, too, Parth," said Jayson.

For once, Parth had nothing to say. He just grinned.

"Anything you want to add, Melinda?" asked Samaira with a sly smile.

"How did you know?"

"Just a hunch."

"We were going to wait a bit to say anything—until after Riyoko has her baby," explained Dr. Kitzinger. "I guess it's out of the bag now. Melinda is about six weeks along."

The rest of the table raised a toast to the couple to celebrate their good news.

"How is Riyoko doing, by the way?" asked Luping.

"Very well," assured the doctor. "Although I wish I could convince her to stay here. We've converted a couple of carts into sturdy, comfortable beds, and the clinic building is complete, but she insists she's fine over at the fishpond."

"How much longer?" asked Samaira.

"Two or three weeks," replied the doctor. "It's almost time for me to show some value around here."

"You built half the clinic—with a little guidance," reminded Parth. "So I'd say you've done just fine."

"And it looks like there's no shortage of work now," added Jayson. "The baby boom is coming."

"I hope so," said Melinda with a suggestive glance at Samaira.

Samaira pretended not to notice.

"Anyone feel like playing a game while we talk? Cards, or something?" deflected Jayson.

"I'm too tired," said Melinda. "I'm going to turn in early."

"Me too," agreed the doctor wisely.

They said goodnight, and the two rose with their dirty plates and utensils to wash them in the basin. Those remaining wasted no time changing the subject to reflect on the earlier meeting.

"It's got to be Olena," started Parth without segue. "Did you see how quick she was to deny any rights to the ship?"

"And the pushback on reaching out to nearby islands," added Jayson.

"I agree," said Samaira. "Not so much about the nearby islands. That could have been genuine fear. But I don't think we have enough yet."

"How can we be sure?" asked Luping.

"We watch her carefully," suggested Parth. "Keep track of when she disappears, or when she's on a device, and see if Matteus can correlate it with activity from that unknown user account."

"Good idea," agreed Jayson. "But if she's a trained spy, or something like that, she might notice if she's being watched. Counter-surveillance, or whatever."

"What do you know about that?" asked Parth skeptically.

"Just what I've read in spy thrillers," admitted Jayson, "but it could be a real thing."

"What do they do in the books when they're following someone?"

"Work in teams and trade off regularly. Try to blend in—I don't know."

"We don't need to do anything fancy," said Samaira. "We just need to go about our normal work and take mental notes on her behavior." It's not like there are many places for her to go."

"I guess," allowed Jayson. "I'm just a little nervous. I've never done anything like this."

"How do we start?" asked Luping.

"We just do it," answered Samaira with a shrug. "Where is she now?"

"With Kailani, Matteus and Serge," said Parth. "I've been watching her all evening."

"Well, she's not there now," said Jayson.

They all looked over at the same time to see that her place at the table was empty.

"We're not good at this," observed Jayson, shaking his head. "We look like a bunch of fucking prairie dogs."

***

It was always in the back of their minds that they might be chasing a ghost. Despite what Aiden may or may not have been, there was no clear evidence of another spy—just the suggestion from what Matteus had seen in the logs. The morning after their meeting, there was no longer any doubt.

Jayson and Parth woke early to go for a short walk together down by the harbor. It wasn't unusual. The ship was an object of interest for everyone, and people took time to check on progress on a near-daily basis. Sleek and majestic, the boat sat perched on a purpose-built slipway, looking to the untrained eye as if ready to launch at any moment. The rigging was complete, and the sails, though furled, were in place. Despite the early hour, the deck was already alive with various preparatory activities.

At the head of the slipway sat two empty chairs and the smoldering remains of a fire. Evidently, at least two security team members had spent the night guarding the ship. That had never happened before.

"Looks like we're not on a snipe hunt after all," observed Parth.

"Nope," agreed Jayson.

"I'd say somebody told them about our meeting yesterday. They've never felt the need to set up a guard post before."

"Maybe that's where Olena disappeared to after dinner."

"You're probably right, but it doesn't really change anything for us. We still can't be certain."

"No," agreed Jayson. "But I didn't notice anyone else slipping away."

"You're not looking for anyone else," cautioned Parth. "It could have just as easily been the doctor, or Melinda, or someone else you didn't even notice was missing."

Chapter Thirty-Two

It was early on a cool spring morning, just days before the anniversary of their arrival, when Dr. Kitzinger got the hit from Riyoko. Her contractions had started in the middle of the night but were far enough apart she'd decided to wait until first light to disturb him. Her water hadn't broken, and a self-examination revealed no significant dilation to indicate there was any hurry.

He immediately started a video call to see how she was doing, and offered to come and meet her. Seemingly more calm and collected than the excited doctor, she assured him that she and Farzin were fine to journey to the clinic on their own. They'd start on their way soon, and Farzin would bring an empty cart in case she got to the point where the contractions were so painful she couldn't walk.

Excitedly, he roused Melinda from her sleep to tell her the news. Melinda, in turn, went to find Samaira and Jayson. Despite Riyoko's assurances, she asked them to meet the expectant couple halfway, in case they needed help. Of course, they eagerly agreed, setting off immediately while Dr. Kitzinger made preparations.

Four-and-a-half hours later, they arrived together at the clinic. Riyoko was still walking, although with considerable difficulty, having rebuffed all attempts to get her onto the cart. Dr. Kitzinger escorted her to a room dominated by one of the cleverly converted beds, where he and Farzin helped her get as comfortable as possible.

"How close are the contractions?" he asked.

"Between four and five minutes," replied Farzin.

"Cutting it a bit close."

"I'm fine," insisted Riyoko.

"When did your water break?" asked the doctor as he began his examination.

"About an hour ago—during the walk over. Is everything okay?"

"Completely normal," he assured. "Dilation is six centimeters, and the head is down. No reason to expect this won't be a textbook birth."

Farzin breathed a sigh of relief. Riyoko squeezed his hand tightly as another intense contraction caused her to wince in pain.

"Try your best to relax," advised Dr. Kitzinger. "I will tell you when it's time to push."

Samaira and Jayson were waiting nervously in the anteroom. They were unsure of their role once they'd arrived, but now felt somehow involved, and decided not to leave. A cool breeze passed through the open window, and Samaira shivered.

"Are you okay?" asked Jayson.

"Fine. Just a bit of a chill," she assured.

"I don't know how you do it."

"Huh?"

"Women, in general," he clarified. "It must be terrifying."

"Giving birth?"

"Yeah. I mean, how do you go through with getting pregnant when you know where it's leading?"

"I don't think I can speak for *all* women," she replied with a laugh.

"What about you, then?"

"Intellectually, I know childbirth will be painful," she explained, "but it's not really part of how I think about becoming a mother."

"What do you think about?"

"Just about the connection I'm going to have with a beautiful little life. I'm going to be her entire world, and I will feel a love like nothing I've ever imagined before. Whatever I need to go through to experience that seems so trivial—it's not even a consideration."

"Hmm," he nodded.

"And whatever I think it's going to feel like to have that connection, I know the real thing will be ten times stronger."

Jayson's eyes went wide as Riyoko screamed loudly from the next room.

"If you say so," he said with a gulp.

Samaira smiled and squeezed his hand.

"Don't worry," she assured. "You'll get through this, big guy."

***

The first baby of their new civilization, a healthy little girl, was born on April 24, 1175. Her parents named her Jasmine. The community was united in joy and celebration—as if the baby somehow belonged to all of them. Despite their relative dissociation from the rest of the recruits, even the security team took a break to join in congratulating the couple, fawning over the new arrival.

Dr. Kitzinger struggled to stop the steady stream of visitors and clear everyone from the room to give Riyoko some time to rest after the ordeal of childbirth. It was too soon, he insisted, to subject her to so much excitement. Reluctantly, the well-wishers eventually deferred to his expertise and left the couple to bond with their daughter.

However, their excited impatience to have a proper celebration could not be held off for long. Melinda planned a party to recognize both the anniversary of their arrival and Jasmine's birth. Two days later, everyone gathered in the common building—except poor Ted Park. He'd drawn the short straw and stayed behind at the harbor to guard the ship.

Though it broke his heart to do so, Jayson added a special treat to the menu. For the first time, dinner featured roasted herb chicken served with potatoes and fresh vegetables. Though it may have seemed a small thing, the impact of the welcome variety added significantly to the joyous mood. It was almost as though they were one team again instead of two factions with divergent purposes sharing the same island.

Clearly exhausted, Riyoko was beaming, nonetheless. She and Farzin graciously accepted another round of congratulations, and Jasmine endured the fawning with indifference as she alternatively fed and slept at her mother's breast.

As people finished their meals and the clinking of metal utensils died down, Josh stood up and tapped his aluminum cup with a knife. Though it didn't make the same musical sound as a crystal champagne flute, the intent was clear, and the room fell silent.

"To our friend and comrade, Farzin," he started, speaking on behalf of the security team, "we give our most sincere congratulations on the birth of your perfect, beautiful daughter."

Everyone applauded enthusiastically.

"And of course, to Riyoko, who admittedly had the harder part of the bargain."

There was some laughter that died down as Josh's face went serious.

"Today also marks a bittersweet anniversary. A year ago, when we arrived in paradise, we lost a colleague and a friend. I would like to propose a toast to Aiden."

"To Aiden," echoed the assembled team.

"But I want to keep this celebration happy, and focus on new life and new hope," he continued. "Tomorrow morning, we will launch our ship at nine o'clock, and we'd like you all to be there."

The security team initiated the applause; the others joining in with varying degrees of enthusiasm.

"In honor of our latest arrival—a living symbol of why we are here—I would like to announce we will name our ship 'Jasmine's Hope.'"

This revelation drew even more enthusiastic applause, and everyone rose in a standing ovation.

Samaira leaned over to Jayson as they both stood clapping, and whispered in his ear, "outstanding PR move. There's no way people will react negatively to the ship now."

***

The following day, everyone gathered at the harbor to watch the launch. Though they had no champagne, a christening of some sort was a mandatory maritime tradition, ensuring good fortune and safe travels. Josh stood on the deck with fellow security team members Isiah O'Neal, Paul Suryana, and Miroslava Sirotkin, holding a coconut in one hand and an aluminum cup in the other.

It was a warm, sunny day, and the water was calm; perfect for a maiden voyage. Josh raised the coconut and cup above his head to signal the beginning of the ceremony. The crowd fell silent.

"Welcome, friends and colleagues, to the culmination of a great deal of effort and sacrifice. I would like to thank everyone here for making it possible. I know some may disagree with the priority placed on this effort, but I assure you that will change when we share the benefits."

Still holding both over his head, he emptied the coconut into the cup before passing it around among his colleagues on the ship. They each took a sip and handed it back to Josh.

After taking a sip himself, he poured the remainder onto the deck and called out, "I christen this vessel Jasmine's Hope," before throwing the empty cup into the crowd for good luck in a tradition predating that of breaking a champagne bottle against the hull.

Ted Park swung a hammer to knock out the final block holding the ship in place, sending it rumbling down the slipway before it hit the water with a splash. Despite what some may have felt about the effort to create it, the crowd erupted in unified cheers over the successful launch of Jasmine's Hope.

Holding a line attached to the bow, Jen guided the craft over to the sturdy wooden dock near the slipway where the rest of the crew scurried up a pair of rope ladders. She gave the bow a hard shove before mounting the nearest ladder as the ship drifted slowly into the harbor. Except for Farzin, who stood next to Riyoko giving his newborn baby daughter at least as much attention as the launch, the entire security team was aboard.

"We're going to take a few days to circumnavigate the island and get familiar with how she handles before we decide what to do next," announced Josh.

He shouted out a few commands and, within moments, the sail was unfurling into the gentle southeasterly breeze. Those crew members not occupied with the task of getting underway waved briefly to the crowd before turning their attention seaward.

"That's it? They're just taking off and leaving us for a few days?" whispered Jayson.

"It looks like it," agreed Samaira.

"They've only left Farzin, and he's already been away from the fishpond for a few days. I imagine he'll be wanting to head back soon."

"I'd be willing to bet on it."

"What do you mean?"

"This is as much a test for us as it is for the ship," she said.

"How is it a test for us?"

"To see how we'll react with no security team around."

"Ah," realized Jayson with a nod. "While the cat's away."

"Exactly."

"What should we do?"

"Stay on our best behavior and carry on like normal," replied Samaira simply. "And ease off on watching Olena. Let's not give her any reason to think we're suspicious."

As predicted, Farzin reluctantly left Riyoko and Jasmine behind to return to the fishpond. Riyoko had intended to go with him, but Dr. Kitzinger managed to talk her into staying in the clinic for a few more days until she was more comfortable with breastfeeding. Besides, Farzin would be busy, and there were many people at the main camp willing to fawn over Jasmine while her exhausted mother caught up on sleep.

***

Though improvements would continue for generations, the most important buildings were weatherproofed and comfortable enough to serve the community's immediate needs. Construction efforts shifted to completing the fortified structure in the crater housing the servers, communications hub, and quantum stack. Eventually, the site would grow to include the university, where future generations would learn to use, maintain, and develop their technology.

A few family residences began to take shape on the slopes of the crater. Within a year, there would be permanent, comfortable shelter for everyone, assuming the security team was finally willing to help, but the first units would go to those already expecting children. Samaira and Jayson were pouring the concrete foundation of the newest residence when they heard Zaina shouting, and saw her pointing towards the bay. Four days after departing toward Diamond Head, Jasmine's Hope was returning to harbor from the west, having successfully circumnavigated O'ahu.

Those working within view of the harbor paused their efforts to meet the returning ship at the dock. Herman and Olena caught a pair of lines thrown by the crew and hauled them in. Park scurried down the ladder to grab the rope from Herman and tie it off for him.

One by one, the security team alighted the craft. They were, without exception, grinning and laughing. Apparently, the test had gone well, and they'd been delighted by the opportunity to get back to sea.

"How'd it go?" asked Herman.

"Incredible," replied Josh. "She handles like an absolute dream."

"See anything exciting?" asked Jayson.

"Just the whales and the open ocean," he said. "And that's plenty for me."

"What's next?"

"Not sure yet. We'll take stock of the situation and decide from there," he answered. "For now, we'll start with some lunch."

Josh worked his way through the crowd on the dock, followed by most of the crew. Paul Suryana remained aboard alone, securing the lines and sails. It seemed they would not be leaving Jasmine's Hope unattended.

"Did you notice anything interesting?" whispered Samaira as the crew departed.

"No," replied Jayson. "But I'm getting used to it."

"Ted went to help Herman tie off—like he didn't trust him to do it right."

"So?"

"Nobody helped Olena."

"You're right," he realized. "They must have reason to trust she'd do it right."

"I think we're beyond the point of reasonable doubt. It's got to be her."

***

305

Most of the security team spent the next several weeks more engaged with general infrastructure projects around the new settlement. While they'd taken charge of the shipbuilding, they were more than happy deferring to Parth and Serge when it came to urban planning and construction.

The navy recruits were unequaled in their pure strength and ability to put their heads down to focus on a task. Despite providing only a quarter of the workforce, their efforts doubled the rate of progress. Although appreciated, it added to the frustration when it became evident some of them were preparing food and supplies for a significantly longer voyage, and the help was only temporary. The newly increased pace of development would be short-lived.

They converted several sealed equipment containers for water storage, supplementing them by constructing some wooden barrels. Farzin salted and dried a few hundred pounds of fish while Riyoko planned what they'd need to avoid significant nutrient deficiencies on their long voyage.

Jayson was incensed when they began picking through the crops, helping themselves to whatever they thought they needed. He'd have gladly assisted if they'd only bothered to ask. He and the others hoped their departure would somehow present an opportunity to uncover and undermine whatever they were doing, and if he could hasten it, he was happy to do so.

Finally, near the end of May, the preparations for departure were complete, and Josh announced plans for the voyage one evening at dinner.

"As you know," he started after getting everyone's attention, "we chose O'ahu as our home because it offered the best balance of isolation and access to resources. However, the lack of significant metal ore deposits limits our development. We intend to set sail for China and establish a trade relationship to fix that problem."

"How does that fit with your insistence on staying isolated?" asked Kailani.

"We have no intention of telling them where we're from, or inviting them to visit us here," explained Josh. "Isolation is still very much part of the plan."

"And you're confident we're safe here without you?" asked Samaira.

"We're leaving two people behind to keep you safe. Considering the lack of inhabitants and the absence of visitors, it should be more than enough."

"Who's staying?"

"Farzin, of course, and Jen—and they'll be well-armed to handle anything that might come up."

To Jayson, the last statement seemed like it might have been a threat, but he was aware it was just as likely an inference on his part.

"How long will you be gone?" asked Dr. Kitzinger, knitting his brow.

"It's hard to say," replied Josh. "We don't want to push our luck with the weather. I'd guess it'll be just over a year. Eighteen months at most."

"What? That seems like a really long time to be gone."

"You have to remember, we're sailing. Seven or eight knots is going to be around average for us."

Dr. Kitzinger blinked in silent disbelief at the news.

"We'll also be looking for other opportunities to improve our quality of life with this mission," continued Josh.

"Like what?" asked Jayson.

"A little more food variety. I was hoping we'd find wild pigs when we arrived here, but it seems we were too early. Maybe we can bring some back with us."

"I'm not sure that is a great idea," he cautioned. "They're technically a non-native invasive species."

"Lighten up, Jayson. A nice pig roast is just what we need to make this really feel like O'ahu."

The cheers of agreement, mainly from the security team, convinced him to drop his opposition. It wasn't likely they were going to listen anyway.

People chatted about the mission and the upcoming prolonged absence of the security team as they finished dinner. Gradually, the crowd thinned out, and only a few scattered clusters of recruits remained—playing games or talking. In a rare break from their practice of keeping to smaller groups, all of the co-conspirators gathered at a table in the corner.

"At least we know imperial jade isn't a code name," said Luping.

"How do we know that?" asked Parth.

"It's for trade with China. High-quality imperial jade is worth more than gold or diamonds or anything else I can think of."

"Really?" asked Jayson. "From a thousand years in the future, and the best we can do are some colored rocks?"

"It's not about what we value," explained Samaira. "It's about what we know *they* will value."

"What I value is having the security team gone," said Kailani. "I don't care where they're going or what they're doing."

"What difference does it make?" asked Parth.

"At least we won't have to look at them—knowing what they're part of."

"Do we even know what they're part of? I mean, maybe they didn't know about compass guy either."

"They know," insisted Samaira. "Otherwise, they wouldn't need to lie to us and put spies among us to make sure we don't interfere with whatever they have planned."

"Interfere with what? Trade? Even with advanced weapons, it's not like ten people can do much harm out there."

"If we can figure out what they're bringing, maybe we can figure out what they're doing. Let's keep an eye on the containers they load up to compare them with the manifest."

"It's going to be tricky," reminded Serge. "I've seen them repurposing some of the empty containers for food and water storage."

"Look for containers set apart from the rest of the cargo. There can't be a whole lot other than food and water going with them, since we couldn't bring a lot through the portal in the first place."

"I'll do it," volunteered Parth. "I've been showing professional interest in the construction from the beginning, so they won't find it suspicious when I'm checking things out."

"Be careful," warned Luping.

"Don't worry. I'll be fine."

Chapter Thirty-Three

TEN SECURITY TEAM MEMBERS boarded Jasmine's Hope and cast off on the last day of May. It was too late in spring to guarantee the best sailing conditions, and their late start had the potential to place them in the path of an early typhoon before finding safe harbor somewhere in the orient. The crew, however, seemed confident in their abilities, and the hundred-foot ship was far from a fragile pleasure craft. It was built to handle some weather.

They started out on a heading of due west, presumably to avoid attracting attention from the inhabitants of the nearby island of Kauai. A small group saw them off at the dock, and an even smaller group stayed behind until the mast disappeared behind Sand Island. When it was gone, they followed the well-worn path through the trees back up to Punchbowl. Jayson and Jen trailed along—well behind the others.

"You feel like getting together later?" asked Jen.

"What?"

"You know what I mean. We could have a little fun—like before."

"Honestly? I'm not feeling up to it."

"What's wrong?"

Jayson hesitated.

"I think I'm in love with Samaira," he said finally.

"No shit. I could have told you that," she said with a laugh. "I'm not looking for a commitment here."

"I know," he replied. "It just wouldn't feel right."

"You didn't bring along any puritanical baggage, did you?" she asked, giving him a light shove.

"It's not that."

"Then what is it?"

He regarded her for a moment.

"What happened to us, Jen?"

"Nothing happened. We both had a lot going on."

"The moment we arrived here, you distanced yourself from me—from everyone. The entire security team did."

"It wasn't deliberate," she said, breaking eye contact. "We just had to focus on the job of keeping everyone safe."

"I don't get what building a ship has to do with that. It would've been a lot better if you could have helped us with shelter and infrastructure."

"See? That's why you need us. You're too naïve."

"What?"

"There's just a handful of us here. Do you have any idea what the world population is right now?"

"No," he realized. "But I don't see how it's relevant. We're isolated for centuries."

"Hundreds of millions," she continued. "Our arrival here has changed history forever. Like a ripple across a pond, soon nothing will be untouched. There is no way to guarantee how well or how long we're isolated."

"I'm no expert," he conceded, "but heading off to China to make contact hardly seems the best way to mitigate the danger."

"We need to do whatever we can to ensure our safety," she insisted. "Our simulations showed this is the best way."

"What is the best way?" he demanded, stopping in his tracks.

"We need more armaments than we could have possibly carried through the portal to secure the island from potential invaders. That's why we need Chinese steel."

"Jesus Christ! I didn't come here to start a war!"

"None of us did," assured Jen. "But you're too idealistic—all of you. It's why you're perfect for laying the foundations of a new society. If you knew what was truly necessary to secure our future, you'd never have come."

"Jesus Christ," he repeated, shaking his head.

"Please believe me," she implored. "We all have the same goals. I want the best possible world for the generations that will follow—just like you."

He didn't respond. Instead, he was trying to imagine what she felt was 'truly necessary.'

"We know where the world is headed, Jayson. I'm willing to do everything I can to make sure we change course."

"Yeah," he said with a nod. "I guess that makes sense."

It was more an attempt to end the conversation than an expression of agreement. They walked the rest of the way back in silence.

When they arrived at the settlement, Jayson sought out Samaira among those busily pouring foundations and erecting living quarters at the base of the crater. He felt the need to share the conversation he'd just had with Jen—except, of course, the part about wanting to hook up.

"It's been pretty dry the last couple of days," he started upon finding her hard at work helping Herman raise a wooden framed wall. "Think you could give me a hand with watering?"

"You good, Herman?" she asked.

"Go ahead," he assured. "I've got this."

As they started down the path leading to the nearby fields, Jayson glanced back to see if anyone was watching them leave. Everyone was preoccupied with their work and didn't seem to notice.

"Help watering, huh?"

"It seemed like a good excuse."

"What's up?"

"I just walked back from the dock with Jen."

"Hope you gave our friends a nice sendoff."

"Yeah. Just wanted to see them leave with my own eyes."

"Do you feel any different now that you have?"

"I guess. Jen certainly seemed different."

"Really? How?"

"Like she was relieved."

"You mean like she's glad they're gone?"

"No. Nothing like that. The closest thing I can describe is the feeling you get after final exams are over. That's how she seemed."

"Did she say anything revealing?"

"Kind of. It was weird. She basically admitted they've been planning on an aggressive strategy for our safety all along. We weren't told because we're 'too naïve.'"

"What kind of aggressive strategy?"

"Not much detail. Just that they're getting steel from China to build armaments. I get the feeling there's more she's not saying."

"That doesn't give us a lot more than we already knew," said Samaira.

"It's how she said it," explained Jayson. "She's not a bad person, Samaira. She really thinks she and the others are doing the right things for the right reasons."

"You believe that? They're basically good people?"

"I do," he said. "At least Jen and Farzin."

"Yeah," she agreed. "I get that feeling about Farzin, too. I don't think he's faking his love for Riyoko and Jasmine."

"I think we should tell them what we know—about the compass, Aiden, and Olena—and ask them what the hell is going on."

"Not yet," she cautioned. "We still don't know what Parth was able to figure out about their manifest. The more we know, the better. Then we need to plan how to approach them carefully."

**

That evening, Jayson and Samaira dined with Matteus, Luping, and Parth to discuss the day's events. Samaira was particularly anxious to hear what Parth had learned about the manifest. He did not disappoint her. Bravely, or perhaps recklessly, he'd taken some surreptitious photos while conducting a pre-planned 'emergency' video call with Luping as his excuse for walking around the dock with a tablet raised to his face.

"Here are the two boxes I was talking about," he said, zooming in on one of the photos. "Paul carried them onto the ship and brought them straight into the hold. They stacked everything else on the dock for an inventory check."

"Interesting," said Matteus. "Let me check the numbers against the original manifest."

He took the tablet from Parth and navigated to a folder where he'd hidden copies of the unencrypted security team documents, opening the one containing the detailed list of what they'd brought along.

"The numbers match two hardened cases on the manifest," he announced. "The larger one is imperial jade, and the smaller one is Scylla."

"Something else they can trade?" wondered Parth.

"According to the master list, there's another box of the same stuff somewhere," said Jayson. "Why don't we just try to find it and look inside?"

"They've got a locked room in the building up top where I've got the servers and communication equipment set up," replied Matteus. "It's likely there."

"Locked?" said Jayson. "Shit."

"It's not really secure. They just screwed a latch from one of the cases to the outside of the doorframe. It's more of a message than an attempt at actual security."

"So we could get in and take a look without them noticing?"

"Yeah. Easily."

"At least now we know it's not some kind of bomb," said Parth.

"How do we know that?" asked Jayson.

"They're not morons," he explained. "No way they'd risk blowing up our tech hub by storing a bomb right next to it."

***

The next day, Matteus went up to the secure building inside the crater equipped with a Torx head screwdriver in addition to his usual tablet. The others worked on construction activities at the base, watching for anyone else climbing to the top. Since the equipment was now secure in a completed structure, it was rare for anyone other than Matteus to make the trek. If someone did, he'd get a hit on his tablet, warning him to put the latch back on and pretend he was doing system maintenance.

He descended several hours later, looking defeated, and joined his coconspirators in the shade of a stand of acacias for a midafternoon break.

"The door lock wasn't an issue," he explained, "but the cases all have combo locks. I dug through the personnel files and tried birthdays, addresses, social security numbers—whatever I could think of. No luck."

"How beefy are they?" asked Jayson.

"Nothing crazy. But there'd be no way to break them without making it obvious."

"Something has to give. We can't just keep pussyfooting around going nowhere," he said, throwing his hands in the air.

"You're right," agreed Kailani. "This is getting old. How long are we going to keep waiting to figure out what's going on?"

"I think we can handle Farzin and Jen," replied Samaira, "but Olena really worries me. I don't know how she'll react to a confrontation."

"We've got to roll the dice at some point," insisted Kailani. "Before we know it, the rest of them will be back, and we'll have missed an opportunity."

"An opportunity for what?" asked Luping. "No matter what we do, they're coming back. Then what?"

"Exactly," agreed Samaira. "Whatever we do has to be so big it can't be undone."

"Like what?" demanded Kailani.

"I don't know yet. Just give me some time," pleaded Samaira.

"Okay," allowed Kailani. "But at some point, we need to make a move."

"We should get back to work now," interjected Jayson.

"Yeah," agreed Parth.

Jayson and Samaira returned to work at one of the residential structures where they'd been installing floorboards in preparation for raising another set of walls.

"I know you're getting frustrated," she said, placing a hand on his shoulder.

"It's not just me."

"I know. We're all frustrated."

"So what are we doing? You must have *some* ideas."

"I'm coming up short," she admitted. "We just don't have any leverage."

"Huh?"

"I can't think of a single thing they can't simply undo when their numbers are more favorable. Even worse, my simulations show they'll crack down once we tip our hand."

"Crack down?" he asked.

"Imagine a kind of military dictatorship. I mean, we're basically living in a self-imposed state of military rule already by not questioning or confronting them. They'll just make it official."

"Shit."

"Yeah," she agreed. "Exactly."

Chapter Thirty-Four

WHILE SAMAIRA MADE LITTLE progress on a plan to flip the balance of power on the island, the team could at least take solace in their progress at building a community. By midsummer, everyone was living in permanent structures on the crater slopes, having packed the last of the tents into storage. With less pressure to finish quickly, they could spend some time beautifying their nascent city to ensure it would be a pleasant and livable one.

They planted shade trees and flower gardens along the broad boulevards and narrower streets. Community gardens sprouted up, providing a significant amount of the fresh vegetables they consumed daily. Not only was this important for sustainability, but Samaira also insisted it was one of several necessary long-term aspects of society to prevent the kind of rural isolation exploited by the unscrupulous to create division. Nobody, she felt, should lose touch with the soil and the gratification of providing at least some of their own sustenance.

With gardens, parks, flowers, and pathways, they'd transformed what had at times felt like a forced labor camp into a proper home. Those oblivious to the evidence of the sinister underpinnings of their society thought themselves in paradise. To the slowly growing number who could be trusted to know more—now just over a third of the researchers—the satisfaction was tempered by uncertainty about what kind of society they were building.

Luping and Parth, with a baby on the way, had their own living quarters with a small, terraced garden cut into the slope behind it. Having been restricted to light work by Dr. Kitzinger following some concerning abdominal pain, Luping split her time between puttering in her garden and planning the next advances in concrete production. After they readied a few more apartments for the security team, she hoped Parth would start work on a lime kiln, allowing them to create stronger concrete for more impressive structures.

While researching the kiln requirements, she received an ominous group hit from Riyoko, broadcast to the entire team.

Send dr k with first aid
Fishpond
Urgent

What's wrong?

Luping stared transfixed at the screen, waiting for a response. When nothing more arrived after a few seconds, she jumped to her feet and hurried out the door.

"Help!" she yelled as she ran as fast as she dared towards the clinic. "Riyoko needs help!"

Jayson jumped to his feet in the garden in the central plaza where he was planting some flowers.

"What's wrong?" he called.

"Riyoko needs Dr. Kitzinger at the fishpond. Where is he?"

As if in answer, the doctor burst from the clinic door with a large pack slung over one shoulder and a tablet in his hand. He had also apparently seen the message, and wasted no time asking questions.

"Jayson," he yelled upon noticing the pair in the plaza, "grab a cart and catch up to me as quickly as you can."

"I'm coming, too," said Luping.

"The hell you are," replied Dr. Kitzinger as he rushed past. "Go back home and sit down."

Luping looked down at her vibrating tablet again to another short message from Riyoko.

Kailani too

"Kailani?" asked Luping.

"What about her?" demanded Jayson.

"She's hurt, maybe? Is Kailani at the fishpond?"

"No. I saw her with Herman and Parth just a few minutes ago. They were taking some timbers over there," he said, pointing to a pathway across the plaza.

"She must mean she wants Kailani, too," realized Luping. "I'll get her."

"I'll grab a cart and meet her here," decided Jayson.

A few minutes later, he arrived with a cart just as Kailani rushed in from the opposite direction.

"I took these full canteens from Herman and Parth," she explained as she tossed one at him.

"Good thinking. Let's go," he urged.

They started at a measured running pace towards the eastward trail. Behind, curious and concerned people gathered in the plaza, talking among themselves.

It took an hour for the pair to catch up to Dr. Kitzinger. Though he was in reasonably good shape, Jayson and Kailani were more athletically inclined, and had maintained a better pace. To make matters worse for the poor doctor, he'd left in such a rush he'd neglected to bring water, even though it was a hot summer day. He slowed to a walk as they arrived at his side and motioned for Jayson's canteen.

"Thank God you brought water," he panted after gulping down a few mouthfuls.

"Any idea what's going on?" asked Jayson.

"None. I checked a couple of times to see if she wrote anything else, but there's nothing."

"Shit. Get on the cart for a bit, doc."

"I'm fine," he insisted.

"You still need to be useful when we get there. I don't. Get on."

The grateful doctor jumped up, grabbing onto a tie-down strap running between D-rings on opposite sides of the frame as he made himself as comfortable as possible. Jayson and Kailani started running again, albeit a little more slowly than before. Though well worn, the trail was hardly smooth, and under less dire circumstances, the bouncing doctor's efforts to hold on as if he was riding a mechanical bull would have been amusing.

Kailani and Jayson traded off pushing the cart whenever one of them needed a break. Dr. Kitzinger did his best to give them both a break from time to time by running on his own until he could no longer match their pace. At their insistence, he remained a passenger for the closing leg of the long journey to catch his breath and steady his hands for whatever awaited.

They emerged from the trees where a low ridge stretched nearly to the beach, and Riyoko and Farzin had built a comfortable hut for themselves on a small piece of high ground west of the fishpond with a magnificent view of the ocean. Dr. Kitzinger jumped immediately from the cart and called out for the young mother.

"Look!" yelled Jayson, pointing to the shoreline.

A small outrigger canoe sat thirty meters away with its bow lodged on the beach, its stern bobbing up and down with the low waves. A thin trail of crimson-stained sand led from the high water mark all the way to the tree line ahead of them. They rushed forward, still calling, as Riyoko leaned out of the trees and waved them over. She cradled Jasmine, screaming and writhing, against her body with one arm.

"Hurry!" she yelled. "Over here!"

"What's wrong?" yelled the doctor. "Is Farzin hurt?"

Riyoko turned away, dropping to her knees beside the form of a man lying in the shade of the tree line without answering. Dr. Kitzinger, with his two companions on his heels, arrived at her side in seconds and threw his pack on the ground."

"Holy shit!" said Jayson. "Who is he?"

A sickly, tattooed man with long, wavy, dark hair, wearing only a torn, knee-length wrap around his waist, lay panting on the ground. His lower left leg and foot were covered with blood. Riyoko had tied a makeshift tourniquet just above the grisly mess to staunch the flow. The doctor began examining him without a word.

"I don't know who he is," she said helplessly. "I saw the canoe drift in and thought it was empty until I looked inside. He was just lying there. I tried to give him some water, and he freaked out."

"Freaked out?" asked the doctor.

"Yeah. He started thrashing around, fell out of the canoe, and tried to swim away."

"He's in no shape for that, obviously."

"He didn't get far. His leg was already pretty bad, and I think he re-opened his cut on the coral."

"So the wounds aren't fresh?"

The blood in the canoe was all dried up," she explained, "but when I finally managed to get him onshore to drag him out of the sun, he was bleeding again—a lot. How does he look?"

"I wish one of the medics was here. This kind of trauma isn't really my area of expertise."

"Can you help him?"

"There's not much I can do here," replied the doctor, touching the man's forehead. "He's running a fever—probably from an infection—and the foot isn't looking good either. I'm going to need to start him on an IV antibiotic back at the clinic ASAP."

"I don't know if he'll make it," she said dismally. "He's really weak."

"Hopefully, any infection isn't too advanced, and we're just looking at the effects of dehydration. I can hook up a saline drip to get that under control while we cart him back."

He dug through the pack and grabbed some saline and an IV line.

"Hold this," he instructed Jayson, handing him the bag of fluid.

He took the prone man by the arm and tried to insert the catheter. His eyes wide with fear, the reluctant patient pulled his arm away and croaked hoarsely.

"E 'ole! E 'ole!"

"What's he saying?" Riyoko asked Kailani. "I thought you might be able to communicate."

"He's saying 'no,'" replied Kailani.

"Can you explain I'm trying to help?" asked the doctor as he tried regain hold of the man's arm.

"I can try," she said.

She knelt down next to Dr. Kitzinger and whispered to the man, "pono mākou e kōkua iā 'oe."

He looked at her with a mix of puzzlement and vague recognition as the doctor tried once more to insert the catheter. Again, the patient pulled his arm away.

"We don't have time for this," complained the doctor. "Hold him down."

"E kala mai ia'u," she said apologetically as she grabbed his wrists and pinned him to the ground.

Dr. Kitzinger pulled out a needle and injected something into his shoulder. In just a few seconds, he was unconscious.

"Jayson, bring me the cart," he directed. "We need to get him back."

Jayson ran back to where he'd left the cart sitting at the end of the pathway and hauled it over to the now unconscious patient. At that moment, Farzin appeared at the nearby mouth of the fishpond and started running towards them.

"What's going on?" he shouted with panic in his voice. "Is Jasmine okay?"

"She's fine," assured Riyoko, rising from her place by the side of the injured man. "We're both fine."

"What is it then?" he asked as he got closer, slowing to a walk.

"This guy washed up in an outrigger, and Riyoko called for help," explained Dr. Kitzinger.

Farzin's relief vanished in an instant.

"Why didn't you come and find me first?" he demanded as he stepped forward and reached for his sidearm.

Riyoko's eyes widened in horror. She stepped between Farzin and the injured stranger, still holding Jasmine in her arms.

"What are you doing?"

"He can't stay," pronounced Farzin, as he pushed Riyoko aside.

Incensed, she kicked him in the shin.

"Don't you *ever* push me," she hissed. "And if you don't put that fucking gun away *right now*, you will never speak to your daughter *or me* again."

Farzin froze, his mouth agape, staring at Riyoko. It took him only seconds to reevaluate his priorities before sliding the gun slowly back into the holster. He took a step back, still staring at her with a look of shock.

"I'm sorry," he said. "I can't believe I pushed you—and Jasmine."

"What the hell were you thinking?" she demanded, her anger unabated.

"He can't stay," repeated Farzin, with less resolve than before.

"He's hurt, and we're going to help him," insisted Kailani. "And who are you to tell us he can't stay?"

Farzin snapped out of the initial shock of Riyoko's rebuke and tried to explain himself.

"He's an outsider, and he represents a threat. It's my job to keep us safe."

"This man is no threat to anyone," replied Dr. Kitzinger with a dismissive wave of his hand. "Make yourself useful and help us get him on the cart."

With Riyoko still fuming beside him, Farzin understood he had little choice. Reluctantly, he helped Jayson, the doctor, and Kailani lift the unconscious man and place him onto the cart. Next, Dr. Kitzinger inserted the catheter and hooked up the saline solution.

"Someone's going to have to hold this up over his head while we take him back. It's going to be a long walk home, and he can't make it without fluids."

"Just a second," said Jayson. "I have an idea."

He cut a branch from a nearby tree with his pocketknife and whittled down one of the short offshoots until it was small enough to accommodate the ring where the saline bag would normally attach to a metal rack. Then, he used the tie-down strap to affix the branch to the cart.

"Hang it up here, doc," he said.

"Perfect. Now let's get moving. It's going to be getting dark by the time we get back."

"I'm coming too," said Riyoko, "with Jasmine."

"Let me take the cart," offered Farzin, still trying to atone.

"No," replied Riyoko flatly, "you can stay here."

***

Although no less urgent, the trip back was, by necessity, much slower. They needed to avoid jostling their patient too much and risk having the IV line pulled out, or worse, having him roll off onto the ground. The now-laden cart was also more challenging to navigate over the small dips and rises of the path. Aside from Riyoko, who carried Jasmine in her arms, they all shared the burden of pushing. Jayson took the first shift, manning the cart while the doctor kept a careful eye on the patient.

"I'm so glad you were able to communicate with him, Kailani," said Riyoko.

"I'm not sure I was," she admitted. "I was just speaking Hawaiian, and I don't think he fully understood."

"But you know his language, right? From your studies?"

"I know a theoretical language he might understand, but it's not something I've ever really spoken."

"Oh. I didn't realize that," replied Riyoko.

"The good news is I can use the algorithms to develop a translator for his language pretty quickly just by speaking with him—if he survives."

"Do you think he will? Survive?"

"I have no idea. He doesn't look good, though."

"People are hitting me to see what's going on, and I don't know what to tell them," she said, glancing at her tablet.

"It's been hours," realized Kailani. "They must be freaking out."

"I guess I should say something."

"No," said Kailani, knitting her brow. "Just tell them everything is okay, and we'll be back soon."

"Why?"

"You saw how Farzin reacted. I'm worried our new friend might be in danger."

"What?"

"Farzin—and Jen, I assume—obviously have orders to prevent contact. I honestly thought Farzin was going to shoot him right in front of us."

"He wouldn't do that," said Riyoko unconvincingly.

"If you weren't there—" started Kailani, shaking her head.

Riyoko didn't answer.

"Does Farzin have a tablet?" asked Kailani. "A way to communicate?"

"No. This is the only device we had."

"Good. Just hit back to the group and tell them everything is fine—false alarm. It'll give us some time to get this guy inside the clinic and set up some protection."

***

It was dark when they arrived back at Punchbowl. Though it had made the last part of the journey challenging, the high clouds blocking out the moon and stars also improved their odds of sneaking the new arrival into the clinic unseen. Jayson and Riyoko provided a distraction.

Emerging from the pathway ahead of the others, they went directly to the common building where most of the team had already finished eating and were unwinding from a day of work and worry. Jasmine immediately attracted a crowd of cooing admirers, and Riyoko recounted, with convincing embarrassment, the false alarm that had caused her to call for help.

According to her story, Jasmine had been crying in pain for hours with a distended belly. Fearing an intestinal blockage, she had called for Dr. Kitzinger in a fit of panic. As he examined the poor child, she released an enormous fart right in his face, and immediately started giggling. Everyone laughed and assured Riyoko she had no reason to be embarrassed. Being a new mother couldn't be easy, especially so isolated from the nearest help. While the cleverly crafted story held everyone's attention, Jayson scanned the room to see who was missing. Though not everyone was there, at least Jen and Olena were accounted for among the crowd. He hit Kailani to let her know it was safe to transport their patient to the clinic.

Dr. Kitzinger kept the lights in the clinic as low as he could without compromising his ability to work. He pushed the cart as close as possible to one of the converted beds and enlisted Kailani to help transfer the unconscious stranger.

"We're going to have to strap him down somehow—for his own safety," said the doctor.

"Yeah," agreed Kailani. "I'll take care of that while you get the antibiotics going."

"Thanks."

The doctor hung the broad-spectrum antibiotics next to another bag—the third one—of fluids. If there was a bacterial infection, he was confident it couldn't resist a treatment of modern antibiotics. Then, he started examining the wounded foot as Kailani worked out a way to use the tie-straps as restraints.

"This isn't good," he observed.

"What is it?"

"Gangrene. There is a lot of dead tissue on his left foot and ankle."

"Are you sure?"

Dr. Kitzinger raised the lights and returned to his examination.

"Come and take a look," he said. "I thought maybe the blackness was from caked blood and dirt, but it's his flesh. It's dead."

"There's nothing you can do?"

"To save it? No," he said, slowly shaking his head. "And to save him, I'll need to amputate."

"He's not going to be happy about that, I imagine," replied Kailani.

"He's never going to be happy *or* sad about anything ever again if I don't do it." She nodded in resignation.

"Okay."

"We'll keep him sedated after he wakes, and maybe he won't notice for a while. That'll give you some time to gain his confidence and calm him down a bit before we tell him."

"Okay," she agreed again.

"Help me undress him and give him a wash-down. I don't want any new infections on top of what he's already dealing with."

Chapter Thirty-Five

THE TRUTH SPREAD QUICKLY among those deemed trustworthy. Jayson had told Samaira immediately following Riyoko's performance, then sought Serge and Matteus to share the news with them. By early the next afternoon, they all knew about Dr. Kitzinger's hidden patient, and Farzin's reaction to his arrival.

Jayson, Samaira, Luping, and Parth took their lunch break together at a newly installed bench in the shade of a tree next to a flower garden on the plaza's west side. The expectant couple had only just learned of the visitor and suggested they gather to talk about it.

"Do you think he's going to be okay?" asked Luping.

"Doc said the surgery went okay," replied Jayson. "Kailani was a little worried, though. She said he kept referring to instructions on his tablet during the procedure."

"He's an OBGYN, Jayson," chided Samaira. "It's probably safe to assume it was his first amputation."

"I know. I'm just telling you what she said."

"We really should train someone to be a nurse," said Luping.

"I'd say Kailani's doing just fine. She stayed through the whole thing. Won't leave his side."

"We need to think about how we're going to keep him safe," she added. "Kailani and the doctor can't do it all by themselves. We should set up shifts around the clock."

"I agree," said Jayson.

"Devil's advocate here," interjected Parth, "but why is it our job to keep him safe? Isn't there a chance this'll create too much conflict with the security team?"

They looked at him with shock.

"What? I said devil's advocate," he said.

"In my experience," said Jayson, "that's what people say when they're about to be an asshole."

"Sorry. I'm not saying we should let anything happen. I just think we need to consider how this is going to play out."

"We need to *control* how this is going to play out," corrected Samaira.

"Huh?"

"This is it—our wildcard," she added. "I've been wracking my brain for a way to flip our situation, but something's always been missing. This is it."

"How?" asked Jayson.

"I don't know yet, but this is it. Nothing this disruptive is going to fall into our laps again before the rest of the security team returns. This has to be our answer."

"Alright. So what now?"

"Luping is right. We need to make sure he stays safe, and give Kailani time to learn as much about him as she can."

"I'll work with the doctor to set up a watch schedule," said Jayson. "Kailani can fill you in on what she learns from him while I'm at the clinic."

"It's a start," agreed Samaira.

***

Jayson arrived at the clinic to find Kailani asleep in a chair beside the occupied bed. There was no sign of Dr. Kitzinger, who was likely getting some sleep after a long night of surgery and post-operative care. The patient was looking around groggily, trying to move his limbs.

"He afa kāu i hana mai ai iaku," he said hoarsely.

"Hey, man," whispered Jayson quietly, "It's okay. Everything's cool."

"O hai' koe," he said with rising alarm, realizing he was restrained.

"Shit," whispered Jayson, gently nudging the patient's sleeping caretaker. "Kailani. Wake up."

Startled, she sat up and looked around.

"What's wrong?"

"Your friend is waking up," replied Jayson quietly, "and I have no idea what he's trying to say."

"O hai' koe," repeated the patient.

"'O Kailani ko'u inoa," replied Kailani in a soothing voice. "Palekana 'oe."

"What is it?" asked Jayson.

"He asked who we are, I think. I told him my name—and that he's safe."

"So you can communicate?" he asked hopefully.

"Jesus, Jayson. I just woke up. Give me a second."

"Sorry."

"'O wau 'o Kailani a 'o ia 'o Jayson," she said.

"Aia i hea waku?"

"O'ahu," replied Kailani.

The patient's eyes widened, and he worked violently against his restraints. Kailani placed her hand on his chest in an effort to soothe him and stop his thrashing. Instead, he yelled out. She pulled back immediately, and he froze, his eyes following her as she backed away.

"What the hell did you say to him?"

"Nothing. I think he asked where he was. And I said O'ahu."

"Well, I think something got lost in translation. Does he even know this island as O'ahu?"

"I'm not sure," she admitted. "What I hear sounds a lot like Hawaiian—and a pretty good match to what we've theorized about proto-Polynesian—but I can't really speak it. I've just been answering in Hawaiian. I might have screwed up."

"Whatever you said, it freaked him out. We need to calm him down."

"I know. I just need some time to let the algorithms refine the translation. We can't get beyond the basics without it."

"How do we do it?"

"We just need to get him talking, and the translations will improve automatically as we go."

Kailani walked over to retrieve her tablet from the countertop where she'd left it to recharge. Opening her custom proto-Polynesian translator, she spoke a few words in Hawaiian.

"'O 'oe pū me nā hoa aloha."

She pressed the speaker icon on the screen, and a soft female voice emanating from the tablet repeated the phrase with a few differences in pronunciation and intonation. The patient, who had seemed momentarily calm, began thrashing in terror again.

"Yeah. A magic talking rectangle. That's not going to be a problem," said Jayson, rolling his eyes.

"Palekana 'oe," she pleaded.

"Does that thing work with English, too?" asked Jayson.

"Fine. I'll change the input language—for you," she said with a huff.

The patient spoke a few words back to them. Kailani selected 'yes' when prompted with the option to recognize the voice as proto-Polynesian. It automatically adopted a man's voice for the translation.

"Are you gods?" it said.

Another dialog box popped up.

"Alternative detected. Would you like to hear it?" read Jayson from the screen.

Kailani selected 'yes.'

"Are you demons?" said the voice from the tablet speaker.

They looked at each other.

"That's not good," remarked Jayson.

"No. We are just like you," said Kailani.

They waited for the translation and response.

"You are not like me," he replied, eyeing the tablet with suspicion.

"We are just like you," she insisted, pointing at the device. "This magic belongs to our god."

"I thought we weren't doing gods," said Jayson.

"You want to explain this some other way? Be my guest."

"Yeah. I'll pass on that."

"Thought so."

The man spoke again, and the translation came through more quickly than before.

"Who is your god?"

Kailani hadn't thought that far ahead and quickly blurted, "Akindele."

"Jesus Christ," lamented Jayson, shaking his head. "Really?"

"Jesus Christ," repeated the patient.

"Shit! No! No!" insisted Jayson, frantically waving off the remark. "It's Akindele. Our god is Akindele."

"Akindele," repeated the man with a slow nod.

"How about you let me do the talking?" said Kailani with a sideways glance.

"We should get Samaira for this," suggested Jayson.

"I understand his culture better than she does, Jayson. I think I can handle this."

"Fine. Keep going. I'll just shut up now."

"What is your name?" she asked the patient.

"I am the sea," came the translation.

Jayson raised his eyebrows and looked at Kailani.

"That's, uh, interesting," he said.

"It's a literal translation," she explained, pointing at the word on the screen. "His name is Kai."

"Kai," repeated the man with a nod. "Aia i hea waku?"

"Where am I?" Came the translation.

"He didn't like this one last time," reminded Jayson quietly.

"You are at our home. You are safe," she replied.

His tension eased only slightly, and he spoke again.

"Why am I—" started the translator.

A message popped up, warning 'translation incomplete.' Kailani looked back and forth between Jayson and the patient, with confusion. Kai pulled on his restraints in a silent reply.

"He wants to know why we've tied him up," said Jayson.

Kailani quickly typed in a couple of options to indicate Kai had likely asked about the restraints. The algorithms would learn from the feedback and refine future translations.

"To keep you safe," she answered. "You were badly injured and should not move until you heal."

He looked at her questioningly.

"Keep it simple for now," suggested Jayson, "until the translations get better."

"I know how this works," she said with irritation, before turning back to the patient. "Your leg is hurt. You should keep still."

He nodded somberly as the translation emerged from the tablet speaker.

"If I am safe, please untie me."

Kailani looked at Jayson. He shrugged deferentially to let her know he would follow her lead.

"We can untie you," agreed Kailani, "but I need to explain some things first."

Kai nodded, but gave no other indication he had understood there were conditions for releasing his restraints.

"This is for medicine," explained Kailani, tracing the pair of intertwined IV lines down to his arm with her finger. "Do not remove them."

He nodded again.

"Your leg is injured. You cannot stand up."

"I remember," came the translation.

"If you try to hurt us or get up, we cannot trust you. Do you trust us?"

"What choice do I have?"

"None," she asserted with a sympathetic look. "But I promise you are not in danger."

She nodded at Jayson, and he began undoing the tie-straps securing Kai's arms. With his upper body freed, he tried to raise himself and fell back down after a brief attempt.

"Would you like to sit up?" asked Kailani.

The translation didn't seem to register.

"Up?" she asked again, making a motion with her hand."

"Yes," he replied.

Jayson went around behind him to adjust the mechanism they'd rigged up on the converted cart now serving as a hospital bed. He raised Kai's torso up to about seventy-five degrees.

"Is that good?" she asked. "Are you thirsty?"

"Yes," he replied, presumably in answer to both questions.

"Can you get him some water, Jayson?"

"Sure."

He walked over to the counter and opened a blue plastic valve enabling cold, fresh water to flow out of a polyethylene tube poking through the wall. He let it run for a moment—more out of habit than necessity—before filling an aluminum cup he'd grabbed from the shelf. Kai watched the entire production with fascination.

"More of Akindele's magic?" he asked via the tablet translator.

"Not magic," assured Kailani. "Just water."

"When you are well enough to stand, I will show you how it works," offered Jayson, as he handed Kai the cup.

The translation didn't seem to land, and Kai offered no response. He just stared at the smooth, metallic surface of the cup in amazement. After a moment, he took a tentative sip and smiled at Kailani.

"It's good," he confirmed before taking another, longer sip. "Thank you."

"You're welcome," she said, returning his smile.

At that moment, a bleary-eyed Dr. Kitzinger walked into the room, reacting with a start when he noticed his patient sitting up unrestrained. Instinctively, his carefully honed bedside manner took over, and he managed to stifle an outburst.

"I see our patient is doing unexpectedly well," he said pleasantly, but with a clear undertone of disapproval.

Kai sensed the tension and gripped his covers tightly, his eyes trained intensely on the approaching doctor.

"Who is this sick man?" he asked via the translator.

"Excuse me?" said the doctor with a frown.

"Just a second," replied Kailani. "It's offering an alternative translation. 'Who is this pale man?'"

"I guess that's better," allowed the doctor, "but I'm not really that pale, am I?"

"It's all relative, doc," laughed Jayson. "Compared to the three of us, you're practically a ghost."

"This is our doctor. Our healer," explained Kailani. "He helped you."

"I hope you've tempered his expectations about what that means," warned the doctor. "Does he know about the amputation yet?"

"Doesn't seem like it," replied Kailani.

"Okay. How has this back and forth been going?"

"Really good."

He looked at Jayson for confirmation.

"Yeah. Really good," he agreed.

"Well, regardless, he needs rest. I suggest we leave him on a high note and put him under again for a bit."

"Okay," agreed Kailani reluctantly.

"And you could use some more sleep, too," he said.

"The doctor says you need to sleep some more. Are you tired?"

"Yes," acknowledged Kai.

Dr. Kitzinger inserted a syringe into a small vial, drawing out a carefully measured dose of sedative. Kai's eyes widened again, and he looked at Kailani for explanation.

"It's medicine to help you sleep," she explained.

He relaxed somewhat, but still followed the doctor's movements with suspicion.

"At least I don't have to jab him with it this time," said Dr. Kitzinger as he reached up and injected the solution into a receptacle in the IV line.

Kai's eyes got immediately heavy. He fought for a short time to prevent them from closing, but to no avail. Within seconds, he was asleep again.

***

Kailani agreed to get some sleep in her own cot on the condition they would not leave Kai by himself. The doctor was still too tired to keep watch, so Jayson volunteered to spend the rest of the afternoon and evening in the clinic. After dinner, Samaira stopped by with a full plate for him and some soft, bland options for the sleeping patient, should he awaken hungry.

"So this is our mystery man," she observed with fascination.

"Yep. His name is Kai."

"How's the communication going?"

"We only had about a half-hour to try. Doc came in and suggested we end it while he was still calm and cooperative. "

"That was a good idea," agreed Samaira. "Did you tell him anything about us?"

"We told him he was safe and we're helping him with medicine."

The look on his face betrayed to Samaira there was more.

"And?"

"The tablet—for the translations—it was obviously kind of hard for him to absorb the fact it was speaking to him."

"Okay."

"We have a limited vocabulary for now, and he doesn't really have any context to understand our technology."

"Okay," she prompted again. "So, what did you do?"

"Kailani told him it was a gift from our god, Akindele," he said with embarrassment.

"That was really clever," laughed Samaira. "The Mighty Akindele has a nice ring to it."

"We didn't mess anything up?" he asked.

"Not at all. We can work with that—and eventually, transition him to a fuller understanding of what it means. But please don't say any more about who we are," she cautioned. "Give me some time to develop what you've said already into a more complete story."

"It's going to be hard to do that. Kailani is going to want to keep talking with him."

"I understand. She feels a strong connection with him, and it will be important not to undermine that."

"So, what do we do?"

"I'll spend some time tonight developing ideas, and then meet with Kailani first thing in the morning to strategize. That way, she'll feel some ownership over how we proceed."

"You're really good at this," he marveled.

"It's just basic psychology, Jayson. And basic respect."

"Yeah, I guess," he agreed.

"Anything else you can tell me about him?"

"He's not what I expected."

"How do you mean?"

"Once we got the whole tablet thing out of the way, he seemed pretty rational."

"And that surprises you?"

"Well, yeah. I expected his reactions to be more—I don't know."

"Primitive?"

"Yeah. Primitive."

"You mean how the first Europeans settlers likely viewed your ancestors?"

"This is going to turn into another psychology lesson, isn't it?" asked Jayson sheepishly.

"This man, Kai, is exactly as smart and capable as either of us. If he'd been dropped into our society as an infant, he would have had the same chance of becoming a doctor, engineer, or scientist as anyone else."

"So he's not as primitive as he appears."

"And we're not as advanced as we like to think," she added. "Your assumptions about him are part of your own primitive nature. We're programmed to view outsiders—and those who are different—as being less than fully human."

"Why?"

"Because then we can feel justified in taking their resources for ourselves. When resources are scarce, we're more likely to survive if we view ourselves as being more worthy by limiting our empathy for those who are different."

"Well, I guess we can't fight our nature."

"If you believe that, then we've wasted our time coming here."

"Huh?"

"We might take a different path, but we're heading to the same destination as the world we left behind if we can't overcome human nature."

"That's a tall order."

"But we can do it, Jayson. The first step is being aware of how your base instincts drive your behavior."

"And the second step?"

"Try to be better than that," she shrugged.

Chapter Thirty-Six

JAYSON AWOKE IN HIS chair with a start the next morning to the sound of an aluminum cup bouncing across the floor. Dr. Kitzinger stood frozen in the doorway with Kailani and Samaira behind him, trying to figure out what had happened.

"You tripped my alarm," explained Jayson, still rubbing the sleep from his eyes.

"Clever," said the doctor, "but I think you scared our patient half to death."

Kai's eyes were wide open, and he was trying to sit up.

"Ua maika'i nā mea āpau," said Kailani calmly. "Mai maka'u."

The doctor prepared some examination equipment while Kailani quickly pulled out the tablet to make sure she'd said something close enough to the calming words she'd intended. Kai seemed to have understood, laying back down on the bed while Jayson adjusted the mechanism to lift his torso, and Kailani and Samaira sat down at his bedside.

"Hello, Kai," she said through the tablet translator. "This is my friend, Samaira."

Kai stared at Samaira with great interest for a few moments before answering.

"Your skin is so dark," came the translation. "Were you burned?"

Samaira smiled broadly and replied, "My ancestors were touched by the sun. This color is my gift from them."

"You are beautiful," he said, nodding in admiration.

"Samaira is our storyteller," interjected Kailani.

"Are you here to tell me your story?" asked Kai.

"Yes," confirmed Samaira. "And to hear yours."

"I am listening," he replied with what appeared to be a degree of suspicion.

"More than a year ago, the god Akindele gathered us from all corners of the earth to bring us here. He touched our tongues and made it so we spoke one language."

"You have only been here for one year?"

"More than one year. Less than two years," she clarified to ensure unambiguous translation.

He affirmed his understanding with a nod.

"Why did he bring you here?"

"He told us someday people will learn to control his magic, and will use it to destroy the world. He told us we must learn it first and teach others to use it wisely."

"Why would people destroy the world? Where would they live?"

"They don't want to destroy the world, but they will not be able to overcome the power of their greed."

"Where does Akindele live? Here?"

"He lives in another world just like this one, where he has already seen the destruction begin."

"Will he come here?"

"He will come after many generations."

Kai took some time to consider what he had just heard.

"This island is O'ahu?" he asked.

Jayson and Kailani exchanged an uncertain glance.

"Yes," replied Kailani.

"Did Akindele remove the evil?"

"Compass guy. Shit," said Jayson under his breath.

"Akindele cleansed the island of evil, but its shadow remains. He warned we must always be wary of its influence."

Kai wrinkled his brow and cocked his head to one side.

"The translation must be too complex for now," said Kailani. "Too much nuance."

"Akindele defeated the evil that controlled this island," tried Samaira.

Kai nodded.

"But gods cannot defeat evil by themselves. We must be wary."

"This is true," agreed Kai through the translator.

"I hate to interrupt," interjected Dr. Kitzinger, "but I really need to check on our patient's recovery."

"Of course, doctor," replied Samaira.

"Our healer needs to examine you," said Kailani.

Kai nodded his head. If not fully relaxed, he seemed resigned to his situation, and did not object.

"Temperature is down to normal," observed the doctor on the readout of his infrared thermometer.

Kai watched with fascination as the doctor wrapped a Velcro cuff around his upper arm and clipped an oxygen monitor to the end of his index finger. The inflating cuff startled him as it began restricting his blood flow. Kailani continued offering soothing words.

"One thirty-five over eighty-five. Not bad, considering how strange this must all be for him. Oxygen saturation is good and heart rate is only slightly elevated."

"So he's recovering well?"

"So far, so good. I need to check the amputation."

Dr. Kitzinger injected something into the IV line, and a cloudy liquid swirled its way down the clear plastic tube.

"Just a little midazolam," he informed them. "If he notices the amputation, he won't remember in a couple of hours."

"We have to tell him eventually," said Kailani.

"I know," replied the doctor. "I'll leave it to the two of you to tell me when you think he's ready to learn about the procedure. Lay him back down now so he can't see what I'm doing."

"Can we still talk to him?" wondered Samaira.

"That would be a great distraction, but he won't likely remember the conversation."

"That's fine. We'll just try to find out a little bit more about him while you do your thing."

Jayson lowered the head of the bed while Kailani explained the doctor wanted to check his injuries. Dr. Kitzinger pulled back the covers and started unwrapping the bandages. When he got to the bloodstained wads of gauze, Jayson went pale.

"I think that does it for my shift," he announced suddenly.

"You okay, Jayson?" asked the doctor.

"Just a little woozy. I think I need to get some breakfast."

"Yeah. That must be it," said Kailani with a smile.

Jayson didn't answer. He left the room quickly without looking back as the doctor uncovered the bloody stump below Kai's left knee.

Once outside, he started feeling light-headed, stooping down with one hand propping him against the wall. A few slow, deep breaths had him feeling a bit better, and he tried taking a few more steps before he doubled over and threw up a small puddle of bitter, yellow bile.

Across the plaza, Olena was exiting the common building after having breakfast. She saw Jayson struggling and trotted over to see if he was okay.

"Jayson," she called as she approached. "Everything alright?"

"I'm fine," he replied quickly, horrified by her sudden appearance.

"You don't look fine. Let me help you into the clinic."

"No. I just came out. Doc says I'm fine."

"Really?" she said doubtfully. "I think you should go back and tell him about this."

"It's anxiety," he insisted. "Hospitals make me throw up. I just need to get away from here and get something in my stomach."

"Alright, alright," she offered soothingly. "Let me at least walk you across the plaza to make sure you don't faint or anything."

"Thanks, Olena. I appreciate it."

***

Jayson tried getting some sleep after breakfast but found his mind was too active to calm down. He needed some mundane work as a distraction. There was always something to do in the fields and slowly developing orchards. Whether harvesting, weeding, watering, or checking for insect infestations, he could always stay busy. Today, however, he didn't feel like being alone, and knew many of the others would be anxious for an opportunity to learn about their new visitor. He decided to join

Parth, Luping, and Serge on their most recent project to expand and beautify the common building.

Just beyond the building's perch at the south end of the plaza, the ground dropped off several meters towards the harbor. Large, open windows offered views of the ocean from above the treetops. The beautification project would see the addition of a lanai like the one they'd enjoyed at the Center for Sustainability Research. It would extend southward over the drop-off to offer even better access to the spectacular view. To prepare for the supporting structure, Parth was overseeing the construction of footings to bear and distribute the weight of the addition.

Of course, Luping's role was limited by her condition. She spent most of her time sitting comfortably while researching on her tablet, occasionally doing rounds to make sure Serge and Parth's canteens were full. The two men were grateful when Jayson arrived and offered to help. Mixing, carting, and pouring the concrete was exhausting work.

"Was this project really necessary?" asked Jayson, as he dumped another load into one of dozens of footings.

"Food, water, and shelter are necessary for life," replied Serge. "But what is necessary to make life worth living? Yes, we need to supply water, build sewers and composting facilities—but we also need beauty."

"Think back to a year ago, Jayson," added Parth. "We were living in tents—eating fish for breakfast, lunch, and dinner. Now, look what we have."

"You could learn more from your friend, Samaira," said Serge. "A balance of the practical and the beautiful keeps everyone motivated and happy to be here. This lanai is no different from the flowers you've planted around the square as a way of making us feel at home."

Serge grabbed his tablet from a nearby rock and showed Jayson some renderings of the finished project.

"Wow," remarked Jayson. "This is going to be awesome."

"Exactly," agreed Serge. "And look at the view."

He tapped his finger on a person modeled into the simulation, and a window popped up showing the ocean view from her perspective.

"Incredible."

"What do you think about our project now?"

"I love it," agreed Jayson. "I guess we can wait a little longer for private bathrooms and running water in our apartments."

"That's going to be a big job," said Parth, looking at something just beyond Jayson. "And you're not the only one asking me about it."

Jayson turned to see Luping standing behind him.

"Don't worry, Parth," she said. "I'm not here to bother you about the bathrooms again."

"What's up?"

"I can't believe I even have to ask. I'm here to find out what's going on with our new friend. Have you learned any more about him?"

"Not really. Doc drugged him pretty good, and he slept all night while I was with him."

"Can Kailani communicate with him?"

"Anyone can—to a degree," he replied. "The translator is pretty good—and keeps getting better the more we use it."

"What does he look like?"

"Like any native Hawaiian you've met, I guess. He's built, too—like a one-legged Jason Momoa."

"Oh," remarked Luping, betraying a great deal of sudden interest.

"You *did* hear the 'one-legged' part, right?" asked Parth.

"A one-legged Jason Momoa is still more than enough for me," she said with a wink.

"Oh, please," he said, waving his hand dismissively.

"That is going to be quite an adjustment for him," interjected Serge. "I don't imagine many people survive such injuries here."

"Do they have any concept of prosthetics?" wondered Jayson.

"Perhaps," allowed Serge. "There is evidence to suggest some cultures have been using them for more than a thousand years already."

"Yeah. But they'd be nothing like what Paralympians have now—in the future, I mean."

"We could rig up something pretty cool for him, actually," realized Parth. "It could be an interesting project—and maybe help us win him over."

"Do we have the parts and tools to pull it off?" asked Jayson.

"Those lower legs—blades, they call them—are pretty simplistic," he replied. "Tons of research has gone into making them effective, but they're not complex mechanisms at all. They're basically leaf springs."

"We have access to all of the design specifications in our internet archives," added Serge.

"I wish Hitarthi was here," lamented Parth. "She'd be able to help us figure out how to get the right spring-back properties from the materials we have lying around."

"We can figure it out," assured Serge. "It will just take a bit more effort."

"This is going to be fun," said Parth, rubbing his hands with excitement.

"I guess the lanai is on hold?" asked Jayson.

"There's nothing we can do until he's well enough to get some measurements, so we may as well keep working on this"

"It was worth a try," he said with a smile.

"When can we find out more about—" started Luping. "What's his name, again?"

"Kai."

"When will we know more about Kai?"

"Kailani and Samaira are talking with him right now, as far as I know. Let's try to hook up with them for dinner."

"What's a few more hours of waiting?" she asked with a rhetorical shrug.

"At least there's lots to do to pass the time," added Parth.

"That there is," agreed Jayson.

He scraped the remaining concrete out of his cart and went to mix another batch while Serge and Parth muscled a thick wooden post into the next hole and set about making it plumb.

***

Hard work and good company helped pass the remaining hours before dinner. Luping, having not exerted herself to the same extent as the others, secured a quiet table in the corner farthest away from the food line while the others cleaned themselves up. She busied herself as long as possible with research to distract from the gnawing desire to learn more about Kai.

One by one, Parth, Serge, and Jayson joined her among the growing crowd arriving for dinner, but there was still no sign of Kailani or Samaira.

"I can't take it anymore," said Luping. "I'm going to hit them to see if they're coming."

Coming for dinner?

Yep
5 mins

"Oh, thank God," she said.

"They're coming?" asked Jayson.

"Yeah. Five minutes, they said."

After passing another ten minutes with small talk and regular, anxious glances at the door, they breathed a collective sigh of relief when Kailani and Samaira arrived with Melinda. They waved and went to the food line to pile some of the evening's offerings onto their plates. Kailani and Samaira joined the others while Melinda walked back out the door with an especially full plate of food.

"Our friend is hungry," explained Samaira as she sat down.

"That's a good sign," observed Luping.

"I think so. He's going to have something to eat, and then the doctor will probably sedate him again."

"Who's with him now?"

"The doctor and Riyoko."

"Speaking of Riyoko—any word from Farzin?" asked Jayson.

"Nothing. She figures he'll be here tomorrow on his regular delivery schedule."

"Do we have anything to worry about?" asked Serge.

"Riyoko doesn't think so," assured Samaira with a laugh. "She says she 'owns his ass.'"

"Yeah," agreed Jayson. "He looked like a kicked puppy when she told him to sit and stay back at the fishpond."

Kailani had yet to offer anything beyond a cursory greeting. She sat mindlessly chewing some food as she stared off into the distance.

"You okay, Kailani?" asked Luping.

"Huh? Yeah. I'm just processing."

"Processing what?"

"We had a long talk with our visitor today, and I'm still kind of reeling."

"What's wrong?"

"Nothing's *wrong*. Just surreal. It's like a legend come to life."

"It was intense," agreed Samaira with a nod.

"Tell us," pleaded Luping. "The suspense has been *murder* all day."

"You good to explain it, Kailani?" asked Samaira. "I can try if you're still processing, but you've got a better understanding of the historical perspective."

"I'm fine," she insisted. "I just don't know where to start."

"Start with the history—for context," suggested Samaira.

"Okay," agreed Kailani. "The first thing you need to know is the settlement of the Hawaiian Islands by Polynesians was a process—not an event—that we think consisted of two or three major waves over hundreds of years. None of the histories are definitive because there is no good documentation. We rely a lot on legends and oral traditions."

"The Moolelo Hawaii," interjected Parth. "I started reading those before we left."

"That's part of it, yes," agreed Kailani. "What we tend to think of as native Hawaiian culture—the strict caste and kapu systems, human sacrifice, and all that—didn't actually arrive until the last wave of pre-contact settlement. Before that, Hawaii was four separate island kingdoms ruled by inter-related monarchs who had arrived in the previous migration."

"How does that align to where we are in their history now?" asked Serge.

"I'm getting to that," assured Kailani. "The most broadly accepted timeline is part of the reason I was so convinced we'd find a thriving culture here when we arrived. The kingdom of O'ahu—along with those of Maui, Hawai'i, and Lanai—should already be well established."

"Which is where compass guy fits in," added Jayson.

"Exactly," said Kailani. "We've learned from Kai that the other three *do* exist—and O'ahu did as well."

"What happened to it?"

"It was taken over by a demon that cast out everyone it did not kill."

"Just one?" asked Jayson. "Even with modern weapons, that's hard to imagine."

"That's not even the strangest part. According to Kai, it happened a long time ago—like nine or ten generations."

"Between two or three hundred years? And they still won't touch the place? If this guy was alone, what the hell did he do?"

"I'm not sure. We didn't get into that yet."

"Sorry. I didn't mean to interrupt. Keep going."

"Anyway," she continued, "the oral traditions tell us the four kingdoms were overthrown by new arrivals from Tahiti or Samoa in the final wave of migration, and their leaders were replaced with transplants. That was estimated to have happened somewhere close to the year eleven hundred."

"So it's already happened?"

"Apparently not. Historians were only able to *estimate* the timeline because the stories used generations as milestones, not years. It turns out they were off by quite a bit—and the third wave is happening now."

"What?" exclaimed Parth. "Poe and that other guy I read about in the Moolelo Hawaii? They're here now?"

"Pa'ao and Pili. Yes," replied Kailani. "They've recently overthrown the island of Hawai'i and established a new kingdom there."

"Wait. Who are Pa'ao and Pili?" asked Luping.

"According to legends—and all but confirmed by Kai—Pa'ao was some kind of priest and navigator. Pili was the first of the line of kings that still ruled the islands when Captain Cook arrived. He's a direct ancestor of Kamehameha the Great."

"Incredible," marveled Parth.

"What's more incredible is that Kai was there to witness their takeover of Hawaii himself, as a teen, when he was among the last to flee to Maui with his father."

"And this next bit is the part that sent a chill down my spine," prompted Samaira.

"What?" demanded Luping.

"His father was Kapawa," revealed Kailani, "the last in the line of rulers overthrown by the new arrivals. Their flight, along with other nobles, from Hawai'i to Maui is a well-known part of our mythology—and it appears to be true."

"Wait," said Parth. "According to the stories, wasn't Kapawa a major dick? Like, totally corrupt? I thought the arrival of Pa'ao and Pili was basically a liberation, and most of the people welcomed it."

"Where have I heard that before?" asked Samaira, rolling her eyes.

"Huh?"

"The victors write the history, and they're never the bad guys. Ancient cultures might not have had a name for propaganda, but they understood the basics. They carefully crafted their legends to reinforce the legitimacy of the victors. "

"So maybe Kapawa wasn't so bad?" asked Parth.

"Not according to his son," replied Kailani.

"But he could be lying."

"It's unlikely he'd have been able to craft those sorts of lies under the influence of the midazolam," explained Samaira. "For sure, he could have some bias that makes him remember his father's rule in a better light, but what he told us wasn't an outright fabrication."

"What he described," added Kailani, "was a harmonious, semi-egalitarian society. The chief, nobles, and priests definitely enjoyed higher privilege, but there wasn't the kind of rigid stratification we see under a caste system. Under Pa'ao and Pili's rule, the vanquished were mostly relegated to 'untouchable' status while the upper echelons of society were taken over by newcomers. Only some priests who submitted to the new gods kept their status."

"These priests are likely the basis for the story that Pa'ao and Pili were welcomed and made life in Hawaii better," added Samaira.

"Based on what Kai described, the Hawaiian oral traditions seem to be a clever mix of truth and propaganda. It's true Pa'ao arrived first with a small group, and they were welcomed as friends. He brought a new religion, built his own temple, and converted a number of the locals—just as we've always learned."

"What's the part that's not true?" asked Parth.

"I'm getting to that," said Kailani. "According to legend, the local priests asked Pa'ao to help them overthrow Kapawa and free them from his despotic rule. After the victory, he sent for Pili—from either Samoa or Tahiti—to be the new ruler because of his pure, royal bloodline."

"Yeah. I remember that."

"Kai tells it differently. He said small numbers of Pa'ao's followers kept trickling in over a few years. Then, suddenly, Pili showed up with a fleet of huge canoes filled with warriors, women, children, and animals—basically an entire floating civilization. They established a beachhead and immediately started fighting. Pa'ao and his followers joined the battle on the side of the invaders and cut off retreat from behind, but Kai, his father, and a few others escaped. Over a few weeks, the survivors retreated all the way from Hilo to the northwest tip of the Island and then fled by canoe to Hana."

"He's pretty far off course to end up here," remarked Jayson.

"This was a few years ago—when he was still a teenager," reminded Kailani.

"So, how *did* he end up here?"

"Pa'ao and Pili have advanced to Maui. In the spring, they landed at Hana and pushed their way across the island to Lahaina, where Kai was injured in battle a few days ago. He and dozens of other holdouts were forced to either flee or face execution at the hands of Pa'ao's zealots."

"Holy shit."

"Kai took to the water, and was trying to get to Lanai, but he lost consciousness and ended up here instead. He said everyone who got away was eventually going to regroup on Moloka'i."

"Pa'ao could come here, too," realized Luping, her eyes suddenly wide.

"Kai said the same thing," said Samaira. "Moloka'i's not very populated, and won't be able to offer much in the way of resistance. They were going to evacuate to Kauai before they get overrun."

"Not here?" asked Serge. "We're so much closer."

"They're scared shitless of this place," reminded Jayson. "Probably they were hoping Pa'ao would make the mistake of coming here, and run into the demon."

"Exactly the plan," confirmed Kailani. "He was actually disappointed to learn the demon is gone, but hoped that Akindele's magic could help us defeat Pa'ao."

"So, with most of the security team gone, we could face an invasion?" asked Luping. "Why would they leave us vulnerable to this?"

"Because they thought all of this happened a hundred years ago," explained Samaira. "When there was nobody here, they must have assumed O'ahu was still deemed off-limits, and we'd be safe."

"This is terrible," said Serge, shaking his head.

"Look at the positive side," offered Samaira. "We don't have to manufacture a crisis anymore. We've got a real one."

Chapter Thirty-Seven

JAYSON JOINED KAILANI AND Samaira at Kai's bedside for the next shift in the morning after breakfast. Riyoko, having spent the night, was still there. All were happy to see their patient was recovering well and had regained a healthy appetite. Kailani had to return for a second serving of breakfast after he downed the first plateful of eggs, hash browns, and mixed berries.

"I feel well enough to stand up today," he insisted via the translator.

"This afternoon," promised Kailani.

Parth was making some crutches, and Serge was modeling a simulation of the new prosthetic design with his CAD tools. They'd planned a way to demonstrate how he would perform without his left foot while they broke the news about the amputation. Then, they'd give him the crutches to get him moving around.

"You told us a lot yesterday about how you were hurt in the battle at Lahaina," reminded Samaira.

"I don't remember that," he replied, furrowing his brow.

"It was the medication. You don't need any of that today."

"Good."

"Today, we want to ask you more about O'ahu. About the demon."

"What do you want to know?"

"How did he chase the people from here? Why did they never come back?"

"The stories say the work of the demon started slowly. People who wandered into the trees alone would often disappear, and their bodies would be discovered in pieces. Many believed it was the work of warriors from Maui trying to take the island from the descendants of the Nanaulu."

JAMES PELKMANS

"Nanaulu?" asked Jayson.

"Before the arrival of Pa'ao and Pili, the four kingdoms of Hawaii were divided between two royal lineages," explained Kailani. "The rulers of the Big Island and Maui—which included Lanai and Moloka'i—were of Ulu lineage. O'ahu and Kauai were ruled by chiefs of the Nanaulu line."

"Got it."

"Please go on," prompted Samaira.

"When strange magic appeared, people knew it could not be the work of man."

"What sort of strange magic?"

"People's heads would break open for no reason at all, spraying those around them with blood and gore. The eggs of monsters would land among them and burst apart in a flash of light to rip the flesh from anyone nearby."

"Sniper rifle and grenades could explain that," suggested Jayson.

"Agreed," nodded Samaira.

"That's awful," added Riyoko with disgust.

"And then a great sickness came over the island. The demon made it clear he wanted everyone to leave—and so they did. Those that survived abandoned O'ahu and joined their Nanaulu brethren on Kauai."

"Biological warfare?" wondered Jayson. "Or just coincidence?"

"What was the sickness like? Can you describe what happened to the afflicted?" asked Kailani.

"No. There are no descriptions of the victims of the first plague."

"First plague?"

"The second was much worse."

"What happened the second time?"

"Some years later, the ruler of Maui foolishly decided the god Kaulu had chased the people from O'ahu because he favored the Ulu chiefs. He sent warriors from Moloka'i to investigate the island and see if the gods would accept their presence. The violation enraged the demon, and he reacted with terrible violence."

"What did he do?"

"He brought the stars down from the sky to turn night into day. He even threw one of the fallen stars among the cowering warriors to rob them of their vision and senses. While they stumbled about, blinded and dumb, he walked among them to shatter their skulls."

"How did people learn of this?"

"According to legend, he killed only the warriors. Two fishermen who had come to provide food were allowed to escape with their lives."

"And the second plague?"

"A third fisherman, his face shattered and disfigured, was returned to Moloka'i in the middle of the night by the demon himself. Shortly after he arrived, his body broke out in weeping sores that lasted many days. Then, he began to bleed from every part of his body before succumbing to death."

"That is some trail-of-tears-level bullshit, right there," said Jayson with a sneer.

"It spread across Moloka'i in a matter of days, killing all but a few isolated hermits and farmers."

"Did it spread anywhere else?" asked Kailani.

"No. When boats from Moloka'i arrived on Maui to deliver the news, the priests noticed the ill among them, and refused permission to stay. They were turned back without exception and without mercy. On that day, the priests declared O'ahu a forbidden place."

Jayson was clenching his fists in rage when Kai finished his story.

"It's pretty fucking obvious what happened," he fumed.

"Calm down, Jayson," urged Samaira.

"Calm down? Are you kidding? Kamaras used biological warfare to clear this place out for us."

"We don't know that for sure."

"And he's probably not above doing it again."

"We definitely don't know that," cautioned Samaira.

"Enough bullshit. I'm going to find out, once and for all."

He stormed out of the room with Samaira on his heels.

"Wait! What are you going to do?"

"I'm going to find out what's in those locked containers."

"And then what?"

"We have to have a confrontation eventually, right?"

"Yes. We do, but—"

"If those containers are what I think they are, then I'm going to be in the right frame of mind for a fucking confrontation."

"Calm down and be rational," she said.

"Don't you get it, Samaira? It's the same bullshit as always. People like Kamaras just take what they want. If they have to wipe out an 'inferior' civilization in the process, who cares?"

"How is acting rashly going to help?"

"If I can destroy that shit, I can stop history from repeating—or prepeating—or whatever you want to call it. The sooner, the better."

He pulled his arm from her grip, left the clinic, and strode across the plaza to the lanai construction site. There, he grabbed a pickaxe from among the tools he'd been using the day before. Bolt cutters would have been better, but he was pretty sure they didn't bring any. Satisfied with the heft of the crude instrument, he made his way back past the clinic and began the ascent to the secure building on the plateau above.

At the top, he didn't bother with the charade of removing the exposed screws on the locked outer latch. He simply took a swing with the pick and knocked the whole assembly to the ground with a single blow.

"What the hell, man?" blurted Matteus, peeking out of the comms room to see what was going on.

"Got the combo right here," explained Jayson, holding up the pick for Matteus to see.

"What?" he as he followed Jayson into the small room.

Immediately, Jayson took a swing at the combo lock on one of the boxes. He missed, piercing the floor instead, and then struggled to extract it.

"Christ, Jayson. What if there are explosives in there?"

"It's not explosives," he assured, delivering a glancing blow to the lock. "It's much worse."

"What?"

"I think it's a bio-warfare agent."

"Then maybe don't swing a goddam pick at it," suggested Matteus, raising his hands to his head.

"You got anything better in mind?"

"I don't know."

"Then this'll have to do," insisted Jayson, winding up for another blow.

This time, the head of the pick scored a direct hit, shattering the lock to pieces.

"It's open! Stop!" pleaded Matteus as Jayson prepared for another swing.

He threw the pick to the floor and caught his breath as he stared at the unlocked box.

"Well?" prompted Matteus.

Jayson kneeled down to remove the broken shackle from the box. He unlatched the lid and slowly raised it. Inside, neat rows of stainless steel cylinders were nestled snugly in a block of foam. Jayson pulled one out to examine it."

"Fucking assholes," he said, shaking his head.

"What is it?"

"Meet Scylla," said Jayson as he held it aloft so Matteus could see the biohazard symbol engraved on the side.

"Holy shit. What are we going to do?"

"I'm taking this one down to show everyone," resolved Jayson. "I need you to take the rest of the shit and hide it somewhere safe until we can figure out how to destroy it."

"Okay," he agreed. "I can do that."

***

Jayson descended from the crater to find a commotion developing in the plaza outside the clinic entrance. Jen was there, arguing with Samaira, Kailani, and Dr. Kitzinger. A few steps away, an exasperated Farzin Khan was absorbing all manner of abuse from Riyoko while Melinda Middleton, standing well out of the fray, soothed baby Jasmine with soft cooing sounds and rocking her gently back-and-forth.

Approaching from outside Jen's peripheral vision, Jayson joined the confrontation just as Jen pushed Kailani roughly aside and stepped towards the clinic door.

"I'm going in," she announced.

Jayson leaped forward without hesitation, violently crosschecking her with the handle of the heavy pickaxe. Caught off guard, she bounced off the doorframe and tumbled to the ground.

"What the fuck is going on?" he demanded as he stepped into the doorway, blocking it off.

"Get out of the way, Jayson," warned Jen, clutching her shoulder as she rose to her feet.

"No way."

She took a menacing step forward, and he countered with a swing of the pick.

"Are you fucking kidding me?" she demanded as she easily dodged the blow.

"I'm not kidding at all," he warned. "You're not getting in here."

Jen pulled out her sidearm and pointed it at his chest.

"Are you sure about that?"

The onlookers gasped in shock at the sudden escalation. Jayson's hands trembled—not with fear but with fierce anger and determination.

"Go ahead and shoot me. Killing doesn't seem to be a problem for you."

Jen sighed and lowered the gun.

"Fine," she said, stepping towards him again. "We'll do this the hard way."

Jayson swung again to keep her at bay, but she rushed him as soon as the pick swung harmlessly past her torso. He had no time to stop the momentum to fend her off again, and she pinned him against the wall, gripping one of his wrists.

"Drop it!" she ordered.

"No!"

Keeping a firm grip to prevent Jayson from wielding the makeshift weapon again, she backed off just enough to deliver a quick jab to his kidney with her free hand. He doubled over in pain and dropped the pick.

"Sorry I had to do that," she said as she stepped over him towards the door.

From his knees, Jayson lunged at her again with perfect timing, wrapping his arms around her ankles. She braced herself against the doorframe to avoid knocking her head against the wall as she fell. Before she could get up, Jayson was on top of her.

"For fuck's sake!" she yelled. "Stop fighting this."

They tumbled around on the ground for a moment, but Jayson was no match for her strength and experience. Within seconds, she had him in a submission hold with his arm twisted awkwardly behind his back.

"Do you want me to snap your fucking arm in half?" she yelled.

"Let him go!" demanded a voice from behind.

Jen looked back to see Kailani pointing a gun at her head. She felt for her holster without looking, and realized with frustration it was empty. She hadn't closed the snap, and Kailani had somehow managed to grab it while she was distracted. Jen released her hold and rose slowly to her feet.

"Don't be stupid, Kailani. You're not going to shoot me."

"The hell I won't," she replied with a sneer. "Back away from that door, or I will kill you."

For the first time, Jen seemed to doubt her level of control over the situation.

"Uh, Farzin? A little help here?" she called.

"I can't help you," he replied with a glance at Riyoko. "I'm out."

Riyoko smiled and clutched his arm.

"You're *out*? What the fuck does that mean?"

"I've realized," he explained, motioning around, "this is my life now. This is my community."

"That is *not* what you signed up for."

"Maybe not," he allowed. "But that's how it is."

"You know it's not that easy, Farzin," she warned.

"I know. I'll talk to Josh and the others when they get back. I'm sure we'll find a way to make this work."

"Right," she said with a laugh. "I don't think Josh is the one you have to worry about."

Farzin looked around nervously and said nothing more.

"Listen, Jen," said Samaira, holding out her palms in a gesture of peace. "There's no need for us to fight. We're all here for the same reason, right?"

"I'm here to make the best possible world for us," she replied, choosing not to answer with a simple affirmation.

"If you agree to take a few steps back and just talk with us for a bit, I'm sure Kailani will put the gun down."

"I'll stop pointing it at her head," allowed Kailani. "But I don't think I'm ready to put it down just yet."

"That's a good start," said Samaira.

Jen walked a few paces into the plaza before turning back to face them with her arms crossed defiantly. As promised, Kailani lowered the gun to her side in response.

"Do you even know how to use that thing?" taunted Jen.

"Come and find out," invited Kailani.

"Please," begged Samaira. "Let's be rational."

"I'm completely rational and ready to talk," assured Jen. "Let's start by explaining why nobody told me about our new guest."

"Farzin's first reaction was to pull a gun on him," said Kailani. "We didn't want to take the chance you'd do the same thing."

"It's our job to evaluate potential threats," explained Jen.

"He's not a threat," interjected Jayson, guarding the doorway once again with his pick. "The only threat I see here is you."

"You're not qualified to make that determination, Jayson. What are we supposed to do now? Let him go back to tell his friends about us? Keep him as a prisoner? A pet? Jesus Christ. Where did you think this would go?"

"When a human being needs help, I don't start planning contingencies—I help," replied Kailani.

"And the next thing you know, we're overrun," said Jen. "That's why you're not in charge of security."

"That's just it," replied Samaira desperately. "We *are* going to be overrun!"

"What?" demanded Jen.

"We're in the middle of a war," she continued. "Kai, the man in the clinic, was injured in battle."

"How do you know that?"

"We can communicate—really well, actually—using the proto-Polynesian translator Kailani was developing with her thesis advisor."

"Can I talk to him?"

"You're not going anywhere near him," warned Kailani.

"I think it's important they meet, Kailani," advised Samaira. "Just not yet."

"Fine," agreed Jen. "Tell me more about this war."

Kailani related the story of Pa'ao and Pili, explaining Kai's belief they would soon bring their warriors to O'ahu after finding Moloka'i abandoned.

"There are hundreds of them," she concluded.

"Shit. How do we know all of this is true?"

"There's no way he made the entire thing up," offered Dr. Kitzinger, finally regaining his composure after the fray. "I had him drugged up during the exchange so I could examine his wound."

"Shit," repeated Jen.

"We need him," said Samaira. "We need his help if we're going to survive for a year without the rest of the security team."

"I need to talk to—to someone," said Jen, shaking her head.

"Olena?" offered Jayson.

"What?" asked Jen, raising her eyebrows.

"How stupid do you think we are?" he demanded.

"Fine," she sighed. "I need to talk to Olena about this."

She looked around to see if Olena was among those gathering to witness the commotion in the plaza.

"Has anyone seen her?"

"She was just here—watching with the rest of us," said Melinda, still bouncing baby Jasmine in her arms. "But I don't see her anymore."

"Just perfect," huffed Jayson. "We're going to need to keep this clinic locked down until we know where she is."

"I'll talk to her," assured Jen. "I give you my word that we'll all have a chance to work this out together before—"

"Before what?" demanded Jayson.

"Before we decide what to do. That's all I was going to say."

"I don't know how we can possibly trust you right now."

"Come on, Jayson. We might not agree on everything, but we're on the same team."

"Bullshit," he spat. "I would never be on a team that uses this."

He pulled the stainless steel cylinder from his pocket, holding it up for everyone to see. Those who were too far away to make out the symbol soon learned from the gasps and whispers of the others in the crowd what it was.

"You fucking bastards!" said Kailani, raising the gun again.

"Put it down!" pleaded Samaira. "We have to talk about this. Get everything out in the open."

"We can't talk about this," replied Jen, slowly shaking her head.

"If we can't talk, we can't trust—ever," said Kailani as she lowered the gun. "You have to decide what kind of society you're going to be part of."

"What a bunch of fucking hypocrisy," said Jen.

"What are you talking about?"

"You. That's what I'm talking about. Not five minutes ago, you were explaining to me Pa'ao and Pili, the conquerors of Hawaii, were on their way to wipe us out."

"So?"

They're *your* ancestors. You owe your culture—your very existence—to the genocide they are committing *right now*."

"Well, not here. Not this time," she said. "We need Kai and his people to help fight off what's coming."

"They might need us, but we don't need them."

"Really? We have enough weapons, ammunition, and bodies without Josh and the others?"

"And without this shit?" asked Jayson, holding the container up again.

"That's not your decision to make," she cautioned.

"I already made it. The rest of the stuff is gone," he revealed without mentioning Matteus.

"You really don't know what the fuck you're doing, do you, Jayson?"

"I'm stopping a war crime."

"Jesus Christ. War is nothing *but* crime. Brutal, bloody crime after brutal, bloody crime."

"I thought we came here to be different," said Samaira.

"I came here to *make* things different," replied Jen. "Not to *be* different. To the victors go the spoils. It's always been that way."

"What exactly is this stuff for?" demanded Jayson, fearing he already understood the answer.

"Do you really think we can make a better world just by wishing for it? We have to make cleaner energy, use more environmentally friendly materials, lower our impact on the planet—that's why you're all here. I'm here for a different reason."

"What is this stuff for?" repeated Jayson, his hand shaking as he continued holding it aloft.

"No matter what we do to conserve resources, other societies are just going to keep breeding like fucking mindless animals, and use them all up, anyway. They're going to cover this planet—fill its oceans and skies—with their filth. The stuff you're holding is going to fix that. It's going to keep this planet clean for *us* and for *our* children."

"How do you figure we have the right to do that?" marveled Samaira.

"Anton Kamaras created this world and gave it to us. We can do whatever we want."

"Anton Kamaras made this world for himself," she countered. "Do you really think he cares about us or our children? If we do his bidding, we—and the generations that follow us—are nothing more than his slaves."

"We are his beneficiaries," insisted Jen.

"Do you really believe that? He's obviously a psychopath. If he can treat an entire world full of *real people* like some kind of ant farm where he can play God with their lives, what makes you think he won't do the same to us?"

"Why would he?"

"I told you. He's a psychopath. You might as well ask why rivers would flow to the ocean. It's just what they do. You might think you're making the world better and cleaner, but you're also making it vulnerable. There will be no civilization equipped to deal with him and his technology when he arrives."

Jen stood silently, contemplating Samaira's warning.

"I—I need to think about this," she stammered.

"I say to hell with Kamaras," continued Samaira. "He's not here, so this is not his world. We don't have to do his bidding."

"It's already too late," replied Jen, still in shock. "Where do you think Josh and the rest went?"

"Fuck," lamented Jayson.

"More than a third of the world's current population lives within reach of our ship," she explained. "As our range extends, we'll hit more and more places with Scylla. When that stops working, we'll switch to Charybdis."

"And then?"

"And then another window opens, and it starts all over again with new tech and new weapons."

"Fuck," repeated Jayson.

"And you didn't—not even for a moment—stop to think maybe we'd be vulnerable to whatever comes next? That Kamaras might use it against us?" asked Samaira, shaking her head.

"He won't," asserted Jen. "He even vaccinated all of us against Scylla and Charybdis as a precaution. It was in the boosters we got before we left."

"That won't protect our children," reminded Samaira. "Even if he doesn't target them intentionally, our descendants will almost certainly be collateral damage."

"I have to talk to Olena," insisted Jen again.

"I agree. We need to get her to understand."

"And we need to keep her the hell away from Kai in the meantime," reminded Jayson.

"I'll help with that," said Farzin. "She's more likely to listen to Jen and me."

"Yeah," agreed Jen. "I'll help too. At least until we figure everything out."

"Nice try," said Kailani, "but you're not getting in there."

"Fine. I'll sit outside."

"We'll both do shifts—outside," assured Farzin. "You can stay inside with him if it makes you feel better."

"No guns," added Kailani. "I don't want either of you anywhere near him with a weapon."

"No guns," agreed Farzin, holding his hands up in front of him in the universal sign for submission.

They had arrived at an uneasy but welcome détente. As tempers eased, the crowd dispersed, and the two members of the security team remained with Samaira and the others to negotiate the arrangements for Kai's continued safety.

Chapter Thirty-Eight

LATER THAT AFTERNOON, PARTH and Serge went to the clinic to show Kai how they planned to replace his missing foot. Dr. Kitzinger hadn't yet revealed the extent of the surgery, but the patient was quickly becoming more alert and active. It wouldn't be possible to hide it much longer. The doctor hoped Serge and Parth would temper Kai's reaction by convincing him he wouldn't suffer any limited speed or mobility.

True to her word, Jen was sitting just outside the door to make sure nobody entered without authorization. They greeted her awkwardly as she waved them in, having witnessed the confrontation earlier and not knowing quite how to react to the strange new dynamic with the security team.

At Kai's bedside, Kailani introduced both of them generically as scientists—in English—and allowed the translator to relay the message. Evidently, she'd found a word combination to convey their role as working to understand and apply the use of magic. By now, the use of English was for the benefit of those around her. Because of the similarities with modern Hawaiian, and a couple of days of nonstop practice, she could now communicate most concepts directly in his native language.

"Hello," greeted Kai through the translator.

"Nice to meet you," replied Parth for both of them, as Serge raised a hand in salutation.

"He's coming off the meds now—except for the antibiotics," explained the doctor. "I want to keep that going for another couple of days."

"Have you told him about the amputation?"

"No. But I think he knows it's pretty bad by how we've been hiding it from him."

"How do you want to play this?"

"He trusts Kailani most," said Dr. Kitzinger. "I'm going to let her explain it, then we'll show him, and then I turn it over to you. Sound good?"

"If you say so."

"I've delivered my share of bad news, unfortunately. I try to stay empathetic and just get on with it."

Kailani reactivated the translation app.

"You are getting much better," she started, "but your foot was badly injured."

"I know," he replied somberly, closing his eyes.

"The doctor had to remove it so the rest of you could survive."

Kai took a deep breath and exhaled slowly. Though obviously unwelcome, it seemed the doctor was right, and the news was not a complete surprise.

"Let me see it," he said.

Dr. Kitzinger raised the head of the bed a few more degrees and then came to Kai's side, placing a hand on his shoulder. He made deliberate eye contact, and the two men exchanged a slight nod before the doctor raised the covers and exposed the bandaged stump. Kai took another deep breath as Dr. Kitzinger began unwrapping the dressings. When he'd fully exposed it, he took a step back to allow his patient some time and space to absorb his new state of being.

"If I am no longer a warrior and a protector, what am I?" he wondered aloud after a few moments.

"You can still be those things," interjected Serge with his typical passion.

"How?"

"Look at this," said Parth, showing him the tablet.

He tapped on the thumbnail of a video showing an athletic-looking amputee running around an obstacle course with ease—a prosthetic blade in place of her missing lower leg.

"What is this? What am I seeing?"

"I think showing him a video might raise more questions than it answers," offered Kailani with a hint of sarcasm.

"Shit. I guess I never thought about that."

"The magic allows us to see our memories again," tried Kailani.

"Not exactly how I would describe it," replied Parth.

"I have to use a context he'll understand," explained Kailani. "I can't refer to photos, videos, or recording. Those things have no meaning."

"Makes sense," he agreed.

"You have seen this?" asked Kai. "This is your memory?"

"Not mine," replied Parth. "Somebody else's."

"And this woman can run and leap without her foot?" he continued, now accustomed to accepting such fantastic pronouncements about magic without question.

"Yes. And so will you."

Serge took the tablet from Parth and pulled up the same application he'd used to model their settlement and experience the view from the lanai through the eyes of a simulated person—the one he learned while building virtual Singapore during his internship at Dassault Systemes years earlier.

"Here," he showed Kai. "This is a representation of you."

Kai furrowed his brow at Kailani. She tried a few different ways to relay the concept of a representation before he finally nodded and turned back to Serge.

"This is your injury," he continued, removing the left foot and lower portion of the leg from the modeled human. "And this is what we will build for you."

Serge then opened a 3D model of a simple blade design he and Parth had devised based on their research, and using materials they had on hand. He affixed it to the simulated human, playing through several pre-defined scenarios to show how it would behave.

"You have done this for me?" asked Kai.

"Not yet," replied Serge. "But we soon will. For now, we have another gift."

Parth retrieved a set of crude crutches from where he'd propped them against the wall near the door on the way in, and then demonstrated how to use them as he returned to Kai's bedside.

"This will allow you to move around until we can finish your new foot," he explained. "Would you like to try?"

Kai looked hopefully at Dr. Kitzinger.

"It's time to get you out of bed and moving," agreed the doctor.

Dr. Kitzinger helped his patient sit up and swing his legs over the side of the converted hospital bed. Gingerly, Kai transferred his weight to his right leg and stood as the doctor and Kailani supported him from either side. Parth helped by slipping the crutches under Kai's armpits and showing him how to grip the handles. He took a few tentative steps forward; the doctor following close behind with the bag of antibiotics raised high in one hand.

"I thought of that, doc," said Parth, pointing to a bamboo extension with a hook at the end protruding up from one crutch.

He took the IV bag from the doctor and hung it from the hook.

"Not bad," said Dr. Kitzinger with a nod.

"Can I go outside?" asked Kai after completing a few successful circuits of the small room.

"Of course," replied Kailani. "You are not a prisoner."

"What about you-know-who—outside the door?" asked Parth.

"I'll take care of that," offered Kailani. "Give me a minute and then bring him outside."

Kailani went to where Jen sat outside the main door.

"Move back," she demanded.

"What's going on?"

"Kai's coming out for a walk, and I don't want you getting too close."

"I'm not going to do anything," she said, shaking her head. "I'm not even armed, remember?"

"Just stand back, okay?"

"Fine," agreed Jen.

Parth peeked out before taking a couple of steps into the plaza once he was satisfied Jen was out of the way. Behind him, Kai emerged from the doorway and paused, taking a deep breath of the fresh outside air. Jen stared in amazement. Even on crutches, the warrior was an imposing sight. Tall, muscular, and adorned with intricate tattoos, he looked like something out of a movie.

"You arrived so recently and built all of this?" he marveled as he looked around the square. "How many of you are there?"

"Don't answer that," warned Jen, the voice from the tablet translator loud enough for her to hear from a few paces away. "It's a matter of security."

"Forty," replied Kailani, narrowing an eye at her.

"Jesus Christ, Kailani."

Kai looked at Jen with curiosity.

"You are a warrior," he stated. "I can see it in your manner."

"Yes," she agreed with a steely, unblinking gaze.

"A woman—yet so fierce."

The translator did not capture emotion well, but something about his eyes and tone of voice conveyed admiration rather than disapproval.

"Are you hungry?" asked Kailani, anxious to keep any encounter with Jen as short as possible. "We will serve our evening meal soon."

"Yes. Thank you," he replied. "But first, I would like to—relieve myself."

"Of course," laughed Dr. Kitzinger. "Please come with me."

The doctor led him diagonally across the plaza to the communal restrooms, showing him the long, wooden trough that served as the men's urinal. A steady stream of water entered at one end and drained from the other. Valves were in short supply, and water conservation was not yet a priority. Kai looked at him questioningly.

"I'll show you," offered the doctor.

Taking some time to overcome the discomfort of being watched, he eventually managed to demonstrate the intended use of the trough. Then, he showed how to sit on one of the composting toilets—in case he hadn't quite met Kai's immediate needs. Finally, he showed Kai where to wash his hands when he'd finished.

"I'll be outside," he concluded with an appropriate gesture, having left the translator with Kailani.

"How'd that go?" asked Parth.

"I didn't stick around to find out," shrugged the doctor. "I'll leave it to you to go in after and find out if anything went wrong."

A few minutes later, Kai appeared, shaking the excess water from his hands.

"Come on," urged Kailani. "Let's go get some food and see who's there to meet."

***

They entered the common building in the early stages of dinner service when there were only a few people there. Whatever conversations they were having stopped abruptly when they noticed Kai. Luping, having received a hit from Parth to let her know they were coming, was already sitting with Melinda, checking the door with anticipation every few seconds.

"Over here," she called as Parth entered the room just behind the imposing warrior.

"This way," advised Parth with a gentle tug on Kai's arm.

They joined the two pregnant women and sat down. Kai struggled briefly with his IV lines, propping the crutches beside him.

"Hello, Melinda," he said in English.

"Hello Kai," she replied with a blush. "Let me get you a plate of food, since I know what you like now."

"Please," he replied, this time through the translator Kailani still held, "I will gladly eat whatever I am offered."

"Good looking *and* charming," marveled Luping, raising an eyebrow at Parth.

"Yeah, yeah," he joked as he pointed at her belly. "A little too late for you."

"This is Luping," said Kailani. "She is another scientist."

"Hello, Luping," he greeted in English again.

"Hello," she replied, offering her hand.

He shook it awkwardly; having not yet mastered the skill he'd only just learned was a traditional greeting among his new friends.

"Another scientist?" he asked.

"We are many scientists," she explained. "There are many kinds of magic we study."

"And warriors?"

"We have warriors," she assured.

At that moment, Melinda returned to the table with a plate for Kai, and Jen walked into the building. She glanced over at them as she went to the food line.

"Can we invite your warrior to eat with us?" asked Kai.

"I don't think so," replied Kailani. "She is suspicious of you."

"She is right to be suspicious," he said with a smile. "Otherwise, she is not a clever warrior."

Jen filled a heaping plate of food and looked around for a quiet place. As she sat, Kai called out to her.

"Kai pū me mākou."

Perplexed, Jen looked to Kailani for an explanation.

"He wants you to eat with us," she translated reluctantly.

"Do you mind?" asked Jen as she approached.

"Yeah, but it would be rude not to indulge our guest. You still unarmed?"

Jen showed her empty holster without answering, and Kailani gestured to an empty chair opposite herself and Kai.

"What is your name?" he asked via the translator as she sat.

"Jen."

"Hello, Jen," he said, clearly proud of the one English phrase he'd learned.

"Hello, Kai. Nice to meet you."

"How many warriors do you have here?" he started.

"No small talk with you, huh? Straight to the point."

Kai looked at Kailani for guidance on the strange translation.

"Try not to use figures of speech or clichés," she advised. "The translator's not good with those."

"Let's talk about something else," tried Jen again.

"I am not your enemy," he assured.

"Why should I believe that?"

"Because I am grateful to you for helping me, and because we will soon have a common enemy."

"Pa'ao," said Jen simply.

"Yes. Pa'ao. I know his strength. I know how he will attack. Let me help you prepare."

"Why would you do that?"

"Because my people do not have the strength to fight him alone. If you cannot fight, then we will all die, or live like animals under his rule."

"If Pa'ao is not afraid of this island—if he comes here—we will fight," she assured.

"We will fight together," he suggested. "I can bring my people here from Moloka'i to stand by your side."

"We don't need your people to defeat Pa'ao."

"But his people need us," interjected Kailani.

"Listen. There's no point in having this conversation until we talk to Olena."

"Where the hell is she?"

"Farzin's looking for her now. I'm sure she's close."

***

After dinner, the group gave Kai a tour of the Punchbowl settlement. They didn't climb the crater wall to see what was hidden in the bowl itself, both because of Kai's limited mobility and Jen's insistence they maintain at least some critical secrets. They did, however, take a walk down to the harbor to see the dock.

"What is this?" asked Kai.

"It's where we dock our ship," explained Kailani.

"Just one? It must be big."

"Do you think Pa'ao and Pili will attack us here?" asked Jen, changing the subject.

"No," he replied immediately. "It is enclosed, and they will be vulnerable before they can exit their canoes. They will choose a long, shallow beach to come ashore."

"Waikiki," suggested Parth.

"More likely, the other side of Diamond Head or even Waimanalo," replied Jen. "They're closer to Moloka'i. If Kai's people really plan to bug out for Kauai, then Pa'ao should make it across Moloka'i pretty fast. After that, it's a straight shot over to the southeast side of O'ahu."

"That's some good news, I guess," said Parth. "At least they'll be far from our infrastructure."

"We need to set up watch on the ridge above where we arrived at Aiden Point," continued Jen, without listening. "Do we know if we can catch the signal from Diamond Head from there?"

"Not sure. We'll need to ask Matteus."

"Better yet, we should test it out. We'll set up watch on Diamond Head, too. It's higher, and might give us a better chance to spot them early."

"We're going to get spread thin," warned Kailani. "We could really use help from Kai's people to cover all the potential landing sites."

"We'll talk to Olena soon," assured Jen.

"I hope so," replied Kailani. "It's creeping me out that she's disappeared without saying anything."

***

The opportunity to move around in the fresh air had been a welcome change for Kai, but he grew tired from the exertion and was ready to rest again. They followed the path through the trees up the gentle rise towards the crater, and the tired warrior struggled his way up the last few steps of the steeper incline by the common building.

On their way across the plaza, Farzin caught up with them, pulling Jen aside to speak with her away from the others.

"I can't find Olena anywhere," he said. "I tried hitting her, too, but didn't get a response. I don't even know if she has a device with her."

"This is weird."

"Yeah. I guess she's not happy about being outed. Probably trying to figure out what to do."

"Come and talk to us. That's what she should do. I didn't even see her leave during the argument at the clinic. Did you?"

"I didn't see exactly when she left, but I looked around when Kailani pulled the gun. She was already gone then."

"Went to get a weapon?"

"She'd be back by now."

"Maybe not. The weapons we're not carrying on us are all secured up top. If Jayson really took the boxes of—of the other stuff—she'd have noticed."

"Shit. You're right. She's going to be on the warpath," realized Farzin.

"And she doesn't know about the threat from Pa'ao, just about Kai."

"Do you think we need him and his people?"

371

"With everyone else gone, and miles of coastline to watch? Yeah. I think we might. And Olena probably still wants to kill him."

"We'll just stick to the plan and keep watch to intercept her before she can do anything. I'll take over now so you can get a bit of sleep," he offered.

"Yeah. Sounds good," she agreed.

Farzin jogged towards the clinic and caught up with the others just as they arrived at the door.

"Hey," he called. "I'm taking watch for a bit."

"Stay outside," reminded Kailani coldly.

"Come on," he protested. "Haven't I earned your trust yet?"

"No," she replied, turning to walk inside without him.

Kai, already inside, stopped in his tracks and maneuvered himself awkwardly back towards the door on his crutches.

"I know your voice," he said, looking outside. "You were on the beach where I arrived."

Farzin didn't immediately respond. He knew they were communicating with the injured warrior through a translation app, but hadn't seen it in action yet. The instant, well-phrased words caught him off guard.

"Yes," he said finally.

"You were angry. Why?"

"I didn't think you belonged here," he replied candidly to the unexpected interrogation.

"What about now? Do you think I belong here?"

"I'm not sure yet."

Kai didn't respond. He simply nodded his acceptance of the earnest reply before retreating to his bed. Kailani narrowed her eyes at Farzin and turned to follow the warrior inside.

Chapter Thirty-Nine

HERMAN AND JAYSON CAUGHT the late end of dinner that evening. After the tense encounter with Jen, Jayson had gone to do some work in the fields as a way to calm himself down. Having lost track of time while personalizing his newly completed residence, Herman had missed out on the first part of the earlier commotion, arriving closer to the uneasy conclusion.

"Quite a lot of excitement today," started Herman to prompt his quieter-than-usual companion to fill in some blanks.

"I'm still shaking a bit," he revealed.

"Angry?"

"Damned right, I'm angry. I can't believe people would go along with murdering off the population of an entire planet."

"It's not *all* their fault, Jayson."

"The hell it's not," he shot back, "everyone makes their own choice."

"It's not that simple. You know my own country has a terrible, terrible history with this kind of thing."

"You seriously want to justify that people are going along with this?"

"Not justify," clarified Herman. "Understand. In Germany, every child learns the unvarnished truth about the Holocaust. No matter how I try to describe it, the words are inadequate to capture the tragic enormity of our failure as a society. We learn this not so that we feel some kind of eternal shame, but so we remain vigilant against it happening again. Even so, we have neo-Nazis marching in the streets—more of them every year, it seems."

"Fucking fascists crawling out of the woodwork everywhere. That's one thing I don't miss at all."

"I'm sure Samaira would agree when I say humans are terribly easy to manipulate—to drive into a state of pure, irrational madness," continued Herman. "Did you notice the words Jen used earlier in the plaza?"

"What do you mean?"

"She talked about 'filth' when referring to the inhabitants of this world. For a German like me, this kind of phrasing sets off immediate alarms. We recognize the parallels—the deliberate word choices used to dehumanize broad categories of people. Jen has been programmed to see the people here as less than human, and not worthy of empathy."

"I guess Kamaras didn't count on the rest of us figuring it out."

"He knew some would," shrugged Herman. "All part of his calculations, I assume."

"Huh?"

"He doesn't need as much support as you might think. Of those we've exposed to the conspiracy, how many are as worked up as you and me?"

"I don't know. Maybe half?"

"Exactly. So we have a bit less than a third of our total population—the ones with the guns, by the way—convinced the inhabitants of this world are not worthy of living."

"I guess," agreed Jayson.

"And maybe another third, including you and me, that finds the notion abhorrent and will resist."

"Maybe," he shrugged.

"It's the last third that's critical," explained Herman. "The ones who choose not to get involved."

"The ones who do nothing are critical?" he asked.

"Exactly. Those willing to sit on the fence—the ones who are proudly and ignorantly apolitical—they are the ones that allow evil to succeed."

"I bet you wish you hadn't signed up for this."

"If I knew what this was *really* about, I would not have agreed to come," admitted Herman. "But now that I am here with a chance to do something? I wouldn't leave even if I could."

"Really?"

"Whether or not we will admit it," explained Herman, "every German eventually asks themselves who he would have been under the rule of the Nazis. I have a chance to answer that for myself."

"That's a lot of baggage to carry."

"I don't know," shrugged Herman. "Every nation has something like this in their history. We just haven't forgotten ours yet."

"I guess," allowed Jayson.

"What are we going to do about the bioweapons?" asked Herman, changing the subject.

"Destroy them," replied Jayson. "I had Matteus hide them for now."

"Matteus?"

"He was up there working on something in the comms room when I busted into the security team storage."

"Alone?" asked Herman, wrinkling his brow.

"Yeah. Why?"

"Have you checked on him since you were up there?"

"No."

"Olena is on the loose, Jayson. Didn't you think she'd start by looking for a weapon?"

"Shit!" realized Jayson.

He leaped to his feet and ran to the door with Herman on his heels. Fueled by panic, it took only minutes to climb to the top of the crater. Cresting the rim, they could hear Matteus calling for help inside the building.

"Matteus!" called Jayson as he burst through the door.

"About fucking time," he panted.

He was standing on his toes with his arms extended above him, lashed to an overhead beam, his ankles bound. His face was bloodied and bruised.

"What happened?" demanded Jayson as he and Herman began untying him.

"What do you think happened? Olena came up here and kicked my ass."

"The containers?"

"To hell with the containers. What about me?"

"You'll be fine," assured Jayson. "Did you hide them?"

"Why do you think she was so pissed off?"

"Okay. What did you tell her?"

"I'm a computer geek, Jayson," reminded Matteus. "Not a soldier."

"What did you tell her?"

"I told her you took the stuff and went north with it."

"Good thinking," said Jayson with relief.

"You're not mad?"

"If you hadn't done that, she'd have beaten the hiding spot out of you."

"Well, now she's going to beat it out of you—if she hasn't already found it."

"How would she find it?"

"I don't know. Following my tracks? I don't know how any of this shit works," he said with a shrug. "We're in over our heads on this."

"Try to relax, Matteus," suggested Herman. "You're just a bit shaken up."

He slumped down onto the floor, rubbing his sore shoulders, and eyed Herman.

"Easy for you to say."

"Catch your breath and have some water," said Herman, passing him a canteen from the desk.

"I don't want to catch my breath. I want to get the hell out of here before she comes back."

"That's a pretty good idea," admitted Jayson, with a glance at Herman. "We need to rethink everyone's safety—not just Kai's."

***

Everyone except Farzin and Kailani gathered for an update on the situation. The two stayed behind at the clinic to ensure their guest was comfortable and safe, while the others learned of the troubling assault on Matteus. They decided everyone would spend the night together huddled safely in the common building with

Jen guarding the door. Given the uncertainty over Olena's next move, safety in numbers seemed the best approach.

"I'll stay in the clinic with Kai," decided Jayson after explaining the full story of the day's events in case anyone, unlikely as it seemed, was unaware of the earlier confrontation and revelation of the terrible nature of Scylla and Charybdis.

"Why?" asked Samaira.

"Kai and I are her most likely targets," he explained. "The clinic is smaller, easier to defend, and it'll put fewer people in harm's way if the two of us are together."

"How would she even know where to find you?"

"We have to assume she's watching us by now," replied Jen. "She's special ops, and she knows what she's doing."

"Fuck *me*. This just keeps getting better and better," lamented Parth, shaking his head. "You didn't think to tell us that before?"

"There's a lot we have to talk about," admitted Jen, "but now is not the time. We need to bring Olena back in first."

"I'm heading to the clinic before it gets dark," decided Jayson.

"Are you sure it's safe?" asked Samaira.

"It's only a couple of hundred meters across the plaza," he assured. "And it's not getting any safer if I don't go now."

Jayson squeezed past Jen, already standing in the doorway looking nervously around outside. Farzin nodded from the far side of the plaza, and Jayson tried his best to look confident as he jogged over to meet him at the clinic entrance.

"Anything?" he asked as he passed through the door with visible relief.

"Nothing," confirmed Farzin. "Could be a long night."

He continued past the lobby and found Kailani sitting alertly by Kai's side.

"You should go to the common room," suggested Jayson. "It'll be safer there."

"I'm not going anywhere," she asserted.

"It's just that—"

"I said I'm not going anywhere, Jayson."

"Fine," he relented, heading for a chair in the corner. "Guess I'll make myself comfortable over here."

"You're scared," observed Kai.

"No," insisted Jayson. "Just concerned. Everything is fine."

"What is happening?"

Jayson hesitated, not wanting to reveal the potential danger.

"One of our warriors is missing," said Kailani, "and we're afraid she's not ready to accept you here. We'll keep you safe until we find her."

Kai nodded, and did not ask about it further as he contemplated the implications. Jayson slumped in the chair and let out a long sigh, betraying his own feelings were well beyond mere concern.

***

The moon and stars illuminated the plaza in an eerie, pale blue light. Above the building entrances all around, small LEDs provided some additional light that was almost unnoticeable on clear nights when the bright Milky Way cut across the sky like a distant, jagged scar. Though hours had passed with no sign of Olena, Jen and Farzin remained vigilant.

A little after 3:30 in the morning, a loud bang against one of the closed shutters where the new lanai was currently under construction startled Jen to alertness. A few of those sleeping closest woke at the sound, whispering worriedly among themselves. Jen quietly hurried to the back of the room and urged them into silence while she listened for signs of a forced entry.

On the other side of the plaza, Farzin jumped from his chair upon hearing his name whispered urgently from somewhere out of sight.

"Olena? Is that you?"

"Yeah. It's me," she whispered, appearing from around the corner. "What's going on?"

"You're what's going on," he replied quietly. "Where the hell have you been?"

"Trying to track down our missing supplies. What are you doing here?"

"Just guarding the clinic."

"From what?"

"From you."

"Have you forgotten who's in charge?" she whispered harshly. "You don't get to guard things from me."

She tried to step around him, but he maintained his position between her and the door.

"Get the fuck out of my way," she hissed.

"I can't do that," he whispered. "I made a promise I wouldn't let you in. Not until we all talk this through."

She stared at him icily without saying a word.

"Things are getting complicated," he continued. "Kai has some intelligence you really need to hear."

"He has a name now, does he?"

"Yeah," replied Farzin, glancing at the ground.

"We were warned about this," she said, shaking her head.

"It's not just about him anymore," protested Farzin. "We're going to have real problems here if we're not reasonable."

"I understand," she said, with a nod.

"You do?"

"Of course," she assured, putting her hands on his shoulders.

Before he could say another word, Olena drove her knee into his groin. Clasping her hand over his mouth to muffle the cry as he doubled over, she slammed his head back against the wall. Farzin slid to the ground.

She glanced across the plaza to make sure Jen hadn't witnessed the attack. Fortunately, she was still investigating the cleverly improvised distraction on the far side of the common building. Crouching down, Olena hoisted the limp body of her colleague back onto his chair and set him upright. Farzin's head slumped forward in a decidedly unnatural way. She pulled his chair a few inches from the wall, propping his head up to make him look alert to a distant observer. With one more glance across the plaza, she slipped quickly into the clinic.

Inside the dimly lit room, Jayson was asleep in the corner chair with his head tilted back, snoring softly. Kailani, too, was finally asleep at Kai's bedside after hours of fighting her fatigue. Occasionally, her head would slump forward and startle her into momentary wakefulness while she readjusted her position. The recovering warrior, troubled by Jayson's apparent fear, lay in that state of restful alertness familiar to all soldiers in the calm before battle.

Olena burst suddenly through the door, knife in hand, triggering the improvised warning device Jayson had fashioned from an aluminum cup and a piece of
string. She was moving so quickly the cup never had time to clatter against the
floor as intended. Instead, it swung across her upper thigh, wrapping the string
around her and throwing her slightly off balance as she sprinted for the bed.

Kai rolled quickly away from his approaching attacker just as she fell to her knees
and drove her blade into the empty mattress where he'd been lying only a split
second before. He crashed down onto the floor on the far side of the bed, ripping
out his IV line and knocking the wind out of himself.

"Fuck!" screamed Olena as she jumped to her feet and attempted to vault over
the bed.

As she braced her arms to jump, Kailani lunged out of the chair and tackled her.
The two women crashed to the ground and began grappling with one another.

"Farzin!" yelled Jayson, rushing towards the sounds of the scuffle. "Get in here!"

He struggled to discern the shapes wrestling on the floor, rightly deciding the
one quickly gaining the upper hand was Olena. He kicked at her center of mass and
caught her in the ribcage with his boot. She looked up at him wide-eyed, snarling
like a feral animal.

"You!" she spat, rising to her feet over Kailani's now motionless body.

He backed away as she took two slow steps toward him.

"Calm down, Olena," he pleaded. "We need to talk."

"You need to fucking talk unless you want me to gut you. Where did you put
the stuff you stole?"

"I—I don't," he stuttered as he found himself backed up against the wall with
nowhere to go.

She raised the knife menacingly to reinforce the seriousness of her threat.

"If you kill me, you'll never find it."

"I'm not going to kill you," she promised. "But I'm going to make you wish I
had."

At that moment, Kai appeared behind her and swung one of his crutches with
both hands, striking her raised arm to send the knife clattering across the floor.
Hopping on one foot, he somehow kept his balance to wind up for another swing.

"Mother*fucker*!" yelled Olena as she turned around.

Kai's second swing was weak, and she easily caught his improvised weapon as it brushed past her face. She thrust the crutch back into his chest, knocking him off balance as he tried valiantly to stay upright while maneuvering on one leg. Falling awkwardly to the ground, he struck his head on a table leg.

Before he could regain his senses, Olena was on top of him with her fingers wrapped around his neck. He thrashed about violently, clawing at her face in a desperate attempt to loosen her stranglehold. His arms grew weak and heavy as his face turned purple. Sensing he was almost finished, Olena leaned down on his throat to choke out the last bit of life.

Suddenly, her eyes widened in shock, and she tried to say something. Instead of words, only blood emerged from her mouth, dripping onto Kai's face. With the last of his strength, he heaved her lifeless body to one side, her fingers slipping from around his neck. Jayson was standing there, hovering over him, staring at the blood-covered knife in his hand.

"Ua 'eha 'o ia," gasped Kai as he fought to catch his breath.

"Huh?" asked Jayson, still in shock.

"Kailani," he said.

Jayson snapped back to reality with a quick shake of his head and hurried to the light switch by the door. He cranked it up all the way and looked over to where he'd last seen Kailani during the skirmish. She was still lying in the same spot, panting, with a growing pool of blood beside her.

"No!" he cried as he scrambled to her side.

She looked at him and moved her lips, but no sound emerged.

Jayson quickly lifted her bloodstained shirt and discovered the knife wound in her stomach.

"No, no, no," he pleaded.

"Kailani!" panted Kai in desperation as he crawled up beside her.

He looked at Jayson helplessly.

"Kōkua koe iā ia!"

"Press here," instructed Jayson. "I'll get the doctor."

"Kōkua koe iā ia!" repeated Kai frantically.

"Look, I don't know what you're saying. Press here."

381

He demonstrated what to do, unsure if it was even the right thing under the circumstances, and then positioned Kai's hand in place of his own over the wound before jumping to his feet to get the doctor. Passing Farzin's slumped form in the chair, he didn't bother stopping to see if his failed protector was okay. He started yelling for help as he ran across the plaza, and Jen shot out of the common building.

"What's happening?" she demanded as she closed the gap in seconds.

"We need the doctor," panted Jayson, pushing past her. "Now!"

"What is it?"

"Kailani's been stabbed. Olena fucking stabbed her," he cried. "She needs the doctor."

"Where's Olena?"

"She's dead. Kailani needs help."

Dr. Kitzinger had overheard the commotion and rushed out into the plaza just as Jayson arrived.

"Kailani's been stabbed—in the stomach," he explained urgently as he began tugging the doctor toward the clinic.

Murmurs rose from inside the building as Jayson, Jen, and Dr. Kitzinger took off at a sprint.

"Farzin!" called Jen as they approached.

He didn't respond or move.

"What happened to Farzin?" she demanded.

"No idea," replied Jayson. "And I don't care right now."

He maneuvered himself between the doctor and Jen as they closed the last few meters, rushing Dr. Kitzinger past the unresponsive guard and through the door while Jen stayed behind to check on him.

Inside, Kai was still pressing his hand against Kailani's stomach and speaking comforting words to her when the pair arrived at her side. Jayson and Dr. Kitzinger could hear her faint responses, but could not understand the exchange.

"Let's get her onto the bed," suggested Jayson.

"No. Leave her here," cautioned the doctor as he pulled away Kai's hand to survey the damage.

After a brief inspection, he scrambled off to gather some surgical tools.

"Can you help her?" demanded Jayson as the frantic doctor threw a few things onto a metal tray and grabbed a bottle of antiseptic from the shelf.

"I'm not a trauma specialist, Jayson," he replied as he arrived back at Kailani's side.

As Kai leaned back to give the doctor space to work, he took one of Kailani's hands and clasped it in his own. Jayson crouched beside the doctor, holding the other one. She looked at him and struggled to speak.

"Thank you," she said weakly.

"For what?"

"For saving Kai. He told me what happened."

"Don't worry about that right now. Just keep breathing, okay?"

"I'm trying. But it's hard," she replied as a tear formed in the corner of her eye and rolled down her cheek.

"Don't give up," he urged.

"Promise me, Jayson," she whispered, "that you'll help him."

"I will," he assured, squeezing her hand tighter. "We both will."

She shook her head almost imperceptibly.

"No," she replied as another tear fell, "but I did what I could. I did something."

"Yes," he confirmed with a nod. "Yes, you did."

Her breathing continued to get weaker and shallower until it was nothing more than a series of desperate gasps.

"Come on," pleaded Dr. Kitzinger under his breath as he worked furiously to repair the damage.

Kai lowered his head and sobbed. Kailani had stopped breathing altogether.

"Doc!" cried Jayson. "She's not breathing! Do something!"

He stopped working and shook his head with dismay.

"There's nothing I can do to get her back and keep her alive, Jayson. We're not set up for this. I'm not *trained* for this."

"You've got to try!"

"I fucking did!" he yelled as he grabbed the tray of instruments at his side and flung it across the floor. "I'm not supposed to be dealing with stab wounds. I'm supposed to be delivering babies. We have almost no blood supplies—and with our fucking medics off doing who-knows-what, we've got no surgical team either. I can't do this myself!"

Jayson, still kneeling, released Kailani's hand and turned to the helpless doctor.

"I'm sorry, Ezra," he said, placing a hand on his shoulder. "I know you tried."

The doctor embraced him and began to sob.

At that moment, Jen came into the room.

"What's going on?" she demanded.

"That bitch killed Kailani. That's what happened," spat Jayson.

Kai grabbed onto the nearby table and raised himself up, staring menacingly at Jen the entire time.

"Shit. And what happened to her?" she asked, pointing at Olena's slumping body.

"Doesn't matter. She's dead now."

She searched his eyes momentarily and decided not to press the issue.

"I need some help with Farzin, doc," she continued.

"Fuck Farzin," spat Jayson.

"He's not to blame here. He was trying to help."

"He did a shit job of it, didn't he?"

Dr. Kitzinger wiped his eyes with his sleeve and took a deep breath.

"It's okay, Jayson. I'll check on Farzin," he whispered.

Kai continued glaring at Jen until she was out of the room. Jayson looked, shaking his head sadly at the angry warrior. Closing his eyes, he lay down on the cold clinic floor beside Kailani and wept.

Chapter Forty

THE HEAVINESS OF LOSS is impossible to escape in a small community. The nature of Kailani's violent death added to the sense of shock and helplessness felt by the Gamma recruits in the days following the unspeakable events in the clinic. Despite her culpability, Olena's death was, in some ways, even harder for them to absorb. Though many had shared the suspicion she was lying to them, it didn't prepare them for how the ultimate proof had manifested. The blinders were off, and no one could continue pretending the security team was either benevolent or benign.

The island itself seemed to mourn along with its new inhabitants. For days, unseasonably cold and persistent rain fell from a weeping sky. The air carried a chill, forcing the team to close the shutters in the common building and gather in the sterile coldness of the artificial lighting.

"We need to make some glass," observed Parth absently as he pushed some food around on his plate. "I feel like we're sitting in a cave."

"Or a coffin," added Jayson without realizing the implication.

"I wish this rain would stop," deflected Samaira. "A little sunshine would go a long way towards helping us feel better."

"How's Kai doing?" asked Jayson.

"Not well," she replied. "He blames himself for everything that happened."

"It's not his fault."

"Of course not," agreed Samaira, "but it's a normal reaction."

"I guess," shrugged Jayson.

"Speaking of normal reactions, how are you doing?"

"Same as everyone else, I suppose."

"Jayson, you killed someone," she replied. "I know how it feels, and I'm worried about you."

"Honestly? I don't feel anything about that."

"Lying to yourself isn't going to help you get over it."

"I'm not lying," he assured her. "I wish I was. It feels weird. I play it over in my mind, and I just don't care. I don't care that I killed her."

"You're still processing. When it hits you, and you need to talk, come find me."

"I will."

"I mean it, Jayson," she insisted. "Day or night—come and find me. You don't have to go through this alone."

The group was quiet while they made half-hearted efforts to eat the day's lunch offering.

"The blade is ready," offered Parth, breaking the uneasy silence.

"Huh?" said Jayson.

"For Kai. The prosthesis."

"Oh. That's good," he replied without enthusiasm.

"I know it's hard to be excited," allowed Parth, "but it might help him feel better."

"I'm sorry. It's great. It really is great that you guys did this. I don't imagine we have much time before he needs to get moving."

"What?"

"He has to go to Moloka'i to get his people before it's too late."

"Are you crazy?" demanded Parth. "He's not ready for that."

"Not alone," agreed Jayson. "But he and I can do it together."

"You *are* fucking crazy."

"Parth, it has to be done," added Samaira.

"What? You think either of them is ready for this?"

"They have to be," she insisted. "This is what they have to do."

"Did you talk him into this?"

"I promised Kailani I would help him," interjected Jayson, hitting the table with his fist. "As she lay on the floor dying in a pool of her own blood, I promised her."

Parth backed off and sighed.

"Holy shit. Have you guys talked to Jen and Farzin?" he asked.

"I'm done giving a shit what they think," answered Jayson for both of them. "If they want to stop us, they can come and try."

"Jesus Christ. This is nuts. You're not really willing to die for this, are you?"

"I am," he said flatly.

"Me too," added Herman from across the table. "If I have to."

"And me," agreed Samaira. "But I don't think it'll come to that. They're done."

"Farzin is done," agreed Luping. "Riyoko and I have been talking about it."

"What about Jen?" asked Parth, looking at Jayson.

"I don't know," he shrugged. "And I don't care."

"Jesus Christ," repeated Parth, still shaking his head.

***

The first blade fitting was not the celebration they imagined when they'd started the process days earlier. Nonetheless, Parth and Serge were proud of their work, and hopeful it would offer Kai a life-affirming opportunity for normalcy. Dr. Kitzinger and Samaira were at their side, watching with curiosity, as they demonstrated the technique for wrapping the stump and securing the prosthetic blade in place with a long, lace-up sleeve made from clothing they'd salvaged from Aiden so many months prior.

Although it looked nothing like a foot, Kai had seen the videos evidencing the astounding abilities of the blade-wearing athletes. Clearly, he was hopeful—and determined to make his new prosthesis work.

"It's going to take some time to adjust," warned Serge, as he and Parth helped Kai rise slowly from the bed.

He took a tentative step forward onto the blade, backing off quickly as it bent under his weight.

"It's not strong enough," he said.

"It's okay," assured Serge. "It is supposed to bend a little. That's how it works."

"Okay," replied the warrior doubtfully.

He again leaned tentatively onto the blade, immediately taking another step forward to get back onto his right foot. Instead of continuing his gait, he froze as his momentum carried his upper body forward, and his brain told him he had no left foot with which to continue. Parth was there to catch him as he started to topple.

"It'll be fine. You just need to practice."

"Let's give him the crutches," suggested the doctor. "That way, he can move around freely while he gets used to it."

"Yeah," agreed Parth. "I think that's a good idea."

Samaira handed him the crutches and urged him to follow her outside.

"I have something I want to show you," she said. "But you're going to have to come for a walk."

"I will," he said with a determined smile—the first one Samaira had seen from him in days.

Outside the clinic, they turned north toward the looming crater wall.

"There?" he asked via the translator on Samaira's tablet.

"Not all the way. Not yet," she laughed. "We're just going up a little bit."

She walked forward twenty paces and turned back to watch him follow. He managed with ease, still relying on the crutches and only gingerly testing his weight on the blade. Where she stood waiting, the pathway up the crater intersected another one running along the wall where most of the living quarters were located. Hardly giving him a chance to rest, she led him westward past a collection of buildings.

As he mounted a step in the path, it caught one of the crutches, and he stumbled towards her.

"Don't fall down!" she said with alarm, rushing forward to catch him.

"Fall down?" he asked in English, as he recovered his balance and caught himself. The translator had evidently not handled the phrase well.

"Fall down," she repeated, motioning with her arm.

"Hāʻule i lalo," he said, mimicking her motion as if to reinforce the meaning.

"That's right," she said with a smile.

Samaira continued the tour, leading him past a small open area with a few flowers and vegetables growing in neat rows. She paused at the building just beyond it.

"This is where Parth lives with Luping. She's going to have a child soon. The next one is the home of the doctor and Melinda."

"She will have a child soon as well," recalled Kai.

"Yes. That's right."

A little further along, Samaira showed two more apartments.

"This one is mine, and the next one belongs to Jayson."

"You are alone?"

"For now," she confirmed with a smile.

Next to Jayson's living quarters, they paused where another dwelling was taking shape. The roof was in place, shielding it from a light rain, and some tools sat just inside the open door.

"And this one?" he asked.

"This one is for you—and your family."

"Here? Among you?"

"Of course," she confirmed, leading him through the doorway.

"It is not necessary. I have no family," he said.

"But you will," she assured him, "and you can raise your children right here."

"You are cruel," he said with a sudden look of sadness. "I am not a man anymore, and will not have a family. I do not even know if my people will still accept me as their leader."

"Why not?" she demanded.

"I am broken," he replied, pointing to his missing foot. "I am not a man."

"That is ridiculous," she said. "Honor and action define a man, not a foot."

"I wish that were true. But a man must be complete."

She took his hand and kissed him gently on the cheek. He closed his eyes, a single tear running down his face. She placed the tablet on the countertop and kissed him again. This time on the lips. Her hands caressed his muscular arms and bare chest as he kissed back with passion. Kai dropped one of his crutches to the ground, grabbing her by the waist to pull her closer. Encouraged by his reaction, Samaira slipped a hand under the wrap tied around his waist to tease him to attention.

"See?" she remarked with a grin. "You are definitely still a man."

He went to kiss her again, but she placed a palm on the confused warrior's chest, pushing him gently back. Without a word, she grabbed his other crutch and tugged it a few times until he released it to her. She threw it to the ground, still smiling coyly. He now understood it was a game—and he was more than willing to play along.

She slowly removed her top and then slid her pants and underwear to the floor, flinging them aside with her toe. Instead of moving toward him, she backed away until her naked body pressed against the far wall.

"Take it off," she demanded, pointing at his wrap.

He wordlessly obeyed, revealing himself to her while managing to stay balanced without the support of his crutches.

"If you want me, you'll need to come over here."

Kai laughed and nodded approvingly at her ploy as the translation emerged from the tablet beside him. He took a tentative step forward, pausing briefly to regain his balance before continuing. Slowly, he made his way to her and braced himself against the wall with one hand before kissing her deeply once more. Samaira wrapped him in a passionate embrace, determined to banish any lingering doubts Kai might have about his manhood.

***

The shutters were open for the first time in days, allowing sunlight to stream into the common building at dinnertime. Though some conversations among the gathered recruits were returning to more mundane and welcome topics, the ominous warnings from their curious new guest still weighed heavily.

When he entered the room, trailing behind Samaira, everyone was silent. He'd abandoned his crutches and was walking carefully on his own towards the table of recruits most familiar to him. Halfway there, he stumbled, and Samaira quickly caught his arm to steady him. Something about the way they looked at each other at that moment sent a jolt through his mind, but Jayson promptly dismissed it as an overreaction.

"I was looking for you guys," he said. "Where'd you go?"

"I was just taking Kai on a tour to show him where he'll be living."

"What'd he think?"

"Why don't you ask him?" prompted Samaira, placing the tablet on the table.

"How do you like your new home?" he asked.

"It is too much," he said. "I have brought you nothing but pain, and you repay me with such kindness. Why?"

"Because all people deserve to be treated with kindness until they prove otherwise," he said simply.

"I will do my best to deserve it, then," he said with a solemn nod. "Thank you."

"Your people," continued Jayson, "are they in danger now?"

"I admit I have lost some days," said Kai. "How long have I been here?"

"Ten days," said Samaira.

"By now, Pa'ao and Pili have returned to Hana to reunite with their canoes. They will be ready to travel to Moloka'i soon."

"Then we don't have much time," replied Jayson. "Are you ready to go to your people?"

"I have no choice except to be ready."

"Then I'm ready, too."

"You?"

"Yes. I will paddle with you to Moloka'i to get your people. Two are better than one, right?"

"Two are better than one," agreed Kai.

"Jayson will show them the people here are flesh and blood—like them," added Samaira. "You need to convince them there are no demons on O'ahu."

"I will not convince everyone," he warned, "but maybe those who fled Hawai'i will trust me as the rightful voice of the Ulu people."

"Then we leave tomorrow at first light to get them," resolved Jayson.

Kai nodded again.

"Let me get you some food," offered Samaira. "You're going to need all of your strength."

Another jolt coursed through Jayson as she stood and traced her fingertips up Kai's arm before going to the food line. This time, it was not as easy for him to dismiss.

***

At dawn the next morning, equipped with food and water for their trip, Jayson and Kai set off by foot for the beach near the fishpond where Farzin had dragged the canoe all the way ashore. Samaira and Riyoko—with baby Jasmine in her arms—accompanied them. The young mother had decided that it was time to reconcile with Farzin and join him in their small hut by the beach, where they would be a family again.

Kai started the hike with a single crutch for support, but discarded it shortly after leaving. Though still awkward on uneven ground, he was beginning to trust himself to stay upright, even enjoying a couple of short sprints. It didn't take nearly as long as Jayson had feared for them to travel the considerable distance to the beach that would mark only the beginning of their journey. If they were lucky, they'd be in the water before noon, and reach the shores of Moloka'i before dark.

Upon their arrival, Farzin rushed from the hut to embrace his family and then lofted Jasmine up to nuzzle her belly with his nose. She giggled with delight, unaware of any lingering tension between her doting parents. Kai went immediately to examine the outrigger and make sure it was seaworthy.

"How does it look?" asked Jayson.

"Better than me," he replied with an approving nod.

"Let's get moving, then. I'd like to get to your people before nightfall."

"My people will be on the far side of the island. We won't get there by nightfall."

"So we will arrive in the dark?"

"No. We will have to make camp alone tonight and meet them tomorrow. If we arrive at night, they might think we are shape-shifting demons and try to kill us."

"But we'll be safe in the day, right?" asked Jayson.

"Maybe," replied Kai.

"Don't lose your resolve now, Jayson," said Samaira. "You know how important this is."

"I'm doing this," he assured her, "but you'll have to forgive me if I'd rather not be dismembered in the process."

"I will keep you safe," promised Kai. "Just as you kept me safe."

There was a resolve and an earnestness to his response that comforted Jayson, and eased his momentary doubts.

"Need a hand with that thing?" called Farzin as he approached the small group standing around the canoe.

Kai raised an eyebrow at Jayson.

"It's alright. He just wants to help."

Riyoko, nursing Jasmine at her breast, came over to see them off as well.

"Grab the back," said Jayson to Farzin as he took hold of the outrigger's bow.

Kai, struggling a little to adapt to walking in the sand, lifted the boom, and the three men waded into the water. Once they'd loaded the provisions, Samaira handed Jayson the tablet.

"You'll need this," she reminded him.

"Yeah. I just hope it doesn't get wrecked."

"If Andrew was right, that should be pretty hard to do."

"Does it float?"

"Try not to find out," she advised.

Jayson sat down in the front of the canoe and turned back to see Samaira squeezing Kai's hand. Then, she kissed him before he waded back into the water to take his seat at the back. Jayson's instinctive reaction to the display of affection betrayed his heartbreak. Samaira offered him an apologetic look as she waved goodbye to the two men.

"Good luck," she said. "We'll be ready for you at the harbor in a few days."

Farzin saluted while Riyoko gently guided Jasmine's tiny hand in a wave of farewell. Jayson turned forward in his seat and began paddling without looking back.

Chapter Forty-One

THE FOLLOWING DAY, ON the east side of the central plaza, Herman and Serge rummaged through the stores building where the recruits kept spare parts and supplies that were not currently in use. Outside, two carts were quickly filling with the necessities to set up a camp. The same tents that had gradually come down to be placed into storage as permanent living quarters took shape were now to host a new set of occupants.

Samaira and Parth prepared a clearing south of their settlement to host the encampment. There wasn't much to do to get it ready—just removing some overgrowth and marking the layout of the tents and pathways. Samaira also insisted on beautifying the area with some flowers and equipping the large gathering tent with LEDs to ensure their new guests would feel welcomed and inspired. Leaving Parth to finish concealing the wiring, she went to fetch a cart so she could continue putting up tents. When she arrived at the storage building, she was annoyed to find Jen there interrogating Herman and Serge.

"Hey guys," she interrupted. "Is one of these carts ready to go?"

"Just about," replied Herman.

"You're helping, Jen?" she asked.

"Maybe if I knew what I was helping with."

"Should be pretty obvious. We have guests arriving."

"How many, exactly?"

"There's no way to be sure. Kai didn't know how many would be willing to come."

"Dozens? Hundreds? We've got to have an idea of the order of magnitude, right?"

"What does it matter?"

"Seriously? If a few hundred people show up, we're overrun."

"He estimated somewhere between twenty and one hundred. Does that help?"

"Jesus Christ," sighed Jen. "I wish you would talk to me about these things."

"I'll be honest, Jen. We don't trust you enough for that yet."

"Whether you trust me or not, the security of everyone here is still my priority. You're setting up a potentially hostile camp right on our doorstep. Couldn't you put them farther away?"

"Put *them* farther away?" asked Samaira. "I don't think you get it yet."

"What don't I get?"

"There's not going to be a *them*. Just an *us*. I'm giving up my place in case there are some families coming. I'll be living in a tent down there until we build some more apartments."

"Are you serious?"

"Me too," added Herman as he dropped another armload onto a cart.

"And me," agreed Serge from inside the store.

"You guys have lost your fucking minds."

"What did you expect would happen?" asked Samaira.

"I don't know. They'd help us fight off Pa'ao and then leave. Maybe some would stay behind to help us with fishing and farming—stuff like that."

"Like slaves?" asked Samaira, narrowing her eyes.

"No. Of course not," replied Jen. "I mean, they'd do their thing, and we'd do our thing. Like neighbors, or something."

"So more like separate, but equal?"

Herman winced at the impact of Samaira's rebuttal as if he'd just witnessed someone getting kicked in the testicles. Jen threw her hands in the air in exasperation.

"Fuck, Samaira. It's not like that. How can you possibly expect them to integrate? They're—"

"Primitive savages?"

"Are you going to twist everything I say?"

"If you're going to make it this obvious, then yes, I am. The older adults may never adjust fully, but the children—and those not yet born—could become our next great scientists, doctors, or engineers. We're shooting ourselves in the foot if we don't take advantage."

"You really believe that?"

"I do. In a couple of generations, we'll be completely integrated, and stronger than Kamaras ever imagined. When he does finally show up, he'll be facing a totally different situation than anything he's been able to simulate."

"And Josh and the others? When they return?"

"In a year? We'll be so intertwined, they won't be able to do a thing about it."

"How did everything get so screwed up?" asked Jen, shaking her head.

"Kamaras's plan from the outset is what's screwed up," reminded Samaira. "We're just trying to un-screw it."

Jen took a deep breath to compose herself.

"How can I help?" she asked.

"You can grab this cart and take it down to the site," interjected Herman. "It's ready to go."

"Okay," she nodded. "Fine."

Samaira raised a doubtful eyebrow at Herman as Jen walked off, pushing the loaded cart in front of her.

***

Jayson and Kai had already set off on the second leg of their journey after a night of surprisingly restful sleep on a sheltered beach partway along the southern shore of Moloka'i. Having already paddled past several small villages, soon they'd be navigating the strait separating the island from Maui and the danger that lurked there. Even though they hugged the near shore of the fourteen-kilometer-wide stretch of water, Jayson was nervous about being so close.

"We should have gone around the other side of the island," he remarked as he glanced uneasily to the east.

"The waves and currents there can be dangerous. This is the best way," assured Kai.

"What's the plan when we get to your people?"

"I will do my best to convince them we can be safe from Pa'ao with you on O'ahu. There is nothing more I can do."

They paddled on in silence, as they had for most of the journey. It was partly because Jayson had to turn his head awkwardly and stop paddling to be heard by the tablet propped up in the bottom of the canoe behind him. Mostly, however, he didn't feel like talking. He was angry with himself for letting Samaira slip away into the arms of someone else for a second time, and was trying to understand what he'd missed. Her budding relationship with Kai had come out of nowhere.

The mindless rhythm of paddling was hypnotic. Lost in thought for hours, Jayson hardly noticed as the villages on the coastline grew sparse, and finally disappeared entirely as they approached the northeast tip of the island. When they rounded the point, an enormous bay lay before them, and he could see a large settlement at the mouth of a river.

As they got closer, a crowd gathered on the beach. So far, the people they'd encountered along the shoreline seemed like simple fishermen—unadorned and wearing nothing but loincloths. The men gathering on the beach in front of them were different. Like Kai, the stern-faced warriors sported tattoos and wore colorful wraps with intricate patterns—and many of them carried primitive, fierce-looking weapons.

Jayson looked back at Kai to see his reaction, and so he could hear any translations coming from the tablet.

"There is no need for weapons, friends," called Kai. "Do you not know me?"

None of the resulting chatter was clear enough to register with the translator.

"Where have you been, Kai? And who is your companion?" called back a tall, muscular man.

"I was injured," he replied. "This man and his people saved me."

"I saw you fall, Kai. We mourned your death."

"I escaped," he replied as the outrigger ran aground on the beach among the onlookers.

"Such a strange-looking man, your friend. Where did his people find you?"

Kai did not answer. Carefully bracing himself, he stepped out of the canoe into the shallow water amid gasps from the gathered crowd. Jayson grabbed the tablet and got out as well. Together, he and Kai pushed the craft safely onto the sand as those closest cocked their weapons and took a step backward. Everyone was staring at the strange prosthesis with a mix of horror and fascination.

"If you saw me fall, Kameha, my friend, then you know how I was injured," said Kai in anticipation of the obvious question. "This man, Jayson, and his people made me whole again."

Jayson hadn't thought to turn down the volume on the tablet. As the English translation emerged for his benefit, the startled warriors turned aggressively towards him, but did not advance closer.

"Fuck!" he said, as he tried frantically to deactivate the app.

Before he could, it spat out what it decided was an appropriate translation for his expression of frustration. Jayson froze. Kai strode from the water and placed an arm around his shoulder.

"See? He is not so strange," said Kai with a broad smile. "He speaks like a warrior."

There were a few laughs among them, but Kameha was unconvinced.

"He did not speak any words I can understand," he protested. "It was that thing he carries."

"Yes," admitted Kai. "It allows him to speak with us. His language is different from ours."

"How is that possible?" demanded Kameha. "Is he a shaman?"

"No," interjected Jayson, following instructions from Samaira not to elevate his own position and risk undermining Kai in front of his people. "Just a man, like you."

"This thing is one of many gifts from his god, Akindele," explained Kai. "I have seen others, too."

"Where?" demanded Kameha.

"O'ahu," he said simply, waiting for the inevitable reaction.

"People do not go to O'ahu for help. They go there to die—or to spread death when they return."

"That was true," admitted Jayson, "until Akindele cast out the demon and brought my people to make O'ahu a place of gathering and peace."

"We have come here because Pa'ao and Pili will not give us peace," continued Kai. "None of us."

"And your god will defeat them?"

"No," replied Jayson. "Our god gave us magic so *we* can defeat them. And we will share that magic with you, if you join us."

"This is a trap," announced Kameha to the others. "A disfigured apparition of our friend, and a stranger talking of magic. The demon of O'ahu calls to us, but we will not listen."

"If you will not agree to return with us, then kill us where we stand," challenged Kai. "Because we will all die, anyway."

Jayson stared at him in disbelief and looked back at Kameha. The angry warrior seemed to favor the second option.

"Of course we will not kill you, brother," assured a shorter, stocky man emerging from the crowd. Beside him appeared another identical man.

"Mano! Malo!" greeted Kai with a sudden smile.

They walked forward to embrace their friend, despite a look of disapproval from Kameha.

"We will speak with you, brother—and feed you—as is our custom," said one of the twins in a rebuke of their companion's rudeness. "And you will tell us more of your plan to defeat our enemy."

Jayson breathed a sigh of relief. Perhaps he would still die on Moloka'i, but at the very least, they'd granted him a temporary reprieve.

***

Farzin, Riyoko, and Jasmine arrived back at the crater that same afternoon with various fresh and cured fish. It was enough, they hoped, to see them through any imminent attack. Their isolated hut was too exposed for them to stay, and Farzin would be too busy preparing defenses to do any more fishing for at least a few days.

He found Jen at the campsite and pulled her away to talk.

"This is nice—what you're doing," he said, "but we need to talk about our defenses."

"There's not much to talk about, Farzin. It's not like we have a lot of options."

"When Kai and Jayson return, we'll know for sure."

"We need to assume they're not coming back—and prepare accordingly."

"Yeah," he conceded. "Prepare for the worst case."

"The best thing we can do is extend the line-of-sight network and set up sentries. At the first sign of danger, everyone gets into the crater, and we mow them down as they come over the top."

"It's the only way to avoid spreading too thin and exposing our lines to penetration," agreed Farzin. "There's no way we can support more than one front."

"They're going to come from the southeast," she asserted. "Let's put the network gear up on the high ground above Aiden Point, where it can see the one at Diamond Head."

"Makes sense."

"If we're lucky, we can put a sentry where they can see Waimanalo and Wawamalu at the same time. Add someone at Diamond Head, and we've got the most likely landing spots covered."

"Is that enough?"

"I'd like someone near Akupu—up in the mountains to the west. They'd be able to cover Ewa Beach, the western beaches, and the central plain in case they want to be sneaky and come in from the north."

"Agreed," said Farzin with a nod. "I'll go over it with Matteus to see what we need for hardware."

"I've done my part here to extend an olive branch to the bleeding hearts," said Jen. "I'll drag all the carts up top. If we flip 'em on their sides, they'll make good enough walls for the weapons we'll be facing."

***

"I'm pretty sure the one at Diamond Head will be fine for anyone perched up here," explained Matteus as he and Farzin examined a three-dimensional map of the mountains above Waimanalo. "We shouldn't need to add a second relay."

"What about Akupu?" asked Farzin, panning over to the west.

"Theoretically, the one here at Punchbowl could work," replied Matteus doubtfully. "But it's pretty far, and the speeds would be slow. Any kind of weather could mess with it."

"Any downside to putting a relay up there just to be safe?"

"I can't think of any. Plus, it would give us coverage of the central valley and most of the west coast."

"What do you need to get it done?"

"Time," said Matteus. "And a companion that's done some climbing. This looks a lot harder than Diamond Head, and Denmark isn't exactly known for its mountaineering."

"You'll probably want two people, then. We'll need a volunteer to stay up there."

***

The volunteers gathered supplies and equipment, setting off in groups to climb the three peaks defining a perimeter around Punchbowl. Diamond Head was the most straightforward ascent, and closest to the settlement. Farzin and Samaira established themselves there so Farzin would be well-positioned to do additional recon at the most likely landing points and then get back to assist with the defense of their home.

Zaina and Parth perched themselves high above Waimanalo Beach, where the very top of the ridge offered a clear view of the network relay at Diamond Head. From there, they'd been able to send and receive hits from the rest of the team. The panorama from their peak was unequaled. They could see half of the eastern coast, and all the way to China Walls, jutting into the sea on the southeast side of the island.

Matteus, Herman, and Serge headed for Akupu. Herman would remain alone while Serge guided Matteus back to Punchbowl to look after the comms and computer networks during the critical days ahead.

***

The negotiations among Kai and his brethren were tense. Not only did it seem unlikely Kameha would allow anyone to join the defense of O'ahu, there was also some debate about whether he would allow Kai and Jayson to leave at all. Kameha had assumed the mantle of leadership of the remaining warriors from Maui and Hawai'i, and did not want to relinquish it or suffer any defections in favor of Kai. He declared the two men demons, suggesting they be put to death to prevent the spread of evil from the cursed island.

At the urging of the twin warriors, Mano and Malo, their uncle took a position in defense of Kai and Jayson to plead their case in front of the priests.

"This is the son of Kapawa," Moke reminded them. "He may not have a kingdom, but he is the last of the Ulu line of royal blood."

The priests declared only the gods could end the Ulu line. If Kai was meant to die, he would do so at the hands of Pa'ao or the demon on O'ahu. Adding to the insult of Kameha's loss in the debate, the priests decided all should be free to choose if they would flee to Kauai with Kameha or join in the defense of O'ahu with Kai.

As an outsider, Jayson could not take part in the discussions. While Kai and Kameha made arguments to persuade the men to join their disparate causes, he waited nervously outside by the fire under the watchful eye of a single guard. Occasionally, curious onlookers would stand at a safe distance to see the stranger from O'ahu. Jayson did his best to look non-threatening, offering them a deferential smile and wave as they stood staring at him.

As the debate continued into the night, the steady stream of spectators dwindled until it finally stopped altogether. Jayson stared absently at the glowing embers of the dying fire, occasionally throwing a small twig into their midst to watch it smolder before spontaneously erupting into flames. The sounds of a hushed

403

argument got his attention, and he looked over at his guard. The warrior gripped a young woman by the arm, issuing what sounded like a whispered admonishment. She responded harshly as she pulled her arm from his grip. Ignoring his pleas, she walked over to Jayson and regarded him curiously.

"Aloha," he said with a disarming smile.

She didn't respond immediately, so Jayson powered on the tablet, which he'd turned off to conserve battery power.

"Hello. My name is Jayson."

Evidently, she'd heard about the curious stone, because she didn't react with surprise when his strange words re-emerged from it in her own language.

"Hello, Jayson. I am Luni."

"I am happy to meet you, Luni."

She furrowed her brow as if the intent of the expression had not translated well. Her confusion passed quickly, and she spoke again.

"We are to choose if we will go with you and Kai to O'ahu or stay with Kameha."

Jayson was relieved. He'd not yet had an update from Kai, and was unsure if perhaps he was still arguing for their lives. If Luni was right, they'd moved beyond that.

"Yes," he replied simply, hoping she would reveal more.

"What do you think we should do?"

"Return with us," he said without hesitation. "Together, we can defeat Pa'ao and Pili."

"How do you know?" she asked. "Are you a warrior?"

"No," he admitted.

"I did not think so. What are you, then?"

"I provide our people with food. I grow things."

"So you are a farmer?" she asked. "I don't believe that either. Who would send a farmer with such an important message?"

"A farmer and a scientist. I help our people grow food, and we share in the task of collecting and preparing it."

He knew Kailani had taught the translator a scientist was someone who studied and applied magic. It wasn't strictly honest, but it would work in the short term. Luni regarded him through narrowed eyes as she digested the information.

"So you are like a shaman to your people?"

"No," he deflected quickly. "We are all scientists. Well, most of us."

"All of your men work with magic?"

"Everyone does—the women too. In our society, we share tasks equally."

Luni cocked an eye at him.

"The warrior leading the preparation of our defenses is a woman," he continued. "Her magic will keep you safe if you come with us."

A murmur rose as a crowd of warriors and older men filed out of the large hut on the opposite side of the pathway. They dispersed into small groups, still debating among themselves. Excusing himself from a group of men, Kai joined the pair at the fire.

"Hello, Kai," greeted Luni, looking at the prosthetic blade. "It's true, then, you lost your foot in battle?"

"Hello, Luni," he replied without answering the question.

"You move very well."

"Thanks to Jayson and his people, yes."

"Your friend is strange, Kai," she said with a smile. "But I think he is honest."

"He is honest," agreed Kai.

"What happens now?"

"In the morning, we will leave with all those who wish to come to O'ahu. Jayson and his people will teach us to use their magic, and we will teach them how we live on these islands."

"And I suppose someone has already decided what I wish?"

"Talk to your father and brother," advised Kai.

"I will," she assured him. "Goodbye, Jayson."

"Goodbye Luni," said Jayson. "I hope I will see you again."

Luni nodded and walked off into the night.

"You will not see her again," said Kai. "She is the sister of Kameha, and will go with him to Kauai. We should sleep now so we will be ready in the morning."

***

Just after dawn, Jayson and Kai set out from the beach in the northeast notch of Moloka'i with a group of forty-five men, women, and children in the largest outrigger Jayson had ever seen. Kameha, with several loyalists, was there as well to make sure he didn't suffer any additional defections.

Only after they'd pushed off and put some distance between themselves and the beach did Jayson relax. Surveying the occupants of the canoe for the first time without the unnerving distraction of Kameha hovering over them, he noted about twenty warriors and an approximately equal number of women. The remainder, about a dozen, were infants and children.

To their right, waves crashed against the steep cliffs rising from the water immediately beyond the beach. Though the sea was relatively calm, there was a sustained violence in the assault of water against rock—as if the two were enemies cursed to fight one another for eternity. Not usually one to note such things, Jayson was struck by the contrast between his growing calmness and the thunderous cacophony less than one hundred meters away.

The distant green peaks of Maui's northern rainforest came into view as they rounded the tip of Moloka'i, and the cliffs to their right gave way to low hills and rocky, isolated beaches. A pair of fishermen in a small canoe waved at them from near the shore. Jayson waved back. Then, they began shouting, their waving becoming more frantic. The fishermen were paddling toward them in an attempt to intercept the faster outrigger.

"Stop!" shouted Kai. "Those are not fishermen."

After hearing the translation, Jayson looked more closely. The approaching pair was not wearing traditional loincloths. They were dressed as women. When they shouted again, he realized they *were* women.

"What are you doing, Luni?" demanded Kai.

"My sister and I are coming with you," she shouted back.

"Your brother has already decided," he replied solemnly as the small canoe pulled up beside them. "You must go back."

Ignoring him, she tossed a bundle of her belongings onto the boat before helping her sister clamber aboard. Then, Mano and Malo grabbed Luni by the arms and pulled her up, too.

"Fine," said Kai with a shrug. "I will take you back to Kameha myself."

"It's too late for that," said Luni, pointing to the southeast horizon.

Kai and the others squinted against the still-rising sun. A speck on the water turned into two, then three. Before long, they could make out eight distinct craft approaching from the northwest tip of Maui.

"Paddle!" shouted Kai. "If we are lucky, they have not seen us yet."

Along with those women unburdened by infants, the warriors took up their paddles, quickly establishing a rhythm. The outrigger accelerated and resumed course along the Moloka'i coastline, heading toward O'ahu. Though they were undoubtedly moving at a more urgent pace, to Jayson, it suddenly seemed they were going glacially slow.

***

After almost two days, there was still no contact from Matteus, Herman, and Serge. While working with the rest of the recruits to fortify the crater, Jen kept nervously checking her tablet for a sign they'd made it to the ridge above Akupu safely. Finally, in the afternoon on the fourth day since Jayson and Kai had departed for Moloka'i, the hit arrived.

Relay showing green
Anyone getting this?

Yes. How's visibility?

Spectacular
We can see Kauai

Ok. Matteus get back ASAP with Serge

Ok

She breathed a sigh of relief. Although they'd not likely have to worry about an attack from that direction, it was better to be sure. The tablet buzzed again. This time, it was Farzin.

Canoe incoming

How many?

Just 1
Maybe 15 clicks out

Jayson and Kai?

Can't tell
Bigger canoe
Way bigger

ETA?

Not sure yet
Maybe 2h?

Ok. Keep updating

Yep

She furrowed her brow. A single canoe, no matter how large, didn't seem like much of an invasion—but she felt it was better to be safe, calling everyone up to the crater. She sent out a hit to every tablet and then set out on a tour of the settlement to make sure nobody missed the warning.

***

Farzin handed the binoculars to Samaira, and she scanned the water in the direction he was pointing.

"See it?"

"Yeah, but it's hard to make anything out at this distance."

"How many people do you see?"

"I can't tell for sure."

"We'll know more in the next hour or so," he assured.

"Wait," she said. "There's another one."

"Where?"

"Behind, and to the right," she directed, handing back the binoculars.

"Looks like it," he agreed. "Good catch."

"I can't tell how many people are on it."

"Me either. They're still too far."

Farzin scanned the horizon intently for several more seconds.

"Shit," he said under his breath. "And another one to the north."

"Should we tell Jen?"

"Let's wait until we know what to tell her."

***

Descending the crater into the main square, Jen noted everyone she passed on the way down. Dr. Kitzinger and Melinda ascended with an armload of supplies from the clinic. The poor doctor was already exhausted from multiple trips back and forth to remove critical equipment from potential harm. At Jen's urging, others had been doing the same with their own equipment and supplies from the stores. Despite warnings from the doctor, even Luping had made several slow trips with food and water before he'd finally convinced her to stay put.

Since Jayson's departure, everyone had been on alert, so it was no surprise to Jen there were no stragglers. She found everything around the plaza and all of the residential buildings were empty when she checked each one in turn. She'd ascend once more to do a final headcount and make sure everyone was accounted for before reconnecting with Farzin to get a clearer understanding of what they were facing.

***

"That's a really big outrigger," said Farzin after another ten minutes with the binoculars. "Maybe a few dozen people on it? They're all so jumbled up, it's hard to get a count."

"I'll hit Parth and Zaina," suggested Samaira. "They're closer, right?"

"Yeah. A lot."

> Hey
> You there?
>
> *What's up?*
>
> Got 3 boats incoming from southeast
> You see them?
>
> *Just a sec*

A minute later, Parth responded back.

> *Zaina's got them now*
>
> How many people?
>
> *Closest 40-50 people*
> *Other 2 are bigger*

How many in those?

~100 each

"Two hundred and fifty people in total, according to Parth."

"That's a lot more than Kai said he could get," replied Farzin grimly. "This could be something else."

"If those are Pa'ao and Pili's warriors, that means they've already overrun Moloka'i," realized Samaira.

"Let's hope not," he replied, examining the approaching craft through the binoculars.

The tablet buzzed again, and Samaira glanced down to see another message from Parth.

"Shit," she said. "There's another one."

"Got it," confirmed Farzin. "A bit behind the others, it looks like."

"This really is an invasion, isn't it?" asked Samaira in disbelief."

"I think so," he agreed. "Time to update Jen."

Chapter Forty-Two

GLANCING BACK EVERY FEW minutes, Jayson realized the men in the approaching boats must have spotted them. Three of them had broken off from the rest, and were in pursuit. Despite the head start, outriggers of that size—manned by warriors—would undoubtedly overtake them. It was only a matter of time.

Infants were left in the care of the youngest children while mothers and older children grabbed paddles to join in the effort for survival. Even so, the massive war canoes closed the gap steadily, hour-by-hour, as they crossed the open water between Moloka'i and O'ahu.

"We will not make it back to your settlement," said Kai grimly.

"We're more than halfway now. How long before they catch us?"

"We might make the nearest shore, but we won't get to your harbor."

"So let's do that. Land at the near shore."

"With women and children? We'll be run down long before we can get to safety."

"Maybe we can get some help at the beach," suggested Jayson, dropping his paddle beside him.

He picked up the tablet and realized with horror it was down to only five percent of power remaining. He should have shut it down during the transit, or at least turned off the active listening mode in the translator application. Hopefully, there would be enough power to ping the relay he and Matteus had set up on Diamond Head and get a message to someone. It was far away but still had line-of-sight to Jayson's location out in the middle of the strait.

413

Anyone getting this?
Hello?

"Shit," he said under his breath.

"What is it?" asked Kai.

"We're still too far to contact the others," explained Jayson. "I need to shut down the translator for a while."

"Why?"

"It's almost out of—of magic."

Kai did not ask for an explanation, but simply nodded. Jayson picked up his paddle and resumed his efforts to help keep them ahead of the dogged warriors in pursuit.

***

Samaira and Farzin continued watching as the small fleet got closer. No more canoes appeared on the horizon behind them, but it was hardly a relief. The approaching force of three hundred and fifty invaders was no minor threat to the recruits and their two remaining protectors.

"It really seems like they're heading right at us," said Samaira, looking through the binoculars.

"Yeah," agreed Farzin.

He took the binoculars for himself and had another look.

"Wait a sec," he added. "It looks like there are kids in the first one."

"Really? That doesn't sound like an invasion at all."

"Hard to be sure, but that's what it looks like."

"Let me see if Parth and Zaina have a better view."

You see kids on first canoe?

Yeah

Just talking about that

What about others?

Can't see any
Closing fast but still too far

"They see kids, too," she confirmed. "On the first boat."

"Still could be an invasion," said Farzin. "Remember Kai said Pili arrived with an entire floating civilization."

"Maybe," allowed Samaira. "But I don't think they'd land the kids first."

"Good point."

The tablet buzzed in Samaira's hand.

Anybody there?

"Holy shit!" exclaimed Samaira. "It's Jayson."

"What? How can you tell?"

"I mean, Jayson just hit me."

"What?" demanded Farzin again, lowering the binoculars to look at the screen.

Yes
Where are you?

Canoe southeast of Aiden Point

We see you
At Diamond Head with Farzin

Need help
Bad guys catching up

What do you need?

Miracle
They're almost on us

Who?
Pa'ao?

Don't know

Farzin grabbed the tablet from Samaira and responded.

Farzin here
Aim for Diamond Head
Follow shoreline on west side
Land at Waikiki and run for the trail
We will be there

Can't make it

You have to
Paddle like hell

***

Jayson relayed the message to Kai, who then urged on the others. The exhausted refugees bore down on their paddles with renewed hope that salvation awaited on O'ahu.

"Kōkua ma laila?" asked Kai.

The tablet offered no translation. Its battery was dead. With nothing more to be said, they put every remaining ounce of strength into outrunning their pursuers.

***

Farzin initiated a video call with Jen and Parth to share what he and Samaira had just learned, and to strategize the best way to help Jayson. Parth and Zaina appeared on the screen first against an expansive backdrop of sky and ocean. Moments later, Jen joined in, looking calm amid the activity of recruits behind her, stowing their tech and preparing defenses.

"We just got a hit from Jayson," started Farzin.

"I know," said Jen. "I saw it too—a few minutes after it arrived. When I tried to reply, it got bounced."

"Same here," revealed Parth. "He must have turned his tablet off."

"He doesn't really have time to chat," said Farzin. "He's got more important things to focus on. He's in that first boat with Kai's people, and they're losing ground fast."

"Do we know who's running them down?" asked Parth.

"He's not sure. Maybe Pa'ao."

"What else did he say?" demanded Jen.

"Not much. I told him to come past Diamond Head, make for Waikiki, and run like hell for the trail. Then he dropped."

"Are they going to make it?"

"Hard to say. They've picked up the pace a bit since we spoke, but it's going to be close."

"Okay. What's the plan?"

"I'll head down to the shoreline west of Diamond Head to hide in the trees," replied Farzin. "I brought sniper gear—got a few dozen rounds in the magazine. It'll give me the best chance to neutralize a few threats as early as possible. I'll have a broadside view, and should be able to get a few clean shots as they go past me."

"What do you want me to do?" asked Jen.

"I need you hidden on the beach to lay down cover fire as they're landing."

"There's three hundred of 'em, Farzin. I don't care if they just have rocks and sticks. That's a lot to handle."

"I know. If they're determined to run into a hail of bullets, no matter the cost, you're as good as dead. We have to hope they're smarter than that."

"Fuck me," she said. "That's not much of a plan."

"Best I could do in two minutes. You got any better ideas?"

"I can help," offered Parth. "Bring me a gun, Jen, and I'll meet you at Waikiki."

"You're too far away," she countered. "It'll all be over long before you get there."

"I could be there in time," interjected Samaira.

"It's not like the movies, Samaira. An untrained person with a gun is more of a liability than a help. Farzin and I will handle this."

"What do the rest of us do?" she protested.

"Keep watch for more trouble," replied Jen.

"They can't be more than a half-hour out," reminded Farzin. "Better get moving, Jen."

"On my way," she confirmed before vanishing from the screen.

"What about us?" asked Parth.

"Keep watching," advised Farzin. "We have no idea what's going on until we can debrief Jayson and Kai."

"Okay," he agreed. "We'll hit everyone else with an update to let them know what's going on."

Closing the cover, Farzin shoved the tablet into his pack and quickly gathered up his canteen, binoculars, and weapons.

"I'm going down with you," insisted Samaira.

"It's too dangerous," replied Farzin, shaking his head.

"If you're taking the tablet, there's nothing I can contribute from here."

He pulled a flare gun out of his pack and tossed it at her.

"There's nothing you can contribute down there, either," he said. "You don't know what it's like to be in battle. Even with primitive weapons, a determined force of that size is no fucking joke. If you see anything else, just fire off a flare to let us know."

"If you lose down there, I'm dead anyway. It's just a matter of time."

"We don't have time for this argument."

"You're right. We don't," she agreed, gathering up equipment and stuffing it into her pack.

Farzin shouldered both of his rifles and checked for the sidearm on his hip.

"Fine," he said. "Do what you want, but I'm not slowing down for you."

There being no safe way to quickly descend the outside wall of the crater on the southwest side, he started down to the interior plateau with Samaira trailing behind, trying to match his hurried pace.

***

O'ahu filled his peripheral vision, and Diamond Head loomed high above. Jayson was almost home. He was delirious from the effort of sustained paddling and probably from dehydration as well. Nobody dared take even a moment for rest or water in their desperate bid to make the shoreline ahead of their pursuers. Though he felt oddly isolated without the benefit of the translator, no communication was necessary to strategize or plan. They were already doing the only thing they could to save themselves.

In a recurring nightmare, he hung from his fingertips miles above the unseen ground below, fighting weakness and fatigue. One by one, his fingers would slip from the beam above, and he'd plunge into the abyss. At that point, he'd wake with a start, covered in sweat, his heart pounding in his chest. He kept hoping he would wake from his current nightmare in the same way before his body failed him, and he could paddle no more.

He imagined what his death would feel like. What would be the sensation of the spear penetrating his body and driving into his heart? Would he have time to experience the pain? Time to acknowledge the nature of his end? Perhaps, instead, it would be sudden. A whack in the head from behind might render him unconscious; mercifully unable to experience the final death blow. These were the thoughts that filled his head as he fought to keep his paddle moving in rhythm with the other desperate evacuees.

He could hear the calls of the advancing warriors behind him. Though he couldn't understand the words, he recognized them as taunts and attempts at intimidation. The sooner they could make their prey give up and accept the inevitable, the sooner it would all be over. He did his best to tune it out, but could not resist the occasional glance over his shoulder. They were no more than a couple of hundred meters behind. Jayson estimated about two kilometers to Waikiki and, hopefully, salvation. They just had to stay ahead, out of projectile range, for another twenty minutes. Ignoring the taunts and fatigue, he pressed on.

***

After jogging about three kilometers down the main pathway towards the fish-pond, Jen veered off down the less-used path to Waikiki Beach. She wasn't pushing too hard; just enough to make sure she arrived with time to position herself in a concealed spot and recover her breath. She was armed with only a pistol and an assault rifle, her pack loaded with every spare magazine she could get her hands on. Though unlikely, maybe she could stay hidden long enough to reload a magazine or two, if it came to that. Binoculars and a tablet rounded out her equipment, and she had a full canteen over her shoulder.

Already familiar with the beach, she had an idea where she'd be able to seclude herself among the vegetation about fifty meters from shore without having to expose herself to get there. According to the plan relayed by Farzin, Jayson and his group of refugees would run past on her left side onto the trail, leaving a clear line of fire to their pursuers. Farzin, she assumed, would close the distance to the beach from the south after doing what he could with the sniper rifle, and catch the attackers in a deadly crossfire. If everything went well, they might just survive.

***

Farzin had opened a sizable gap on Samaira by the time he crested the northern wall of the crater to begin his descent. When she reached the top, he was nowhere to be seen. She searched the tree-covered slope vainly to locate some sort of movement in the canopy below that might betray his location. She dared not call out for him for fear that he would backtrack, losing critical time in his effort to get into position to help Jayson and Kai.

From the rim, she could see Waikiki Bay to the west. She noted the position of the sun, knowing that, without a compass, she could get hopelessly lost in the dense greenery between her and the beach. If she kept the sun ahead and just a bit to the left relative to her bearing, she imagined, it shouldn't be too hard to stay on the right course. Committing herself with a deep breath, she began the descent into the trees.

***

Arriving at the edge of the beach, Jen could see the approaching canoes only a couple of kilometers away. Through her binoculars, it seemed there was very little distance between them. She scanned the shoreline immediately below the west side of Diamond Head for signs of Farzin and pulled out her tablet to send him a hit.

In position
You?

There was no response.

***

Farzin dodged his way through the dense vegetation, glancing at his compass every couple of minutes to make sure he was heading in the right general direction. He knew Jayson and Kai would be alongside the shore at any moment, and they would need his help to cover the final sprint to Jen's trap at Waikiki. The sound of small waves breaking gently against the shoreline rose over the sound of rustling leaves and his own heavy breathing. He was almost there.

The glinting turquoise of the bay appeared among the trees, prompting Farzin to move more carefully to avoid being seen by the approaching enemies. Crouching down, he made his way to an outcropping of rock obscured by trees from the south. The canoes were close—just less than five hundred meters, he estimated.

He quickly tossed his pack aside and readied the sniper rifle, propping the barrel on its bipod. Although he was trained to use the modified SR-25, he was not an expert sniper. His heart pounding and his arms still shaking from the exertion of getting to his spot, he knew there'd be no heroic, long-range, pin-point shots to save the day. He'd do the best he could within the limits of his ability to give Jayson and Kai a few more seconds to get within range of Jen's position.

***

A scream from right behind Jayson rose above the raucous taunts of their pursuers. He looked back to see a spear embedded in the canoe only a few inches from the right leg of one of the children. Mano and Malo, stationed at the back, abandoned their paddles and took up shields and spears in their place. The O'ahu shoreline and Diamond Head were beside them to the east, and Waikiki beach was tantalizingly close, but probably still too far to reach in time.

One of the pursuing canoes was drawing alongside them, positioning itself between the fleeing outrigger and the shore. A second one, directly behind, was nearly upon them. A pair of attackers perched on the bow seemed prepared to leap aboard at any moment, while the twin warriors, Mano and Malo, did their best to hold them at bay. All Jayson could do was paddle and hope his waiting colleagues had a plan to save them.

***

The canoes were almost directly opposite his position, approximately two hundred meters away. Farzin could see through his scope the situation was dire. Pulling alongside Jayson and Kai, the canoe on the nearside was the most significant threat.

The one immediately behind, however, seemed already engaged in some sort of attack.

He ruled out taking any shots that would put Kai's people in the background of his line of fire. He simply did not have confidence in his accuracy and feared he might wind up killing friendly targets. Instead, he decided on a course of action that might remove both of the most serious threats at once.

Training his scope on the line of paddlers on the nearside of the canoe immediately behind Jayson and Kai, he began squeezing off shots. It took a few tries to find his range before he started connecting with targets. One by one, several warriors slumped over—some falling inside the canoe and others towards the edge. Their shocked colleagues stopped paddling to investigate the nature of the sudden injuries, hauling in those in danger of falling into the water.

Those paddling on the far side of the enormous war canoe didn't immediately notice, and kept going at full speed. As a result of the imbalance, the craft veered to the right and struck the rear quarter of the canoe pulling up alongside Jayson and Kai. The warriors in both canoes stopped paddling amid the confusion and began to lose speed, allowing their prey to open up a gap.

Farzin used the opportunity to pump a few more rounds into both canoes before swiveling to the third, trailing outrigger, and delivering a few deadly shots into the line of paddling warriors nearest him.

Standing in the middle of the third war canoe, a man adorned in colorful feathers bellowed a command before crouching down. Immediately, a wall of ornate, oblong, koa wood shields rose along the nearside of all three boats. Paddles emerged below them, and the craft resumed their pursuit towards Waikiki Beach. Farzin continued firing randomly into the wall of shields, but could not tell what effect he was having on those hidden behind it.

***

When Jayson first heard the alarmed shouts of a commotion behind him, he assumed they were being boarded and the slaughter of Kai's people had begun. Looking back for the first time in several minutes, he was surprised—and relieved—to see his pursuers dropping back. There were bodies in the water, and several onboard seemed injured or dead.

"Thank fucking Christ," he panted under his breath.

He didn't know exactly what had happened, only that they were now at least partially under the protection of his friends. If there'd been shots fired, there was far too much noise and confusion for him to have noticed.

He glanced back a second time to see Mano and Malo had dropped their weapons to resume paddling. Some warriors on the canoe behind were rushing to the starboard side with shields to protect the remaining paddlers. The distraction meant they couldn't maintain their previous pace, Jayson realized. He and Kai's people would make it to the beach.

***

Jen watched helplessly from her hiding place among the vegetation at the edge of the sandy expanse of Waikiki Beach; the action on the water far out of range of her assault rifle. Through her binoculars, she'd seen Farzin creep into position and begin firing. It had been hard, from her perspective, to tell exactly how close the attackers were getting to Jayson and Kai, but the fact several people were standing up told her combat was underway or imminent. She hoped Farzin wasn't too late.

She'd feared for a few moments the fight would be over long before she had the chance to help, and even wondered if she should reveal herself to sprint down the shoreline and get closer. When one canoe veered, knocking another off course, she breathed a sigh of relief. They were dropping back under Farzin's attack. She sent him another hit.

Nice work

A minute later, he responded.

Hope it's enough
Out of ammo

Bad guys dropping back

Yep
They should make the beach

I'm ready

Ok
Heading your way now

Keep your head down

***

Exhausted and trembling, it took Jayson a few seconds to realize what was happening when his paddle finally struck the sandy bottom of Waikiki Bay. Part of his brain had already accepted he would not make it. Around him, Kai and his warriors began leaping from the canoe and pushing it forward. Jayson jumped out to help but was not ready for the transition. His rubbery legs failed him, and he stumbled to one side, falling into the water on his hands and knees.

Kai glanced back to make sure he was okay, but kept pushing the canoe, along with the others, to drive it up onto the beach. Submerged to his waist and panting, Jayson looked back to see if the pursuers had given up. They hadn't. The war canoes were less than two hundred meters away—and bearing down quickly.

The moment the canoe stopped moving, its bow lodged in the sand of Waikiki Beach, the women and children began frantically disembarking, with Kai and the other warriors assisting them. Jayson struggled to his feet and sloshed through the shallow water to help. The canoe empty of passengers, he grabbed the spent tablet before going ashore with the others.

"Alaka'i aku iā lākou," shouted Kai at Jayson, pointing towards the trees.

Jayson did not need a translator to understand Kai wanted him to lead them to safety.

"E hāhai iā ia," he added, instructing his people to follow their new ally.

Jayson motioned for them to follow as he jogged up the beach towards the trail. He stopped at the tree line to urge them on, and ensure he wasn't leaving anyone behind. To his surprise, only the women and children were following. With Kai in the middle, the dozen warriors had formed a line between the escape route and their attackers.

"What the fuck are they doing?" hissed Jen from her hiding place a few meters away.

Jayson swung his head around with a start.

"Jesus, Jen. You scared the shit out of me!"

"They're in my line of fire," she continued. "Don't they know the plan?"

"I told them everything I could," he said, holding up the tablet. "Battery died an hour ago, and I lost the translator."

"Fuck. Take mine," she said, tossing her tablet at him.

"It's a little late for that now," he replied, throwing his hands in the air.

Several attackers jumped from the two lead war canoes, pushing them towards the beach, while the third held its position offshore. Kai and the others backed away slowly, inadvertently cutting off more of Jen's line of fire. Each had a shield and short spear meant for close-quarter combat.

"I'm going to have to take down a few friendlies, Jayson," warned Jen. "I can't afford to wait until there's two hundred warriors on top of me."

"No! Let me try to get them out of there."

He urged the women and children further back into the trees and called out to his new ally.

"Kai!" he yelled, waving his arm frantically. "Come on!"

Kai glanced back only long enough to wave him off before returning his attention to the advancing enemy. Jayson activated the translation app on Jen's tablet and tried again. The maximum volume of the small device was no match for the sound of the surf and the din of the shouting attackers. Four lines of hostile warriors formed at the waterline but did not advance. Kai and his brethren stood firm less than twenty meters away. Everyone fell silent in anticipation of the imminent clash.

The man adorned in feathers, now standing in the middle of the third canoe, yelled out. Jayson could not hear what he said, nor did the translator pick it up. It did catch Kai's defiant response.

"Never!" he said simply.

Jayson imagined the man, their apparent leader, must have issued some sort of offer or ultimatum.

"I don't have a shot," warned Jen.

"Then get down there! You have a fucking machine gun."

"I'm going to take a spear to the chest before I get to use it if Kai doesn't get out of my way."

Kai and his comrades edged a few more backward steps towards the trees as the enemy leader stood in stony silence, considering his response.

"Get those people back to Punchbowl," ordered Jen. "Now!"

"What are you going to do?"

"Farzin's coming up from the south. He'll have a clear shot in a few minutes."

"That's too long," he protested.

"Listen. This is all for nothing if you don't get those people out of here. There are weapons back at the crater. Use them—if it comes to that."

"Okay," he realized. "You're right."

As he turned to join his charges on the forest path to guide them to Punchbowl, he heard an angry yell from the enemy leader. Jayson glanced over his shoulder to see the warriors along the shoreline charge forward amid cries of battle. He started running, but froze in his tracks when the clamor on the beach went suddenly silent.

***

Farzin watched helplessly as the plan fell apart. Dodging his way through the shoreline vegetation, he paused every so often to see how things were developing. He knew where Jen had stationed herself, and saw that Kai and several warriors stood between her and the advancing enemy. He resolved to get as close as he could before laying down some fire. He knew he was still too far out of range to provide effective cover, but a distraction was better than nothing.

As the assembled attackers began their charge, Farzin burst from the trees and unshouldered his assault rifle. Throwing himself to the ground, he prepared to unload on them from the rear, but froze just before he squeezed the trigger. An apparition materialized on the beach just to the right of the enemy force, halting their advance and silencing their war cries.

"What the fuck?" panted Farzin under his breath, reaching for his binoculars. To his horror, he realized it was Samaira—walking towards the point of attack. "Jesus Christ. What is she doing?"

***

After getting herself lost in pursuit through the trees, Samaira had stumbled onto the beach—closer to Jen's position than Farzin's—just in time to see the impact of the first volley of shots from his sniper rifle. She'd watched with relief as the invaders fell back for a short time. Resuming the chase behind the cover of shields, it was only a matter of time before Jayson and Kai would be in range of their attack once more. She ducked back into the trees and made her way towards the pathway where she knew Jen would be waiting.

Samaira didn't know what she might offer in response to the quickly developing situation. She only knew she wanted to get to the spot where Jayson and Kai would soon be ashore, and do whatever she could to give them a better chance at survival. The sound of gunfire from behind ceased, and she knew Farzin had done all he could. It would now fall to Jen—and herself, if necessary—to do the rest.

She was halfway around the curve marking the northeast boundary of the bay when she heard the shouts of the landing refugees. Peeking out from behind the safety of the trees, she saw Jayson leading a group of women and children onto the trail. The invaders in the nearest canoes leaped into the shallow water and pushed their craft onto the beach. Kai, easily identifiable by the blade in place of his left foot, backed away from the water with his colleagues, defending Jayson's retreat with the women and children.

As the attackers lined up on the beach, Samaira waited for Jen to do something, but nothing happened. She threw down her pack, rummaging through it for anything that might cause a distraction. The bright orange flare gun caught her eye. Picking it up, she found some equally colorful shells hanging on a plastic strip attached to the handle. She opened the breech and inserted one of them into the barrel.

A shout rose from the direction of the beach, followed by a cacophony of war cries. Abandoned by Jen, Samaira realized she was Kai's only hope. She took a deep breath. Raising the gun over her head with both hands, she walked calmly onto the beach towards the pending melee.

***

Jayson was horrified. Samaira walked slowly towards the enemy force armed with nothing more than a flare gun, momentarily bewildering them with her unfamiliar complexion. How long, he wondered, would it take for them to regain their composure and attack?

Kai, too, seemed paralyzed with fear. Although in his case, it was likely the fear Samaira would be hurt or killed.

"Fall down!" she shouted at him.

He furrowed his brow in confusion.

Taking one hand from the flare gun, she gestured a falling motion and desperately repeated her plea.

"Fall down!"

Not waiting for him to react, she put both hands back on the gun and squeezed the trigger. The glowing red flare shot into the sky with a loud report and a puff of smoke. Jayson heard Kai whisper harshly to his stunned colleagues.

"Hāʻule i lalo!" he commanded them as he dropped to the sand.

Though clearly confused, they followed his lead, throwing themselves at the ground. Jayson started with fright as gunfire erupted from the trees beside him. With Kai and his companions down, Jen finally had a clear line of fire to the enemy.

The bodies of his warriors falling into the water under the light of a burning, red star, the apparent leader of the enemy force in the third canoe, still well offshore, began shouting orders at his men. Paddles hit the water, and they changed course for the middle of the bay. As they retreated, the man kept calling, urging the others to follow.

Most of the remaining attackers closed ranks, ducking behind their shields to provide cover for their colleagues to drag the massive outriggers off the beach and load up as many of the wounded as they could. All the while, Jen continued firing into their midst—splintering shields and shattering bodies until her magazine was empty. Quickly, she shoved in another before raising her weapon again. Jayson grabbed her by the shoulder before she could resume firing.

"It's over," he pleaded. "They're leaving."

Staring intently through the scope with her finger quivering above the trigger, she finally relented and lowered the gun without a word.

***

Farzin watched the spectacle in bewildered amazement. Not only had Samaira survived her foolish gambit, she'd also opened up the line of fire for Jen, putting the attackers on their heels. All three canoes were now retreating past him, although further offshore than their initial approach. He peered through the scope and thought about squeezing off a few more rounds, but the panicked faces and desperation of the fleeing men gave him pause. Only one man—the apparent leader—remained relatively calm amid the retreat. He stood in his canoe, glaring back at the beach.

Chapter Forty-Three

NONE OF THE DEFENDERS on the beach dared talk or move for several minutes as the attacking force withdrew into Waikiki Bay. They waited, chests heaving and bodies shaking, for the enemy canoes to get out of visual range—oblivious to the moans and feeble movements of the injured men at the water's edge.

Farzin stepped from the trees on the east side of the beach and ran towards Samaira. She was trembling and fighting back tears.

"That was incredible," he said, taking her in his arms.

She didn't respond. Instead, she buried her face in his chest and began sobbing.

Kai eased himself slowly to his knees as he looked out across the water at the retreating outriggers growing smaller in the distance. Sensing it was safe, he stood up and signaled his brethren to do the same. He bounded over to Samaira and gently eased her from Farzin's arms into his own.

"Masalo iā 'oe," he whispered.

As Samaira and Kai embraced, Jayson glanced in their direction. Instead of joining in the bittersweet reunion, he felt compelled to survey the carnage along the waterline where the blood-tinted surf lapped gently against the bodies of the fallen. Jen rose from her concealment, following a few paces behind.

"I know this is awful, Jayson," she said. "But it was necessary."

"I know," he replied absently.

An injured man moaned and tried to raise himself to his knees before collapsing back down on the sand.

"We need the doctor. Now," realized Jen.

"Yeah," agreed Jayson, surveying the dead and injured warriors with a blank stare.

"You have the tablet," she reminded him.

"Oh, yeah. Sorry."

"It's shock—and it's normal," she assured as she pried the tablet away to call for help.

Beside them, the evacuees streamed out of the trees. Kai's warriors embraced their wives and children, and all cried with relief. Miraculously, no one had suffered injuries in the close encounter during the final sprint to safety, and the standoff on the beach.

Farzin, Kai, and Samaira approached the shoreline to survey the aftermath of the brief battle. Samaira, still crying, had yet to say anything. When they reached Jayson, she pulled away from Kai and ran to him.

"I'm so glad you're safe," she said, wrapping her arms around him.

"Thanks to you," he replied.

"No shit," agreed Jen. "You really saved our asses."

"What do you mean?"

"Kai and his men were blocking my shot," she explained. "Until you got them to hit the ground."

"Right," she said with sudden realization.

"I have to admit, that was a pretty gutsy play, Samaira. I didn't know you had that kind of steel in your belly."

"It was desperation more than anything."

"Don't be modest," countered Jen. "That was legendary."

Kai arrived beside them, taking Samaira once more into the comfort of his arms.

"Who was that?" asked Jen through the translator app.

"That was the warrior-priest Pa'ao," explained Kai. "He and Pili spotted us as they moved to attack Moloka'i, and split their force to give chase."

"What did he yell at you before the attack?"

"He told me if I surrendered the island to Pili, I would stay to rule it in his name."

"We should start helping the injured," interrupted Samaira. "And bury the dead."

"Doc's on his way," assured Jen. "But you're right. We should start triaging."

Some of Kai's men were already dragging the wounded from the water, while several women investigated their injuries. While his colleagues began searching for survivors and tending to those most in need of immediate help, Jayson stood transfixed at the water's edge, watching the torn bodies rise and fall on the gentle waves.

***

In the aftermath of the brief battle, the Gamma recruits and their new allies transported the handful of surviving enemy warriors to the clinic, where they remained under guard in the care of Dr. Kitzinger while their injuries healed. The community gathered to dedicate a memorial to the dead at the terminus of the Waikiki Beach trail, interring beneath it the cremated remains of the invaders.

In the presence of the survivors well enough to attend, Kai spoke a few words in what Samaira called an essential first step in an eventual reconciliation with their aggressive neighbors. When the recovering men were strong enough, they'd be offered the opportunity to build a canoe and return to Maui. Hopefully, the mercy and hospitality shown to the vanquished would be viewed as an olive branch and an invitation to dialog.

Upon arrival at the settlement, the families of newcomers with young children were given housing among the recruits on the slopes of Punchbowl. The rest stayed in the temporary encampment where Samaira, Jayson, Herman, and Serge joined them while construction was underway for additional permanent housing. Now experienced builders, the recruits made quick progress with the addition of a score of strong men eager to learn and contribute to their new community. Only two months after their arrival, the twins, Mano and Malo, helped Jayson dismantle the last of the tents and other temporary structures and return them to storage.

As they pushed the final cartload into the plaza, they paused to watch Melinda directing the children in a game next to a garden. She'd outlined some numbered squares on the ground, and the excited youngsters were hopping one-legged from one to the next, pausing for instructions in between. Their teacher had taught them how to count, and they were engaged in some basic addition and subtraction to determine which square to jump to next.

"My daughter, La'akea," said Mano in English with a smile as he pointed to a jubilant young girl.

"Maopopo ia'u," answered Jayson with a nod.

After the children were asleep in the evenings, Melinda led the adults in more challenging games of bilingual charades and Pictionary. Never failing to generate copious, genuine laughter, they made silly mistakes trying to learn the basics of each other's language. The new friends often communicated in a mix of both without the aid of the translator as they engaged in daily work to reinforce their learning.

Luping, her pregnancy now showing more obviously, sat peacefully shaded from the late afternoon sun under a tree, watching the games in the plaza with Samaira and a pair of the newly arrived mothers by her side. When they saw Jayson and the twins, they waved a friendly greeting, and Samaira excused herself to go and speak with them.

"Aloha, Mano. Aloha, Malo," she greeted.

"Good afternoon, Samaira," replied Malo for both of them.

"Do you have time for a walk, Jayson?" she asked.

His heart skipped a beat, knowing it meant she likely had something important to tell him.

"Sure," he replied. "Where to?"

"It doesn't matter. How about going down to the harbor?"

"Sounds good."

The twins began unloading the cart while Jayson and Samaira strolled past the common building, down the sloping path towards Honolulu Harbor. It seemed so familiar to Jayson as he thought back to the day they'd first met at the Center and explored the pathway around Waipi'O Peninsula together. By the end of that first walk, he felt like he'd known her for years. Now, after everything they'd been through since arriving on the island, it seemed to him they'd spent a lifetime together. Although part of him recognized it was in vain, he hoped she would announce she felt the same way, and that they should be together.

"This is where it'll all come to a head," she announced as she paused on the slope overlooking the dock. "They'll return here in a year or so, and either accept or reject what we've done."

"What do you think is going to happen?"

"I've been running the simulations for a while to figure that out."

"And?"

"Olena and Kailani are dead," started Samaira, "and Farzin and Jen don't have the will to fight any of this."

"So, what does that mean?"

"It moves things in our favor," she said with an absent nod.

"Do you think it's enough?" he asked.

"There's more," she said, taking a deep breath.

Jayson furrowed his brow, but said nothing. Something about the way she'd made the statement implied he wouldn't like what she was about to say.

"They'll return to find a living symbol of the unity in our new society," she continued.

"What?"

"I'm pregnant, Jayson," revealed Samaira. "With Kai's child."

He said nothing for a while, determined to get his emotions under control so as not to convey the devastating betrayal he felt.

"Do you love him?" he asked finally.

"He's a good man, Jayson," she replied.

He nodded. Kai *was* a good man.

"I know this hurts, Jayson. It's why I wanted you to be the first to know—so I could explain it to you."

"You don't have to explain yourself," he said more aggressively than he'd meant to. "It's not like l have some claim over you. You don't owe me anything."

"But I know how you feel. And I know this must be hard."

"Yeah," he acknowledged.

"There's too much at stake here," she continued. "What happens in the next year is going to determine the future of our civilization."

Too much at stake for what? He thought about pushing her to find out, but decided it would be easier for him to live with the ambiguity left unresolved.

"Congratulations," he said after a few more moments of silence. "That's what I should have said in the first place. I know you're going to be an awesome mother."

"Thanks, Jayson. That means a lot to me."

"When are you going to tell Kai?"

"This evening. And then I'll announce it to everyone else tonight at dinner. Try to act surprised?"

"Yeah," he promised with a smile that was equal parts forced and genuine. "I'll act surprised."

She squeezed his hand, breathing a sigh of relief.

"Watch the sunset with me?"

"I'd love to," he said, glancing to the west, where it was already making its stunning transition from yellow to orange above the mountains west of Waipi'O.

Epilogue

RICHARD SAT IN HIS office, staring absently at his laptop. On the screen before him was the complete digital mockup of the prototype Columbia class ballistic missile submarine he needed to validate the weight distribution for Delta. As fascinating as the highly classified data was, it didn't have his full attention. His thoughts were focused on securing his rightful place on Epsilon.

Appealing to Kamaras's sense of humanity or fairness was a losing option. His only hope was to demonstrate to his boss that he was irreplaceable, and that shipping him off before Epsilon would put the entire operation at risk. And he knew exactly how to do that. Well, maybe not exactly. But he knew that somehow undermining Akindele was the key.

There was a knock, and Andrew leaned in.

"You wanted to see me?"

"Yes, Andrew," he said with a smile. "Please come in. I'd like you to take a look at something."

He spun the laptop around and leaned back in his chair.

"What do you think?"

"Cool. What am I looking at?"

"This is Admiral Daniels' newest toy. It'll be leaving dry dock in Connecticut in six months."

"What's it got to do with us?"

"This is your ride, Andrew, for the next part of the mission. I need you to run a few load optimizations to make sure everything goes smoothly."

"My ride?"

"Well, you and about a hundred others—plus supplies," he said with a shrug. "But let's not kid ourselves. Those grunts are mostly replaceable. You are not."

"I appreciate that, sir, but aren't you coming?"

"Not this time, Andrew," he said with a smile.

Scan here to see the next book in
Countdown to Epsilon

Scan here to see my blog and
join my reader list.